YOU BEAUTIFUL THING, YOU

Bad Boys of Bardstown
Book 1

SAFFRON A. KENT

Blurb

Nineteen-year-old *Tempest Jackson* wants a baby.
No, her biological clock isn't ticking, but she's desperate for unconditional love. Rejected by all except her brother and soon to be married off by her father for financial gain, she aches for someone to hold close and call hers.

Enter *Ledger Thorne*. Soccer god, devastatingly handsome and her brother's rival.

Once upon a time they had a thing. A beautiful thing. But while Tempest thought she was madly in love, Ledger was only using her for petty revenge.

So Tempest has a plan: seduce the sexy jerk who broke her heart, use him to get pregnant and then leave him in the dust like he left her, to marry a stranger.

Only the problem with making babies is that it doesn't feel like revenge. It feels a lot like that thing they used to have: Hot and stormy, and intense and intimate.

But Tempest isn't a fool. She'll stick to the plan.
Because wasn't it Ledger who turned their beautiful thing into something ugly?

Now it's her turn…

NOTE: This is a STANDALONE set in the world of Bardstown, a St. Mary's Rebels spin-off.

Cover Art by Najla Qamber Designs
Editing by Olivia Kalb and Leanne Rabesa
Proofreading by Virginia Tesi Carey

October 2023 Edition

Published in the United States of America

To all the romance girlies: We run the world. We change the world. We make this world a beautiful place. Don't let anyone tell you otherwise.

To my husband (and the new daddy): Who makes me believe in romance every single day.

To my baby girl, Adora: You beautiful thing, you. Thank you for choosing me (and your dada) and coming into our lives. I loved your little kicks in my tummy and I love you even more now that I get to kiss your little kicking feet.

To me: You did it! You wrote the book, your hardest and most personal. You wanted to give up so many times but you didn't. Always remember that you can do whatever the fuck you put your mind to. Again, don't let someone tell you otherwise.

Author's Note

Ledger and Tempest's story has been in my head since 2020 (ever since I conceived the idea of writing St. Mary's Rebels, a group of girls sent to a reform high school.) I knew Callie, from A Gorgeous Villain (book 2 in the SMR series) will have four big brothers and all those brothers will have their individual stories. I knew her brother, Ledger, would be the first to get a story once I was done with the St. Mary's series.

This book was supposed to come out much earlier this year. But in March, while I was just beginning to write it, I found out I was pregnant. I was ecstatic and thrilled and of course, very, very sick for the first 15 weeks. Writing was impossible; I just wanted to make it through my first trimester, which for a while I didn't think was possible.

Once I got better, I started writing and my only goal was to finish this book and release it this year. Of course my body wasn't a hundred percent. Pregnancy is hard and extremely real and I'd like to take this moment to impress upon every single girl out there: if you are doing it, you are magical and filled with endless strength.

Many times I thought I would have to give up when my fingers would get achy and swollen after hours of typing; when my back would act up; when I'd have bump pain, pain in my ribs, neck pain, headaches. You name it, I had it.

Many times I cried myself to sleep when I saw others moving ahead and celebrating their successes while all I had to show after a long hard day of work was about a 1000 words and an achy back.

During those times, there were people who came to my rescue and I'd like to thank them here: Jennifer Mirabelli, Christina Santos, Katie Conde, my sister, my husband. Their encouragement, their support was what kept me going. This book wouldn't be here without them. I'd also like to thank my editors, proofreaders for always accommodating me and reading this book as many times as I wanted them to. My cover designers (for all the million covers that I had made for this book); the artists that brought my vision to life. All of you inspired me to keep going so I could finish.

Lastly, I would like to say that many of the pregnancy things that Tempest goes through in this book are taken directly from me. Some are fictional though. Hope you enjoy this book. And if you don't, well I am still proud that I wrote it, finished it exactly 16 days before my due date. Writing a pregnancy book while being pregnant is WILD and I will never forget this experience.

Bad Boys of Bardstown

You Beautiful Thing, You
(Bad Boys of Bardstown 1)
Ledger and Tempest's story!

Oh, You're So Cold
(Bad Boys of Bardstown 2)
Stellan Thorne and Isadora Holmes' story!
Pre-order Now

A Wreck, You Make Me
(Bad Boys of Bardstown 3)
Shepard Thorne's story

Bad Kind of Butterflies
(Bad Boys of Bardstown 4)
Ark Reinhardt's story

For you, I fall to Pieces
(Bad Boys of Bardstown 5)

I'm Hopeless, You're Heartless
(Bad Boys of Bardstown 6)

Add the series to your TBR

Other Books by Saffron A. Kent

The Unrequited

Gods & Monsters

Medicine Man (Heartstone Series Book 1)

Dreams of 18 (Heartstone Series Book 2)

California Dreamin' (Heartstone Series Book 3)

St. Mary's Rebels Series

Bad Boy Blues (SMR book 0.5)

My Darling Arrow (SMR book 1)

The Wild Mustang & The Dancing Fairy (SMR book 1.5)

A Gorgeous Villain (SMR book 2)

These Thorn Kisses (SMR book 3)

Hey, Mister Marshall (SMR book 4)

The Hatesick Diaries (SMR book 5)

Part I

Chapter One

Three years ago

IF THEY ASK me how I met the love of my life, I'll tell them it was at a soccer game.

I'll tell them it was fate.

Because I wasn't supposed to be there, see.

I was supposed to be back in New York, at school, attending my last class for the day. But in a moment of wildness, I ditched it and snuck out of school to go see my brother play in Bardstown. I thought I'd surprise him. Mainly because it's very rare for me to go see him play. Not only do I live at a boarding school in New York and can't attend most games, but also because he's always insisted that he didn't want me around his asshole teammates; he's super protective like that.

But on that day I thought, why not?

I'd just received an early sixteenth birthday present from my parents: a sleek black car. And while I shouldn't technically be driving yet, that still wasn't enough of a reason for me not to go.

So I went.

And there he was.

My brother's teammate.

It happened in a flash.

Like in the romance novels that I eat up for breakfast, lunch and dinner.

I saw him flying across the field, his powerful legs taking him at a speed that seemed humanly impossible. His long-ish hair whipping in the wind, his uniform sticking to his tall and muscular body. And the way he kept scoring goal after goal, dribbling the ball, heading it, dodging the players of the opposing team, flipping himself in the air like gravity didn't hold him down like it does to the rest of us.

And I just… fell.

For him.

I know people say love at first sight isn't really a thing.

But meh, what do people know?

They don't know how *electric* I felt in that moment. How thrilled and euphoric and just so fucking enamored by him. They don't know that I wanted to jump and scream on the bleachers that day. Cheer and clap for him when the game was over and they won.

Oh, and they absolutely do not know, and hence can never understand, that amidst all the cheers and excitement at the victory, he *looked* at me.

He saw me across the space.

His eyes landed right on me and that was it.

That was the moment our love story began.

But all epic love stories have a problem, don't they?

Something that keeps lovers apart.

Some hurdle that threatens to destroy their happiness and leave them brokenhearted forever.

Our does too.

And one of the problems in our love story — quite possibly the biggest, or let's say the second biggest — is that it's imaginary.

It's fake. It's made up.

It's all in my head. And my heart.

In my sick, obsessed, love-drunk heart.

Although to be fair, it's not *all* imaginary.

I mean, the soccer game is real. My loving, protective brother is real and I did go see him play. And his teammate is real too. Not to mention, all the things that my brother's teammate made me feel, those are real as well.

But the moment at the end, where he saw me and instantly fell in love?

Yeah, that never happened.

It's just something I read in one of my romance novels once. And I liked it so much — that he saw her and only *her* in a room full of people — that I decided to use it for my own story.

In reality, he doesn't know that I exist.

He doesn't know that at this very moment, I'm crouched behind the thick shrubbery that lines this strange and unknown backyard and that I'm watching him as a party rages on around us. That I've been watching him since the game last week. I skip my classes here and there, drive down to Bardstown without a license and follow him around town. I follow him into parties and observe.

From a distance.

It all sounds very stalker-ish.

But it's okay.

I'm harmless. I have no bad intentions.

It's not like I'm going to approach him and say hi. Or flirt with him — which I'm very good at, if I do say so myself — and ask him to hang out with me. I'm not going to make any advances toward him, or any sort of contact, even.

I can't.

Even if I wanted to.

It's just how it is.

And so this is all I have and will ever have.

Me watching him from afar while he goes on about his life.

As he drinks from a beer bottle, shoots the shit with his friends, chuckles with them. Although I have to say that I haven't really seen him laugh yet.

And the longer he makes me wait for it, the more I feel like I'm going to love it when he does laugh.

What I don't particularly love though is the plethora of girls around him.

The plethora of girls that are *always* around him. And since I've been following — or semi-stalking — him for the last few days, I've come to recognize a few. There's a redhead who finds everything hilarious; a brunette who looks up at him like she's gazing at the moon; a mocha-skinned black-haired beauty, whose ass is to die for and she never lets him or anyone else forget it; and a couple of other girls that I call transient brunettes because they come and go.

I'm not going to lie, this little groupie group that he has pisses me off a little.

The only solace is that he doesn't seem to be interested in any of them. I mean, he talks to them and shoots the shit with them as well but he doesn't look at them like he wants them.

Which is a very good thing.

Very good.

And I think… wait.

Wait, wait, *wait*.

It looks like my solace was temporary because right in front of my eyes, here comes a new addition to the group. A girl I've never seen before, and as soon as she arrives, his eyes focus on her. They practically devour this new blonde with a short sleek haircut. She's got a skinny, model-like body that reaches up to his sculpted jaw, and she has a killer red dress on.

And I can't help but notice that the one girl he's taken any romantic interest in is the complete opposite of me.

I have long dark tresses that go down to the small of my back. I'm not very tall. Not by myself at least. In four-inch heels, I can be five seven. If I stand up on my tiptoes, I can stretch myself up to a solid five eight, but that's it. And I'm definitely not skinny.

But neither am I curvy, per se.

But for someone as short as me, the meat that I do have on my bones — on my ass and thighs, my chest which is a decent 32C and my hips too — appears to give me a compact curvy sort of look.

So as I said, the complete opposite of me.

Is that what his type is then?

Is that why he never paid attention to his other groupies, because they aren't reed thin blonde bombshells?

I'm offended on their behalf.

I'm *enraged* on mine.

And oh my God, oh my *God*, where is he going with her?

Where the *fuck* are they going?

I watch as he grabs her hand and pulls her behind him as he starts walking. He crosses the pool area and dumps his beer bottle in a trash can without breaking stride. Meanwhile the drunken crowd around him gives him back pats and high fives as he moves through them with ease.

As if he's royalty or something.

Well, he *is*.

From what I've heard and seen.

The soccer royalty that not just the school but the whole of Bardstown bows down to.

But that's not important right now.

What's important is that it looks like he won't stop until he gets to where he's going and I think he's going somewhere with privacy. But when he reaches the back deck that leads inside the house, he pauses and I swear to God my heart pauses with him.

Then standing there, on the raised wooden deck, he turns a little. And holy shit, his eyes hone in on the shrubs lining the backyard. They hone in right where I am hiding.

As if he knows I'm there.

But that's... that's *impossible*. That's...

My thoughts cease to exist because just as quickly as he'd paused and 'looked' in my direction — which is insane; there's *no way* that he knows — he turns back and resumes his purposeful strides with the blondie in tow. And as soon as he disappears, I spring up from my hiding position and go after him.

Bad, *bad* thing to do.

Very bad.

And if I stopped for a second, I'd be able to come up with all the reasons why it's so bad.

But like him, I'm not stopping. I'm jogging through the misty grass in the backyard, rushing along the pool where people are frolicking, crossing his group of friends and reaching the back deck, all ready to go into the house. But I'm stopped right at the threshold by two guys that flank the glass sliding doors.

Or more specifically, two drunk guys.

Who may also be high.

Given the strong whiff of marijuana coming from them.

"Hello there," one of them says.

Before I can respond, the second one goes, "You look new."

I do, yes.

Because I am.

And now that I've come to a halt, I finally have time to think things through and realize *why* this is a bad thing. Number one: they're both wearing soccer jerseys, which could mean that they're on the team. And if they are they must know my brother, and if they're *here* — at this party I mean — then they must not be big fans of his, to put it mildly.

"And pretty," the first one keeps going.

The second one looks me up and down, all lazily and drunkenly. "Yeah, pretty hot."

Yikes.

I start with the long-hair guy. "Hi." Then I move on to the goatee guy. "Not sure calling a girl 'pretty hot' in your sleazy way's a good way to start a conversation but," I smile, "thanks. I know."

The goatee guy's undeterred though. "Well, I speak the truth, babe."

"Yeah, not your babe either," I tell him, wrinkling my nose slightly.

He leans forward. "Not yet. But you will be."

I raise my eyebrows. "Is that the truth again?"

"You bet your pretty little ass it is." Then he actually *looks* at my ass by bending further forward. "Not little. Tight though." Grinning, he continues, "You bet your pretty tight ass it is, babe."

Okay, can I just smack him a little?

He's so drunk that I'm sure one's enough to put him in his place.

I resist though. Only because I don't want to make any waves and draw attention to myself.

Or who I am or who my brother is and all that.

Although to be honest, the chances that these people will recognize me are very low. As I've mentioned before, I don't live in town and I've hardly been to any of their games before.

But still.

"Right." I somehow keep my smile in place. "As much as I'd love to stay and chat with you guys, I really want to catch up with my friend tonight. So can you," I gesture with my hands, "make way, please."

The goatee guy smirks. "We can. If you tell us your name."

"Krista," I say instantly.

Of course it's a lie; I'm not going to tell them my real name.

"Krista," he repeats.

"Yup."

He looks me up and down. "Very pretty. Suits you."

"Pretty name for a pretty girl, right?"

His smirk widens. "I'm Rocky. This here is Joe."

I swing my eyes over at Joe, who hasn't said anything since his initial greeting. And the reason, as I find out after looking at him, is that *he* is looking at me weirdly. As if he's trying to search for something on my face.

Fuck.

Please tell me he isn't trying to place me or something similarly disastrous.

Still I keep my cool. "Hi, Joe. Hi, Rocky."

"So who's your friend, Krista?" the goatee guy, Rocky, asks me.

I bring my focus back to him. "That wasn't the deal."

"How about you tell us and we'll let you go."

"You don't know her."

"We know everyone at this party." He raises his brows, which I think was meant to look all arrogant and sexy but due to his drunkenness looks kinda sloppy and comical. "In fact, you're the only person we don't know and —"

"No, we know her."

Joe speaks for the first time, and Jesus, this is what he decides to say?

"What?" Rocky frowns at him.

Joe frowns back. "Yeah, we do."

"No, we don't."

"We do, asshole."

"Yeah? Then who is she?"

At this, Joe frowns harder. "I think she's…" His frown becomes even thicker. "Bobby's sister."

Rocky throws him a flat look, or what passes for one while inebriated. "Fuck off. Bobby's sister is Barbara."

Joe's brows twitch with confusion. "All right then. But she's someone's sister."

"Duh, fuckface," Rocky snaps. "She *has* to be someone's sister."

"Or girlfriend."

Rocky gets super upset at that. "Fuck you, Joe. She isn't anyone's girlfriend."

"Or she could be someone's side piece."

Rocky gets up in Joe's face. "Yeah. She's going to be mine."

"What, your girlfriend?"

"Why the fuck not?"

"Because you've already got one. And I don't think Simone's gonna like you fucking around on her."

"Simone's not here, is she?"

"Because she's fucking cramming for a test," Joe reminds him.

"Yeah, which ain't exactly supporting her boyfriend who's just won a game."

Now Joe is the angry one. "You never deserved her, you fucking pig."

"Fuck you again, Joe. And I don't want her. I've already got what I want in front of me."

They argue some more.

And all through this my emotions go from fear when Joe looked like he recognized me — especially when he said that I was someone's sister, which I am — to amusement at Rocky and Joe fighting idiotically to actual anger on this Simone's behalf. Of course I don't know the girl, but there's a thing called sisterhood. And this asshole jock boyfriend of hers is ready to break her trust.

I'm with Joe here. This guy does not deserve her.

"Hi, excuse me," I chime in, deciding to break up this argument and move things along, and thankfully they both stop talking. "Can we focus on me for a second, please?" I first address Joe. "You're right. I'm someone's sister, but you don't know them, okay? And you don't know me. I don't go to your school. I don't even live in town. I'm visiting. There. Does that satisfy your curiosity?" Then I turn to Rocky. "And as flattering as all your drunken and pot-infused attention is, I'm not interested. I wasn't interested from the get-go, but now that I know you've got a girl, who by the way sounds really responsible and amazing, studying on a Saturday night instead of wasting her time partying with you, there is no chance in hell that I'll ever be interested in you. Are we clear now? Can I go say hi to my friend?"

Or the guy that I've been semi-stalking for the past week.

Who at this very moment is with a girl, doing God only knows what things.

Well, I know too. God's not the only one in the know here.

And every second I spend on these morons, he's spending it with her.

"Now listen here," Rocky goes. "Don't try to play games when we both know you're into me."

I draw back, shocked. "What?"

"You've been smiling at me, flirting with me since the beginning."

"Look, buddy." I glare at him. "If I was flirting with you, you'd know. I'm quite the flirt, all right? My smiles were meant to be polite. That's it. So again, can I go now?"

Anger crackles on his face which makes me roll my eyes. "Don't be a fucking tease, all right?"

I stab a finger at him. "Why don't you stop being a self-centered asshole first?"

His hand strikes from out of nowhere and grabs my wrist. "Don't make me angry, Krista. You're mine and —"

13

I'd say I don't know what caused him to halt mid-speech and so abruptly at that, but I'd be lying.

Because I do know.

It's the same thing that causes him to let go of my wrist. Again, abruptly. As he stares — him and Joe both actually — at something over my shoulder with wide eyes and an open mouth.

I want to turn around and look at it too.

Or rather him.

It's a him.

Him.

But I'm frozen in my spot for some strange reason. And the word 'frozen' itself could mean that I'm cold. That I have a chill running down my spine. That I may be turning blue, my blood going icy.

It's not true though.

Even though it's February and technically winter, I feel what I felt that day.

At the soccer game.

I feel like the air has turned heavy and swollen. Humid. Like it does before a rainstorm. A *fierce* rainstorm that brings with it a thunder so loud and crackling, so bright and blinding that you have to cover your ears and clench your eyes shut. That you have to run and take cover, protect yourself from it.

Not me though.

I don't want to take cover. I don't want to run.

I want to tip my face up and open my mouth to drink it down.

I want to open my arms and let the lightning strike me.

Because I know it won't hurt me. Nothing will.

I'm as charged up and electric as the thunderstorm. I'm as liquid and shapeless as the rain falling from the sky.

I'm heated with excitement and burning with thrill. And when the thunder actually strikes, I go up in flames.

"No," a growl comes from behind me, "she's mine."

I spin around then.

I have to.

Because I have to see. I have to stare into the eye of the storm.

The dark and gleaming, *angry* eye of the storm.

And holy fuck, it's beautiful.

He's beautiful.

He's more beautiful than anything I've ever seen in my life. Than anything has a right to be.

Then, he switches his focus over to me. "You."

His growl makes me clench my belly and whisper, "Yes."

Those dark angry eyes darken further at my breathy reply. "Come."

With that, he turns around and begins to walk away.

And I go.

Wherever he is going.

My brother's teammate.

No, not a teammate but my brother's rival. The *one* guy my brother hates to his core.

Ledger Thorne.

Chapter Two

MY BROTHER'S RIVAL.

Yeah, did I forget to mention that?

If I did, here it is: Ledger Thorne is not only my brother's teammate but also a rival.

Let me explain what it means.

So once upon a time, in a town called Bardstown, there were two soccer players: Reed Jackson, who also happens to be my big brother, and Ledger Thorne, the guy I've been obsessed with for the past week. They were both great in their own right. So great that they'd been given nicknames based on their playing styles: the Wild Mustang, because my brother is supposedly erratic and unpredictable on the soccer field and because he drives a white Mustang; and the Angry Thorn, because Ledger is known for his hothead-edness and his anger that he mostly keeps in check when on the field — *mostly* being the operative word — sticking to a very structured approach, and because his last name is Thorne.

They've been playing together for years now.

Always on the same team. And hence always on the same side.

However, instead of being friends or even cordial teammates, they are enemies.

They're rivals. Adversaries. Foes.

Competitors.

No one knows how it all started, but what they *do* know is that the Angry Thorn, despite the name, values his cool head on the field. He's the team captain, the authority, and he likes to set an example. Which doesn't sit very well with the Wild Mustang, who probably also wanted to be a captain since they're both equally good. Which means the Mustang does everything in his power to make the Thorn lose it on the field. Which in turn, doesn't sit right with the Thorn — that he does in fact lose it because of a player on his team — and so the Thorn, as the captain, does everything in his power to make the Mustang's life miserable off the field.

So it goes on and on in a vicious cycle.

But that's not all. They also have this very official-sounding unofficial bet that's been going on for years.

To see who could score more goals.

At the end of each season, the number of goals made by each of them individually are tallied, and a winner is declared. And apparently, since Bardstown is a soccer town, this 'winner' gets not only bragging rights — which could be further used to provoke each other on and off field — but also the town's respect, all the girls that you could think of, all the fanfare and free drinks and food throughout the year.

All of this, to a non-soccer fan, would look very surreal. It does to me for sure.

But that doesn't mean that it's not true.

It's *so* true that there are actual sides, or camps, if you will.

The Mustang camp, made of everyone who worships my brother. And the Thorn camp, made of the disciples of Ledger Thorne.

So anyway, remember the second problem in our epic love story that I'd mentioned?

I mean, apart from it being imaginary.

It's *this*.

Their legendary rivalry.

Which I knew nothing about up until last week. Since I don't attend any games and my brother has never uttered a word about it to me. But I saw it firsthand on the field, my brother and *him* facing off. Actually my brother and him, practically coming to blows in the middle of the game over I don't even remember what. Something about my brother not passing the ball to a striker so he could take the winning shot himself.

But that's not the point.

The point is that I know about it now.

I know how much they both hate each other.

And even though I think it's stupid and childish and ridiculous and *really fucking idiotic* to be fighting over something as trivial as sports, I still have to pick sides. And since I'm a Jackson, I am automatically Team Mustang. I will always be Team Mustang. I can betray *anyone* in this world, but not my big brother.

Never ever my big brother.

Because all we have is each other, and that's always been the case. Us against the world. Us against our parents. Who can't really be called parents because I don't remember the last time they acted like it. When my dad's not busy earning millions, he's off screwing everything with a skirt. And when my mom's not busy with her pool boys, she's off globe-trotting and spending the said millions.

That's why I promised myself that I'd stay away from *him*. I promised myself that I'd stay at a distance.

I'd look but never touch.

I'd dream but never wish for it to come true.

But look what I did tonight, what I'm *doing* tonight.

I not only blew my cover and entered, without a thought or a plan, into what is essentially the enemy camp — I mean, what was I going to do if and when I found him with that blonde girl? What was my plan of action? — but also, now I'm following their leader to parts unknown.

Just because he said — no, *growled* — 'come.'

What am I, a dog?

I mean he could've phrased it nicely and…

No, wait.

Wait a fucking second.

Because that's not all that he growled back there, is it? He growled something else.

He said…

But then I go crashing into something hard and I lose my train of thought.

Also my footing.

The latter I get back though. Very quickly.

And it's all because of the hand on my bicep.

His hand.

Strong and heated.

Just like the thing that I crashed into — which I'm suspecting was his back — not two seconds ago.

So heated that I feel it through the thick layer of the Italian cashmere coat that I'm wearing.

Breathless and hot, I go from his long fingers wrapped around my arm, up *his* arm that looks all kinds of dense and solid, to his shoulders that again appear all corded and muscled — and all this, through his brown leather jacket — all the way up to his face.

And I say, "I'm not yours."

Because that's what he had said. Back there.

Along with growling at me to 'come,' he'd called me 'his.'

Which I'm clearly not.

"You said that, back there." I lower my voice a little and try to mimic him. "*She's mine.* She's not yours. I mean, *I'm* not yours. I'm sure you probably said it to save me from them. And thank you for that, but —"

"No."

"What?"

Now that I've managed to get my breath and thoughts back, plus my footing, I realize that there's no reason for him to keep a hold of me, but he still is. In fact his grip has grown tighter in the last couple of minutes.

As have his features.

Which is saying something, because his face already appears to be carved out of stone.

It was one of the first things I noticed about him after the game was over and I rushed down the bleachers to get a good look at the guy who played like thunder and went toe to toe with my brother. Something that I'd never seen anyone do.

Even relaxed after his win, I could tell that the bones of his face, the structure of them, are forged in steel. The arches of his cheekbones. The jut of his square jaw. His stubborn forehead. Even his arrogant nose.

And it's all very broad and masculine.

Beautiful.

King-like.

And as I've said before, he *is* the king.

The Angry Thorn.

Although I don't know if that nickname is appropriate for him anymore.

After following him around for days and witnessing his beauty from all angles, I think his nickname should be something else. He may be a hothead — and he clearly looks angry right now — but what he is more is beautiful.

The Beautiful Thorn.

That is what people should call him.

Because pair his kingly face with his glittering dark eyes, his dark hair — thick and wavy, falling all over his forehead and the side of his face, completely mussed up and crazy beautiful — plus his leather jacket that bows down to the broadness of his shoulders and his washed-out jeans, he's the most beautiful thing I've ever seen.

"Didn't do it to save you," he explains, his face dipped toward me.

Oh and let's not forget about his voice.

I've heard it before, here and there, from a distance, polluted by the noise of traffic or crowd. But this is the first time I'm hearing it from up close, and it's beautiful as well.

Rough and low and gravelly.

Reminds me of dipping my toes in sand.

"So then w-why did you?" I ask, flexing my toes in my boots. "Call me yours if not to save me."

"That I could've done, and *did*, with one look," he goes on, ignoring my question.

Believe it or not, it's the truth.

If he wanted to save me — and he did — he didn't even have to open his mouth.

And that's because they're all afraid of him.

Afraid of his temper. His reckless anger.

I should be too, right?

But I'm not.

In fact his anger for some reason makes me feel… safe.

Like nothing could touch me when I'm around him.

No disaster, no calamity. No bullets, no arrows. No snowstorms, no hurricanes.

Because he's the thunder himself.

Something that I've only ever felt with my brother. Definitely not my parents or anyone else.

"Because they're all afraid of you," I say, my breath going haywire again.

His eyes gleam. "Yeah."

"Because you're the Angry Thorn."

Something flickers over his features that I can't read. "I see my reputation precedes me."

Even though his expression is a mystery to me, I somehow still think that it may resemble… hurt. And before I can stop myself, I say, "I think that's the wrong nickname for you though."

"Yeah?"

"Yes." I nod. "You should be called something else."

"And what's something else?"

"Beautiful Thorn." I lick my lips. "B-because you're beautiful."

His eyes dip to my mouth for a second. "And what should I call you?"

"K-Krista," I say, cringing on the inside.

Usually I'm pretty good at lying and I didn't feel the same hesitation back when I told Joe and Rocky my false name. But telling it to him feels wrong.

What feels even more wrong is when he repeats it. "Krista."

"Uh, yeah. Krista." I smile slightly. "That's me. Nice to meet you."

"Must be."

"What?"

"For you."

"I don't —"

"I mean from what I understand, it does get tiring."

"What gets tiring?"

His fingers flex around my arm. "Following me around all the time."

"What?"

His eyes rove over my features before he says, "You do that, don't you?"

My heart's thudding in my chest. "I… I don't know what you're talking about. I —"

"You're the pretty little stalker."

I try to twist free from his grip and step back. "I'm not —"

"*My* pretty little stalker," he says, his dark eyes glittering something fierce. "So technically you're mine. Which is why I said it."

"I'm —"

"Have been for the past week. Since the game."

Before I can stop myself, I blurt out, "So you… did see me at the game?"

"Black dress and a bright purple coat," he murmurs. "Who probably cheered for me and every goal I made. Yeah, I saw you."

I did.

I did cheer for him and every goal that he made.

I did feel guilty about it though. Because every goal that he scored was one goal less for my brother, and I could see that that frustrated him. But I couldn't stop myself.

Like I can't stop myself now from saying, "You were amazing on the field. The way you ran, it was like your feet didn't even touch the ground. You were flying. Like you had wings or something. Something that the others didn't have. I just… I thought that was beautiful. I thought you were beautiful."

He takes his time replying back.

Probably because he's busy staring at me. Studying my upturned face. And I let him, because that gives me the time to let the news sink in.

The great big news.

That he *did* see me at the game.

He did.

All this time I thought that he didn't know that I existed. That he had no clue, but he did.

He did have a clue.

Oh my God. Oh my God. *Oh my God.*

"So is that why you've been stalking me for the past week?" he asks at last. "Because you think the way I kick a muddy ball around is beautiful?"

"No," I reply.

"So why don't you enlighten me then?"

Right.

Why *have* I been following him?

Well first, he *is* beautiful. He's the most beautiful guy I've ever seen. And then there's the fact that he makes me feel the things that no guy has ever made me feel — electric, euphoric, excited. Just the way I do when I'm reading my romance novels.

But that's not all.

That's not why I'm obsessed with him or in love with him.

I think I'm in love with him because I have a suspicion he's like me. Or at least our stories are somewhat similar.

So in all my stalking and observing and asking around about him, his legendary temper isn't the only thing that I've come to find out. Turns out he comes from a big family of siblings. He's got three older brothers and a baby sister. And like Reed and me, they have no one else but each other.

While our parents are still technically around, his father abandoned the family when he was a kid, and then a few years later, their mother died of cancer.

And since then they've been taking care of each other by themselves.

In fact they've single-handedly — by they, I mean all the brothers, including Ledger — raised their baby sister and taken care of her. And people say that the Thorne brothers would do anything for their sister. They say that the way these siblings stick together is the stuff of legends and very rarely heard of.

And I just… I just want to hug him, you see.

I just want to tell him how amazing he is, how freaking wonderful for not only taking care of his sister like only a few people can ever do, but also for beating all the odds and becoming one of the best soccer players with such a bright future.

In fact, he reminds me of the only person in my life who's ever made me feel safe.

My brother.

And yes, I know my brother would flip his shit if I ever told him that he's like his greatest enemy.

But anyway, those are the reasons why I've been thinking about him, obsessing over him, following him around.

Not that I'm going to tell him that.

I'm not an idiot.

I know how strange it will sound to him.

As strange as I sound to people that I know and grew up with.

So the people I grew up with or go to school with come from a very specific and strange society. The society of the rich. Where things like love and family and good parenting and so on aren't very high on the list of priorities. In my world, everyone's more concerned about dresses and jewelry and parties and cars and exotic vacations. Husbands cheat on their wives and wives on their husbands. Children get handed from one nanny to another until they grow up to be self-centered and materialistic. And then, they marry the same kind of people and behave the exact same way as their parents.

I don't want any of that.

I want something different.

I realize that I not only *don't* have lofty goals like the girls in my world, but also like the girls in the rest of the world. I don't want to be an engineer or a doctor, a lawyer or a teacher or any of those things. All I want — all I've ever wanted for as long as I can remember — is the kind of love I read about in romance novels. I want a man who loves me, who makes me feel safe, and I want to make a family with him.

As simple as these wishes are, they're super controversial in my world.

And anything or anyone who thinks differently is branded as crazy.

So that's what I am to them.

A crazy girl living in her own world.

And while I don't give a fuck — in fact I flaunt it, my abnormal way of thinking, just to annoy them — about what they think of me, I do care about what *he* may think if I tell him that I've fallen in love with him at first sight.

So I try to stall. "Well first, I don't think you could call it stalking. What I've been doing for the past week."

"No?"

"No," I inform him sagely. "Stalking sounds intense. Stalking sounds wrong. *Stalking* implies criminal behavior. And I'm not a criminal."

His eyes rove over my face once again, something flickering in his eyes. "So what are you," he pauses a second before saying, "Krista?"

I cringe again.

I wish he'd stop saying that name. I wish he'd say *my* name.

Even though I can't tell him that.

And even if I could, I would never want him to call me by my name.

It's tragic, my name.

Shakespearean and catastrophic.

I lift my chin. "Actually, before I answer your question, what I'd like to know is, if you thought I was stalking you, which I clearly was not, why didn't you say anything before tonight?"

His grip flexes around my arm again. Then, "You mean, why'd I let you run after me in your sky-high heels all this time?" My feet teeter in my sky-high heels and he gives me my balance back once again. Then his gaze drops down to my boots for a second before lifting. "When you clearly don't know how to walk in them."

"I know how to walk in them."

His eyes go to his grip on my arm then. "I beg to differ."

"Actually you know what," I try to twist free from his hold again, "I think I'm okay. You can let go of me now."

And again, he doesn't let me. "Why don't you answer my question first?"

"Why don't you answer mine?" I say curtly, rolling my shoulders, struggling harder.

He barely pays attention to my puny struggles. "I'm not the one trying to get free."

"This is harassment," I tell him then.

"I call it self-defense."

"What? Self-defense from *what*?"

"From my pretty little stalker."

"If you're so afraid of me, then why don't you just let me go?"

"And have you jump all over me in the throes of your stalkery obsession?" His voice, on the other hand, sounds amused. "Nah, I think I prefer to keep you trapped."

"I'm not going to jump all over you."

"Can't take that chance, can I?"

I growl.

Then, "Listen, okay? I'm sorry I stalked you. I'm sorry I followed you around this past week. I'm clearly not going to make the same mistake again. So why don't you just let go of me so I can leave and you can go back to that model-like blonde," then before I can stop myself, I add, "who I have to say has very bad taste in shoes."

"Does she now?"

"Yes," I reply. "I'd never pair those silver sandals with the red dress that she's wearing."

He hums, still not letting go me. "Can't say that I'm interested in her shoes though."

"Well clearly not. Otherwise you wouldn't be with her."

"Or her dress."

My heart squeezes. "Why, because she won't be wearing it for too long?"

"Why, does that make you jealous?"

My heart squeezes harder. "No."

At this, his lips pull up on one side and I watch his face become even more beautiful. Which I didn't think was possible at all. But there you have it.

The Beautiful Thorn can become even more beautiful.

And I can become even more breathless and obsessed with him.

Even when I want to smack his face and stomp on his foot.

He leans down a little, his gaze boring into mine. "It's okay. There's no need for you to be jealous."

"I —"

"There's plenty of me to go around. And you can have a taste once I'm done with her."

I blink.

Then I gasp.

And *then* I rear back, wanting to hit him. "You're disgusting."

Not that he's afraid of me or my venomous words. Chuckling, he says, "But for tonight, that blonde was just a cover."

"A cover for what?"

"To draw you out of your hiding place."

It's a testament to how frazzled I am that it takes me a second to understand what he's talking about. And then I remember something from earlier. When even though he was dragging that blonde behind him with single-minded purpose, yet he'd stopped at the back porch to glance over at the bushes.

Shock runs through me then.

At the realization that he knew I was hiding behind the bushes.

Even though it shouldn't.

I mean, he's already admitted to knowing all along, but still.

"Because you knew where I was hiding," I say finally.

"I did."

"All this time."

"Yeah."

"You probably also knew where I was hiding at the last party."

"Behind the tree. By the rose bushes."

"And the party before that."

"Under the living room window."

Ugh.

I can't believe he knew.

I *cannot believe* that he knew all along that I've been following him.

Or how poor my stalking skills are.

God, how fucking embarrassing.

"But you still chose to not say anything," I say.

"Yeah, I chose not to."

"Probably because you've been having too much fun laughing at me with your friends, right?"

His jaw clenches at my assumptions. "I'm not a very friendly person."

"What, that's —"

"And laughing at someone behind their back isn't really my style."

"I don't —"

"What I'm not," he says then, cutting me off yet again, "is a very patient person. So again, why the fuck have you been following me for the last week like bad fucking mojo that I can't seem to shake?"

"B-because I've got a crush on you," I blurt out.

I don't know why I said that.

But then again, what else could I have said?

Plus I don't think he's going to let it go. So the best course of action is to just tell him — a very mild version of the truth — and leave.

Although my answer has only managed to tighten his grip on me and bring him closer as he murmurs, "Is that right?"

Something about his eyes and the way he's watching me makes goose-bumps rise on my skin, and with trembling breaths, I say, "B-but I can see that my following you around — I'm still not calling it stalking, no matter what you say — has caused you distress. So I won't do it anymore. And if you —"

"You won't anymore," he says, his eyes narrowed now.

"No, I won't," I say, promising that to myself as well.

Because honestly, that way only lies betrayal of my brother and heart-break. So it's best that I quit now before it goes any further. And God forbid *he* finds out who I really am.

"So if you just let me go, I can get out of here and —"

"No."

"What?"

"Not letting you go."

I look at his fingers on my bicep again before going back to him. "But you just said that you would."

"I lied."

My heart's pounding in my chest. "Ledger, let me go or —"

"Not yet." He squeezes my flesh. "Krista."

"I swear —"

"Not until I tell you that I've been watching you too."

I freeze. "What?"

For the third time tonight, his gaze sweeps over my features. He takes me in but this time it feels lazier, his perusal. Slow and deliberate. As if he's cataloging things about me and my face.

"Especially your eyes," he says a few moments later.

"M-my eyes."

"Yeah." Then, squinting his own as he looks into mine, he continues, "Which I thought were gray, but they're not."

"They… They're not?"

"Not all the time."

"I don't understand."

"Sometimes," he tells me, still looking into my eyes, "they are blue."

"I don't think that's true. My eyes have always been g-gray."

Something that I share with my brother.

Along with our dark hair.

"Mostly in the sunlight," he says though, breaking into my thoughts.

"Oh," I breathe out.

"Or when you laugh."

"I —"

"Which is pretty much all the time, isn't it?"

"Well, uh, I-I think so?" It comes out as a question but I don't know what else to say.

He hums. "Especially when you're eating cotton candy."

"You know that?" I say, again stupidly because hasn't he just admitted to watching me?

"Which again is pretty much all the time, isn't it?"

"I l-love cotton candy."

I love you.

Do you also love me?

Is that why he's been watching me?

Oh my God he's been watching me.

Me.

All this time.

All this freaking time, and oh my fucking God, please tell me it means what I *think* it means.

Please tell me it means that he's…

"And then there's your dark freckle," he says, dropping his eyes down to the side of my neck. "Siting right at your pulse. Beating like a heart."

"What about it?"

"Sometimes it's there and sometimes it's not."

"How's that possible? How —"

"Sometimes your long, thick, endless hair hides it. But then sometimes you'll flip your hair or the breeze will whip it back, like right now, and there it is. Like a hidden fucking diamond that I can't look away from. Can't look away from you. From how fast your heart is beating."

Since he's still looking at that spot, I *know* that he knows.

Exactly how fast my heart's beating.

The answer to which is very fast.

Extremely fast.

My heart is going supersonic in this moment.

It's going so fast through time and space that it may disappear at any moment.

That *I* may disappear at any moment.

So without volition, my hands go to his t-shirt — a faded navy thing that makes you think more of punk rock and electric guitars than of soccer players, but I guess that's why it looks so good on him — and hold on lest I vanish from this surreal moment.

"L-Ledger," I whisper on a broken breath when he doesn't say anything.

It makes him snap his eyes up.

As if waking up from a dream.

As if he *didn't like* that I woke him up.

He wanted to keep staring at my mole, my hair. He wanted to keep sleeping and dreaming.

"And *then*," he continues, picking up the thread of conversation. "Then there's you."

"Me."

"And your tight-as-fuck dresses and sky-high heels."

He says it so violently, so angrily that I can't help but reply, "There's nothing wrong with my dresses or my heels."

"No," he says with clenched teeth. "Except your dresses can barely contain your tight ass and your heels make it look even tighter. And when you strut down the street in something that can barely contain you and makes you look twice as juicy, the entire town has to stop what they're doing and watch you. The entire town has to stop and *hear* you go click-click-click down the street. They have to nail their eyes on your curvy little body, watching it bounce and jiggle as you pass them by. Watching that gap between your thighs, probably placing bets on who gets to stick their hand up there first. Or maybe stick it down from the top. Because it's not as if your dresses are doing a better job of hiding your tits either. In fact, if anything," his eyes go down to my chest, "your dresses lift them and offer them up like candies for every hungry motherfucker out there."

I don't think I'm breathing at all.

I think I'm suffocating.

I think *he's* suffocating me. With his words, all dirty and heavy and sticky like syrup.

A syrup so sweet that I have no choice but to guzzle it down instead of air.

"But they're fools, aren't they?" he says, his voice still low, his eyes still dark and his jaw still clenched.

"Why?"

He squeezes my arm again, "Because they don't know that you're mine."

Current runs up and down my spine and my fists become tighter in his shirt. "No."

"They don't know that I'll fuck them up, if they keep watching you."

"What?"

"If they keep wanting to touch you."

"I-I'm —"

"And you know I can do it, don't you?"

I swallow. "Yes."

"Tell me why."

"Because you're the Angry Thorn."

"I am."

"And you belong to me."

I sway on my feet a little. "Yes."

"No one can keep us apart."

"No."

His lips pull up in another smirk and in the back of my mind I think that this smirk from him seems different. It feels different too. "And do you know who I'll enjoy fucking up the most, if he ever came between us?"

"W-who?"

"Your piece of shit brother."

I blink. "What?"

His smirk only grows. And I realize it's different because it's cruel.

It's cold.

So cold that it burns me.

"And I'm pretty sure he will," he keeps going, his eyes burning me too. "Because he's an asshole like that. But it's okay. I can take him. In fact, I've been wanting to take him for years now. And now that I have you," his heated eyes go up and down my body, "I won't hesitate to break his bones and play ping pong with his eyeballs, if it means keeping you." Then, even lower, "Tempest."

I flinch.

At him using my real name.

My stupid Shakespearean name that I've hated for as long as I can remember. Because Shakespeare was a fool who wrote tragedies and reveled in destroying happily ever afters. He probably didn't even believe that they existed. Exactly like the people who I've grown up with.

But more than that, I flinch because the name that I've always hated sounds so... beautiful in his voice.

As if he's got the magic of turning ugly things into beautiful ones.

Even though he's using it mockingly.

Even though he's breaking my heart into a million pieces.

And he is, isn't he?

By how callous he sounds. How cruel. How he knew all along, which seems to be the theme of the night.

That he knew.

Who I was. Who I really was, all this time.

And he's using it against me.

"Who would've thought, huh," he continues thoughtfully, "that the guy I can't stand, the guy that I've hated for years, the biggest piece of shit I've ever met, *that guy* has such a pretty little sister? I mean, where was he hiding you? And he was, wasn't he? That fucker. Probably because he knew. One look at his pretty-as-fuck sister can turn a man into a giant rabid horndog. So maybe I can't blame him. But it doesn't matter now, does it? The deed is done. You're mine. And the best part is," he leans in further, "that you don't wanna go anywhere either. My pretty little stalker."

"Let me go," I growl.

"Yeah?"

I twist my fist in his t-shirt and push at him. "Let me the fuck go."

He doesn't budge. "I don't think I want to."

"I swear to God, if you —"

"I *think*," he speaks over me, "now that this opportunity has fallen into my lap, I want to use it."

"What?"

"Use you." He tilts his head to the side. "To fuck with your brother."

My heart has dropped to my stomach. "Don't you dare."

"No?" He chuckles then. "But come on, it'll be fun. All you have to do is pose for the camera and kiss me a little."

"What?"

"Which I bet you've been dying to do anyway."

I push at him again. "*Let me go.*"

"Are you saying that you haven't been dying to kiss me, Tempest?" He tsks. "Because if you are, then I find that very hard to believe. Especially given the fact that you've got a crush on me. You have, haven't you?"

"No, not anymore. I don't —"

He tsks some more. "See, I don't think I like you lying to me, baby."

"Don't you call me baby. I'm not your fucking *baby*."

He puts his other hand on his chest, where his heart is. "Well that hurt a little. But we're going to let it slide, baby, and focus on important things."

"You —"

"Such as you and me. And that kiss in front of the camera."

His words, his smirk. Those eyes.

They're stabbing me, stabbing my heart like sharp thorns.

Making me bleed on the inside.

Making me weep and gush out all the soft, pink emotions that I had for him.

But I'll be damned if I let him see that.

I'll be fucking damned if I let him see anything other than my anger at him.

"Listen here," I begin, stepping closer to him, glaring, "you fucking asshole, if you even think about using me against my brother, I'm going scratch your eyes out. And then I'll stomp on your fucking feet with my sky-high heels and I'll do it so hard that you won't be able to play your beloved game for the rest of the month. Do you understand? So I want you to let me go before I hurt you like no girl has ever done before."

Still, he takes his time looking me over. Then, "You're a firecracker, aren't you?"

"Yes." I push at him again. "And I'll set you on fire, if you're not careful."

He chuckles again but this time it's softer, more like a puff of air as he keeps taking me in. "Although you don't feel like one."

"I don't —"

"You feel more like a" — a curious frown emerges from between his brows — "Firefly."

I go still then.

Because his tone has changed, become something akin to... reverence.

Which I'm sure is wrong but I don't know what else to call it.

"Fragile and bright. Glowing in the dark."

And since he sounds reverential — which as I said is wrong and ridiculous — I push at him the hardest. And by some miracle — either he wasn't expecting it or he was getting tired of my pushing and snapping — he lets me go.

But it makes me stumble and teeter on my four-inch heels.

Like he was the only thing holding me and keeping me tethered to the ground and now that he isn't there, gravity has got me in its clutches and I fall.

Down on my knees.

My bones hitting the pavement with a crunch.

It must be painful but I don't feel it.

There's a much larger pain in my chest.

Like before, he wraps his fingers around my bicep and hauls me up. But unlike before, he doesn't keep his grip on me. Or maybe I'm too ferocious in this moment to *let him* keep his grip on me and he can sense it.

"You really don't know how to fucking walk in heels, do you?" he growls then. "What the —"

"Don't," I snap, wiping my hands on my skirt, hardly feeling the gravel rubbing across my skin. "Don't touch me. Ever. I don't know what I was thinking. I don't know why I thought…" I swallow. "I thought that you had more to you than what people say. I don't know why I thought you were… different. You're not. Clearly. And you know what, my brother's right to hate you. And I hope he fucking beats you in your stupid contest."

With that, I turn around and start walking away.

I start walking to my car.

I don't look back. I don't think about catching a last glimpse of him.

I simply get in my car and get out of there.

Twenty minutes later as I'm waiting for the garage door to open, I think I spy bright headlights in the rearview mirror. I think I know those headlights. I know that vehicle. It's a beat-up black truck that I've been following around for the past week.

But before I can confidently conclude that, my garage door slides all the way up and I decided to not dwell on it, choosing to drive forward.

Because nothing about him should matter to me.

Nothing about him should be important or vital or life-changing.

He's not the guy I should be in love with.

He's the Angry Thorn. Soccer royalty of Bardstown. Soccer god.

My brother's rival and enemy.

And I will do whatever it takes to get over him.

Chapter Three

HER BEAUTIFUL THORN

Long-as-fuck hair.

Creamy skin. Mouth plump and pink like cotton candy.

A short fucking dress partially hidden under the winter coat but not enough to hide how tight it was.

Not enough to make me forget.

The trail of blood running down her knees. Because of her fall.

Or that her blue-gray eyes were misty and wet when she left.

Truth be told, it's none of my business. That she left here bleeding and crying. Heartbroken.

What else did she expect?

Given who she is and who I am.

Given who her fucking brother is.

For all I know this was one of his dirty tricks. Using his sister to distract me from next week's game so he could win this year's contest. So he could fuck with me on the field like he always does.

Even as I think it though, I know it's not true.

If there's one thing that asshole loves more than himself, it's his little sister.

And as much as I hate to admit it, I get it.

I get it big time because I've got a baby sister too and I'd blow my fucking lid if she ever got close to him. I'd blow my *fucking lid* if I found out that he ever — *ever* — set his dirty eyes on her. Or worse, watched her from afar.

Like I have been doing. To his sister.

For the past week I mean.

Like I *did*.

A year ago.

When I saw her for the first time.

In my defense, I had no idea who she was.

She was sitting on the hood of a car, her legs dangling, watching people go by on the street. I don't exactly know what made me look at her in the first place. Was it the fact that she had a pink cotton candy in her hand or that she matched it in her pink dress and sandals? Or maybe it was the fact that her dress was more like a bigger version of a fucking tube top, leaving her delicate shoulders and the tops of her milky thighs bare.

She actually looked like a bowl of cream and candies.

Or it could've been the fact that she was laughing at something while taking bites out of that pink sugary cloud. And as sappy as it makes me sound, her laughter had a tinkling quality. Like the wind chimes that my sister likes to hang on our windows all over the house and drive us all crazy with the annoying sound.

Only on *her*, it wasn't as annoying.

On her it was... musical.

Or some shit.

Nonetheless, it pissed me off. I do remember that.

It pissed me off so much that it made me stop in my tracks.

Especially because I was exhausted after a long-as-fuck practice day. I wanted to go home and soak in ice water. I also wanted to eat whatever I could get my fucking hands on. My sister had been nagging me to get her cupcakes from her favorite store, Buttery Blossoms, for dessert, and since I'd lost a bet with one of my brothers, I had to be the one to go pick 'em up.

Which means I was busy and I had places to be.

I didn't have the time to stand on the sidewalk, frozen and immobile with a cupcake box in my hand, and watch a Barbie lookalike eating something that I wouldn't touch with a ten-foot pole. I also didn't have the time to intimidate the other people who stopped to watch her too. A group of guys, shooting the shit in front of the coffee shop next door, that had their eyes trained on her. That, in turn, scattered like cockroaches when I shot a low-whistle and a glare their way.

But what I remember the most is *him*.

Reed fucking Jackson.

The fact that he arrived at the scene only a few seconds after I'd sent those douchebags scurrying away. And the fact that as soon as she saw him, she jumped down from the hood, her entire petite but curvy body jiggling, and she threw herself into his arms, laughing like wind chimes in a fucking hurricane.

Which was when I noticed that the car she'd been sitting on was his.

Meaning she'd been waiting for him.

Meaning she was his. His flavor of the week. His piece of ass. His fucking groupie.

For a few seconds, as I watched them together — her grinning up at him, him chuckling; her chattering non-stop, him listening to her patiently; her reaching up to kiss his cheek, him smiling and ruffling her hair — my world was covered in a red film. My chest was burning. My gut was burning and the sounds of my own body were loud.

In the midst of all this, I watched him bend down and kiss her.

On her forehead.

Which, I will admit begrudgingly, was the only thing that had saved him that day.

Because why the fuck would he kiss her forehead when she had a mouth all sugared up and pink from cotton candy.

It almost looked... brotherly.

Something clicked in my brain then and I looked at them, *really* looked at them.

I noticed how she was watching him like he hung the moon, like he was her hero — something my own sister does with me and my brothers — and how he was looking at her, like she wasn't a hot piece of ass but she was something precious, something to be cherished and protected at all costs — something that my brothers and I do with our sister.

And it hit me.

She *was* his sister.

The infamous little sister that Reed Jackson adored to pieces.

She went to a boarding school in New York and so no one had ever seen her.

People speculated though, about the sister, Reed Jackson's only weakness.

Once the realization set in, my red haze cleared and I could breathe. But then it occurred to me that I'd been standing there, watching Reed Jackson's little sister.

My *enemy's* little sister.

Disgusted, I got out of there.

And honestly, I never expected to see her again.

Which was just as well because for the life of me, I couldn't get her out of my head. In fact in the year since, I thought about her so often — something that I'd never admit out loud — that when I did see her again, at the game last week, I thought I was hallucinating.

I thought I'd gone crazy.

But then I saw her again. And I kept seeing her.

Around town. On the streets. At that cupcake shop. At parties.

Always around. Always with her eyes on me.

I've got a crush on you.

I mean, what the fuck.

34

What in the *fucking fuck* is she thinking?

Either she's extremely stupid and naive.

Or really fucking brave, stalking the enemy.

Doesn't she know how dangerous I am? Doesn't she fucking know that I could do things to her?

Use her, abuse her. Goddamn ruin her just to fuck with her brother. Just to take out years and years of frustration that her piece-of-shit brother has caused me. Just to be the goddamn best soccer player in town. Which I already am, but it would be nice to crush the fucking competition.

Good thing I sent her home bleeding and crying.

Even though it still makes me want to punch something and then kneel at her feet so I can bandage her wounds, I'm glad that I scared her enough that she'll keep her distance from now on.

Which again makes me want to punch something.

But whatever.

I'll survive.

In fact, I'll thrive. Now that this chapter has been closed, I can forget about her and focus on what's important: the game. My career. Being the best. Being better than the best so I can get out of this shitty town and never look back.

When I return to the party, after making sure that she got home all right — something that I shouldn't have done but couldn't stop myself — I go in search of my targets. I find them by the pool, more or less in the same spot as before. Their eyes widen when they see me approach, almost ready to flee. But they're drunk and hence slow, and I'm faster than the entire team put together. So I reach them before they can take more than two steps back.

Grabbing both their collars, I growl, "You ever talk to her, touch her, or even look at her, I'll break your fucking body, yeah?"

Joe and Rocky nod instantly and vigorously like bobbleheads.

Fucking idiots.

"And you tell that to everyone on the team." I shake them to emphasize. "*Every fucker* on the team here tonight. No one touches her. Or they deal with me."

They both sputter and nod again, stumble over their own and each other's words.

Satisfied, I let them go and they scuttle away.

Then turning around, I stalk out the way I came, completely over this fucking shitshow of a party. I need to get back home anyway. I've got an early practice tomorrow — earlier than these douchebags — and my coach, who also happens to be my brother, is going to fucking shit a brick if I'm late.

Actually he's going to shit a brick if I'm not ten minutes early.

Because I'm the team's captain and as such I need to work harder than the others.

I've got a crush on you.

I get in my truck, slamming the door loudly in the wake of her words.

Stupid, naive, *annoying* words.

Of the girl I saw last summer.

Made of cream and candy.

Who glows in the dark like a firefly.

My rival's little sister.

Tempest fucking Jackson.

Part II

Chapter Four

Present

IF THEY ASK me how I met the love of my life, I'll tell them it was at a hospital.

Granted, it's not a very popular meeting place. But fate is fate. And love is love, isn't it? You never know when and where it's going to strike.

In our case, it struck us at the most unlikely place. At the NICU ward. I saw her tiny little body — even tinier and littler than the usual babies because she was a few weeks early, a preemie — hooked up to wires and tubes and instantly fell in love.

The kind of love that I knew at the moment — still do actually — will last a lifetime.

The kind of love that's massive and pure and absolutely life-changing.

A beacon.

Just like her name: Halo.

Halo Cora Jackson.

She's five months old and she's the love of my life.

Oh, and she's my niece.

Her eyes are big and blue and twinkling like jewels and she's got the cutest laugh ever.

Strapped to my chest in a cute little baby sling, she blinks up at me and I tell her, "Isn't this nice, just you and me?"

"Pah."

I bend down to kiss her sweet-smelling forehead. "I know, I know. I'm being selfish, taking you away from your mommy and your other aunts just so you and I can have some alone time. But can you blame me? You're my bestie."

"Gah. Gah. Pah," she replies as she flails her fist at me.

I catch it and place a kiss on it. "Plus I know you love me too, don't you? You love your auntie Tempest."

Halo blows a spit bubble at me, as if in agreement.

I chuckle. "Yeah, you do, my cute little birdie."

More spit bubbles and this time they're accompanied by some cute little kicks of her chubby feet that get me in the ribs. I don't mind though. I love when she wiggles her tiny little body.

I kiss her little fist again. "Best friends forever."

At this, she not only kicks me again but her entire body flails and jiggles in happiness. Plus she laughs. And then I have to kiss her fist again and again, and a bunch more times because how can I not?

She's my baby boo.

"What are you doing?"

I startle at the voice and look up.

Standing at the mouth of the kitchen — where I'm hanging out with Halo, and of course, doing other unsavory things — is my other BFF, Callie.

Usually I'd be happy to see her. Given that not only is she my BFF, she's my *very first* BFF ever since we bumped into each other at a soccer game three years ago. Plus she's my sister-in-law too. But since I was trying to get away from her, at her house no less, I'm kinda feeling guilty.

"Nothing."

She frowns, walking in. "You've been gone forever. Everyone's waiting for you."

Everyone includes my posse of other BFFs. Courtesy of Callie because I met them through her.

"Well, I went to the bathroom." Then, "I'm allowed to go to the bathroom, aren't I?"

Damn it.

That sounded super defensive.

And suspicious.

I wasn't doing anything wrong. It's just that sometimes I can get a little possessive of Halo and I don't like to share her, even with her mommy. And now that she's here, I'll have to give up Halo.

"What's going on?" When she reaches Halo and me, she peers down at the little bundle strapped across my chest and runs a finger down her pink cheek. "What's going on with your aunt, Lolo?"

"Gah. Gah. Ahhh."

Accompanied by some fierce wiggling and pumping of her fists, trying to leap onto her mommy. Which is something that I knew she'd do so I'm already halfway through loosening the sling wrap from around my body so Callie can go for Halo.

Despite being a possessive aunt, I don't blame Halo.

Or Callie.

For doing that.

I also don't blame Halo for giving her mommy the biggest smile as Callie settles her against her chest. A smile that lights up the entire room. And the smile that Callie returns possibly lights up the whole town of Bardstown. And then Halo, or Lolo as Callie calls her sometimes, launches into a series of babbles and coos that Callie nods at like she understands everything.

I just wish I had someone to give me a smile like that.

"Well, Lolo says," Callie says, looking up at last, "her aunt needs another cupcake."

Despite myself, I smile. "She's right. Or maybe she's giving you a signal that she's ready to taste your cupcakes."

"Absolutely not." Callie shakes her head. "She's only five months old. No solids until six months."

Halo blows another spit bubble — this time in protest, I'm sure — and out of nowhere, Callie produces a burp cloth and wipes off Halo's chin and lips. And she does it all without even looking.

I raise my eyebrows. "Is it because you're afraid that she's growing up too fast?"

Callie's shoulders droop. "She is, isn't she?" She peers down at Halo again. "I mean, she was just inside me, you know? Like yesterday. She used to kick and punch and," she smiles, "hiccup. And then she came. She could barely hold her head up. Hardly maintain any eye contact. She was all scrunched up like my little monkey. And now look at her, she's cooing and her eyes are so big. The other day, she even pointed at a dog in the park like she knew what it was. Like, how? How is she getting so big and smart? Shouldn't she be pressed up to my chest and just suck on my boobs and sleep? I think she's growing up faster than other babies." Finally, Callie looks up at me with the same blue eyes as Halo. "Don't you think?"

I give her a sympathetic look.

But she sighs dejectedly. "You think I'm crazy."

Halo coos again, probably trying to soothe her mommy.

Her mommy gives her a little kiss on her chubby cheeks.

"No, I think you're a mommy," I tell her, my throat feeling slightly choked up. "Actually you're the best mommy in the whole world."

Callie looks up then, her eyes shiny, a small smile on her face. "Thanks. I love you."

I smile back. "I love you too."

Then comes a voice from the living room.

"Where *is* everybody? We need to finish what we started."

We both look at each other, slightly guilty that instead of doing what we're supposed to do, we're standing here wasting time. Actually it's my fault so I say, "Shit. Let's go."

Patting Halo's diapered bottom, she says, "Yup. Duty calls."

In the living room, we find everything exactly as we left it: brown leather couches covered in heaps of clothing and accessories, and when I say heaps I mean it. I think I practically brought my entire wardrobe tonight. Then there are shoes littering the hardwood floor, again heaps of them because I also brought almost my entire shoe collection with me too: heels, strappy heels, wedges, peep-toes, booties, high-heeled booties, mid-heeled booties, pencil heels, block heels and everything else that you can think of.

And in the middle of it all, sitting on the floor among dresses and shoes, are the rest of my BFFs: Echo, Jupiter — she's the one who hollered just now — and Wyn. Although Wyn is in a computer screen set down on the coffee table because she's in New York and wasn't able to make it in person.

I'm very proud and happy to say that these aren't all of my BFFs. I've got two more but both of them were too super busy to even FaceTime and hence couldn't make it. For someone who grew up with people who branded her crazy, hence not worthy of their friendship, I've certainly made a lot of friends. And it's all because of my very first BFF, Callie.

She's the one who introduced me to every single one of them and I couldn't be more grateful to her.

"Okay, tell me you know how to do this," Jupiter says as soon as Callie and I resume our seats in our little circle. She has a makeup brush in her hand and she's pointing it at Echo like she's going to stab her eye with it. Then, "Because let me tell you, contouring is not my strong suit at all."

I shake my head. "Here, gimme." I turn to Echo who turns dutifully to me. "Now, just close your eyes and relax."

She looks skeptical but does as I say. "Okay."

And since Jupiter has already cleared her face with the kickass cleanser and toner she brought, I grab the bronzer and the highlighter and get to work. Although I have to say there is not much work to be done here. With her honey blonde hair and her light brown eyes, Echo's a natural beauty. Her cheekbones are already high and so her cheeks are sunken the right way and the right amount. All I have to do is darken them a little bit so they are the first things people see on her face. And maybe accentuate her jawline a little more than it already is.

Piece of cake.

Ten minutes later, she's ready to take on the world.

"Now open your eyes," I tell her and hold a mirror in front of her.

She does and as soon as she sees herself, she gasps. "Oh wow. That's…" She squints at herself, turning her face this way and that. "I can't… I can't believe that's me. I can't believe I look so pretty."

I smile at her. "It *is* you and you *are* that pretty. Makeup just jazzed it up a little."

"Exactly." Jupiter looks at her with wide happy eyes. "Girls don't need makeup to be beautiful because we already are. Makeup just gives us a little *oomph*."

Jupiter raises her palm for me to high five and I do, feeling warm.

I have to say, when Callie introduced me to all these girls, I wasn't sure if they'd be so welcoming. Not because they're not all friendly and awesome. But because they're already so tight with each other and also because until recently, I lived in New York and only visited Bardstown every so often.

Plus all these girls went to school together.

And it wasn't a normal high school either. It was an all-girls reform school called St. Mary's School for Troubled Teenagers. Which means it's a school for delinquents, troublemakers and rule breakers. Which also means that going to that school, graduating from it like they did this year, is no easy feat.

There's a stigma attached to it. Plus there are a million rules from when to wake up to how to do your homework and get good grades to graduate. It's basically like a prison, and when you're in prison together, you develop lifelong bonds. So I thought since I had a different high school experience, I wouldn't be able to jell with them and do it so quickly and easily. But I did and now here we are.

"I think this is perfect," Callie says while Halo is bundled up in her arms, playing with her golden blonde braid.

Wyn chimes in from the computer, tacking on to Callie's statement. "For what we have in mind."

Callie looks at her. "I know. This is going to be amazing."

"Right?" Wyn grins from the screen. "And here I was worried that our days of planning and plotting were over."

Callie grins back as Halo coos with happiness, probably watching her mommy smile. "It's never over when there's a guy involved."

"A grumpy, hot guy who won't have sex with you," Jupiter adds in, grinning as well.

"Well, I'm glad my misery is so amusing to all of you," Echo says, frowning.

Callie throws Echo a sympathetic look. "You're not gonna be miserable for long. Trust me. He'll see you like this and he'll lose his mind."

Wyn nods. "And all his inhibitions and reservations."

Jupiter smirks though. "Which is very ironic. Given how you ended up in this situation."

Oh yeah, the situation.

Well truth be told, it *is* kind of amusing.

So the reason we're all gathered here today, at Callie's house, is because Echo's boyfriend, Reign — a very hunky and grumpy soccer player — won't have sex with her. It's not because he's bored of their relationship. He can't be; first, because they've only just gotten together like, a couple of months ago. And second, because he's been wanting to get together with her since the first moment he saw her six years ago. But she started dating his best friend and so Reign backed off, thereby ensuring years and years of tortured pining on his — and turns out, hers as well — part.

The reason why Reign won't have sex with Echo is because last time they had sex, they got caught.

By Echo's parents.

Like actually got caught, almost buck-naked, doing it in her childhood bedroom, by Echo's mother.

I mean, oh my *God*.

It led to a lot of parental drama and heartache and tears. It's a miracle that they're together today and that her parents somehow calmed down enough for Echo to date Reign. Whom they still don't trust fully. And since it led to all the problems in their relationship, Reign, misguidedly, has taken it upon himself to prove himself. To her parents.

Which means no sex.

He says it's for a little while. Until her parents start to trust him and this new relationship.

But man, it's been like two months. And all they've done is some hand holding, some kissing and *that is it*. He won't even take them to second base. And get this: they both live in New York, where they're going to college. Echo is in her freshman year and Reign is a senior. So it's not as if there's any chance that her parents will even know that they're having sex, let alone catch them in the act like before.

But still, Reign won't budge.

Which is why since Echo is visiting this weekend, we all offered to help.

Jupiter brought makeup. I brought clothes and shoes. Callie brought or rather baked cupcakes and made butterscotch milkshakes; mine and Jupiter's are laced with a little vodka while Callie is drinking a virgin since she's breastfeeding. And Wyn, who also lives in New York with her boyfriend, brought moral support and her own diet soda.

Even though the situation is serious, we all can't help but snicker a little.

And Echo's frown becomes thicker, which she aims at Jupiter first. "I hate you." Then, to all of us, "I hate all of you." Then, just to Wyn, "I can't believe that you're laughing too. You're the kindest of them all, Wyn."

She's right. Wyn *is* kindest of us all. She's gentle and soft-spoken and she never ever laughs at anyone. She's basically a saint.

Wyn purses her lips, muttering, "Sorry." Then, "And you're right, I *am* the kindest of all. So shut up all of you and let's figure out what our next move is going to be."

We all purse our lips then and try to get back to business.

Callie's the first to respond, gently swaying Halo who seems to be falling asleep in her arms, still playing with her mommy's hair. "I say you dress up like that on your next date and then *you* make the move."

"Exactly," Jupiter says. "At the end of the date, tell him to come inside your dorm room."

"But he won't go," Echo says, her shoulders drooping. "He always just drops me off in front of my building and takes off. He won't even come through the door, let alone go up to my room on the *third floor*." A pause, then, "Well, first he insists that I go in, and when I do get inside, *that's* when he takes off. Like a stubborn, hands-off bodyguard protector."

"How about you tell him you need something fixed?" Wyn offers. "Like, in your room."

"I've tried that," Echo says. "I told him that I couldn't open this jar of peanut butter and that I needed his superior strength skills. And he looked at me and told me to stop. And when I asked him, stop what, he said, torturing me, and then he just took off. He didn't even wait for me to get inside and I didn't even get my goodnight kiss." She throws up her hands. "So basically I'm torturing him by trying to seduce him."

"Well I mean, he's not wrong," Jupiter says.

Echo narrows her eyes. "What?"

"In the sense that if your seduction attempts were working, there wouldn't be any torture. Because you both would get relief. But since so far you've failed, it *is* torture."

Echo stares at Jupiter for a second before chucking a piece of cookie at her; oh, because Callie also made chocolate chip cookies. "Gee, thanks for the explanation, Jupiter Jones."

The piece lands in her lap and she pops it in her mouth, grinning. "You're welcome, Echo Adler."

They're about to argue some more when I chime in, "I think I have a plan." Every eye in the room focuses on me and I explain, "You need something better than peanut butter. As in, more drastic than peanut butter."

"Like what?" Echo asks.

"How are your acting skills?" That gives her pause, but I keep going, "Doesn't matter. He can resist you asking for fake help for a peanut butter jar, but he won't be able to resist if you cry out for help in distress. Even if it's fake distress. Guys are weird like that. Especially the ones who are in love with you. So next time on your date, you wear that dress, you put that makeup on, and you wear my killer Dior heels. And at the end when he's dropping you off, you pretend to stumble and you pretend to stumble badly. And you cry a little, okay? And it doesn't matter how fake it is because if he loves you, there is no way he can resist carrying you in his arms and bringing you to your third-floor dorm room. And as soon as he does that, you lock the door and you jump him."

Echo is speechless.

All of them are, actually.

They're all staring at me with wide, wonder-filled eyes.

Then Callie says, "Did you read that in one of your romance novels?"

My heart constricts slightly. "Yes."

Jupiter leans forward. "Which one is it? Can you lend me a copy?"

"Sure," I tell her, my heart constricting further.

"No, me first," Echo says, "I'm the one with a crisis in her love life." Turning to me, "Can I please borrow it?"

"Uh-huh," I try to sound enthusiastic instead of squeaky and freaked out. "I'll bring it by tomorrow."

She beams. "Yay. Thank you."

First, I just want to say that I love how supportive these girls are of the fact that I read romance novels. They actually encourage me to read love stories; all of these girls even bought me a bunch of paperbacks for Christmas and my birthday last year. Something that I never even dreamed would happen given how I grew up, and it just makes me love them so much more.

But the thing is that I don't read romance novels anymore.

Haven't read them in a year.

Actually *over* a year. Thirteen months to be exact.

I've not only *not* read them but also I don't like to think about them or talk about them. So this conversation is making me a little uncomfortable. Of course they don't know that though. If I told them, I know they'd just get worried and fuss over me. Which I absolutely don't want because there's nothing to worry about at all. I'm just taking a break from romance.

A permanent sort of break, but yeah.

Thankfully though, I'm so glad we've moved on from the topic of romance novels, and now Callie's saying, "I can absolutely vouch for Roman losing his cool every time he thinks I'm distressed. And it has always been that way. Right from the start. And I can't tell you how many times his worrying and ranting about me not taking care of myself has led to us doing —"

"Okay." I point a finger at Callie. "No. Don't. I don't want to hear about *Roman* and you doing stuff to each other, okay? That's my brother."

My big brother, that is.

Well, his name is Reed but Callie calls him by her own name, Roman. And he calls Callie by his special name, Fae. Short for Fairy. And while I'm over the moon ecstatic that my brother and my very first BFF got married and have a beautiful little baby girl, I'm not going to sit here and listen to their sexy adventures. A sister has her limits.

Callie's eyes twinkle. "I was just saying that your idea has merit."

"Shut up."

"I don't think it's only the guys in love that do that," Wyn says then. "I think it's the guys in love from *Bardstown* who do that. I think it's something in the water here. Boys of Bardstown are uber possessive and protective. I can attest to that too. Because Conrad has always been —"

46

"Shut up," Callie goes. "If you say one more word about my brother —"

"Ha!" I stab my finger at Callie again. "Now you understand."

We narrow our eyes at each other but I'm right. *Now* she knows how it feels, because Wyn's boyfriend is Callie's older — oldest; Callie has four older brothers — brother Conrad. Like me, she's thrilled that one of her BFFs hooked up with her brother, but a sister has her limits.

Which Wyn completely understands, because she swivels her gaze to me and winks.

In fact, the only girl in our group right now who isn't hitched is Jupiter. Well, apart from me. But I have it on good authority that she's got her eyes set on another one of Callie's brothers, Shepard. Who unfortunately has a girlfriend.

Ouch.

I wish I could help her or at least talk to her. But given that I'm no expert in these things, loving and getting the guy to love you back, I haven't yet broached the subject with her.

In any case, after that we discuss the nitty gritty of the plan and how Echo is going to corner Reign and make him give in. There's copious amounts of laughter, cupcakes and butterscotch milkshakes and even more hope that this plan is going to work out. At some point, the girls leave and Callie puts Halo down in her little bassinet in the master bedroom. She says she's still afraid to let Halo out of her sight and let Halo sleep in her big girl crib in the nursery.

I help Callie with the clean-up even though she insists that she can do it. But she's a new mommy and as competent as she is at the job, it does show that it's taken a toll on her.

Then like clockwork, I hear the crunch of tires outside and a car coming to a halt. I already know it's a white Mustang and those thumping footsteps jumping out of the car, bounding up the stairs to the porch, belong to my big brother. The joy that comes over my best friend's face is a thing of beauty. It's on the same level as when Halo smiles at her and she smiles back.

But she doesn't move from her spot at the sink to go greet him.

Because again like clockwork, as soon as he opens the front door, there's a sharp, distressed cry from the bedroom. And so my brother — the new dad — rushes over to the rescue. It's like this every time he comes home from work. Halo, without fail, wakes up from her nap and causes a ruckus until her daddy calms her down.

And it always makes me choked up.

Exactly like when I see Halo and Callie reach for each other.

It makes me pine for things.

Things that I've long since buried.

My life-long dream of a family, love. A baby.

My thoughts break when Reed finally enters the kitchen with Halo in his arms. And look at that little bundle of joy/terror, she looks so content with her dark-haired head on her daddy's shoulders, sucking on her fist, her eyes droopy and her cheeks flushed. While only a few moments ago, she was bringing down the whole house. All she needed was my brother's attention because she's her daddy's little diva.

"You know you're a total pushover for her, don't you?" I say to my brother.

He gives me a look. "Hello to you too, Pest."

I stick my tongue out at him for calling me by the worst nickname ever. And dutifully turn my back as Callie approaches him, to give them a little privacy. I get busy with my job until I hear a smack and Reed's hiss. Followed by, "What the fuck?"

I turn to see Callie glaring up at my brother. "Don't curse, Roman."

He glances down at his hand that I think Callie swatted at. Then, "She's asleep."

"Still." She shakes her head. "Babies can hear everything. What if it settles into her subconscious and that's her first word?"

He scoffs. "Her first word is going to be da-da."

"Oh, you know that, do you?"

"Fuck yeah."

Callie breathes out sharply and Reed smirks.

Actually he does something else too. Or rather his eyes do something else that a sister shouldn't be a witness to and so I turn back once again and focus on my dishes.

Meanwhile the bickering continues behind me.

"What?" Reed asks, somewhat pissed.

"I told you these are not for you," Callie goes.

"I don't care," he says. "These cookies are mine because you're mine."

"You don't even like oatmeal raisin cookies."

"Yeah, because they're shitty cookies."

Another sound of smacking. Then, "So then why do you want them?"

"Because you made them."

"Roman." I can imagine Callie shaking her head. "No. You only want them because I made them for Ledger."

"Yeah, and why does he get to benefit from my wife's baking skills? You're mine and everything you bake belongs to me."

"You know, you really need to find a way to get along with Ledger. He's my brother and you're my husband, okay? We're married. So he's part of our family. This whole high school rivalry is getting really old and…"

Oh, did I not mention that before my best friend was my sister-in-law, Calliope Jackson, she was Calliope *Thorne*?

As in one of the infamous Thorne siblings.

The baby sister whom all the Thorne brothers cared for and raised.

And whom my brother fell in love with.

Much to everyone's dismay.

Especially *his*.

My brother's rival.

Whose name my best friend just mentioned and it was so jarring — so out of the blue — that I tuned her out after that. I also gripped the edge of the sink right away, that I'm still gripping now.

But I whirl around abruptly and blurt out, "I'm leaving."

Reed frowns. "What?"

"Um, dishes are done," I tell Callie. Then, to my brother, "Which means I'm going to go."

"Why?" He's confused. "You can just stay here."

Which is what I'd normally do rather than going back to my apartment.

But not tonight.

I wipe my hands with the dishtowel. "Yeah, no. It's not that late and I'm not that tired. I can make the drive."

It's not necessarily a lie.

It's just not the whole truth, or the real reason I want to leave.

But before they can argue some more, I quickly bid them both goodbye, kiss Halo on the forehead and practically run out of there. I get into my car and peel out. I'm probably going to have to explain my sudden departure to them later, but for now, it's okay.

I know I'm acting like a lunatic.

I *know* that.

And there's not even a good reason for it.

So yes, my best friend forever uttered the name of the guy that I was once upon a time in love with.

Why wouldn't she?

She's his little sister. Of course she'd say his name, bring him up in conversations, keep us all — including me — updated on things happening in his life. Like how he's a pro-soccer player now, living in New York City; how amazing he's been doing. Like me, she has very little interest in soccer but since she's a good sister, she always talks about his achievements with pride.

So it's not new, me hearing his name mentioned.

That's the first thing.

The second thing is that whenever I do hear it, his name, I'm okay with it. Yes, I get a little jarred but it's not that bad. Mostly because I'm over him.

Yup.

I'm completely and irrevocably over that asshole.

Three years ago, he showed me his true colors. He showed me who he was and I promised myself that I'd get over him, didn't I?

And I did.

I moved on. I got over him. End of story.

So again, I'm acting like a lunatic.

My phone chimes with a text, barging into my thoughts.

Dad: Where are you?

Dad: I need you at the house.

Fuck.

Fuck, fuck, *fuck*.

What are the chances of me blowing him off and him taking it nicely? Probably zero, right?

I tap my fingers on the steering wheel, pondering.

I'm also pondering what this could be about. But then I think I know.

I mean what else could it be about, other than my upcoming wedding?

Oh again, did I not mention that?

I'm getting married.

Yes, I am. I have a fiancé.

We haven't set a date yet. Mostly because he travels a lot for work so his schedule is a little unpredictable. But it's going to happen next summer. Which further goes to show that my behavior tonight was beyond ridiculous. Because look at me, I'm going to be a married woman soon and I couldn't possibly be any more moved on than I am.

Now if only I didn't want to strangle myself every time I thought of my impending nuptials.

Chapter Five

I KNOCK at my father's study door like a good little daughter.

Something that I never thought that I'd call myself. Not because growing up I made it my mission to be bad and make my dad's life miserable or whatever. But because I was hardly ever on his radar. If I didn't know better, I'd say that he never realized he had a daughter. Only a son.

But it was a good thing, trust me.

Now that I am on his radar, he won't leave me alone.

Even so, it takes him at least a couple of minutes to answer my knock. And even then it's not him, it's his secretary. With disheveled hair and wiped off lipstick and a skirt that she keeps pulling down as she looks at me with a shy smile.

"Good evening, Miss Jackson," she says in a chirpy voice. "I'm sorry, we just got busy signing some paperwork."

It's a lie.

Even if I couldn't put two and two together — by two and two I'm referring to the delay in opening the door and her obvious attempts at putting herself back together — there's no file in her hand to suggest that this was in any way a paperwork signing meeting.

But still, I smile at her like I smile at all my dad's secretaries. "That's okay. I'm used to my dad signing a lot of paperwork."

She chuckles. "He's a brilliant man, isn't he?"

I don't know how I keep smiling but I do. "Yes. Very brilliant."

"Well, I'll leave you two to it then."

"Uh, just… You can call me Tempest," I tell her as she passes me by. "No need to be so formal."

"Okay." Then she grins. "Plus you aren't going to be Miss Jackson much longer anyway, right? Your dad told me about your engagement. Congrats."

I still keep smiling. "Thank you."

Finally she's gone and I enter the room, my smile dropping as I see my dad sitting on his throne-like chair, his eyes on his phone. He hasn't bothered to put himself together like his secretary has. His hair — dark and so much like mine and my brother's — is all mussed up and his tie is askew. I don't even want to know what's happening with the rest of his outfit, so thank God he's sitting behind a large mahogany desk.

I close the door behind me and he looks up.

His face splits into a smile that I'd call handsome if he wasn't so... sleazy and evil.

Before he can say anything, I ask, "Is she new?"

He sets his phone aside. "Yes. Part-time while she goes to school. But I think she may be full-time material."

Yikes.

"How old is she?"

He tsks. "Now, Tempest, you know it's rude to ask a girl's age."

"Not if she's not legal," I retort. "Is she? Legal."

His smile's still in place. "Why, are you afraid of your old man going to jail, baby girl?"

Double yikes.

In fact I think I threw up in my mouth a little.

His nickname for me has to be the most offensive and sleaziest thing ever. Not because it's sleazy by itself but because he is saying it. And I hate it. I'd much rather be called by my tragic name.

"Well," I raise my eyebrows, "if I knew there was even a single cop in this town who'd arrest you, trust me I'd be beating down his door right this second."

At this, his smile drops, not all the way but still, and his true face shows through. Which is basically hard gray eyes and tight displeased features.

"I'd be very careful what I say next," he says. "No one likes a smartass. Especially when it's coming from a puny little girl."

Ah, the misogyny.

Isn't he wonderful?

"What can I say," I still go on, "I'm your daughter. I learned it from you."

"Which is the only reason I haven't put you in your place yet," he says, his voice promising retribution. "And you know I can do it, don't you?"

Still standing at the door, I clench my teeth.

Because yes, I do know he can put me in my place any time he wants.

And he won't do it by hurting me, per se.

But by hurting the people I care about.

Namely my brother.

"What do you want?" I ask grudgingly.

Knowing that he's put me in my place, he smiles again and sits back in his disgusting chair. "Just wanted to see what my soon-to-be-married daughter has been up to."

"You know, this is the classic example of 'this meeting could've been an email'," I tell him, unable to keep the sarcasm from creeping into my voice. "You can always text me and ask."

"And deprive myself of the pleasure of seeing you?"

"Funny how you deprived yourself of the pleasure for the last nineteen years," I say, "until I became useful to you."

He steeples his fingers together, watching me. "I'm glad you remember that. That you're useful to me. I'm sure you also remember how useful you are to your brother, don't you?"

I look at him for a few seconds.

Look at his merciless face, his calculating eyes.

Growing up, there were times when I'd cry to Reed about why Dad never noticed me. I'd ask him what was wrong with me. Why our dad didn't care about me. In fact, I used to get jealous of my brother because my dad always kept his finger on him. He always kept a watchful eye over what my brother was doing.

It was only later, when I grew up, that I understood that our father's finger was really his thumb. He was keeping my brother under his thumb. Making him do things that he didn't really want to do.

And Reed did them for me.

To keep me safe. To keep me out of harm's way.

All our childhood, he protected me from our father's wrath.

And I honestly don't know what I would've done without him.

He's the best brother in the world.

And yes, I know how useful I am to him now.

How I'm the only person standing between him and our dad.

"I do remember, Dad," I say, my heart beating furiously in my chest. "I couldn't care less about being useful to you. In fact, if it were up to me I'd leave you to rot, and I mean that from the bottom of my heart. But I do care about my brother. I do care what happens to him. Which is the only reason I'm doing this. The *only* reason I've agreed to your dishonest scheme."

He watches me for a few seconds before chuckling. "Well, I can't say I don't appreciate your honesty. Thank the big Lord then that you've got a brother, or I'd be screwed, wouldn't I?"

I throw him a mock smile. "Yeah, you would be."

He chuckles again. Then, "Well the reason I wanted to see you is that I've set up a meeting between you and Ezra with his secretary. Tomorrow for dinner at six."

"What, why?"

"Because you're engaged," he says in what I think of as his *duh* voice. "And as wonderful as that is, engaged isn't married. Engaged isn't even close to what we need. So you'll meet with him; you'll bring out the Jackson charm that I'm sure you have somewhere deep down and get me a wedding date, an advanced wedding date, before he leaves town for business next week. So I can get these fuckers off my back."

I fist my fingers at my sides. "You mean those debt collectors."

My father narrows his eyes at me. "Why don't you leave the details to the grown-ups and focus on looking pretty? I can handle the money aspect."

My nails are digging into my skin. "But aren't grown-ups the ones who got us into trouble in the first place, Dad? So you had to come to me, a dumb puny girl who's only good for looking pretty, to get you out of your gambling debts."

Yup, that's exactly what's happened.

Apparently my father, along with screwing barely legal girls, is also a gambler. Something that I never knew. Granted I never knew a lot of things about my dad, but still. And even more apparently, he has been running himself into debt for years. But now the hole's so deep that he needs help pulling himself out.

Enter me, his young daughter that he can marry off to a rich family — the Vandekamps — so he can partner up with them and steal all their hard-earned money by selling them his company that's secretly bankrupt. Oh, and since the Vandekamps have expressed the desire to announce the acquisition of Jackson Enterprises on the day of the wedding, kinda like a double celebration, my father is dying for a wedding date.

An advanced one because those debt collectors are breathing down his neck. Apparently, it needs to be mentioned that they are Russian and so somehow that makes them even more dangerous.

In any case, I don't think this is the first time he's done this.

Stealing money, I mean.

While I can't prove it, I do think my father's business — he's a real estate mogul; not as big as the Vandekamps, but still — is not entirely legit. I think he's been involved in a lot of shady, criminal behavior over the years. But since he's richer than sin — only in theory right now — he's got all the cops and judges and lawyers and all the important people in his pocket.

Well, except for these Russian debt collectors.

But I can't really point fingers, can I?

I'm helping him dupe a perfectly innocent family. Yes, I'm doing it under duress. Because my father has promised retribution on my brother if I don't. And I know he'll carry out his threat. I know he'll destroy my brother's new business — a garage for vintage cars called Auto Alpha — and/or hurt his new family, his own daughter-in-law and granddaughter.

And after everything that my brother's done for me, I cannot let that happen.

Ever.

But I'm still complicit. I'm still a bad guy like my dad.

And God, I hate him.

I absolutely fucking hate my father for making me do this.

"You like running your fucking mouth, don't you?" my dad says softly, threateningly. "I'd ask you to refrain, but then I think I like it. I like that you're trying to be a brave little mouse. Because then I really get to show you what I've got in store for your brother. For leaving me and the family business."

Despite my anger, fear stabs my chest.

I knew it.

I knew my dad's been looking for a reason to hurt Reed ever since he managed to distance himself from our dad. When I said that Reed put himself in between me and my dad, I really meant it. He did everything that our father demanded of him, including working at our father's company even when he hated it. And for years, he was miserable. Until he found a way to separate himself from everything and do what he really wanted to do.

And I can't be the reason that everything that's he's built for himself over the last few months is destroyed.

Or worse, he gets pulled back in.

So as much as I want to smack my own father's face, I say, "I told you that I'd do it, didn't I? I *am* doing it. I am fucking engaged to the man you want and I'll get you that wedding date. So I'd appreciate it if you stopped threatening me every two seconds."

His lips pull into a cold smile. "Not you, baby girl, your brother. I'd never hurt you."

I pull in a deep breath. "Is there anything else?"

Slowly shaking his head, he goes, "Not right now, no." Then, "And don't be late tomorrow. You don't want to keep him waiting."

Free at last, I walk out of his office but unfortunately run into a different kind of monster.

My mother.

While my dad always ignored me growing up, my mother both ignored my existence and seemed annoyed that I'd want to spend time with her. She'd look at me like I was a nuisance, following her around, when she had so many better things to do such as parties, going shopping, fucking guys and so on. So then I took to trying out her makeup and her shoes, copying her dress sense so that she'd think we're similar to each other. Never happened, but yeah, I tried a lot with her.

"Tempest, sweetheart," she says when she sees me.

"Hey, Mom."

She's wiping her brows after what looks like a yoga session; she's dressed in her athletic gear that's mostly to show off her still tight curves and there's a very hot yoga instructor trailing behind her. She gives him a flirty kind of smile — which gives me a little glimpse into what kind of body contorting she's been doing — and waves him away as she approaches me. The guy gives me a once-over and for the second time tonight, I throw up in my mouth a little.

Maybe there was a time when my mother loved my father. But years of his betrayal has turned my mother into a feelingless and hardened woman who finds joy in materialistic things.

"I'd hug you but I'm all sweaty," she says, her blonde hair and blue eyes shining under the chandelier.

"That's okay. I'm fine."

She looks at me for a few seconds, a smile lingering on her face. "Look how you've grown up." Then, reaching out to touch my hair, "Although I keep telling you to go blonde. This dark color makes you look like a corpse sometimes."

I keep smiling and politely remove her hand from my hair. "Thanks, Mom. I'll look into it."

She sighs. "But never mind. It's not important."

"You know what, I think I'm going to —"

"I wanted to talk to you about the luncheon everyone's planning for next week," she says, cutting me off.

"What luncheon?"

"At the club," she clarifies, her eyes now on my dark maroon knit dress, perfect for fall. "In your honor."

"Yeah, I'm —"

"Everyone's so excited about your engagement," she says. "No one ever thought that it would happen, you know. *I* never thought it would happen. What with your stupid books and crazy ideas. I thought you'd be one of those unmarried spinsters that everyone sends to live in France or Italy. But look at you now, soon to be a bride. It's going to be wonderful."

Yeah, I'm sure it will be wonderful.

But only for my mother and all these other women who want to wish me well.

Because it will give them a chance to gloat. A chance to say, *we told you so.*

Because they did. All my life.

They told me that my romance novels are bullshit. That I was crazy to believe in something like love. In something like family. That I was even crazier for *wanting* it, for wishing for it. Instead of wishing for better things, practical things like money or jewelry or vacations and parties.

And I'd roll my eyes at them.

I'd look down upon them. I'd tell them that I wasn't like them. That I wanted something real in my life. I didn't want to end up like them, screwing around on their spouses behind their backs, neglecting each other, neglecting their children.

I'd tell them that they're the ones who are crazy, not me.

And that one day, I'd escape this meaningless existence.

I won't now though, will I?

Not only because I'm getting married soon — to someone from my world — but also because they were right. All these people who called me crazy. There's no such thing as love. There's no such thing as escaping the existence that I was born into.

Not for me at least.

That's why I'm so proud and thrilled that my brother got out of it. That he has all the things that I wished for myself and also for him. A loving family, and so I need to protect it with all that I am.

Although I will say that ever since I got engaged, I've been thinking about one aspect of my dream. Look, it's a given that I'm never going to have the kind of love or family that I want. But that doesn't mean I can't have something to love and cherish.

A baby.

Right?

I can still have that.

Or at least that's what I think. Until the moment I start seeing a baby with dark wavy hair and dark eyes, resembling someone I don't want to think about.

But anyway, that still doesn't mean that I want to be present for the gloating.

"You know what, Mom, I think I'm going to have to check my schedule for next week. But I'll let you know, okay?"

Before she can say anything, I get out of there.

I escape like I escaped from my brother's house.

But instead of going back to my apartment in town – something I rented with my grandfather's trust which my dad can't touch so I don't have to live in this hellhole of a mansion – I go to a bar called The Horny Bard because I don't feel like being alone right now. It's a dingy sports bar with really tacky and neon-y red light reaching and covering every inch of this place. There's loud bass-heavy music and lots of curses and verbal abuse flying around at the mounted TV screens, displaying a soccer game.

Ugh. Soccer.

I never liked that sport, *never*, and I hate it even more now. But I'm here because the booze is good and they'll let me in with a fake ID. Like they do all the other underage patrons, either college or high school students.

Taking a seat at the bar, I carefully avoid touching the sketchy-looking countertop and order a cosmo. And since I don't want to look at the TV screens like all the other soccer fanatics in here, I decide to look around. Which goes uneventfully for a few seconds until I have to stop.

Abruptly.

Mostly because for the second time tonight, I feel like I've been jarred out of my body.

I've been cruelly thrust out, pushed out, *removed* from my own self.

And this time, it's even more forceful than before.

It's even more violent than when I heard his name spoken out loud.

Probably because this time, it's not just his name.

It's him.

Here.

In the flesh.

What the fuck is he doing here?

I mean yes, he's in town right now apparently. As evidenced by Callie making him his favorite oatmeal raisin cookies. But why the fuck are we running into each other?

Shit. Shit. *Shit.*

But that's not even the big problem.

The *big problem* is that he is here and he's not alone.

He's got company.

Of the female variety, of course.

And as always, she's exactly his type: reed thin, blonde and tall. And of course, she's touching him.

She's also leaned over him so that her shoulder-length blonde hair is grazing his left forearm that's resting on the bar-top table. He's sitting there with a beer bottle, his elbows resting on the table, his broad shoulders made even broader because he's bent forward.

It's a familiar posture.

I've seen it hundreds of times before.

And every time I see it, I can't help but think that this casual pose does nothing for him. In the sense that it can't hide the barely leashed intensity in him. The sheer strength and power contained in his muscular body. The heated energy, the electric danger that runs just under the surface of his bronzed skin.

Three years ago when I saw him for the first time, I thought that he was the most intense guy I'd ever seen.

And three years later, nothing has changed.

He's still the most intense guy I've ever seen.

A force of nature. A fierce thunderstorm.

The Angry Thorn.

So maybe I can't blame her, the girl who looks so enamored with him.

Nothing is more beautiful than the Angry Thorn, resting all casually but not really, and his hair.

The dark and thick and unruly strands of his hair.

His crazy hair.

That tonight looks even thicker and wavier and crazier.

And longer than what he usually maintains.

She's almost there too, her fingers reaching out, almost touching the wavy strands fallen over his forehead. And despite not blaming her at all for her actions, I grip the skinny glass of cosmo so hard that I'm afraid I'll break it.

But the glass is saved in the last second when his hand snaps up and his long fingers curl over her svelte wrist, effectively stopping her in the process.

"Oh, thank God," I whisper, my grip loosening from the glass.

As irrational as my response just was, I gave it too quickly.

Because as soon as I said those words, it's as if he heard me.

It's as if he knew I was sitting here, watching him.

So he watches me back.

He pushes the girl away and his gaze swivels over to me.

Across the crowded and red-tinted space.

And holy fuck, I duck.

Like I did all those years ago. The night he caught me stalking him.

Well, he'd already known about it. So let's say it was the night he forced me to come out of my hiding spot.

The only difference is that that night I took cover behind a shrubbery, while tonight it's a beefy guy who's so engrossed in the game that he doesn't notice I'm using him to hide myself.

Like a stalker.

Which, I'd like to point out, I'm not.

Tonight I'm *not* a stalker.

But after how frazzled I've been — both from my trip to Callie's and then at my parents' — I don't need the confrontation right now. I can't take it. So ducking and hiding and running out of the bar is my only recourse. Quickly, I walk down the cracked and empty sidewalk, my heels clicking and clacking, to get to my car at the parking lot adjacent to the bar. But as soon as I reach my car, I find that I can't *really* reach my car.

Because there are two guys leaning against it.

They're chatting and laughing, completely oblivious to the fact that this isn't their vehicle.

Breathing deep, I say, "Hey, guys."

They both halt mid-conversation and turn their attention to me. Their eyes run up and down my body and they like what they see because they both lean away from my car as if coming alert and there are small — also silly and drunken — smiles gracing their lips.

"Hey there," one of them says, or rather slurs.

"Need a hand with something?" the second one asks, or again, slurs like his friend.

"Because we'd love to give you a hand," the first one goes, without waiting for my reply.

"Yeah. Our hands are very capable," the second one tacks on.

"Especially for a pretty girl like you," the first one finishes.

And then they both laugh.

Like they've cracked the most hilarious joke of the century or something.

God, please, I do not *need this right now.*

Still I paste a patient smile on my lips. "That's... great. Because I do need a hand with something." Both their eyes grow wide and shine but before they can start another volley of lame jokes, I continue, "I'd love it if you guys moved away from that vehicle. Because that's my car and I need to get out of here."

They both do a slow blink as if confused and then together, they both turn and look at the car behind them. It's uncanny how their movements are in perfect unison.

Then the first one goes, "This your ride?"

"Yup."

"You're fucking with us."

"Nope."

Even though I'm a little annoyed right now, I still can't help but feel a hint of pride at the wonder in his voice. My car tends to do that. It's a 1967 Chevy Corvette and it's the prettiest car ever made. And not only because it's painted cherry red. I've had it for about a year now; got it as a present for my eighteenth birthday from my brother.

Who restored it himself at his amazing garage.

"And you want us to move away from it," he continues, breaking into my pleasant thoughts.

Okay, now they're back to annoying me. Sighing, I reply, "Yup."

"So you can get out of here."

"That's pretty much the gist of it, yes."

He opens his mouth again but the second one beats him and goes, "How about we *all* get out of here?"

My gaze snaps over to him. "I'm sorry?"

He shrugs, and for some reason he doesn't look as drunk as he did only moments ago. "You wanna get out of here. Turns out, we wanna get out of here too. And you've got a killer ride. How about we all slide into it and see where it takes us?"

"Fuck yeah," the first one says, jumping onboard quickly. "The night's still young."

The second one takes a step forward. "And we can have some fun, you and us."

Right.

I should've known.

Even though according to them the night is young, it's still late. And the parking lot is empty save for the three of us and for some reason, guys think it gives them license to be pushy.

"What kind of fun?" I ask.

The second guy — I'm thinking he's the bolder of the two of them — replies, "The kind where there's a happy ending." Then he leans forward again. "For all of us."

Even though I don't like the fact that in the last several seconds this sleazy-looking and drunk-sounding guy has gained several inches between us, I still stand my ground. I still stand tall in my heels and look him in the eyes as I say, "I'm not a happy ending kind of girl."

"You're with us now," he says, "we'll make you a convert."

I look at his swaying body up and down. "You sure you're up for that?"

"More than anything."

"Because from the way you're swaying and slurring your words, I don't think you have it in you to give yourself a happy ending, let alone me and your friend over there."

He goes still for several seconds along with his friend.

Actually, his friend is still, except he's blinking really fast. Then, "What the... He didn't... There's no fucking happy ending for me."

"That's what I'm afraid of," I agree with a mock pout.

He shakes his head. "There's no fucking happy ending between us. There's nothing..." He shakes his head again, disgusted. "There's nothing between us. Not like that."

I raise my palms up. "Hey, there's no judgement here, dude. Love is love."

The first guy sputters some more, unable to form any coherent words. But the second guy comes out of his stupor and advances on me, grabbing one of my raised wrists. "You think you're so smart, don't you?"

My heart jumps to my throat in fear but still, I hold on. I twist my hand in his grip. "Let me go."

He sneers. "Although not so much right now." He tightens his grip and gets even more up in my face. "Are you?"

"Listen..."

I trail off because I feel the air change around me.

I feel it become heavy and hot and static.

Electric.

Oh no. No, no, no.

Damn it.

Why's he here?

Why —

"She's mine."

What, no.

Absolutely not.

Why would he say that? Why would he say the exact same words that he said three years ago?

Why is it that we're in a similar situation as three years ago?

Why?

As angry and irritated as I am right now, his growled words do the job.

And the guys in front of me flinch as if an angry thunderstorm has just crackled across the sky.

I've seen it happen several times over the years. How people flinch and shake as soon as they catch sight of him. How when he stares down at them — because somehow he's always the tallest guy in Bardstown — they cower and hunch into themselves.

And like a fool, his anger, his reputation, his dangerous aura made me feel safe.

Like nothing could touch me as long as he's around.

I'm not a fool anymore though. I don't find his power, his authority attractive anymore.

I *don't*.

Even when the guy who's been holding my wrist prisoner not only loosens his hold on me but also scrambles back, his spine hitting my Chevy. And his friend, who's also cowering, actually moves away from him. As if he doesn't want to be associated with the guy who goes around grabbing girls' wrists.

"Y-you're the Angry T-Thorn," he says, stuttering.

The second guy simply blinks and gulps.

"We're huge f-fans," he continues. "Although sucks what happened —"

Then comes another growl from behind me. "Leave."

And they do.

As if they were waiting for his command.

And then we're alone, him and me.

Exactly the thing I didn't want to happen.

Chapter Six

HE'S STANDING BEHIND ME.

Still.

Those guys have been gone for ages now. Well, probably for ten seconds or so but he's *still* standing the fuck behind me.

Without making a move.

Without saying a word.

I can hear his breaths. I can hear how loud they are. How thick and *heated* as they graze the back of my neck, my shoulders and upper back, waking goosebumps on my skin even through my dress. How they end in a low growl like that of an animal.

A wild, angry animal.

I'm angry too actually.

About a lot of things. About the fact that he called me his when I'm clearly not. About the fact that he came to my rescue when I was totally handling everything. And that he *followed* me out to the parking lot when I didn't want any confrontation with him tonight.

When I just wanted to go home in peace.

Fucking *asshole*.

But you know what, I'm not going to give in to it. I'm not going to give him the satisfaction of riling me up. He has done that in the past; riled me up, that is. Because as I've said before, he's my BFF's brother. It's not uncommon for me to hear about him from her. It's also not uncommon that we run into each other from time to time, like once every few months or so.

And every time that we've had family encounters, it's always ended badly.

With him provoking me by appearing all confident and arrogant, and me playing right into his hands — even though I've moved on — and then regretting it later.

But I'm not going to do that anymore.

Because I realized something tonight. I realized that Callie was right; he *is* family now. He's my sister-in-law's brother and we're going to see each other, hear each other's names all the time. I can't let him get to me like that.

So I fist my hands at my sides and take a deep, deep breath.

Before I whirl around and paste a smile on my face.

"Hey," I say cheerfully. "Fancy seeing you here."

I don't expect him to say, *yeah, how are you.* Or *long time, no see. Are you okay?*

I already know that assholes like him don't have manners. So I'm not surprised when all he does is stare down at me, his features all blank, and in the face of my own cheerful smile they look even more wooden.

But I keep going as if he has spoken.

"That was…" *Totally unnecessary.* "Wonderful. What you did." Again, I don't expect him to say *oh, it was nothing* but I continue having this one-sided conversation. "How you saved me I mean." I press a hand to my chest. "But I'm okay. All thanks to you." Then, still smiling, "But boy, those guys were something, huh? And they were your fans. How about that? You must feel extremely proud," and then, just because I can't help it, "and *humbled* at their love for you. Although I don't know what he was talking about? Like, what sucks and —"

"No," he says at last.

I ignore how his one-word reply is identical to the one that he'd given me three years ago and just feel the relief that at least he said something. And I don't have to keep going with the ridiculous one-sided conversation.

I also ignore that his voice sounds gritty.

Unused.

Like he hasn't spoken in a long while. Probably in three years.

I still keep the smile in place as I politely inquire, "No?"

"I'm used to it," he replies, his dark eyes still pinned on me.

All arrogantly.

Of course.

He's used to people worshipping at his feet and how like him to remind me of that.

Again, I'm not going to let it affect me. "Agreed. You've always been a superstar."

"And you've always talked too much."

Asshole.

"Again," I say chirpily, "agreed. I do have a talking habit."

Finally, I see something change in his expression.

It goes from being blank to being all tight, his eyes narrowing slightly.

Which is both a good thing and a bad thing.

Good because at least he's showing some reaction to my conversation rather than annoyingly staring down at me with no recourse in sight. Bad because his changing expression has forced me to pay attention to the little nuances of his face.

Something I usually avoid when we have the misfortune to run into each other.

Here's the thing: he's always been beautiful. There was never a question about it. His features sharp and defined. His skin all bronzed from playing under the sun.

But over the years, especially over the last year, something has changed.

His features have grown sharper. His cheekbones like jagged peaks of a cliff; his jaw razor-sharp. His eyes have grown darker and more intense and the lines around his mouth are more pronounced.

He looks edgier somehow.

More dangerous. More powerful. More kingly.

It could be a side-effect of going pro and his increased popularity. Or it could be something as inconsequential as the fact that he keeps a thick stubble now. On his jaw I mean. Thicker than a five o'clock shadow but not so thick that it can be called a beard. Actually, now that I think about it, I haven't seen him clean-shaven in a year.

In thirteen months to be exact.

I wonder if…

No, I *don't* wonder.

I *do not* wonder about him.

"Are you drunk?" he asks then.

My smile slips a little. "What, no."

"High then."

My smile slips some more. "I don't… No. Absolutely not."

His gaze studies my features and his frown only thickens. "What about cotton candy? You had too much sugar and it finally broke your brain."

Okay, I just want to go on record and say that *this* is why I get provoked and go off on him. It's not all my fault.

He does this on purpose.

He tries to get a reaction from me on fucking purpose.

And even though I'm on to him, it's still very difficult to hold on to my cool. "Nope. My brain's all intact and fine, thanks for asking though."

He grinds his jaw. "So then why the fuck are you smiling like you're in a toothpaste commercial?"

"Because I'm trying to be friendly, you asshole," I snap before I can stop myself, my hands fisted at my sides and my teeth clenched.

"Friendly."

"Yes."

"Why?"

"Because believe it or not, I don't like fighting with you."

SAFFRON A. KENT

"No?"

"No."

"Strange," he murmurs, "because it usually gives me a hard-on."

"Well your stupid hard-on is going to have to find a different way to survive." I lean forward, glaring. "Because we're family, all right, and I'm freaking done fighting with you."

I realize though that that's exactly what I'm doing.

Fighting.

Damn it.

Even though I've moved on from him and my little mishap in judgement for falling for him, I hate that he can so easily make me lose my cool. I hate that he has such control over me while I basically have none. So I straighten up and take a deep breath. I also tuck my hair behind my ears, pat down my dress and just try to get my composure back.

"Family," he says, making me pay attention to him.

His expression is something I don't understand.

It's not as wooden as it was before and it's not amused either. Like it was only a few moments ago when he was winding me up like a doll only to watch me dance for him.

But I don't waste my time trying to solve the mystery as I reply, "Yes. Because my brother is married to your sister. Meaning we'll be seeing each other, running into each other all the time. We can't always be fighting with each other. So we need to make the best of it and just… keep the peace."

I'm ashamed to admit that it hadn't occurred to me before.

Reed and Callie have been married for like three months now and this is the first time that it's hitting me. That he and I, we're family. We're forever bound to each other now whether we like it or not. Maybe that's why I got so freaked out back at my brother's house. Because Callie mentioned his name and family in the same sentence. Or it could be the fact that I simply don't want any more friction in my life. I already have tons of complications, tons of drama, and I just need some calm.

Whatever it is, I just want to go home now.

Stuff my face with cotton candy and vodka and fall asleep.

But apparently he has other plans because he asks, "So who are you?"

"What?"

"To me," he explains. "Now that we're family."

It's a good question.

I think about that. Then, "I don't know. I mean, I'm your sister's sister-in-law and uh, you're my brother's brother-in-law. Something I bet you hate. Actually you both hate that but that's not what we're talking about." I shake my head. "Anyway, maybe you're my…"

What?

Yikes.

No.

66

Please tell me I wasn't going to say the B word here. No actually, please tell me he didn't catch my drift.

"I'm your what?"

But of course he did.

And I have a feeling that he isn't going to let it go.

Still, I reply, "It doesn't matter."

"It kinda does."

"It's not important what you are to me."

"It is."

"What's important is that we're family now and —"

"Answer me."

"We shouldn't fight no matter how much we hate each other."

I feel something hitting my spine and I realize that it's my Chevy. Although it's a mystery to me how I got to my car when I know for a fact that I was standing at least four paces away from it.

But more than that, how is it that he got to my car as well?

How is it that there's hardly any distance between us?

How I went from looking at him from a respectable distance to him leaning over me, my neck craned up, his eyes, his crazy dark hair, his *crazy* beautiful face, filling my entire field of vision.

Despite myself, my fingers tingle with the need to touch it.

Touch his stubble.

I know I've denied it in the past, this urge to touch his stubble, trace it with my fingers. I've denied its existence every time we've seen each other and I'd notice that stubble covering his killer jawline.

But tonight, denying it is much harder.

Probably because he's closer to me than he's been in a long time, and it's potent, his closeness.

So much so that even though I'm standing still, I still teeter on my six-inch heels.

And when I do, he's there to catch me.

His fingers wrap around my arm and I lose my breath at his touch. The first one in a year.

Thirteen months to be exact.

Don't go there, Tempest. Not now.

Not when he's so close and you're especially fragile tonight.

"Still don't know how to walk in heels, do you?" he murmurs, his fingers squeezing my arm.

"I know how to walk in heels," I protest, even though my voice sounds breathy.

His eyes flicker down to his grip on me for a second before he says, "I beg to differ."

"Well, whatever." I twist my arm, trying to get free from his grip. "You can let go of me now. I'm fine."

"Not until you tell me what you were going to say."

I swallow. "Why are you pushing this?"

"Because I can."

I exhale sharply. "Fine. Brother. I was going to say that you're like my brother now."

His grip on my arm tightens. "Like your brother."

I blush. "Yes. But clearly that was a mistake. So can we just forget about it please and —"

"No."

Blushing harder, I try to jerk my arm out of his hold. "Let me go. You said you'd let me go if I told you."

"I lied."

Asshole.

I pull and jerk my arm again. "Let me go or I swear I'll —"

"Uh-uh." He tsks, shaking his head slightly. "Can't threaten me, remember? We're family now."

"You —"

"Besides, I'm like your brother, aren't I?" he says in a lowered voice. "Surely I'm allowed to touch you a little."

A shiver runs down my spine at how he says 'touch.'

Like touch isn't just an innocuous word but something very, very dirty.

"Actually, no," I tell him, swallowing. "You're not allowed to touch me. It's highly inappropriate."

He hums. "Is it?"

"Yes."

His thumb moves then. In a repeated up and down motion.

As if caressing me.

Good thing the dress that I'm wearing has full sleeves or I'd be feeling his scrape-y touch on my bare skin.

"How about now?" he asks. "Is this inappropriate?"

"Yes," I reply, my breath starting to come fast. "*And* you're not supposed to be standing so close to me either."

"No?"

"No."

"Why not?"

"Because…" My breaths break for a few seconds when his thumb makes a particularly long swipe on my arm. "Personal space, okay? You're supposed to respect my personal space, not fuck with it."

That was absolutely the wrong thing to say.

Because now he's latched on to it, his eyes flashing. "But I do so enjoy fucking."

I clench my teeth, fighting against another shiver. "See? This is what I'm talking about. You're not supposed to say these things to me."

"You mean, if I wanna be a good brother."

68

"Yes. It's rude and vulgar and just… inappropriate."

"Clearly I know nothing about being a good brother."

"No, you don't. So why don't you take my advice and step away?"

"Nah." He shakes his head slightly. "I think I'll stay right here and soak in all the knowledge."

"I —"

"So what else shouldn't I do?" he asks, his eyes sweeping all over my face. "If I want to be a good brother."

"Call me *yours* in front of every guy you meet," I blurt out.

Just like the B word before, I wasn't planning on saying this either.

Even though it's been bothering me ever since he said it.

But before I can regret my slip of the tongue, he goes on, "But you are mine, aren't you?"

"I'm not. I'm not even *close* to being yours."

His lips pull up in a small smirk. "If you weren't, you wouldn't have run out of there like your ass was on fire just because a girl was hanging onto my arm."

"I did not run out of there because of —"

"And if you think calling you *mine* is inappropriate," he cuts me off like he isn't interested in listening to my excuse, "you're certainly not going to like what I was planning to do to make sure they know who you belong to."

"What exactly were you planning to do then?"

His answer is slow in coming because he's busy taking my breath away with his heated eyes. "Stick my hand under your tight dress and grab hold of your even tighter ass. Just to make sure they know whose hand goes up there. And when they learned that it's not theirs like they clearly wanted, I would've picked you up like that, thrown you over my shoulder and walked away."

I was wrong.

My breaths were fine before this. Even though he was staring at me with intense eyes, he was letting me breathe.

Now he's completely choking me.

Not only with his dirty words but his imagery.

His super masculine, caveman type of imagery.

Like these things actually happen in real life. Like a normal guy, a guy who isn't *him*, is capable of doing things like that.

I swallow. "Y-you —"

"But now that I know I'm like your brother, I probably would've done something else too."

Despite myself, I can't help but ask, "What?"

His fingers squeeze my arm and he grows even closer to me. "Instead of just grabbing your tight-as-fuck ass, I would've spanked it."

I flinch. "What?"

"Only because we're family, you see," he rasps. "And family looks out for each other, doesn't it? So I would've made it hurt. Probably shaken loose a few tears and screams. Made your creamy skin all pink as cotton candy. But I want you to remember something, okay?"

"I don't w-want to —"

"It would've hurt me more than it hurt you."

"You need to move away from me."

"Unless," he continues thoughtfully, "you think spanking is better doled out by the man of the house and not by someone who's just like your brother." I wince again and hiccup as well as he keeps going, "Because if that's the case, then I'm not opposed to changing our *familial* relationship a little bit and being the new daddy in town."

"Get away from me," I say quietly.

Dangerously.

"No."

"Or I am going to scream," I tell him.

"Yeah, I don't think it'll do you any favors, drawing people's attention."

"No, it won't do *you* any favors."

"Because when they *see* who my new sister is, they won't blame me for putting my hands on her. In fact," he licks his lips, "they'll help me hold you down so I can do my brotherly duty and teach you a fucking lesson for strutting your goddamn ass in a bar in the middle of the night."

I grit and grit my teeth, anger running in my veins like hot lava. "You're an asshole, you know that? A disgusting asshole and —"

"Yeah, I am," he says, his own eyes shooting fire now. "What I'm *not* is your fucking family *or* your fucking brother."

Finally I can see that he's angry.

That he's been angry all along.

Ever since he arrived at the scene and saved me.

And that just ratchets up my own anger.

"You're right. You're not. And I'm an idiot for even thinking that," I snap. "But I didn't ask you to come out here and save me. I had it under control and —"

"No, you didn't."

"I did. I —"

"Not with the way you were fucking running your mouth," he bites out, "and if you don't realize that, then you're a bigger idiot than you just called yourself."

"You know what," I get up in his face, "fuck you, all right. *Fuck. You.* You can —"

"You better watch your mouth and clean up your language," he growls. "Because if *I* have to do that, your lips will be swollen and your throat will be sore for a week."

I go to snap back at him, but can't get a word in.

"And before you dig yourself further into this hole, let me tell you that I

70

won't do it because I'm your new big brother. We'll call this one a favor to the world for saving it from your firecracker mouth."

My chest is heaving and I swear I'm growling.

I'm fucking growling with anger.

Not that he cares. "Now, you're going to get in your car like a good girl. You're going to drive away and go back home. And then you're not going to come back here. Not *ever*. Definitely not at night and *definitely* not without some adult fucking supervision. Is that understood?"

I don't give him the satisfaction of answering his condescending freaking question.

Not until he squeezes my arm again, shaking me this time and growling, "Is that fucking understood?"

"Yes," I say through clenched teeth.

"Good." Letting go of me and stepping back, he finishes, "Let's do it then." Then, as if to himself, "The sooner you drive away, the sooner I can follow you back and call it a fucking night."

"What?" I ask, confused.

"What?"

"You're going to follow me back?"

"So?"

"So do you think I'm stupid?"

"Not until tonight."

I exhale sharply. "I don't need you to follow me home, all right? I'm not a child. I can drive myself back and I can do it very well. Because who knows what you'll do with it later. Probably use it as an excuse to exact petty revenge on my brother or something. God knows you've done it enough by being a raging asshole tonight. So —"

"If you *think*," he bites out, interrupting me, "even for a single second that putting you in your place and having a little fun with you is my idea of revenge, then maybe you've forgotten how much of a *raging asshole* I can be."

No.

No, no, no.

He's not saying that. I *refuse* to accept that he's saying that.

"Have you?" he continues, his eyes boring into mine. "You couldn't have though, right? Because it's only been thirteen months."

Thirteen months.

The cursed number. The number with tragedy and catastrophe written all over it.

The number I don't want to think about.

And that's why I don't.

I refuse to think about it.

I refuse to think about what happened thirteen months ago.

"And if you have, then I'd be happy to remind you. I'd be happy to remind you how far I'm willing to go to exact revenge and how exactly I'm going to use you to do that. And it wouldn't be hard, trust me. Given how eager you were to be used. How you panted and writhed and fucking begged me to make all your dreams come true and fucking abuse the shit out of you."

A quickening starts up in my belly.

Thick and heavy.

Overpowering.

As if my body is reaching out to him. My body, my soul, my very center.

My very femininity is reaching out to him to be, yes, used and sacrificed.

Like it did that night, thirteen months ago.

But I don't give myself the time or space to gather my strength, to calm down. I break into action.

I push at him.

And thank God, he moves away.

Thank God he gives me space so I can unglue myself from the metal and make my escape for the third time tonight. And then I'm rounding my car, throwing myself into the seat and flooring it.

I'm running away.

From the past.

From my shame at all the things that I promised I'd never do that night three years ago, but still did.

I promised myself that I'd get over him that night, didn't I?

But I lied.

Because I didn't.

Not that night. Not the next day. Not the next week or month. Or even a year.

I didn't get over him; I didn't stop chasing him; I didn't stop thinking that there was more to him than what people said until thirteen months ago.

Until he broke my heart so irrevocably that I thought I was going to die.

I thought I was going to choke on my own feelings and foolish dreams.

Chapter Seven

Her Beautiful Thorn

WHEN PEOPLE ASK me what my anger feels like, I tell them it's an itch.

If I ignore it, it only grows.

If I scratch it, it grows then too.

And by grows, I mean the little itch that starts somewhere deep in my gut spreads out. It takes over my chest, my throat. It goes down to my legs, my toes. My fingers, my jaw. My teeth. The back of my neck, the heels of my feet.

Until it covers every part of my body like little red ants.

Coating my vision in a red film.

Uncontrollable. Undeniable. Fucking explosive. That's what it feels like, my anger.

And I was kidding before.

As in, when they ask me what my anger feels like, I tell them to fuck off.

Because it's none of their business.

It's none of anyone's business.

Although in probably two point five seconds, it's not going to be true anymore. Because it looks like I may have to make it their business and I don't even care if it gets me in trouble.

More trouble than I already am.

I'm not going to sit here, at this fancy fucking restaurant, and let this jacket — which is one size too small — suffocate me any longer. I roll my shoulders and yank at the collar of my shirt, gritting my teeth.

I'm also clenching and unclenching my fist, hoping that I get to plant it in someone's face.

Or at least in a piece of furniture or on the wall.

"So tell me about it."

The words are spoken by my dinner companion and my agent, Gio.. He's the one who chose this restaurant. Where you can't eat their overpriced and overcooked food unless you're wearing a dinner jacket. And since I never wear a jacket — and fuck, a dress shirt too — they gave me one of theirs. The wrong size and fucking annoying.

Hence the rage in my heart.

Or one of the reasons why I'm feeling pissed off right now.

I watch him carefully cut a piece of his steak.

It's well-done and disgusting.

I don't know how he's eating that. But then again, he asked for well-done and disgusting. I didn't and still got that.

Maybe I should punch the waiter the next time he comes over to top up my water.

For now, I leave my own steak untouched and opt for the scotch. "About what?"

It's a bullshit question.

I know what he's asking me. I'm just trying to stall.

No actually, I'm trying to be a shithead.

A difficult motherfucking shithead. And a pain in the ass.

I think it's fair.

Because it's not as if Gio is being a ray of sunshine right now.

Or even for the past few days, ever since I left New York and moved back to Bardstown for a bit.

He's acting like it's my fault, this move. As if I actually want to be here.

For the record, I don't. I fucking hate this town. I always did. Even though when I lived here, I was a king. A god.

A soccer god.

People worshipped the ground I walked on. They looked at me with awe. They groveled and bowed as I walked by. Which was all great. I'm not going to deny that I didn't love all the attention. But still it was a town that suffocated me. And there are reasons for that.

Three reasons that I'm not going to get into right now.

Suffice it to say, moving back wasn't something I'd planned to do. But here I am.

"About your sessions." Then, looking up at me, he adds, "Mandatory sessions."

Okay, that was deliberate.

Mandatory.

The word and that look.

Like I'm fucking ten years old and need to be punished for something I did on the playground. Which I have to admit has happened. A million times when I was in school.

But that's neither here nor there.

What's *here* is the fact that my own agent thinks that he needs to have a conversation with me about my mandatory sessions. Or rather my agent *has been sent* to have a conversation with me about my mandatory sessions.

So to piss him off even more — and by extension, the one who wants him to spy on me — I say, "It didn't work out."

He pauses in the process of cutting another piece and looks at me. "What?"

I take a long gulp of my scotch. "You need to find someone else."

At this, he puts his cutlery down. "Are you fucking serious?"

I don't bother replying to that and instead take another long drink of my scotch.

He sits back. "You're fucking serious."

This time, I throw him a bone and give him a shrug.

Mostly to just piss him off further.

His bushy brows snap together. "This is the second time. This is the *second fucking time* that you've fired your therapist."

"She preferred counselor. As opposed to therapist," I murmur unhelpfully.

"What's the difference?"

"Fuck if I know." I raise my eyebrows. "Just one of the reasons why I fired her."

"Yeah, what's the other reason?"

"Her office smelled like cheese."

"And?"

"Cheese makes me angry." Another shrug. "Which I thought was defeating the purpose of me being there."

He narrows his eyes. "You're really starting to piss me off, kiddo."

I take another unhurried sip of my liquor. "Then may I suggest anger management therapy? Can't say it did me any good but there's no harm in trying, yeah?"

He breathes out sharply.

Ah, finally.

Some relief from my incessant anger.

But it only lasts a few seconds because Gio speaks, in a quiet voice. "You know, people warned me about you."

And just like that, the itch comes back.

I flex my toes and my fingers. I grit my teeth.

Restless.

My tone is nonchalant though. For now. "Yeah?"

He gives me a small nod. "About your temperament. Your behavior."

"Can't imagine what they had to say." I look him in the eyes. "I'm a fucking delight."

"They told me there's a reason why you're called the Angry Thorn."

When I was a kid, I used to watch this cartoon. Can't remember what it was called but there was this guy on it. Usually, he was mellow and easy-going, an insurance salesman. But any time someone said the word 'papaya' he'd blow up. He'd lose his easy-going persona and transform into an eggplant-colored muscled monster, breathing fire and breaking things with his bare hands.

It was hilarious as fuck.

And even if no one can ever accuse me of being mellow and easy-going, completely relatable.

Because as soon as someone utters my soccer nickname — something they coined back in high school — I want to scratch the itch and smash every bone in their body.

Just to prove them right.

My fingers are curled tight around the tumbler as my own voice goes quiet. "Is that so?"

"There's a *reason* why no one else was willing to sign you," he goes on. "Even though you had the potential to be a first round draft pick. Just like your big brother."

My big brother.

It always comes down to this, doesn't it?

How I'm not like my brother. Or rather *brothers*.

My three big brothers.

To give a little context: I've got not one but three big brothers and a baby sister. All my brothers are very well known in the soccer community. In fact, you could say that they're all legends.

The Thorne brothers.

The soccer royalty. The soccer gods.

My oldest brother, Conrad AKA the Original Thorn, was hands down the best player when he started his college career. Before he made the pros, agents and teams were lining up to get him to sign with them. But when he cut his college career short — he had to — all their eyes turned to my twin older brothers: Shepard and Stellan. And as expected, Shepard — the Wrecking Thorn, because he's a wrecking ball on the field — was the first draft pick. Stellan — the Cold Thorn, because his coldness and calm on the field is what people write poems about — didn't enter the drafts, but when he expressed the desire to join the pros as a coach, he had his pick of teams.

And then there is me.

The Angry Thorn.

The liability. The risk. The rogue Thorne brother.

The brother who might finally end the magical soccer streak of the legendary Thornes.

All because of his temper and his hotheadedness.

This itch that lives inside of him.

But it's *my* itch, remember? It's my curse.

No matter how incessant it has been all my life, I've learned to control it. I've learned to tame it.

Soccer has helped. Soccer has calmed me down over the years. I don't know what it is about it but holding the ball in my hand, standing on the trimmed green field, focusing on the net and visualizing the goal has always helped calm down the restlessness in my gut. Soccer pushes back the red ants and helps put a lid on Pandora's box.

And over the years, I've never let my anger interfere with my game. I've never let it interfere with my ambitions. With how much I bled and sweated and died on the field. But regardless of all that, regardless of how fucking good I am, I wasn't the first choice of any of the teams or any of the agents when I entered the drafts. The reason I got picked at all was because Shepard convinced the owners of his team to bring me on board. He was also the one who convinced his agent, Gio right here, one of the best in the business, to sign me.

"But I did sign you," he goes on, giving me his famous glare. "Not only as a favor to your brother but also because you had raw talent. I could see that. You had that rare quality that only Thorne brothers seem to have. But quality isn't everything, is it?"

For a five foot seven, rotund Italian from the Bronx, he does that glare thing quite well. It's been known to bring unruly players, coaches, the press down to their knees.

Not me though.

I've never been intimidated by much in my life. *I'm* the one who intimidates.

"So why don't you tell me what is?" I ask, my jaw ticking.

"Keeping your cool on the field and not punching a player, for a start." Then, "Especially in a stadium full of people."

Fine, I'll give him that.

When I said that my anger never interfered with the game, I may have lied.

It interfered.

Once.

When I punched Ronnie Rodriguez, the striker of the opposite team, in the face. It wasn't my finest move. I shouldn't have done what I did, especially during a live game. In front of witnesses and TV cameras.

All I can say is that for the first time ever I couldn't control myself.

And well, he pressed charges. The cops arrested me and kept me in a holding cell for a night. My team posted my bail and then I was sent home free. Well somewhat free, because I do have these mandatory anger management therapy sessions.

Forced upon me by the team's board.

Among other people.

On top of that, I've been suspended.

"I've already issued a team-sanctioned apology," I say with clenched teeth. "I spent a night in jail. I'm fucking suspended. They won't even let me set foot on the premises. And all of this *after* I scored the winning goal in the game. *Me.* Nobody else. Not even my saint of a brother."

"It doesn't matter. I told you, it's not enough."

"Yeah, so what's enough?"

"Anger management therapy."

Jesus fucking Christ.

"So sitting in a chair, *talking* about my feelings, crying in a tissue, and breathing *in* and breathing *out* like I'm a fucking pregnant chick in labor is what's enough."

Because I'm not doing that.

I'm not fucking going to therapy.

I don't need therapy.

What I need is to get back on the team and work my ass off like I've always done so I can make it to the European League. Something that everyone's been speculating about even though I've only had one season.

What I *need* is soccer.

So I can calm the fuck down and not think about killing someone every other second.

"Look, kiddo," he begins, sighing, "I get that it's frustrating. I get that this is only your first offense, but what you gotta understand is that your reputation precedes you. Everybody in the soccer world knows about your anger issues. They know you're a wildcard. You're a hothead. Now, is that fair, I don't know. I don't fucking care. What I do care about is getting you back on the team. Getting you ready for the upcoming season. And if in order to do that, you gotta show that you've changed, then you gotta do that. No fucking arguments, all right? No fucking around and firing therapists. You do the therapy. You get cleared and you come right fucking back."

"No."

"What?"

"No. I've done everything that was asked of me but I'm not doing therapy."

"Jesus Christ." He throws the napkin on the table. "What the fuck is your problem?"

"I don't need to be psychoanalyzed to prove my worth to the team. If they can't see it, then I'll just move."

"You'll move."

"Fuck yes."

"First, there's a contract. And second, who'll take you?"

"You're my agent, aren't you?" I shoot back. "Figure it out."

I'm expecting him to argue with me some more. But he goes silent.

And observing.

Which I realize that I find even more annoying than when he's trying to intimidate me.

"Listen," he begins again but this time it feels like I'm going to fucking loathe whatever it is that he's trying to say. "I don't know what's going on with you. What your problem is. All I know is that you have one. Now I'm the kind of an agent who doesn't like to get involved," then after a pause, "unless I like the client. I don't particularly like you. But I don't particularly hate you either. So I'm gonna say this once: you don't have a fucking choice. You need to sort it out. And I'm not talking about therapy right now."

"And here I thought that you were acting like a clingy girlfriend because you were all about therapy."

"Your brothers. That's what I'm talking about."

I stiffen in my seat then.

My muscles lock tight. My itch roars and knocks at my bones.

"I don't want to get into the middle of some family drama," he says, his gaze serious and penetrating. "But I know you've got a problem with them. Especially with your oldest brother. It's plain to see. You've never been a mellowed-out person but you somehow managed to keep a lid on it while you were playing. But ever since Conrad was brought on board as the head coach, you've been erratic. Exhibit A: you fucking punched someone during a game. So I don't know what your beef is with your brother but whatever it is, whatever drama, it needs to go. You need to take care of it."

Family drama.

As much as I hate the term, I don't know what else could describe us, the Thorne siblings, better.

Our piece of shit father left as soon as our baby sister Callie was born, stating that he couldn't take becoming a father once again. Especially when Callie was an accident. His words, not mine or my brothers' *or* our mom's. And then a few years later, our mom passed away from cancer.

While our father's abandonment was sudden and came out of nowhere, our mother's death was slow and agonizing. She'd been sick for over a year, in and out of the hospital, getting chemotherapy and radiation, getting reduced to mere bones before she drew her last breath.

After her death, Conrad, being the oldest and of legal age, quit college and soccer and came back to assume responsibility for me and my siblings. So he's always been more than our oldest brother. He's the only authority figure that we've known after our mom. For Callie and me, the youngest of the bunch, he's probably the only authority figure we've ever known. Since we were both so little when our parents exited our life.

Anyway, for the world, we're the Thorne siblings. Always united. Always standing together and taking care of each other.

And we have and we will.

We'd lay down our lives for each other.

But while my brothers have always been more or less alike, always somewhat on the same page with each other — especially Conrad and Stellan — I'm not like them.

I never was.

I wanted to be, though.

I wanted to be responsible and good like Conrad, who gave up his entire life to be there for us. Or Stellan, who's essentially Conrad 2.0 and, rightfully, Con's righthand man when it came to taking care of us. Or even Shepard, who's always been unfazed and carefree, who likes to have fun but still is the person you can count on when you need something.

In fact, the reason I picked up a soccer ball in the first place — that later became a salvation from my anger — was to imitate my older brothers.

To be more like them.

To be included in their group and not treated like a baby brother, a nuisance.

Someone to take care of. Someone to babysit.

Although that's what I am apparently, aren't I?

I'm a loose cannon.

Because I've been blessed with something called rage.

Anger. Fury. Mayhem.

So they have to go out of their way to keep me in line, to *control* me.

When I was little, it was all these rules about how to behave at school, how to behave with teachers and students. How if I got into one more fight, I'd lose my TV privileges. Or I'd be grounded, sent up to my room for the entire weekend. Then when I grew up and took an interest in soccer, it was about how many hours I needed to practice if I wanted to be the best like my brothers. It was about when to go to sleep, when to wake up, what to eat, how many miles to run, how much to bench press.

And it all came from my oldest brother, my high school coach, Conrad.

Of course, Stellan and Shepard helped.

And it's not as if I haven't obeyed their rules before. It's not as if I haven't always done everything that they've asked of me, even when I wanted to plant my fists in each of their faces and run away from our broken, parentless family.

But I didn't.

First, because it was Conrad's one cardinal rule: we stay together. Always.

And second, because even though I couldn't take living with my overbearing brothers and being treated as less than, I wasn't going to abandon my baby sister like our father did.

Especially when we were all the other had.

But enough is enough, all right?

I've paid all my dues. I've done their bidding. I was there for the family.

Now I want life on my own terms.

Meaning I don't want them to call me or text me all hours of every day.

Which they've been doing for the past month, ever since the incident happened. I don't want them to show up at my apartment unannounced to check up on me, which is why I moved away from New York and came back to Bardstown, into our old childhood house that I hated.

I definitely don't want them to sic my agent on me so he can spy on me on their behalf.

And I'm not doing fucking therapy because it's not the board that wants me to, but them.

All three of them together.

Teamed up against me.

Like always.

Instead of standing by my side and having my back, they're forcing me to abide by their rules like a little kid again.

But fuck them.

Fuck them all.

I'm not a little boy anymore. And it's time they fucking understood that.

"Right," I begin, staring into my agent's eyes. "Now, I want you to listen to me very carefully, Gio, because I'm not going to repeat this. But you will. To my brothers, as soon as I leave this godforsaken restaurant. I'm not doing therapy. And my brothers can't fucking make me. And if my brothers or the board know what's good for the team, they'll pick up their phone and beg me to come back. You've got Shepard, yes, but he can't carry the team on his own. He needs a partner and no one's better qualified for it than me. Given the streak of victories we've had this past season, ever since I came on board, means what I'm saying is the truth. So you go and you tell my brothers and anyone else who has a problem with me that if they want me to help keep it up, they better start doing everything they can to bring me back. And same goes for you too, Gio. Do what you have to do to convince them that I don't need therapy. Or better yet, tell them that I did my time and I'm all better now. Because your twenty percent comes from me, not from Conrad. So you better stop kissing his ass and start kissing mine. Because my anger issues or not, you know I'm going places. And not because I'm a Thorne. But because I'm me. And I'm a fucking god, you understand?"

With that, I rise from my seat, ready to leave this brightly lit space with floors so polished that they have their own glare. But I only make it halfway when my eyes catch something.

A flash of dark hair.

Long and thick. Shinier than the floors below.

Paired with creamy skin. Again, shinier than the chandelier above.

But that's not what keeps me looking.

It's the dress.

A short black dress. Tight. Too tight. Too exposing as always. Which means I can see a fuckton of that creamy skin, her delicate bones, the slope of her shoulders, the arch of her neck. Which also means that I don't have to imagine her rounded curves. For a girl as petite as her, she's got a lot of them. A lot of dips and valleys where hands can settle — *my* hands. A lot of soft, smooth swells where fingers can grab — *my* fingers.

And I bet *every* motherfucker in this place is thinking the same thing.

Like always, I look around and take stock of the place, the people, the *motherfucking* motherfuckers that are looking at her. And there are. At least four of them, stealing glances every few seconds, ogling her body.

My vision starts to turn hazy then.

My body starts to turn heated. Even more so than it was when I was sitting at that table, watching Gio eat that disgusting steak and gab about therapy. A low growl is building up in my chest, moving up to the base of my throat.

Exactly like it did last night.

Which is why I went after her at the bar.

Despite the fact that I make it a point to stay away from her.

Well, that's not very true, is it?

Sometimes it is. Sometimes I *do* make it a point to stay away from her, and I succeed.

But other times I can't.

Other times it's too hard to keep my distance from her, to not get sucked into her orbit, to not rile her up. To light her up like the firecracker she is.

My feisty Firefly.

Not mine, but you get the picture.

And yes, that makes me an asshole. Even more of an asshole because I've done some really jacked-up shit when it comes to her. It's something that I think about often.

Maybe every day even.

Fine, so I think about it every fucking day.

Multiple times a day.

Some days I can't stop thinking about what I did.

Last night though, my intentions were noble. I *had* to go after her.

In the dress that she wore, even tighter and shorter than the one she's wearing now, she was a menace. Launching a thousand boners as she walked by on her ridiculous heels. And good thing I did because of course there were dogs salivating around her.

At the memory, that growl in my chest builds and builds.

What lets it out though and what coats my vision in a red neon film is not her dress or her hair or her wind chime-y laughter or even those motherfuckers who're staring at her like she's the most beautiful girl in the world — she is, just for the record — but the fact that all her beauty and mirth is directed at one person.

One guy.

His back is to me so I don't know who he is but he looks of her world.

Rich and polished and wearing a suit that probably costs more than my old truck. Something that I still drive to this day.

And then my vision turns scarlet, a dark bloody red, when her laughter turns into a smile.

A soft, dreamy smile.

A smile that they probably write about in those fucking romance novels she likes to read. The ones that she'd tell me the stories of, with all the enthusiasm and too much fucking detail. I never stopped her though or told her that I had no interest in hearing about *how* the priest's daughter, apparently rebellious to the core, managed to remain a virgin. I'd rather hear about *how* she lost her virginity to the blacksmith's son in the barn.

But that was way back then.

When those smiles were reserved only for me. That dreamy, moony, goddamn *beautiful* smile that said that I hung the stars for her every night. Like wind chimes and dream catchers.

But apparently, she's giving it away to some rich, slick douchebag sitting in front of her.

Yeah, and whose fault is that, you fucking bastard?

I know it's my fault. I know that I fucked things up.

But see, that's not the point, whose fault it is.

The point is that that smile belongs to me.

It's *mine*.

Other than soccer, it was the only thing that would calm me back then. Her smile, her laugh, her voice. And the fact that she's throwing it at some douchebag is not something I'm going to tolerate.

It's not something that I can allow her to do.

They call me the Angry Thorn, don't they?

Well, I'm going to show her exactly what that name means.

Chapter Eight

HIS HAIR IS blond and his eyes are blue.

His skin has a pinkish hue to it.

But not overly so.

Just enough to prove that he's not a very outdoorsy, sporty person.

He can't be; he'll burn if he stays in the sun for more than an hour or so.

Which is a point in his favor.

Actually a *great* point in his favor, because I'm not a sporty girl either.

The second great point in his favor: he has excellent taste in clothes. He doesn't just throw on a ratty t-shirt that seems too cool for everybody and a pair of jeans that have been washed so many times that they're almost threadbare and as such, display every bulge and flex of the sinew.

Just look at his suit: bespoke, first of all. Armani, second. And since it's bespoke *and* Armani, it fits him like a second skin, showing off his not-too-broad shoulders and not-too-freakishly-muscled biceps. His crisp white shirt also displays his torso that's lean and flat and, again, not packed with ridged and stupid muscles.

Meaning, he takes care of himself only because he likes to.

Not because it's his stupid job or like he's a bodybuilder or God forbid, an athlete.

Not to mention, his shoes. Again Armani. And they're polished to within an inch of their life and laced up just right.

As in, in a butterfly knot.

Which everyone knows is the right way to lace up your shoes.

All in all, my fiancé Ezra Vandekamp is perfect.

If I was going to be blackmailed into marrying someone, I couldn't have asked for a better match for myself.

Currently, we're at dinner. The one that my dad set up. And he'd be happy to hear that I made it in time. Well, almost. I was probably five minutes late but Ezra didn't mind. He was busy with his phone, setting up meetings and whatever.

I take a sip of my cosmo as I ask, "So how's your week been?"

I watch his golden head that's still bent over his phone as if he didn't hear me. Not that I mind. I may have lucked out in the forced engagement department but I still don't want to be here. Probably because I don't really know him — we got engaged like three weeks ago in a private ceremony, up in New York — or have any desire to know him, given our marriage is going to be a sham. But mostly because I don't want to lie to him or dupe him like my father wants.

But it is what it is.

And I'm here to do a job.

So leaning forward, I try again. "Was it stressful?"

Finally, he gives me a non-committal *hmm*.

I keep smiling. "Your week. How has it been?"

Still, he keeps me waiting, his fingers going at such a high speed that I'm afraid they'll break off. But he stops in the nick of time, puts down his phone and looks up at me.

"It's been okay," he says, taking a sip of his drink. "The usual."

I wait for him to explain but he doesn't.

He goes for his food — finally — and gets busy with that.

So not much of a conversationalist. Not that I thought he was the other couple of times that I've met him, but still. I need him to at least pay me some attention so I can start spreading my Jackson charm like my father wanted.

"So when are you going on your trip?" I ask, even though I already know.

My dad made sure that I memorized all the dates.

He finishes chewing, takes a sip of his drink. Then, "Next week."

"And when are you coming back?"

Again I know. This one's a long trip — he's going to Korea for a merger and breaking ground on a new hotel his company is building — and it's going to take him at least a couple of months before he comes back. Which is why my dad wants a new wedding date *now*.

Ezra shrugs, his eyes on his phone as he forks up some noodles. "A few months. Depending on how things go over there."

And then, he goes back to typing on his phone while also chewing his noodles.

Damn it.

I keep hitting a conversational wall.

I'm usually pretty good at talking and getting other people to talk. But Ezra is a tough nut to crack. So I guess maybe he's not all that perfect.

"You're kinda busy, huh," I comment, taking a sip of my own drink.

No answer.

Which was an answer in itself I guess.

Then, "I was thinking, what do you think about a spring wedding?"

Another non-committal grunt.

"I mean I know we have summer in our minds but I always wanted to get married in spring. Winter even actually. Or you know, when is it that you're coming back again?"

This time it looks like he didn't even hear me.

And oh my God, I'm getting super frustrated now.

Leaning forward, I go, "Ezra, are you listening to me?"

Nothing.

I lean forward all the way, my chest touching the edge of the table. "Ezra! You're gay."

That gets his attention.

I knew it would.

It also makes him frown. Very hard and in anger. Although I can see that along with his anger, there's a touch of fear as well. Which is why instead of berating me, he looks around, trying to gauge if anyone heard me.

"No one heard me," I tell him then, feeling a little bad for blurting out his secret willy-nilly.

But I had to do something to get his attention.

He looks back at me, his features reflecting only anger. "I'd ask you to refrain from saying such things in public."

"Look, I'm sorry, okay? I know you're," I search for how to put this, "not open about it and for a good reason, of course. And I swear I made sure to keep my voice lowered. But I've been trying to talk to you and you haven't been paying attention."

He watches me for a few seconds before sighing. "I apologize. This merger is taking up too much of my time and I just came from a meeting. But I'd appreciate it if you —"

"Yes, of course," I say immediately. "It wasn't my intention to upset you. In fact I don't want to fight with you at all. I'm sorry. I really am. And I understand you have work and you're busy. But we're getting married soon. We're going to spend the rest of our lives together. I just... I want us to be able to talk to each other."

At this, all the residual anger leaks out of his frame and his body loosens up. He even goes so far as to put the phone away and nod. "I'm sorry. You're right. We should be able to talk to each other." Then chuckling, "I mean, just because you're marrying me doesn't mean you have to get bored to death. So please go ahead."

"You're not boring," I say truthfully. "Or at least not perpetually boring. I'm sure we can find a way to spice you up a little."

He laughs a little and I breathe a sigh of relief that the ice has been broken.

But then he goes silent and a light frown appears between his brows, this one curious. "Why are you marrying me?"

"I'm sorry?"

"I know why I'm marrying you," he says, looking slightly suspicious. "But I never asked why a beautiful girl like you is marrying me. I'm sure you could have anyone out there that you want. So why me?"

Because my dad is blackmailing me into marrying you for your money and I can't do anything about it.

And I've never felt worse about that than I do now.

Because I know why he's marrying me and it's just as unfair as my reason.

It's because his dad is an asshole.

A *homophobic* asshole.

Apparently, he caught Ezra with one of his bodyguards one day and got so disgusted that he threatened to take away Ezra's inheritance and his position at the company if he didn't get married to a girl.

I thought my father was an evil asshole, but turns out he's got competition in Ezra's dad. Maybe that's why he's such good friends with my father.

Who wants to steal all their money.

But since I can't tell Ezra that, I tell him something else that's true. "Because if I don't marry you, my dad will find someone else for me to marry. And he may turn out to be exactly like him."

Yup.

Ever since my father called me into his study a month back and told me what my fate was going to be, I'd been living in constant fear. I thought my dad would choose someone exactly like him: big and brash and scary and cruel. Someone who'd treat me like an object, abuse me, degrade me just like he's done with my mother. With the rest of us.

But then I met Ezra and all my fears went away.

He was polite, well-mannered and very, very gay.

With the way he couldn't take his eyes off that bodyguard of his.

Although I have to say that while my fears were abolished, my guilt surged up.

I thought if the man I was going to marry was like my father, I wouldn't have any problem pretending to be nice to him to cheat him out of his money. But with Ezra, it does hurt me to do this.

He smiles then and raises his glass for me to clink. "To us. For having the misfortune of being born to the worst two fathers on the planet."

My guilt at its worst, I smile back. "To us."

And then we go back to our food. We eat, eat, eat. Or rather, I eat and Ezra goes back to typing stuff up on his phone.

Until I utter the most bizarre thing ever.

"Have you ever thought about babies?"

Jerking his head up, he looks at me. "What?"

Damn it.

Where did that come from?

Well, I know where it came from. As I said, I have been thinking about babies ever since I got engaged but I didn't mean to blurt it out like this.

But maybe it's a good thing.

Maybe if I talk about it with my fiancé and make a plan, *he* won't barge into my thoughts. Yes, once upon a time I was in love with him and wanted all these things with him but that's not the case anymore. So yeah, good thing.

"What do you think about them?"

"What…" He blanches. "What do I think about babies?"

"Yeah. Do you like them?"

"Do I like them?"

"Yes." I nod, now getting slightly impatient that he's repeating everything. "Do you like babies?"

"Why?"

"Because I've always wanted one."

"I –"

"And because I think a baby might be a perfect thing." Then, I add, "For us."

Actually, yes.

It just occurred to me.

It's more than good. It's genius.

"I don't…"

"Yes." I lean forward again. "If we have a baby, you can convince your dad or anyone else who thinks that you're gay, that you're not. That you're a healthy, straight man with a wife and a baby on the way."

Exactly.

It will be perfect for him.

"And how would we do that?" he asks, his face still looking freaked out.

Then smiling my biggest smile, I say, "We could just, you know, use your —"

My words get swallowed up when his phone rings and he hurries to take the call like he wants to have any other conversation than the one we're having.

I should be disappointed but despite myself, I'm not.

Because I was going to say something that fills me with distaste and revulsion before I'd even said it. It apparently goes against the very fiber of my being.

Damn it.

I hate that having my fiancé's baby — even through in vitro techniques like I wanted to mention — is not something that I want to do at all. It makes me feel… dirty and miserable and just plain sad.

Why. Why, why, why?

Why can't I get *him* out of my head when it comes to my dreams?

I hate him so much.

I hate him for ruining this for me. I hate…

Something stirs in the air then, breaking my freaked-out thoughts. Something familiar.

A familiar heaviness and turgidity.

A familiar electric frisson.

The kind that only an angry god can make you feel.

But that's *impossible*. That's…

Frantically, I look up, ready to search for the source of disturbance, and there he is.

Standing dead center in my line of vision. Standing and *sticking out* in a place where nothing sticks out at all. Where everything is equally blindingly shiny and hence mundane and non-dramatic.

He's dramatic though.

He's the opposite of mundane.

He doesn't belong here with his crazy, unruly hair and his too powerful frame. Too large, too tall as well. But the thing about him that absolutely *does not* belong here — in a place where being civilized and well-mannered and posh is more of a job than anything else —is the fact that his too-powerful frame appears to be made of stone.

But even so I can see that it's seething.

It's practically vibrating.

Ready to crack open and pour down like the thundering and wrathful and violent sky.

And I'm the target.

Me.

Because he's watching me. And from the looks of it, he's been watching me for some time now. And God, *God* I feel a shiver of thrill roll down my spine. At his sudden appearance in this part of the world, my part, the boring part.

But that's not all.

I also feel that familiar quickening in my belly. A familiar throb in my womb. A pulse.

And before I know what I'm doing, I spring up from my seat. I excuse myself, tell Ezra that I'm going to the bathroom, and run out of there.

Chapter Nine

THE BATHROOM IS CLEAN.

Which is great.

Not that I expected anything less from this five-star establishment, but still.

It's also empty.

Which is even better. I *think*.

I'm not sure if it's a good thing that there's no one here to watch me in such an agitated state. Or if it's bad that there are no witnesses. Although why I would need witnesses, I don't know.

Nothing is going to happen, I tell myself.

So what if he's here? So what if he looked pissed off? That's his thing. He's the Angry Thorn. He's always angry at something. It has nothing to do with me.

I should be more freaked out about what just happened between me and Ezra.

He's my fiancé – a forced one but still – and so I should be thinking about babies with him and not... *him*.

The door to the bathroom opens and suddenly, he's standing at the threshold.

Covering it, blocking it. Overpowering it.

Dipped in beauty and rage.

In the back of my mind and extremely uselessly, I notice that his stubble is thicker than it was last night, which means that he *still* hasn't shaved. And my fingers, despite everything, still tingle with the urge to touch it.

Why's that important, Tempest, you lunatic?

"What are you doing here?" I ask, shaking all my thoughts away, my voice high and loud in the empty space. "This is a women's bathroom. And it's occupied, in case you haven't noticed." I wave a hand down my body. "By a *woman*. So get out."

His response to that is getting *in*.

And closing the door.

Which he does without looking away from me.

Even though I know it's an intimidation tactic — keeping his flinty dark eyes on me — I still can't help but feel a frisson of fear in my chest. *Especially* now that we're in an enclosed space.

But as always, I'm not going to show him that I'm freaking the fuck out. He doesn't deserve to know that.

He doesn't deserve *anything* from me.

"Why are you closing the door?" I demand then, in a voice that I'm carefully crafting to sound angry instead of shivery.

Again his response is something worse.

He reaches his arm back and locks the door that he just closed.

I can't see it because his big muscular body is blocking his actions, but I definitely hear the click of it.

I even *feel* it.

It feels like a beat dropping from my heart and thudding down to my stomach.

"Oh my God, why are you *locking the door*?"

In response, he starts moving toward me.

Long, slow, prowling steps.

And I can't help it. I absolutely *cannot* help stepping back — a display of weakness I know — until my spine crashes into the wall.

"Are you insane?" I speak again even though he's hasn't deigned to answer any of my questions yet. "Are you freaking *insane*? What are you *doing*? Why are you here? What if someone needs to use the bathroom, huh? What if it's an emergency and they can't get in?"

Again, no response from him except that he's inching closer by the second.

Watching me.

Stalking me like I'm his prey.

"It's going to be your fault," I tell him, almost hurling the words at him. "Do you hear me? *Your* fucking fault if someone needs to use the bathroom and they can't."

Oh my God, why won't he say something?

Why is he being so scary?

Stupid scary asshole.

"And what if someone calls for help? What if someone calls for security? What are you going to do then? I'm not going to cover for you." I shake my head. "In fact, I'll scream with them. I'll —"

My words melt on my tongue because he's here.

He's reached me.

I look down to see that the tips of his brown boots, which look like they belong on a biker or a rockstar, are touching the tips of my sophisticated, girly silver stilettos. And for several seconds, all I can do is stare down at them. Stare down at how completely wrong his boots are for the outfit that he's wearing, a dress shirt and a too-tight jacket, and yet how they look exactly right for him.

How unfair it is that I think this should be the new trend in men's fashion.

Rockstar boots paired with a jacket a size too small.

"It's all wrong," I tell him. Then looking up, "Your boots don't match your outfit. And it looks like you're going to bust out of your jacket like the Incredible Hulk."

"That's always your threat, isn't it?" he says then, finally and completely ignoring what I just said.

Which is just as well because what I'd said was silly.

"What is?"

"Screaming."

I swallow. "That's because you don't listen to me."

"Yeah, I've got selective hearing when it comes to you."

"You —"

"But I'll still say that it's you," he says, "who doesn't listen."

"What is that supposed to mean?"

"Because wasn't it last night that I told you what would happen if you screamed?"

I swallow, my hands pressed against the wall, trying to keep me steady. "I don't care what you told me. I want you to —"

"I told you," he cuts me off, the look in his eyes messing with my heart-beats, "that screaming won't do you any favors, remember? That they'll take one look at you and understand. In fact, not only will they absolve me of any sins but they'll turn into sinners themselves. They'll hold you down, keep you quiet and let me do what I came here to do."

I'm shaking.

Or at least my thighs are.

I don't know if it's fear anymore though. It's there, sure, but when he's concerned, there's always a hint of thrill. There's always a hint of electricity.

Pressing my thighs together, I ask, "And what is it you came here to do?"

"I came here to ask you a question," he replies softly, casually, belying the dark look in his eyes, that tic in his jaw.

"W-what question?"

He puts a hand on the wall, up above my head, stretching his already too tight jacket to its limit, appearing larger than before. "If I killed that motherfucker out there, the one you were sitting with at the table, would you cry at his funeral?"

My breathing stills. "What?"

"I'm debating two ways," he goes on, still speaking softly, which somehow is making every word he says even more dangerous.

"I'm not sure what —"

"I could either snap his neck," he interrupts me. "Very fast, very clean; he won't know what hit him. Or I could break every little bone in his body, one by one, slowly, *methodically*, until he's crying out in pain and pissing in his pants. And *then* put him out of his misery and strangle him to death."

My breaths that had gone still and quiet before are noisy now. They've become heaving and erratic and my words sound the same. "You're… This is… What the hell are you talking about? What the —"

"I personally prefer option number two. Because I don't think simply snapping his neck is going to be enough for me. I want it to hurt."

"Can you just —"

"But I'm not completely irrational either, you understand. I can be persuaded to have mercy."

"I don't —"

"So if you tell me that you won't care if he dies, that you won't even go to his fucking funeral let alone cry at his death, I'll pick option one. I'll make it easy on him. So," he gets even closer to me, dipping his beautiful face so he can look me in the eye, "which option is it going to be? Option one or two. It all depends on you now."

"One," I blurt out.

A muscle jumps on his cheek at my reply. "One."

"Y-yes."

"Why?"

"Because I won't cry."

"At his funeral."

"Yes. I-I won't even go to his funeral."

"You won't."

"No." I shake my head frantically. "I don't even care about him, okay? I don't…"

"You don't what?" he bites out, that muscle in his cheek still jumping.

If anything, I think I've managed to make him angrier, but I don't understand how that's possible when I'm giving him what he wants. When I'm playing along with him in this twisted game that I don't even know the rules of.

"I just… Just don't hurt him, okay?" I say then, pleading. "I'll do whatever you want me to do. Just don't hurt Ezra. Just —"

"That's what his name is," he says, his jaw ticking. "Ezra."

"Yes."

"Who the fuck is he?"

"N-no one."

He grinds his jaw, his eyes flickering all over my face before saying, "You don't expect me to believe that, do you? After you've so beautifully begged for his life."

"I-I just —"

"Pro tip," he says, coming even closer, dropping his voice even lower. "You don't want to beg for another man's life in front of me, if you in fact want to save it. It's only going to make me kill him more. And that's saying something because I already wanted to fucking erase him from the world because you were *smiling* at him."

"What?"

"That's what you did, didn't you," he rasps, his eyes narrowed. "You smiled at him. You gave him what belongs to me."

Wait a second.

Just fucking *wait*.

Is that what this is about?

Is this about *jealousy*? Is that why he's so angry and acting like an unhinged serial killer?

While I still hate to think about the very complicated past between us — I'd rather pretend that it never happened and that we went our separate ways after that one disastrous night three years ago — I will say that this isn't the first time. That he's been jealous, I mean.

Although 'jealous' is probably the wrong word here.

What I always thought was jealousy and took as a sign of his secret affection for me — because clearly he wasn't saying anything out loud and so I had to make assumptions — is simply his ego talking.

I've always said that I've never met a guy like Ledger.

He's intense, more intense than anyone else I know. He's competitive, again more than anyone I know. Probably even more than my own brother — but please don't quote me on that because my brother has done some fucked-up shit in the name of their stupid rivalry.

In any case, this is not jealousy. This is his Neanderthal response.

To seeing someone else play with his toy.

Which is what I am to him.

Or I was for the longest time and due to my own foolishness.

So the fact that I'm feeling satisfaction right now is stupid. There's no need for that. There's no need to feel excitement or thrill or any of those old things that I used to feel back then.

What I should be right now is enraged.

Which I am, of course. But it's polluted by other things.

Still I focus on my anger and say, "No, it doesn't. It never did. So I want you to stop throwing your weight around and step away from me."

The muscles in his raised arm strain. "Tell me who the fuck he is."

I raise my chin. "No."

His eyes are this close to turning into slits. "Don't fuck with me right now, all right? I want you to tell me who he is or I'm going out there and beating the shit out of him until he tells me himself."

I glare at him too. "First, you won't do anything like that. Because even though you think you're a god or whatever, you're not. What you are is a celebrity. You can't beat someone up and get away with it, okay? Not even you. In fact, it'll only hurt your reputation and your career and —"

"Fuck my career."

"What?"

"And fuck my already fucked reputation."

"What does that mean?" I ask, confused.

"You've got five seconds to tell me who he is or I'm going out there."

"What do you mean already fucked reputation? What —"

"One."

"What?"

"Two."

"Are you —"

"Three."

"No, you aren't."

"Four."

"Tell me you aren't counting right now."

"Five."

Time stops, it feels like.

The earth stops moving too. The people outside cease to exist and I think, crazily, that there's just the two of us here. There's just his pitch black eyes looking into my gray ones, and his cinnamon scent – the scent that I sometimes dream about – mingling with the scent of cotton candy.

There's just him and me.

Locked away in a place with no time or space.

But of course that's not true, is it?

Even though it feels to me like we exist in a different plane, we don't. And he hasn't forgotten that. He hasn't lost himself like I have and so he breaks the trance and takes his hand off the wall, ready to leave.

Ready to do what he promised he would.

And I grab on to his jacket then.

I grab it tightly and firmly, stopping him. "He's no one, okay? Just a guy. I promise. A family friend."

His nostrils flare. "A family friend."

I lick my dried-out lips. "Yes. It wasn't even my idea to see him tonight. It was my dad's and —"

"Your dad." Then, "Your *piece of shit* dad."

Needless to say that when I was crazy for him, I told him everything. Well, most things. And those things included my parental history. So he knows everything about my dad and my mom. Not to mention when Callie and Reed got together, the entire Thorne family came to know about how shitty my father is. While all I know about is family is what I've heard either from my town gossip or from Callie.

Not from him though.

Never from him.

And I thought that it was because I hadn't yet broken the barrier with him and that maybe I should do better. But of course that wasn't the case. He just wasn't into me.

Anyway.

"Yes," I say. "He set up the meeting."

"Why?"

Shit.

We're getting into dangerous territory here. I do not want him to know why.

I do not want anyone to know why.

"Because," I start, grasping at straws. "As I said, he's a family friend. My dad wants me to, I don't know, *mingle*."

He doesn't believe me.

I can see it *clearly* on his face. I can see clearly that he won't let it go either. But before he can force me to tell him the truth, I decide to give it to him anyway — partial truth though — and distract him.

"Look, you already know that my dad's a piece of shit, right? So as such, he's bound to do piece of shit of things." I twist my hands in his jacket, keeping him from bolting as I keep going. "He's trying to play matchmaker, okay? He's trying to push Ezra and me together. He wants us to, I don't know, get engaged, get married but —" His frame jerks and his jaw gets so tight that it hurts even me and so I tighten my hold on his stupid jacket. "But I don't want it. I don't want to marry him. I don't want to marry anyone right now. So I want you to calm down, okay? I want you to rein it in and let me handle it."

His frame jerks again and I almost lose my grip on him as he growls, "Handle it."

"Yes. Because that's what I'm doing."

"I'm going to —"

"No," I tug on his jacket again and say firmly. "You're not going to do anything. Because look." I raise my left hand and show him. "Do you see an engagement ring? That's because, as I said, I'm handling it, and I don't want anyone to interfere, least of all you."

I knew this would happen.

If anyone ever found out — anyone who cares about me that is — that I was marrying according to my dad's wishes, they'd go crazy. Especially my brother. He'd know right away that something was wrong and he'd do anything in his power to get me out of it. That's why I haven't told any of my friends.

Not to mention, good thinking about taking off the ring and stuffing it in my purse as soon as I got into the bathroom.

"Now can you please calm down?" I sigh. "And stop acting like a murderer on the loose. There's no need for it. It's not as if I haven't smiled at guys before today. In fact, I have and…" God, I can't believe I'm saying this but whatever. "I have smiled at guys; I've flirted with them. Deliberately. Just for the purpose of riling you up. And you never went this batshit crazy. So I don't understand what —"

"I did."

"What?"

His jaw is still ticking and I think that's because he still doesn't like the fact that I've asked him to back off. "After."

"After what?"

"When you couldn't see."

I study him then.

His anger-lined features. His pitch black eyes. That crazy hair of his, teasing his frown.

The way he's leaning over me, and I remember something.

I remember that this is what he used to do.

Lean over me, slightly hunch his shoulders, bend his back. So I didn't have to stand on my tiptoes or crane my neck up too much even in my heels, to look into his eyes due to our massive height difference. I used to love that. I used to think he did it to put me at ease. He did it to make things easy for me and the fact that he did it so unconsciously made me love it even more.

Like he wants to smooth things out for me simply based on instinct.

I know better now of course.

It was just something he did and there was no hidden meaning behind it.

But the fact that he's doing it now, in this moment, is making it very hard for me to remember why I shouldn't be anywhere near him.

Not to mention what he just said.

"Are you saying that you went batshit crazy after I went away?" I ask.

I've already said that I'm not proud of the way I've behaved with him in the past thirteen months. Along with arguments and fights, I've also tried to make him jealous. I've tried to flirt with guys, smile at them, talk to them with the clear intention of getting back at him.

But of course he never showed any outward reaction to that, and so I always thought that my schemes, if you will, never worked.

"Yeah," he says, pulling me back to the moment.

My heart's in my throat when I croak out, "W-what did you do to them?"

"Fucked them up."

Now my heart's on the tip of my tongue. "Even your… brother, Shepard?"

Because yes, I've flirted with him as well.

Just once though.

It made me feel really icky when I did that.

He grits his teeth again. "Yeah, you *really* know how to do it, don't you?"

"Do what?"

"Aim for the heart."

I flinch, oddly feeling apologetic. "I didn't —"

"And yeah, even my brother Shepard."

My eye pop wide. "Will you apologize to your brother for me?"

"No."

"But —"

"He's my brother. He grew up with me. He knows how to take a punch."

I swallow. "I never meant for those guys to get hurt. I was just —"

"Trying to hurt me."

I flinch again. "I'm —"

"And you did," he says, although I don't see any anger on him at this, only a weird sort of satisfaction. Like he *liked* it, hurting for me. "More so today when you smiled at him than any time before."

"But it was just a smile and —"

"It was a smile you always saved for me."

I'm so taken aback at his statement that I almost bang my head against the wall. "What? What does that mean?"

His dark-as-night eyes flicker down to my mouth. "It means that you smile a lot. And you've got a smile for every occasion. A tight-lipped, sarcastic smile. An angry smile. An amused smile, usually for things that no one finds funny except you. And then are times when you smile and your eyes shine like little blue diamonds. Your cheeks go pink like cotton candy. Your pulse, that freckle over it, flutters like a hummingbird or something. Your entire face goes soft, dreamy. You light up, like a firefly. And you do it for me.

"You did it when you'd see me. Back then. Either on the street. At my house when you'd come to see Callie. On the soccer field when you went to my games. Sometimes you'd do it even after you'd seen me only an hour before. It was like I lit up the world for you. For *my* Firefly."

Firefly.

The nickname he gave me.

Sometimes late at night, I think about his last words to me. They were ugly. Those words. They always make me cry. But like a lunatic what makes me cry even more is the fact that he punctuated them with 'Firefly.'

I know he gave that nickname to me mockingly, with malice in his heart. And revenge.

Or maybe he gave it to me without much thought, I don't know. At this point, it's a toss-up but it certainly wasn't out of what I initially thought.

Love.

It wasn't because he secretly liked me or adored me and couldn't live without me.

He didn't give it to me because he felt what I felt.

And so before I can really think things through, I whisper, "I loved you."

His body goes still then.

For a few moments, I don't think he breathes.

I don't blame him. I'm not breathing much either. Or at all.

Of all the scenarios that I pictured in my head over the years, telling him in the bathroom of a five-star restaurant thirteen months after he broke my heart, while my fiancé sits outside waiting for me, is not something that ever made the list.

And that list was long. Because I imagined it a lot.

I imagined it day and night, telling him.

Instead of letting him think that I'm some crazy girl with a major crush on him, his rival's little sister, I'm the girl who's in love with him. I'm the girl who can't live without him. Who wants him to love her back. Who wants to be with him for the rest of her life.

Many times, I came close.

But I never could because I was so afraid that he'd reject me. I was so afraid that he'd look at me like I was crazy. Like the rest of the world did. For someone who's always been so brave and reckless and so out there, I acted like a coward, I admit that.

Maybe love is something that changes you.

It gives courage to the cowards and steals it from the brave.

I don't know.

All I know is that I never said it. I never explicitly told him that I loved him.

And now that I have, he isn't breathing.

As if my confession has killed him. Strangled the life out of him.

Well, what a great reaction, isn't it?

Every girl wants this in return. To tell a guy that she loved him and for that guy to look like he's seen a ghost.

"I did," I confirm, wedging the knife deeper in his heart. "I never told you because I was afraid. I was scared that you wouldn't say it back. Every time I convinced myself to say those three words, to tell you the truth, I'd back out. I'd think maybe I needed a little more time. A little more time to make you fall in love with me. A little more time to make you see who I was. The girl in love. So I did everything that I could to make that happen. I did everything that I could to convince you, to show you what was in my heart. The way I chased you around, the way I kept calling you, driving down to see you. The way I kept smiling at you with hearts in my eyes. The way I kept asking you to open up to me. It was all because I loved you and I wanted you to see that. So one day when I did tell you that I loved you, you'd say it back.

"But I'm glad I never said it. I'm glad that I have at least a little bit of self-preservation left in me. Because I was a fool, wasn't I? Because no matter what I did, you never would've looked at me as a girl you could love. To you, I was always your rival's little sister. A pawn. A chess piece. Someone to use against my brother. Someone to abuse for your revenge schemes.

"You asked me last night if I remembered about your revenge schemes, didn't you? I remember. I *remember* how you came to my dorm room thirteen months ago in the middle of the night. I remember how after two years of chasing you, you at last chased me down. Not to mention, I remember *why* you did it. What exactly was going through your head when you knocked at my door and kissed me for the first time. It was my very first kiss, did you know that? And God, it was beautiful. It was the most beautiful thing I'd ever experienced in my life. Until you turned it into something ugly. Until you turned my first kiss into a kiss of revenge."

Tears are streaming down my face and I don't have the wherewithal to stop them. And neither can I stop my words as I continue, "So now you don't get to come in here and ask me about the guy I was smiling at. You don't get to be angry about it, or jealous. You don't get to *remember* the way I used to smile at you because you're the one who destroyed it all. You're the one who changed what could've been our love story into a story of revenge. So it's best that we stay away from each other. From now on, if you see me on the street or at a get-together or anywhere at all, you pretend that I'm not there. And I'll pretend that you aren't the guy I used to love who ended up breaking my heart."

Chapter Ten

Her Beautiful Thorn

SHE THINKS ABOUT IT TOO.

Doesn't she?

Every day.

Every second of every goddamn day.

Like me.

She thinks about what I did to her. She thinks about how I broke her heart. But she's not angry about it.

Well, she is.

Of course she is.

But she feels other things too.

She feels the pain. The heartache. The fucking trauma that she had to go through at my hands.

Jesus.

Why didn't I figure this out before?

Why didn't I see it?

For the past thirteen months, the only way I've been able to live with myself is to know that she had moved on. That whatever I did to her that night didn't leave a lasting impression. That she bounced back. And finally, she realized that chasing after me wasn't something she should do.

It's something that I've been wanting her to understand since the get-go. Since the night of the party where she was hiding behind the bushes.

And I have to admit that it pissed me off.

That she was able to move on so easily when all I could do was think about her. All I could do was think about that night thirteen months ago.

And yeah, I'd deliberately provoked her because of that.

I'd deliberately rile her up so she'd give me her attention like she used to. But now I know that she's like me.

If her tears today, the heartbreak in her eyes are any indication, she's been stuck in the past like me. And all I have done is make things even more difficult for her.

What kind of an asshole am I, huh?

What kind of a fucking asshole am I who'd do something like that?

What kind of an asshole not only breaks a heart but repeatedly stomps on it?

Fuck.

Fuck, fuck, *fuck*.

Chapter Eleven

THREE YEARS AGO, I saw a guy on the soccer field and fell instantly in love.

Despite the fact that he was my brother's rival and someone my brother absolutely hated. Despite the fact that a few days later, at our first interaction, I hated him as well and promised myself that I'd get over him and move on.

I didn't.

At least not right away.

Instead what I did was the exact opposite: I ran after him. I chased him around. I did everything that I could to make him love me back. The only explanation that I have as to why I did all of that is that I was foolish. And naïve, and believed in fairy tales and romance novels. I *believed*, despite all the initial signs, that there could be more to him than being an asshole jock. After all, look what he had to live through and overcome. Look how similar he is to my own brother, whom I love to pieces.

So I decided to give him another chance.

Which meant following him around. Showing up at his soccer games and practices — much to my brother's dismay. Showing up at his house to hang out with his sister, although I will say that me hanging out with Callie wasn't only because of her brother; I would've done that regardless because she was my best friend, but still.

It also meant when I couldn't show up to see him — because I lived at a boarding school in New York and he was in Bardstown — I'd text him or call him, DM him on social media. All in the hopes that he'd see me as more than his rival's little sister.

Because that's how he saw me most of the time.

Most of the time, he called me his pretty little stalker — when he wasn't calling me his Firefly — and dismissed me. I'd show up at his games and he'd barely pay me any attention. I'd show up at his parties and he'd be too busy with his friends to spare me a glance. I'd text him and sometimes he'd answer hours later and when he did deign to answer back, he'd be stand-offish and condescending and low-key threaten me to use these texts against my brother.

He never did though.

He never outed the biggest secret that I'd been keeping from my brother — that I was obsessed with his enemy.

And like a crazy little fool, I took that as a positive sign.

I took it as 'he's got more to him than he wants me to see.'

Especially when he'd do something sweet — out of the blue and totally randomly. Like the time he got really mad at me for driving down from New York for his game when there was a storm. Or when he got jealous and warn his teammates off me at parties. Or all the times I'd go to see Callie and he'd practically order me to sleep over because it was so late.

All those times, I wanted to tell him.

I wanted to say that I loved him. That I'd loved him since day one, since the very first moment I saw him.

But I'd refrain.

I wanted everything to be perfect. I wanted to be confident and secure that he'd say those words back to me.

So when, thirteen months ago, he showed up at my dorm room in the middle of the night, unexpectedly and out of the blue, I thought that was it. I thought that was the night when he'd tell me that he loved me and I'd finally get to tell him too. And my confidence and my happiness only grew when before I could even blink, his mouth was on me, giving me my first kiss and simultaneously taking all my breaths away.

I mean why else would he have been kissing me, right?

He'd never done that before. And neither had he ever come for me or chased me around or initiated any contact with me. I'd been the only one doing the chasing up until that point. So all signs were pointing toward him being there for what I hoped he was there for.

Somehow we ended up on the bed, with me naked and spread open, half out of my mind with joy.

And lust.

And need and love.

But then he said something. Something about not wearing a condom, which multiplied my joy. Because of course that had been my dream, right?

So of course I was on board.

I was eager. Panting, writhing, *begging*.

But then he said something else too, which at last snapped me out of my erotic and happy daze.

"Let's see how much he likes it when I knock you up. His fucking sister but *my* Firefly. *Mine*."

Those were his exact words.

Exact.

And suddenly everything became clear in that moment.

Crystal clear.

It was like I was waking up after a very deep and long sleep, and finally could think clearly.

Why he was there. Why he came to me *then* and not before.

Who I was to him.

It wasn't love that had brought him there, it was revenge.

I wasn't the girl he was in love with. I was still his rival's little sister, and that night he was finally going to use me as a pawn against my brother. Who had just gotten *his* sister pregnant. It was an accident. An extremely unfortunate one at the time because like me Callie was in high school, a *reform* high school, and there had been some talk about expelling her. We'd only found out about all of that a few days before and I guess that was his way of exacting revenge.

Reed had gotten his sister pregnant so he was going to do the same to me, Reed's sister.

Meaning all this time, all along, that was how he saw me.

That was all I'd been to him.

An object. A chess piece. A pawn.

And nothing more.

All those little signs that I'd seen — his sweetness, his jealousy — meant nothing at all. They barely had been signs to begin with. It was me. I imagined the whole thing. I made it all up in my head.

I didn't need to give him time to realize that he had feelings for me.

What I needed to do was *finally* get over my love for him and move on.

Because this was toxic.

What I'd been doing was toxic. My love was toxic. *He* was — *is* — toxic.

Isn't he?

He's the guy made of thunder and thorns.

He doesn't know what love is when all he's ever thought about is revenge and all he's ever known is anger.

And it's better that we stay away from each other.

"Isn't it, bestie?" I say to Halo, breaking my thoughtful silence.

She's strapped to my chest again in that pale pink sling and we're in Callie's and my brother's kitchen. They're enjoying a rare night out, something that I suggested that they do, and I'm on babysitting duty. Meaning, Halo and I are making cupcakes.

Well, *I'm* making cupcakes. Halo is kicking at my ribs and gurgling while I describe each step as I do.

And every time I look down at her, I can't help but notice how she looks like Ledger.

It's something that I know I do subconsciously. And when I notice that I'm doing it, I'm able to thrust it aside and put a lid on it.

But tonight my subconscious is more overt and the lid is nowhere to be seen.

I'm blaming all these stupid encounters with him over the past couple of days. Not to mention, the talk I had with Ezra yesterday. We never got to finish that talk, by the way. Because after I came out of the restroom, all frazzled, he was already gone. He'd paid the bill and told the waiter to tell me that he was going back to the office.

In any case, Halo looks mostly like my brother and Callie. My brother's dark hair — my hair too — and Callie's blue eyes. But her nose is *his*. Completely. Also her forehead. It's stubborn and broad-ish like his.

And tonight I can't help but think, imagine, what *our* babies would've looked like.

Would they have his forehead too?

His nose.

His dark eyes.

Maybe they'd have his stubborn streak or —

The doorbell sounds, startling me a little.

"That's weird," I tell Halo, frowning.

She's sensed my mood — God, babies are so intuitive — and is watching me with wide eyes.

But I smile down at her, rubbing her cute bottom. "It's okay, honey. Maybe Mommy and Daddy forgot something. Let's go see, okay?"

I kiss her forehead and walk out of the kitchen, rubbing her back and patting her little warm body, trying to keep her calm. As I turn the corner of the kitchen and come out into the living room, my feet come to a halt.

Because I can see who it is.

Clearly.

Through the glass door.

And he can see me too.

In fact, his dark eyes are pinned on me so thickly and intensely — as if he knew I was going to be here and he was just waiting for me to turn the corner so he could see me — that my legs start to tremble.

My legs start to feel heavy, made of lead.

My entire body feels like it's made of lead.

And the very first thing that comes into my head is my own voice.

I loved you.

I said that to him yesterday.

I did.

I can't believe that I did, but I did.

I hate that I told him. I hate that I gave him that much power and blurted out the secret that I'd managed to keep from him for three years.

Somehow I make myself move and resume walking.

Which is when he moves too. Or rather, his eyes do.

They flicker down to where I've got Halo snuggled to my chest. He watches me pat her bottom and rub her back, and shifts on his feet. His chest in his typical rocker t-shirt — this one navy blue with faded red stars — moves with a long breath as well and he presses a hand on the door.

Watching and watching me with Halo.

As if restless.

As if imagining the same things that I was.

Before he got here.

My heart squeezes in my chest. My womb pulses. More than it usually does when he's around.

But I ignore it.

There is no way he's thinking about what I was thinking about. He doesn't have the capacity for that. All he knows is how to destroy.

When I reach the door, he finally looks up, his hand still pressed on the glass, and I notice his eyes have gone pitch black.

His eyes have something flickering in them.

Some type of emotion that I quickly look away from and get busy opening the door.

"What," I clear my throat, "are you doing here? Why aren't you in New York?"

He doesn't answer right away.

His eyes are still watching me. Or rather us. Going from my face down to Halo, who's completely oblivious of anything being wrong right now as she happily coos and chews on her fist.

And they're doing it both rapidly and slowly.

As if he's so hungry that he's both taking his time with it and can't stop gorging himself on what's before him.

It's unnerving.

This isn't the first time he's seen me with Halo. Granted, we've maybe seen each other two times or so at family gatherings since she was born and I'm fairly positive that one of those times I was with Halo. So this sight isn't new. I don't know why he's acting like he never wants to stop watching me.

"Ledger," I say to get his attention and stop him from staring at me like that.

It works.

But in a strange way.

Because his eyes snap back to mine and he looks... taken aback.

"What?" I ask, confused.

He licks his lips. "This is the first time you've said it."

I deliberately keep my eyes away from his mouth. "Said what?"

"My name."

Now I'm the one taken aback. "That's not…"

"In thirteen months."

"That can't be true."

"And yet it is."

I don't know what to make of his comment. Or the fact that he noticed something this trivial. Because honestly, I hadn't. And neither did I do it deliberately, *if* it's true.

Maybe it was my mind's way of protecting me after everything.

Don't say the name of the boy who broke your heart.

Who knows.

All I know is that it's strange and mysterious. Much like his expression.

I clear my throat again. "Well, probably because it's a curse that summons the devil."

His lips flicker with light amusement then. "Probably."

"Are you going to tell me what you're still doing in Bardstown? When I'm sure you should be in New York. Practicing until you, I don't know, drop dead or something."

His reply comes after a couple of seconds of silence. "I'm taking a break from soccer."

"What?"

"So I'll be in town for a while."

"How is it that you're taking a break from soccer?" I ask, confused. "You never take breaks."

Which is the truth.

Ever since I've known him, he's been adamant about not taking any breaks. Like ever.

I remember one time he got into this huge fight with my brother and they both ended up in the hospital because of it. While my brother came out with a twisted ankle, he came out with a badly bruised rib. And even *then* he insisted on going to practice. What's more, he even went to his solo practice. Which he usually did *after* his mandatory practice with the team.

So yeah, soccer is this guy's life.

His dream. His ambition. Even his love.

Soccer is the very reason why his rivalry started with my brother. And of course, his rivalry is why, years later, he ended up breaking my heart.

Sometimes I wonder, what if there was no soccer at all.

There'd be no rivalry. No revenge, and maybe we'd be…

"I do now," he says, breaking into my thoughts.

Which is just as well.

I don't want to go down the *what if* path. And neither do I want to appease my curiosity about his strange break from his beloved game. So even though my confusion is still there, I don't try to clear it.

Instead I say, "Fine. Whatever. But what are you doing *here*, at the house?"

He looks at me for a second or two before dropping his eyes down to the cuddly, sweet-smelling bundle on my chest. He reaches out and runs a finger over Halo's chubby cheek and gosh, my belly trembles so badly that I'm grateful I'm still holding onto the doorknob.

"Came to see my girl," he says softly and lifts his eyes up to me.

"I don't think —"

The rest of his response is drowned out because this chubby little bundle on my chest explodes with coos and gurgles as if she's found a treasure. I guess Ledger's touch got her attention and now she's going crazy in my arms. Kicking with her chubby feet, flailing her fists, hitting me in the ribs and boobs.

And it's painful.

She's five months old but she's strong, my baby boo.

If not for the fact that the guy in front of me is also acting like he's found a treasure.

Because his mouth pulls into the biggest smile that I've seen from him.

Usually all he does is smirk or chuckle with condescension. But this is a full-fledged smile and it's a smile of joy. Pure and simple, making my heart race and my gaze all fascinated with it.

I'm even memorizing all the specifics.

The way his lips stretch up, making perfect half-moons. How the lines around his mouth relax. How his cheekbones look less sharp and severe, and his dark eyes shine not with harshness but with something pretty and light.

"And she's happy to see me," he murmurs.

As if I need any further proof, Halo babbles with joy. "Gah, gah, paaaaah."

His eyes on her, he goes, "Hey, Little Berry."

She claps her hands. "Pah. Pah. Da."

"Missed me?"

She kicks me in the ribs again, going, *gah, gah, gah*. But I barely notice it.

Because I'm witnessing something else that's happening in front of me. Something even more fascinating than him smiling like he's discovered gold.

He's melting. Dissolving. Softening up.

Like a lump of sugar in water.

Just because a five-month-old is cooing up at him and holding onto his long finger.

And that's not even the end of it.

What's even more fascinating is that he's cooing back. Or rather, the voice that he's using with her is not his usual voice, rough and scrape-y, coated with sand. It's smooth and deep and rich.

Coo-ey.

The Angry Thorn that everyone is scared of is *cooing* because he's in love with a five-month-old girl. And that five-month-old girl seems equally in love with him.

I don't know how to handle that.

I don't know what to do with this knowledge.

I mean, I knew he loved his niece. Of course I knew that. But I'd never seen it before. The change that comes over him when he's with Halo. Because while he may have seen me with Halo before, I haven't seen him. This is the first time I'm seeing him interacting with her. Probably because she has so many uncles who are always waiting for their turn to play with her. Plus she has a clingy aunt — me, a clingy mommy and a very possessive daddy.

So maybe in all of that I missed seeing them together.

Which I think is a good thing.

Because if I had, I'd be crippled with longing.

I'd be *crippled* with pain. For wanting what I could never have.

As it is, it's so hard to stand here and watch him with her. So hard to not just break down and sob and beg.

Beg to know why he didn't love me.

Why didn't he think that I could be more?

Why couldn't he have seen me as more than a pawn?

Why is it that my dream of a family, a baby with him can't come true?

"You wanna give her to me?" he says, lifting his eyes.

I don't know what I look like right now but whatever it is makes him frown a little. And he goes, "What's —"

"Yeah, here," I say, stepping back from him.

I hold her with one arm and with the other, I undo the Velcro in the front before reaching behind my back to work on the straps. Which is when I notice him stepping toward me, his arm in the process of being raised for some reason, and I jerk back.

He wasn't going to touch me, was he?

Whatever he planned to do, my abrupt retreat makes him clench his jaw and he lowers his arm.

I feel a slight pinch in my heart at rejecting him, or most probably the help he was about to offer. But then I tell myself that I have nothing to feel sorry for.

Quickly, I get the straps loosened and very carefully gather my squirmy bundle and transfer it to the guy in front of me. But I probably didn't gauge the exact amount of intimacy that's bound to erupt when you do something like this. Because I'm left with shallow breaths and a pounding heart as we both lean toward each other, the back of my hand grazing his palms, the coarse hairs on his forearms rubbing up against mine.

Making it known how heated he is.

How his skin is charged with electricity.

It takes only a couple of seconds to make the transfer but it feels longer.

Much longer, and so as soon as Halo is secure in his strong bulging arms, I step away, bunching the sling in my hands and saying, "Callie and Reed aren't here."

He looks away from Halo, who's smacking her palms on his jaw. "I can see that."

"So you wasted a trip. You should go. I'll tell them —"

I'm cut off by the shrill sound of the timer, alerting me that my cupcakes are done.

So I abandon the conversation, as important as it is, and dash over to the kitchen. I pull out the fourth batch of my simple vanilla cupcakes and, whirling around, put them on the island. And of course, he's here.

In the kitchen.

Standing on the opposite side of the island.

His eyes taking in the state of things.

Fuck.

I don't want him seeing what he's seeing. In fact, he's the last person that I want seeing these things about me.

First of all, the kitchen is a disaster. Every inch of the space is covered with something, either baking sheets or baking ingredients or baked goods. There's a heap of cut-up strawberries on the island and of course there's spilled juices like drops of blood that I forgot to clean up. There's also a big bowl of baby pink frosting sitting just by it, and somehow I've used like, three different spatulas to ice my first few batches of cupcakes. That are also sitting on the island. Plus there's spilled flour on the counters and on the floor; discarded packs of cream cheese and butter; sprinkles of sugar everywhere.

And then there's the fact itself that I'm baking.

That I *bake*.

Something I never told him. Or rather something *else* I never told him.

Mostly because I'm self-taught and I don't do really complex baking. Just simple comfort baking like vanilla cupcakes, brownies, apple pies and so on. Plus he already has a sister who's a master baker. In fact it was one of the things that we'd bonded over, Callie and me. Anyway, I just didn't want to be compared and found wanting.

And the fact that he's yet again discovering another one of my secrets is freaking me out and I want him out of here. Not to mention, I told him that we should stay away from each other only *yesterday*. But before I can say all of this to him, he does something… crazy.

He reaches out with his free arm, grabs one of my cupcakes and pops the whole thing in his mouth.

In one go.

Just like that.

"What are you doing?" I ask, my voice high.

He takes his time chewing and swallowing. Then, "Eating a cupcake."

"You can't eat a cupcake."

In response, he grabs another one and pops that into his mouth as well. Again in one go and just like that. When he's done swallowing that down too, he goes, "Apparently I can."

I exhale sharply. "These are not for you."

He goes for a third cupcake as he says, "Yeah?"

"Stop eating my cupcakes," I demand.

He doesn't, of course, because the third one goes into his big freaking mouth as well. Then, "Who are they for?"

"For your sister and my brother."

And another one goes into his mouth. "Why, what'd they do?"

I reach forward and slide the tray away from him before he can grab a fifth one. "It's a thank you gift. For letting me babysit Halo."

He gives me a look. "Yeah, no. I think it should be other way around."

"I don't —"

"Besides, my sister can bake cupcakes for your brother any time he wants. So *this*," he goes for the bowl of frosting this time, "is mine." With that, he dips his long finger in the frosting and scoops it out before popping it in the mouth and going, "Strawberry, huh. Very nice."

"Oh my God, now that whole batch is ruined and —"

I swallow my words when he goes ahead and dips his finger again, scooping another dollop out. But this time, he goes for Halo who eagerly opens her mouth and licks the whole thing, smearing her mouth with pink frosting.

"Are you crazy?" I squeak out, rushing over to Halo with her burp cloth. "You're not supposed to feed her solids yet. And sugar at that. What are you thinking?" To Halo, I say, "I'm sorry, honey. Uncle Ledger is crazy. I don't know what he's thinking."

Halo grins down at me though, flailing her fists, smacking me in the jaw as I wipe her face, going, "Da. Da. Daaaa."

"You can explain to Callie when she comes back how her daughter has tasted solids for the very first time and it happened without her…"

I trail off because when I look back at him, I find that he's already watching me.

And that would've been okay if he wasn't doing it with such single-minded focus. Or with so much intensity and God, hunger.

That's what that is, in his eyes.

That I didn't want to see before when he was at the door and I was walking toward him with Halo.

He was watching me with hunger, like he wanted something from me.

Like he *wants* something from me now.

And no matter how deep I feel it, the tug in my belly, I don't have anything to give to him. Not anymore. So I step away again and say, "I think you should —"

112

"This isn't the first time," he says.

I look up. "This isn't the first time for what?"

His eyes still intense, he tilts his head toward Halo. "That Little Berry here has tasted solids."

"What?"

"Your brother's already taken care of that."

"Reed?" I ask frowning. "He already —"

"Yeah. Behind my sister's back. So I think I'll be okay."

"But why would —"

"Because Callie's acting crazy." He rubs Halo's back; she turns to him and coos. "She's been ready for solids for weeks now."

Which I also agree with.

Halo's been showing a lot of interest in food lately. She can follow what we're eating, grabs on to things, tries to put things in her mouth. And well, last week when I was babysitting her while Callie was in the kitchen, Halo did manage to swallow a very little and mushy piece of peach. I never told Callie, of course, because she would've freaked out, but yeah, little cutie pie here is all grown up and ready to eat grown-up food. Or at least mashed veggies and fruits.

"Just for the record," I say then. "Are you actually *agreeing* with something that my brother did?"

"I can neither confirm nor deny that," he deadpans after a couple of seconds.

Despite myself, my lips flicker with a smile. "No, I think you can. Confirm, I mean."

His jaw clenches.

But I keep going. "That you just agreed with my brother."

His jaw clenches some more.

"Your arch nemesis," I add.

"I prefer sworn enemy," he says finally.

"Why, because sworn enemy sounds so much more mature than arch nemesis?"

"Apparently."

I narrow my eyes at him. "I'll be sure to notify the maturity police."

His lips pull up slightly as well. "Why don't you do that while Little Berry and I finish off these cupcakes here?"

My heart drops a beat and I ask, finally unable to stop myself, "What's Little Berry?"

"Strawberry."

"What about it?"

"She looks like one."

"So that's your nickname for her."

"Yes."

"And because you're always giving people nicknames."

"Not always, no."

"So then —"

His eyes flash. "Only on special occasions."

And I guess three years ago, meeting me was a special occasion for him, wasn't it? His rival's little sister throwing herself at him while he must've been counting his blessings at the opportunity that had fallen into his lap.

"You can't be here," I say, repeating a version of what I said earlier.

"Why?"

"Because as I said, Callie and Reed aren't here," I tell him. "I can tell them later that you stopped by, but —"

"Or I can tell them myself."

"No. You need to leave now."

He stares at me for a second or two before saying, "Can't break my girl's heart."

I know he's talking about Halo. I know that.

And he's right. Her heart would break if he left so soon. She's clinging to him like a spider monkey. But I can't have him around. It's not good for my psyche.

"I think you're underestimating yourself," I tell him. "You're an expert on breaking hearts. I'm sure you'll find a way to let her down gently. So I'd really appreciate it if you left because I don't want you around me."

For a few moments, all he does is stare at me.

His features tight, his jaw ticking.

Then, "I acted like an asshole."

"What?"

He breathes deep, his chest moving up and down and Halo moving with him. "The other night. Back at the bar."

"I don't... understand."

Another breath, not as deep as the last one, but still deep enough to make me think that he's bracing himself. "You were right. My sister is married to your brother now, much to my..."

He's searching for a word here; I can feel it.

"Displeasure."

"That's a very tame word."

"I've got better ones, but..."

"But what?"

"Can't say it in front of her."

By her, he means Halo.

And the fact that he's cleaning up his language for his five-month-old niece when my own brother, her daddy, won't do it, makes me want to smile. Which is crazy, because nothing about this situation warrants any kind of smile.

I fold my arms across my chest and prod, "Much to your displeasure?"

Another exhale. "And I took that out on you."

"Wouldn't be the first time," I say, referring to what happened thirteen months ago.

How he took his anger, his need for vengeance against my brother, out on me and turned me into collateral damage.

"Yeah well, that's why I'm apologizing."

I draw back. "What?"

He shifts on his feet. "I shouldn't have done what I did. Shouldn't have acted like a douchebag. You were trying to make peace and I was fu—" he pauses, "I messed it up. As I said, you were right. We *are* going to be seeing each other. A lot. And there's no use in making an already sh—" he closes his eyes for a second "— bad situation worse. So I'm here to tell you that I'll stop."

"Stop what?"

"Provoking you. Playing with you."

My heart is racing for so many reasons.

For him not only actively cleaning up his language for his niece, whose face is tucked into his neck now as she sucks on her fist, looking sleepy, but also because he's actually apologizing for his behavior. He's acknowledging that yes, he's been trying to provoke me for the last year.

He's been trying to play with me.

"Why did you?" I ask. "Play with me in the first place."

"Because you're bright and flaming and feisty like a firefly."

My breath hitches. "I —"

"And I wanted to light you up and make you glow."

I open my mouth to say something. Although I don't know what I *should* say at this point. I never expected this from him. Apology, acknowledgements, actual admission of his guilt. Something that he's never done before and —

Wait a second.

He has never done this before.

He has never actually *apologized* to me about anything. About seeing me as nothing more than an object when I worshipped the ground he walked on for years. For showing up at my dorm room thirteen months ago to use me against my brother. For leaving me crying and broken, *naked* in my bed and not looking back.

But he's suddenly feeling apologetic about what happened between us two nights ago at the bar?

Does he actually expect me to believe that?

Does he *actually think* that I don't know what's going on here?

Clenching my teeth, I go, "Are you done?"

There's a frown between his brows. "What?"

"Are you done with your freaking crap?"

"I —"

"Do you actually expect me to believe this? This whole fake apology routine."

His eyes narrow. "Fake."

"Yeah. *Fake*." Then, "I know why you're doing this."

"Yeah, why?"

"You pity me."

A flinch goes through him.

A flinch of shock.

Not because I'm right but because he has absolutely no idea what I'm talking about. I can clearly see that on his face. That does give me a little pause and puts the brakes on my wrecking train of a hypothesis. But before I can ponder over any of this, he speaks.

"And what exactly am I pitying you for?"

His voice has been lowered and I swear it sounds… angry.

Unfolding my arms, I swallow. "B-because I said what I said. Yesterday. In the bathroom."

His features are so tight that nothing seems to be moving or animated. "What is it that you said?"

I grip the edge of the counter to give myself some balance that I'm rapidly seeming to lose. "I… I can see that… It's not —"

"What did you say?"

I curl my bare toes, shivering slightly, cringing that I brought this up at all. "I told you that…"

"You told me what?"

Damn it.

"I said the L word," I finally settle on. "Okay? The L word. And it's not a stretch for me to think that this is you pitying me. This is you trying to, I don't know, make yourself feel… less awkward or something. Because you've never apologized to me for anything before and suddenly twenty-four hours after I've uttered the worst thing that I ever could have, you're here saying sorry. So excuse me if I don't believe you."

I don't know what he's thinking because his expression is still blank. And he's not saying anything either.

I wish he would though.

Even if it's to confirm my suspicions. Though as the seconds pass, it's becoming less and less likely that they're true.

Finally, he says, "I can see why you'd think that. But this isn't pity."

"So what is —"

"If I felt pity for you, then you wouldn't be standing in your little yellow dress like you are right now."

"What?"

"You'd be on this island, flat on your back with your dress on the floor. While your bare skin matched the color of cotton candy." Then, "Because I'd finally be giving you what you've wanted ever since you were sixteen and

I found you hiding out behind the bushes. Something that you still want. No matter how much you deny it or dress it up as disgust. It's a thing called D. I. C. K. That people use, in similar circumstances, to pity. F. U. C. K." Then, "So this isn't pity, this is me trying to do the right thing for the first time ever."

Chapter Twelve

HE IS DOING the right thing.

For the first time ever.

I wonder if that was why I let him stay and didn't kick him out of the house like I should have.

Or if it was the fact that I believed him. That his whole unexpected apology wasn't because of his pity. Because I did believe him.

It was right there on his face.

His shock. His obvious anger. The very fact that he went all vulgar and assholish was because he hadn't liked my assumptions. And the relief of that was so big that I didn't want to sour it by fighting. Or it could be because Halo really wasn't in the mood to let go of her favorite uncle. And since she was sleepy and lethargic and it's never a good idea to mess with her when she's like this, I decided to let it all go.

Whatever the case, he stayed.

In fact, he's still here. A couple of hours later.

And things have happened.

Like for example, I cooked dinner.

Something which, like baking, I taught myself — because no one really cooks where I come from; we've got people for that — and again something that I never told Ledger. But I figured that I was going to cook for myself anyway, plus he already knows about my baking, so what's one more secret.

Then after dinner I watched, surreptitiously, as he did Halo's bedtime routine. While I should've been in the kitchen, doing the dishes and cleaning up.

I watched him as he carefully bathed her, his long fingers all sudsy and gentle. I watched him give her shampoo-slick hair a cool mohawk that his

Little Berry absolutely loved and found totally hilarious. Then he blew bubbles and played with her duckie and chuckled and laughed, something he very rarely does, looking all kinds of beautiful.

Once the bath was done, he patted her dry, again all tenderly, and got her into her diaper and pajamas. And then he fed her as he rocked her and paced around the room. At this point, usually Callie and I, we'd read her a story, but he didn't need to do that. Because not only had she been half-asleep before her bedtime routine, but him playing with her and talking to her — in his coo-ey voice — almost put her to sleep.

That was my last straw though.

Hearing his coo-ey voice again.

Something that I couldn't have imagined him capable of doing in a million years. And like everything else that I did in our one-sided love story, I imagined this a lot too.

Him with a baby.

Our baby.

So that was when I fled and went back to the kitchen.

Which is where I am right now.

Doing the dishes.

Scrub. Rinse. Repeat.

Until I feel something. First, in the air that makes goosebumps wake up on my arms. And then half a second later, a tingling in the back of my neck. By the time I whirl around, which takes even *less* than half a second, my entire body is covered in goosebumps and tingles.

Because he's here.

So close.

"What are you doing?" I ask, looking into his dark eyes that seem darker. In response he moves closer to me and I can't stop my gasp as his face, his lips come very, *very* close to me, seemingly heading toward *my* lips. "Oh my God, what…"

But then he passes me by and reaches with his arm, shutting off the water.

Oh.

Okay.

No. Actually, *not* okay.

So when he moves back and props his hips against the island, his arms folded across his chest, I say, as sternly as I can, "I think I've asked you to respect my personal space before."

He watches me for a few seconds, my flushed cheeks, my heaving chest. "And I would if you'd respected mine."

"I've never −"

"Not my personal space, no. But my privacy."

"That −"

"Which I'm sure falls in the same category as respecting someone's personal space."

Shit.

Shit.

Of course he knew. Of course he knew that I was watching him.

It's uncanny. The way he knows.

Thirteen months ago, I would've taken it as a sign and thought that he's so attuned to me and what I do. But I guess the truth is that I'm just not good at stalking at all.

I press my hips to the counter. "I was checking to make sure that Halo was okay."

"Sure."

"She's my responsibility tonight. You've already fed her cupcakes and peaches. So I had to make sure you weren't breaking any other rules made by your sister."

All true.

He did give her a few pieces of my cupcakes and cut-up peaches. I think I'm going to have to tell Callie when she comes back. That her brother is a total rebel and her husband as well. I have no shame in being the tattletale in this case.

His biceps bunch and flex as he shifts on his feet. "My sister is crazy, as I've already mentioned before. And it's not my fault that your cupcakes are fucking delicious and she kept wanting more."

"That's so…" Then, "My c-cupcakes are delicious?"

His eyes bore into mine. "I ate five in a row. You were there for that, weren't you?"

"Four," I remind him like it's so important. "You ate four."

"Only because you took 'em away."

"You got them back though. Later."

"Of course I did," he says. "I told you they were mine."

His.

God, will he ever stop sounding so possessive?

It makes me almost glad that we were never meant to be. If he's so crazy possessive now, when I'm nothing more to him than an object, imagine how possessive he'd be if we ever got together.

So in a way it all worked out I guess.

Yeah, right, Tempest.

Whatever.

The point is that he did manage to get his hands on the cupcakes after we had dinner and he polished off the majority of them, along with feeding Halo here and there. And yes, it did fill me with pleasure and pride and I did think that he may have liked them. Or at least not completely hated them.

But I was so rattled at the time — I still am, by the way — that I didn't let it penetrate.

I'm letting it penetrate now though.

He likes my cupcakes. He really, *really* likes them.

All my worries in the past were for nothing.

Yay.

"Well, thank you," I say, instead of grinning like a fool. "But that still doesn't mean —"

"So since when do you bake?"

"What?"

"And how come I never knew that you did?"

"You don't know everything about me," I retort.

"Actually I think I do."

"Of course not," I scoff. "Of —"

"I know the first time you wanted to kiss a boy," he says, cutting me off.

"What?"

"Viktor Sullivan."

"I... I'm... What?"

"You were five."

I open and close my mouth, unable to form words.

Because... What?

I mean yes, there was a boy named Viktor Sullivan when I was little, but how does he know that?

"Which was the only reason I didn't go after him. Right after you told me."

"What reason?"

"You were five. You didn't know better."

"I don't —"

Then, shrugging, "Besides I found out that he'd moved to the west coast, and since there was no immediate threat, I didn't think it was necessary to hop on a plane."

"What threat?" I shake my head. "What the hell are you *talking* about?"

He doesn't stop to explain things. Rather he goes on, "I know the first time you tasted cotton candy. At the beach with your shithead brother when you were four. And you said that it felt like you were eating a piece of cloud and that you were a unicorn."

"I —"

"For the record, you're not a fucking unicorn. An ugly horn in the middle of your forehead is not what I wanna picture when I close my eyes." He looks me up and down. "You could be a Barbie though."

"I think," I say, breathing haphazardly, "you need to slow down a little and —"

He doesn't.

"I also know the name of your favorite doll: Krista. You had her from the age of three to seven and the only reason you stopped having her was because your mother saw you playing with her and decided to get rid of her because of how ragged she looked. I hope you know that, like your father, your mother's a piece of shit too. By the way, Krista is also the fake name you gave me the night I called you out on your stalking." Then, "I know your favorite movie: any Hugh Jackman movie is your favorite movie because you've got a thing for burly big men. But since he's happily married with two kids, again I didn't think it was important for me to hop on a plane and hunt him down. Although I think he's getting divorced now so maybe I'll hop on that plane after all. Your favorite romance novel; why you prefer Dior over Jimmy Anthony or something when it comes to shoes. I also know that your favorite color is red but somehow you have the least amount of dresses in that color. You like summer the best but you'll take fall too. Because winter means wearing too many clothes and you apparently like wreaking havoc on my psyche more than you like being covered. And if you were given a superpower, you'd want to be invisible so you can spy on Tessa Thompson from seventh grade, who used to make fun of your romance novels the most, and destroy her."

He pauses here for a second so I think he's done, but apparently not because he goes on to add, "By the way, she was dating one of my strikers back in the day. Kinda as a *fuck you* to her daddy. But then we found out that she didn't just have a weakness for soccer players from the other side of the tracks but she also enjoyed snorting a little white powder that's not very legal. And since it's our civic duty to report these things, we did. The last I heard she was in a convent in Switzerland somewhere."

And *then* he's done.

Still standing there all casually and arrogantly and like nothing happened just now.

Like he didn't just blow my freaking mind.

He didn't just turn my world upside down.

By reciting random, completely unhelpful facts about me, facts that I remember now I told him.

Over several texts and phone calls.

But first.

"Did she really?" I ask, my voice sounding foreign right now. "You know, coke."

His lips twitch slightly at my scandalized tone. "Yeah."

"I knew it." I shake my head. "I *knew* she was up to something and something bad had happened. Because no one knew why she suddenly disappeared one day and got into this prestigious school in Switzerland. Prestigious." I scoff. "*Right.*"

Wait till I tell Callie.

She knows all about Tessa and how much I hated her. And how I've always been wondering what happened to her. And now thanks to *him*, I know and…

Oh my God.

What the fuck am I doing?

Why am I more bothered about the gossip rather than what he just told me?

"H-how do you know all this?" I ask, gripping the counter tightly.

"You told me."

"I know that," I tell him, licking my lips. "But h-how do you *remember* all this? How do you…"

"I guess I just have a good memory."

"And…" I try to gather my breath. "And did you really do that? To Tessa. For me."

For this he takes a couple of seconds to answer. Then, "Yes."

"Why?"

"Because she messed with you."

"So?"

"So I messed with her back."

I lick my lips again. "Yeah. B-but why? Why would you care enough to —"

"Because you were my sister's best friend. And because I could."

My heart's pounding and pounding in my chest. "But I thought… I thought I was your rival's little sister. And nothing else."

"Yeah well, it's fucking complicated, isn't it?" he says coolly. "What you were or what you are. I just did it as a favor."

I don't know what to make of it.

What he did and *why* he did it.

Not to mention that it's pretty fucking surreal that he did it at all.

Pair all this with his apology, I can almost start to assume things. I can almost start to hope.

But I'm not stupid, not anymore.

He probably did it because he could, as he said. And as a favor. Nothing to freak out about.

Even so, I can't help but blurt out, "It's not Jimmy Anthony. It's Marc Anthony. You're thinking about Jimmy Choo." His eyes narrow slightly at my correction. "And did Viktor Sullivan really move to the west coast?" His eyes narrow further. "Only b-because I never heard anything about it and…" When his jaw clenches, I change topics. "And eleven."

He watches me for a few beats, his dark eyes penetrating. Then, "Jimmy Choo and Marc Anthony can go fuck themselves. If you want proof of Viktor Sullivan moving to the west fucking coast, I'd be happy to fly over and bring you photos of him laid up in a hospital bed. And eleven *what?*"

I bite my lip at the strong shiver that rolls down my body at the absolute murder I hear in his voice at the mention of Viktor Sullivan. A boy I'd met on the playground when I was five and I didn't even remember up until he brought him up.

See? Crazy possessive.

For absolutely no reason.

"When I started baking," I reply. "The age of eleven."

I thought his eyes were super intense before but at my reply, they become scorching.

Blazing.

I want to say that they feel like the rays of the sun, but with him, there's no brightness or sunshine, only thunder and rain. So it's like looking into the eye of a storm.

"Why did I not know about it?"

"Because I…" I trail off, trying to gather the right words in which to express why.

He doesn't have a problem though with that. "Because you wanted to bake them for me."

I blush, thinking for a second that I should lie. But then, I whisper, "Yes."

"Badly."

"Y-yes."

"And you wanted me to like them."

I blush harder. "I did."

"Again," he says in a lowered voice. "Badly."

I nod. "And so I thought it would be better if I just… never made them. For you."

"You thought wrong," he tells me, his eyes still burning my cheeks.

"It was something…" I swallow again and lick my lips and curl my toes, feeling all kinds of restless. "I read it in a romance novel."

"What romance novel?"

"My favorite."

His eyes flick back and forth between mine. "The one with the baker chick and that douchebag."

"Jason was not a douchebag," I say, frowning even as I tell myself that maybe I'm focusing on the wrong thing.

The right thing to focus on is that he wasn't lying.

He does remember my favorite romance novel.

But then again if I focused too much on that, then that would be make me a fool and not a smart girl.

"Yeah, he was," he says.

"No, he wasn't," I insist.

"Instead of telling the truth like a man, he kept showing up at her bakery and eating her cupcakes like he hadn't eaten in days."

"He kept showing up and eating her cupcakes because he loved her, you idiot."

"No," he explains. "He kept showing up and eating her cupcakes because he wanted to get in her pants."

"What?"

"Which if he had admitted it like a man in the beginning of the book, then we wouldn't have to read three hundred pages of nonsense only to come to the same conclusion at the end."

I lean forward, completely outraged. "It wasn't bullshit, okay? It was swoon-y. Her business was failing. She thought that she wasn't a good enough baker to cut it. So he showed up every day to show her that she was. That she could do it."

I can't believe he didn't see that.

Ugh. Boys.

Such idiots.

"What's swoon-y?" he asks after a bit.

"Uh, something that's swoon-worthy. That makes you swoon."

"Yeah, no. What you think is swoon-y is probably the sound of my balls climbing up inside my body."

"Ew," I scrunch up my nose. "That's disgusting."

"Truth often is."

I roll my eyes. "Well, it doesn't matter."

"Why not?"

"Because I don't read romance novels anymore."

The only reason I know I've said something of significance is because he goes still. All the lightness, the amusement vanishes from his features and they draw up tight.

Even the bulges of his biceps strain and his veins stand taut like strings.

"You don't read romance novels anymore," he repeats in a low voice.

My muscles go tight as well. "Uh, no. But that's —"

"Why?"

"It's not important. I don't want to talk about it."

"Why?" he insists, his voice going even lower.

"I —"

"*Why* don't you read romance novels anymore?" he asks again, a tic forming on his jaw.

"Are you really asking me that?"

He doesn't answer, simply watches me with undisguised intensity and yes, anger.

Like he's mad at *me.*

For giving up on something that I loved.

"Because they're not real, okay?"

A muscle jumps in his cheek at my answer but I keep going. "They're a lie. They're fantasy. They give you wrong expectations. They make you dream about things that don't exist. Things that don't happen in real life. Because…"

My voice is shaking now.

And I don't think I can do this. I don't think I can keep going.

I want him to leave.

I want him to go away because this is too much. His presence, his nearness. All these encounters when I'm only used to seeing him maybe once every three to four months. And even then in passing where we either keep our distance from each other or argue and move on.

"Because what?" he prods, his face still carved out of stone and looking strained.

"Because real life is made of thunder and thorns."

A flinch goes through him.

Small but I know it's there.

And I know that my words have hurt him. Because I know that *he* knows they're for him.

That I'm saying *he's* made of thunder and thorns.

"And not candies and cream."

This time, *I* flinch. Because I *know* he's talking about me. I know he's calling me that. It's in his dark eyes, all penetrating and intense.

So that's what we are then.

A boy made of thunder and thorns. And a girl made of candies and cream.

No wonder we weren't meant to be together.

Not in this life at least.

"No," I tell him, unable to look anywhere else but him. "Real life isn't made of candies and cream. Because in real life when you see a boy in a crowded stadium at a soccer game and fall in l-love with him, he doesn't do the same. In real life when you chase him around, he doesn't stop and let you catch him. He doesn't call you. He doesn't text you, no matter how much you want him to. No matter how you jump at every little beep your phone makes, hoping that it's him. Finally. But it's not. It's never him, is it?"

I don't know why I said that.

Why I had to show him further how desperate I used to be back then.

I mean, is it not enough that I did call him like a junkie almost every night? Or that I did follow him around and show up at almost every party and every game?

"Yeah," he rasps as if agreeing with me, and I squirm in my spot. "It's never him. Because in real life, he's an asshole with an ego bigger than his head. In real life, he's a selfish motherfucker focused on his game, his career, his rivalry. Because in real life, he's *incapable* of focusing on anything else, and that's okay. Or it would've been, if he — *I* — hadn't dragged you down with me. If I hadn't done what I did. Or what I wanted to do for years. All the things that I wanted to do. To you. For *years*."

I think I have a pretty good idea of what he wanted to do to me.

But even so, I can't help but whisper, "W-what things?"

He gnashes his teeth, staring at me, as if he doesn't know if he should say. But then he decides to do it anyway. "Take advantage of you."

I freeze.

As if this is the first time I'm hearing of it.

Which is not true at all but still, it's a shock.

He ignores it, however, and keeps going, "To use you against your brother. And you made it so easy too. You made it so goddamn tempting. Because you were everywhere, weren't you? Everywhere I turned, there you were with your blue-gray eyes and your flowing dark hair. Smiling at me, mooning over me, worshipping the ground I walked on. It was enough to give me a hard-on for days.

"A hard-on to ruin you, wreck you, destroy you, only to brag about it later to that son of a bitch. Only to see his face drain of all color when I told him what I did to his little sister that he loved so much. Because guess what, his pretty little sister is all grown up now and she loves me. And so she'd let me make her fall apart and put her back together, if I wanted. *However* I wanted. She'd let me do things to her that he could only imagine in his head in the dead of the night, when the whole world is asleep and he's awake, jerking himself off to them."

His eyes look so far away, almost glazed over, as he keeps going, "Sometimes I wonder why I didn't. Why I didn't do all the things that I wanted to do. What stopped me. But then it doesn't matter, does it? Because I did end up doing it. I did end up hurting you that night. All so I could hurt him. So I could have my revenge."

He did.

He's absolutely right.

Even though he somehow managed not to do those things to me — and yes, I would've let him, all in the name of love — he did end up hurting me anyway. He did end up ruining me and wrecking me.

And destroying me just like he wanted.

So the fact that I can see — for the first time ever — something very similar to remorse on his face, something very similar to self-directed anger, shouldn't matter to me.

It shouldn't matter at all.

"And so that's why it was never me," he says, breaking my chaotic thoughts, now focused on me. "That's why you waited and *waited* by the phone, jumped at every little beep, thinking that it was me but it wasn't. Because the way I felt about you, the way I wanted to use you to stroke my ego and the way it was *so hard* to stop myself, I didn't think I could handle going after you. I didn't think *you* could handle me going after you. Because look what happened when I did. When for the first time ever I said fuck it and chased you down. I showed up at your dorm room in the middle of the night and left you broken and crying in my wake. Because I don't live in the pages of your romance novels, do I? I'm not your swoon-y, cupcake-eating hero. I am the real life. Made of thunder and thorns. And you're made of candies and cream. And the only way I knew how to keep you safe from me and my twisted head was to keep you away."

Did he say safe?

That he was keeping me... *safe*.

From himself.

Safe.

That was the first thing that I'd felt when I was around him. I'd felt safe. Turns out that it wasn't true in the end, but the fact that he kept me at a distance in his twisted attempt to keep me safe is... I don't know what it is except mind-blowing.

Not the first time I've used that word tonight.

But that's what it is.

The reason he never initiated any contact with me was because he was... *protecting* me. That's what it means, doesn't it?

He was protecting me in a way that maybe a predator protects its prey. A lion knows he's dangerous. He imagines sinking his teeth into the lamb's flesh, tearing her open and eating her heart out. He imagines destroying her in a million ways because that's what he does, that's who he is.

So in order to protect her, he goes against his own instinct, and tries to run her off.

He tries to spare her life.

And if the lamb were smart, she'd take his advice and run away.

But I'm not a lamb, am I?

I'm a firecracker. A firefly.

His Firefly.

And he's always been my Thorn. My Beautiful Thorn.

And that's why here I am, all broken and bent, my wings trashed. Lovelorn and alone.

"I think... I'm —"

"But that's not important," he cuts me off, his face looking determined. "What happened or who am I or what I did. What's important is what I do now."

"What?"

He studies me for a second, my face, my throat, stopping at the freckle on the side of my neck, before moving down to my body that I know I'm holding very tightly now. All my muscles bunched up and alert.

Because whatever he is talking about is giving me a bad feeling.

A *very* bad feeling.

Then in a flash, I'm proven right when he gets so close to me that the next breath I take is laced with cinnamon.

And God, *God*, he captures the next beat of my heart in his palm.

Because he wraps his fingers around my throat, his thumb digging into that freckle on the side of my neck.

"W-what are you —"

"I always wanted to do that," he rasps, taking my face in.

"D-do what?"

"Feel your pulse against my skin."

I swallow against his grip. "I-I —"

He flexes his fingers, making me gasp. "Feel how *hard* your heart races when I'm around. How high your pulse would jump for me and your freckle right on top of it would dance, when I actually touched you."

The answer to that is '*extremely*.'

Extremely hard and extremely high.

I bet he can feel that too.

How my body dances to his tune, and I want him to make it stop.

I want him to stop touching me like this.

"I don't know what you're doing but —"

His fingers flex around my throat once again. "You said it was your first kiss."

I blink rapidly, feeling the pressure around my neck, freaked out and holy God, *excited*. "What?"

"That night," he explains, darkness swirling in his eyes. "When I came to your dorm room."

"I'm not sure why we're —"

"You said it was the most beautiful thing you'd ever experienced."

"L-Ledger, please. I —"

"Was it?"

My chest is heaving but I don't think I'm getting any air in and I'm starting to feel faint. "Y-yes."

"But then I turned it ugly," he keeps going.

"You did."

He rubs his thumb over my pulse then, over my freckle. His eyes rove over my face as if memorizing every little crevice and line, every little thing that makes me *me*.

"I may not be the hero of a romance novel. And I may not be able to turn back pages and rewrite our story. But I can do one thing."

"What one thing?"

"I can make your second kiss even more beautiful than your first, Firefly."

I jolt at him using my nickname.

And that's probably the only reason why I don't say anything, why I freeze and let him put his mouth on me.

His hot and warm and soft mouth.

His wet mouth.

And he's giving me a kiss.

My second kiss.

And despite all the confusion, all the shock and all the reasons why this is a bad idea, I do think that it's more beautiful than the first. I'm not sure why that is but it's true.

Maybe because his lips are more urgent than they were thirteen months ago.

Which is saying something, because they were pretty fucking urgent back then too. They were pretty fucking dominating as well. It felt like he was finally giving in to something that he'd always wanted. Not to mention what I'd always wanted.

And yes, this one feels like that as well.

But there's an added layer to it.

And I think it's familiarity.

It's the fact that he *knows* how to turn my head, at what angle, at what degree to go deep into my mouth with his tongue. It's the fact that when his taste — cinnamon-y — explodes inside my mouth, it's like taking a hit of your favorite drug. The drug that did take you places the very first time you tasted it but you were also afraid to chart an unknown territory.

You were afraid of your own reactions, your own feelings and moans and God, the way your own mouth sucked on it.

On his taste, his tongue, his *mouth.*

There is zero such fear now.

Zero such hesitation and fumbling.

And I don't want to stop. I don't ever, ever want to stop. Which is precisely why I *should* stop. Because this is the worst idea ever. Not only should we not be kissing each other but also we shouldn't be doing it where we can get caught.

By my brother *and* his sister.

Who also have no idea about our history. Back when I was crazy about him, I didn't want to tell Callie because I didn't know if she'd be against it or what and I didn't want to take that chance and potentially lose her. Plus she had her own problems with my brother and so I didn't want to burden her with mine. And by the time I thought maybe I could tell her, she got pregnant and of course the non-relationship relationship I had with her brother had been over.

So yeah, bad freaking idea and I need to put the brakes on it right now.

I move away from him, or try to, and explain my reasons.

But when he doesn't let me, I scratch and claw at his shoulders, at the side of his neck.

I struggle against him.

Against his hold on my neck, the fist of his other hand that I realize is in my hair, tilting my neck back so he has all the control over me. When even that doesn't work, I bite him, his lower lip, and he groans, sucking in a breath, his fingers flexing on my body. And finally, I manage to break away from him.

With our foreheads mashed together, I pant, "Wh-what... We can't. We... My brother... He can come back any second and —"

"And if he does," he says, panting too, his mouth wet, his eyes glazed over. "I hope he gives me what I deserve."

"What —"

This time when he comes for me, I somehow know that he won't stop.

No matter what I do.

Or what I saw.

Or what the danger is.

He's not going to stop because he doesn't care about coming out of this alive. He doesn't care about himself.

He doesn't *care*.

I don't know why I find it both scary and exciting in equal measure. So much so that my lips melt under the heat of his and I can't help but kiss him back. I can't help but let my tongue go exploring when his mouth opens up. As soon as my tongue touches his, I moan and his fingers around my throat go tighter.

As if he's not only trying to capture the pulse of my body but also this keening sound that came straight from my belly.

And why wouldn't he?

I know he likes that sound. I know he likes it when I make noises and moan and whimper.

So I do it again.

Not that it's hard. I guess I'm a moaner — something I hadn't known until that night in my dorm room — which is a good thing because he likes to make me moan.

So every time his tongue swipes against mine, I moan. Every time he sucks on my mouth, I whimper. And when he bites me, my lip, I jerk against him and whine. Which makes him not only groan but also tighten his grip around my throat. And I think it's easy to interpret that as domination.

And it is, of course.

But I also think that it's needy.

His grip on my neck.

It's his attempt to feel me.

To feel what he does to me, how he affects me. As if my reactions are an aphrodisiac to him. As if my reactions are what keeps him alive. Like he really is a devil like I called him and he feeds on my lust. Or a lion who feeds on my pulse and blood and how it all roars for him.

So I give him everything.

It doesn't even occur to me to hold back, or maybe it does but like him, I don't care.

I tug on his crazy hair — that, Jesus Christ, is still as soft and thick as it was thirteen months ago, quite possibly softer and thicker — and he pulls at mine. I bury my fingers in his stubble and he pushes his body against mine.

And yes, it's beautiful.

It's the most beautiful thing I've ever felt.

Just as I think that, I hear a car door slamming outside.

Footsteps climbing the stairs, walking across the porch. The front door opening.

Oh fuck.

Shit. Fuck. *Fuck.*

He's here.

My brother is fucking here. With *his* sister.

And maybe it's the rush of adrenaline or my extremely strong will to protect him — even after everything — or something else that I can't quite figure out in the moment, but I give him such a hard push that he's power-less against it.

He's powerless against me and my attempt to break the kiss.

He stares down at me like he doesn't know where he is and the only thing that was keeping him grounded was my mouth under his. But then I see the comprehension dawning on his face and I know he can hear the approaching footsteps as well.

While his mouth — wet and pink and swollen — stretches up in a satis-fied lopsided smile, my own falls open.

While he lets go of my hair and my neck only to bring his hand up to my face to cradle my cheek like he thinks I'm the most beautiful thing he's ever seen — more beautiful than the kiss he just gave me — my own hands snap away from his body and curl into fists at my sides.

And while he's rubbing his thumbs over my skin so tenderly, so softly that I want to weep, I whisper, "Please."

Which is what makes him move back.

Just in the nick of time because as soon as he does, I hear a thundering voice. "What the fuck?"

My eyes are wide as I stare up at Ledger and he throws me a smile that I can only call satisfied and reassuring. Like this is exactly what he wanted and now that he's got it, he's going to take care of it.

Before I can react to that, my brother demands, his voice even more booming than before, "What the fuck are you doing?"

With a last look at me, Ledger turns and oh my God, I can see that he wipes his mouth off with the back of his hand — or at least I can surmise from his gestures since his back is facing me now — before he drawls, "Hello to you too."

"Answer the fucking question, dipshit," my brother growls, "what the fuck are you doing with my sister?"

"The same thing you probably do every day with mine."

I hear Callie gasp.

Reed growls.

And I finally jump out from behind Ledger's back. "He's kidding."

Not a moment too soon, because Callie is grasping my brother's arm, probably trying to stop him from going after Ledger. Who's standing with his feet apart, his fingers fisted at his sides as if prepared to do battle with Reed.

But I know — I can feel it — that this is one battle that Ledger has every intention of losing.

"He's kidding," I repeat, hoping that my flushed cheeks and my tangled hair don't give me away. "He wasn't doing… anything with me."

Finally Reed deigns to look at me. "Why was he standing so close to you?"

"Because he was helping me with the dishes."

Reed glances over to the sink for a second before coming back to Ledger once again. With his ticking jaw, he goes, "Was he now."

Before Ledger can say anything, I reply, "Yes, he was. He really was. So can you stop glaring at him?"

He doesn't.

In fact he adds, jerking his chin up, "I want to hear it from him."

At which point, Callie goes, "Roman, I think —"

"You're going to let your sister talk for you," my brother cuts his wife off and taunts Ledger.

I can feel the heat, his anger that I know will soon reach a point where it changes the very air around us, radiating out of him. "I don't know, you tell me. You gonna let your wife hold you back from coming at me?"

Reed seethes, absolutely fucking seethes with fury, and takes a step forward, distressing Callie, and I've just had it with the both of them.

"Stop it, okay?" I say sternly, stepping forward on my own. "Both of you. What's wrong with you guys? You're acting like you're still in high school. Which was years ago, okay? *Years*. Why can't you just move the fuck on? I used to think it was soccer. That stupid freaking soccer is responsible for turning you into animals." I shake my head. "But I guess I was wrong. It's not soccer; it can't be. I mean, you don't even play anymore. You have a fucking garage, Reed." Turning to Ledger then, "And you did it, okay? You won. You went pro. You're in the big leagues now. Everyone thinks you're the best. Isn't that fucking enough? Stop fighting. *Please*. You're family now. Stop letting your stupid, boneheaded egos control you."

"Exactly." Callie adds, "There's a baby sleeping down the hall. Your baby, Roman." Turning to Ledger, she goes, "And your niece. Imagine how she'd feel when she grows up and sees her two favorite people fighting like kids on a playground."

Reed's breathing harshly and so is Ledger.

Both their chests moving up and down almost violently as they glare at each other.

God, what a bunch of Neanderthals. How can they not see that they're both essentially the same person?

Just when I think this silent stand-off will never end, Ledger speaks. "I'm leaving."

And gosh, I breathe out a sigh of relief.

That I think I let out too soon because when Ledger goes to grab a container of cupcakes — I'd carefully frosted and put them away in a container for Callie and Reed to enjoy later — Reed growls, "What the fuck are you doing with my sister's cupcakes?"

With his eyes on my brother, Ledger puts his hand, his fingers splayed wide, on the top and slides the box across the island toward himself. I'm not sure if it's apparent to the others or not, but I thought that that gesture screamed possessiveness.

"You want cupcakes," Ledger says, his voice low and bordering on threatening, "you ask your wife to make you some. These are mine."

Chapter Thirteen

Her Beautiful Thorn

WHEN PEOPLE ASK me the second most frequently asked question —
where does my anger come from — I tell them what I usually do when they
ask me the most frequently asked question. Which is basically to fuck
right off.

I don't like it when people try to get personal and poke into my business.

But the truth is that I don't think I know the answer to this question.

I don't know where my anger comes from. I don't sit around, looking out
the fucking window, contemplating the hows and the whys of it all.

I do, however, know what it felt like when I gave in to it the first time.

It was on the school playground and I was about four or so. Our father
had left us a year before and there was this fuckface in my class who
wouldn't shut up about it. Every single afternoon, he'd have something to
say about me, my brothers, my baby sister who was barely two, our mom.
He'd have something to say about how we must've done something to drive
him away. How our own father didn't love us enough to stick around.

Kids can be cruel when they want to be.

For months I'd ignored it. For months I'd let all the steam build up in my
system until one day he smiled at me and barely opened his mouth to start
his bullshit, and I exploded. I threw myself at him and took him down on
the ground. I punched him and punched him and fucking punched him so
many times that I forgot why I'd started in the first place.

All I knew was that I wanted him to shut the fuck up.

I wanted him to never ever be able to talk or make a sound or fucking
smile at anyone.

Anyway, teachers had to be called and I had to be physically pulled away. They suspended me for a bit and I do remember my mother was told to find ways to get my anger under control. That while they understood our home situation wasn't a hundred percent stable, they couldn't have an angry kid wreaking havoc at school. I also remember my mother refusing and telling them that she could handle her own child and that there was hardly anything to handle anyway.

I think she had been the only person in my life who had ever thought that.

That I didn't need outside influence to fix whatever was broken inside of me. Because nothing was.

But that's not the point.

The point is that there was only one time in my life when I'd felt that way. The way I'd felt when I'd beaten up that kid. I'd never felt that amount of rage and fury coursing through my system, like I'd been experiencing it for the first time ever, except that night.

Thirteen months ago.

When I showed up at her dorm room with the intent of getting back at the asshole who had ruined my sister's life. And no, it wasn't fury at him but at myself. For finally crossing the line. For finally committing the crime that I'd been stopping myself from for the past two years.

For at last turning her into an object that I could use for my purposes.

I wasn't lying to her when I said that I had, in fact, been stopping myself from doing what I did that night for years. Probably since the time she'd crashed back into my life — after I saw her on the hood of her brother's white Mustang.

And she made it hard, yes.

She made it very fucking hard to be good and noble because not only was she everywhere I turned but she was also the only thing I could think about. She was the first thought in my head when I woke up in the morning and the last before I closed my eyes at night. Instead of thinking about soccer, running plays in my head, doing everything that I could to get out of this town and out from under the thumbs of my brothers, all I could think about was the color of her eyes, that freckle on the side of her neck, her tinkling laughter, her wind chime-y voice.

All I could think about was I could crook my finger at her and she'd come running. How I could make her dance to my tune, dance on broken glass barefoot and she'd do it with that goddamn beautiful smile of hers. How I could kiss her, bite her, leave her with purple bruises and my teeth marks and instead of being scared and cringing away from me, she'd bare her neck, offer me her wrist, find little corners on her tight body that I hadn't gotten to yet.

Jesus, she fucked with my head.

My focus. My concentration.

That's why I kept her at a distance.

That's why every time I made her wait for a text from me or kept her on the edge of her seat while ignoring her at a party, I hoped and *prayed* that she'd go away. That she finally would get the message that I'd been trying to send ever since I found her hiding behind the bushes two years earlier.

The message that I was a loaded gun, see.

I was only a trigger away from lodging a bullet in her chest and murdering her heart.

But then again, it doesn't matter now, does it?

Because I ended up doing exactly what I'd stopped myself from doing. I did fire the gun and I did murder her heart.

I loved you…

The moment I hear her voice in my head, a rush goes through my body and I remember where I am. At this 24/7 boxing gym called Yo Mama's So Fit in a shady neighborhood of Bardstown. I've been coming here since I was fourteen. It's owned by one of Shep's friends, Ark Reinhardt. A tough looking guy from the wrong side of the tracks who's now one of the richest men in Bardstown. Not only because of this very popular gym but also because he started his own security company.

With me going pro though, I haven't been able to come here at all. But since there's no soccer — yet — I can come here anytime I want and beat the crap out of shit.

Although I have to say it's not all that satisfying when all I get to beat up is this body bag rather than an actual person. Because believe it or not, I did have a real live human punching bag, my friend Reign Davidson. One of my soccer friends who's ready to go pro this coming January. He had his own issues and liked getting beat up. But ever since he got together with the girl of his dreams, Echo Adler, he's been too happy to hang out with the rest of us sad losers.

So here I am, trying to find satisfaction and peace, but from the looks of it, it ain't happening.

Giving up and deciding to go back home, I take a quick shower and change into a fresh pair of sweatpants and a t-shirt in the locker room. I drive back to my childhood home where I'm currently living, wondering for the thousandth time why. Why the fuck am I living in the same house that I couldn't wait to get out of all my life?

I could very easily live in a hotel or something.

Actually I could very easily have not come back to Bardstown in the first place and flown out to practically anywhere in the world in my quest to escape my overbearing brothers. But I wasn't willing to leave Callie completely alone with that jerkface. While all my brothers have kinda come around — there's still some animosity though, between them and Reed fuckface Jackson — I'm the only one who hasn't forgotten what a player he used to be.

And now that they have a baby together and Callie is foolishly in love with him, it's even more imperative to keep an eye on that fucker so that he doesn't fuck up. Like he had in the past, so here I am.

As I'm pulling up in front of the house, I see someone sitting on the front steps.

My brother, Stellan.

I park behind his car and climb out of my truck, my gut tight and my eyes pinned on him.

He stands up as I reach him, his face stern and disapproving, and I say, "Fancy seeing you here."

Shifting on his feet, he replies, "You're not picking up anyone's calls."

"I lost my phone."

His eyes — dark like mine — flicker down to my pocket before he comes up and says, "It's in your pocket."

It is indeed.

Still I say, "Are you sure that's my phone? It could be, as they say, a roll of quarters or a candy bar."

He looks at me for a moment. "Are you using a euphemism to refer to your dick?"

"Are you saying that I shouldn't care about your delicate sensibilities and just come right out with it?"

His eyes narrow with displeasure.

"It's a joke," I tell him then.

"Everything's a joke to you, isn't it?"

"Not everything, no." I shake my head. "Some things are though. You should try it sometime."

His face remains stern. "I think I'll pass."

I shrug. "Your call. But if you go on like this, pretty soon people won't be able to distinguish between you and our big brother."

Again, a joke.

While Stellan, Shepard and I have dark hair and dark eyes, our big brother Conrad has dirty blond hair and blue eyes. He's the only brother that looks even remotely similar to Callie. I guess they both took after our mother while us three, we take after the father who abandoned us.

Anyway, there's no chance anyone could *ever* mistake Stellan for Conrad.

Not in the looks department at least.

Their demeanor, however, is a whole 'nother story.

"Gio said that you're still refusing therapy," he says instead, choosing to ignore me.

The muscles in my gut tighten further. "You should tell Gio that he needs to keep his mouth shut. Or I will shut it for him."

He exhales a sharp breath. "Yes, because that's what you do, don't you? You shut people's mouths."

"Apparently yes." I clench my jaw. "So maybe you should consider yourself lucky that I haven't taken measures to shut yours yet. Although you're cutting it very close."

With that, I bound up the steps, leaving him there, and open the front door.

I'm about to step through when Stellan says, "Ultraflex won't be the last brand to drop you, you know that, don't you? One by one they'll all drop you if you don't play. All your dreams and goals and *everything* that you've worked so hard for is going to go down the drain."

Ultraflex is a company that makes exercise equipment, and before the whole incident happened they'd signed me as the face of their new designs that they're launching next year. They'd just announced it when it happened and apparently they'd gotten so much heat for it that they finally made the decision to drop me. Gio had called with the news last week.

While I haven't been dropped yet by the other brands that I've signed with over the past few months, Stellan is right. If I don't get back on the team, I may as well kiss goodbye to all my extracurricular campaigns.

Not that I care about them.

I'm more concerned with the game, but it still fucking stings.

Turning around to face him, I raise my eyebrows. "Spooky. But Halloween is still a few weeks away, so why don't you go trick or treating somewhere else?"

There's a very small chance that he took my hint and is now on his way back to the car, ready to drive back to New York and tell on me to Con. Because obviously, that's why he's here, isn't he?

To do Conrad's bidding.

Because that's how it always started when we were kids. I'd do something wrong and Con would first send Shep to talk to me. On my level. And make me realize my mistake. If he couldn't do the job, then it would be Stellan's turn. If he proved to be unsuccessful as well, then it was time to bring out the big guns: our big brother himself.

I guess I've finally surpassed Shep's stage and so Stellan is here.

Anyway, I'm still hoping.

Until I reach the kitchen and get out orange juice from the fridge, gulping one third of the bottle down before I take a breath, and hear, "What the fuck?"

Of course he hasn't gone anywhere and is probably taking stock of the living room.

Well, I don't blame him; it looks like a war zone in there.

As I'm screwing the cap back on, I hear from behind me, "What the fuck happened in there?"

I take my time putting the bottle back in the fridge, looking for some quick snack to put together not because I'm hungry — although I could eat — but because I wanna piss my big brother off. He started it by showing up here and pissing me off, so it's only fair.

Finally I turn around and his eyes are slits and his jaw appears to be made of granite. A vein is bursting on his temple and I swear I can see it. Stellan magically turning into Conrad.

"You done jerking me around?" he goes.

I lean against the counter. "Not really. But I guess I can take a short break."

"What the fuck happened to the living room?" he asks again. "Why are there holes gouged out of the walls and where's the coffee table and the bookcase?"

"Your books are fine, in case you're worried about that," I tell him. "I boxed 'em up, put them up in your room. I only broke the bookcase. Coffee table's gone though, completely trashed. I couldn't do anything to save it after I threw it against the window. I did clean up the glass and finished putting in a new window yesterday. And there are holes on the walls because I realized cleaning up after throwing furniture around is not as fun as they make it look on TV."

All true.

Living in my childhood home has turned out to be a little more traumatic than I thought. While I've come back from New York on occasion, I've mostly stayed over a night or two, *if* that. I usually crash at a friend's place or just stay out until all I can do is drop dead on the bed.

Which is pretty much all I've been doing ever since I moved back.

Even so, prolonged exposure to this godforsaken house, where my mother died and our father abandoned us and where Conrad ruled with an iron fist, isn't good for me.

"And who are those fucking roses from?" Stellan asks.

I grind my teeth then. "Why don't you ask the douchebag you shared a womb with?"

Stellan frowns in confusion. "Shep?"

"Yeah," I reply with clenched teeth. "Apparently he thinks it's funny to act like a clingy girlfriend and send flowers three times a day. Because I refuse to answer his texts or calls."

Again, all true.

That jerk is the most annoying human on the planet. At first, it was his incessant calls and texts and voicemails. When I let every single one go without an answer, he resorted to this. Sending me flowers with pink little notes. As if written by a crazy ex-girlfriend.

Hey lover, when are we getting together?
Lover, why don't you answer my calls?
Don't you love me anymore, lover?
Is there someone else, lover?
If there is, I'm going to scratch her eyes out for laying them on my man.
One note had just this: *Loverrrrrrrrrrrrrrrrrrrrrrrrrrrrr.*

I have half a mind to report him to the cops or just call him the fuck back.

Stellan's lips are twitching though, as if he finds it all funny.

"Oh, so this you find funny?" I growl.

He shrugs. "At least he's getting to you."

"Yeah, like he's been getting to you for the past year?" I say, watching him carefully. "Going after the same girl that you like."

I regret it as soon as I say it.

It's not something Stellan likes to talk about. Actually, Stellan doesn't like to talk about anything that's too personal to him. Again, he's like our big brother in that sense. Tight-lipped and private. Although I think Con's improved a little ever since he got together with his girl, one of Callie's friends, Wyn Littleton.

Which surprised the fuck out of all of us.

Con not only going for one of Callie's best friends but also for someone fourteen years younger than him. Who also used to be his student for a brief period of time when he was a soccer coach at St. Mary's School for Troubled Teenagers.

Because Con is nothing if not a rule follower.

In any case, we're all very happy for him — me included, and I'm saying that genuinely.

But that's not what I was talking about.

What I was saying was that Stellan is as tight-lipped as Con and no, we have never talked about him being in love with Shep's girl. So my bad.

But fuck it, he needs to face it sooner or later.

"I don't know what you're talking about," he says, his lips barely moving.

"Is that how you wanna play it?" I shake my head at him.

"No, I don't want to play at all."

I scoff. "Do you think Shep doesn't know? That he's got no clue that his twin brother is in love with his girlfriend? Do you think he can't sense it? The distance between you two. How you hardly hang out with him anymore. How you're always too busy to talk to him, to —"

"Shut your fucking mouth," he growls, his stance tight and battle-ready. "Or I will do it for you. You're not the only one in this family who knows how to throw a punch."

My anger roars inside me then.

The itch that's always there surges up and I feel it happening.

The red ants crawling just beneath my skin.

And they start to sting at my veins when he continues, "Now I came here to talk some sense into you. To make you *see* how you're hurting yourself by acting like a stubborn five-year-old. You have a problem, Ledger. You've always had a problem. And you need help. Do you understand that? You've needed help for a very long time and we should've done this years ago. Because frankly, we're tired of cleaning up your messes. This isn't high school anymore. You need to take responsibility for your actions. You need to straighten yourself out, go to therapy, have some accountability. Or you'll be off the team. For *good* this time."

"Get out."

"What?"

"Get the fuck out of this house or I swear to God, I'll throw you out myself," I growl, my vision almost red now.

And I'll do it too.

But not before I beat the shit out of him. Not before I break every bone in his body and send *that* back to our big brother. As a message.

"You wanna act like a messenger," I continue, "fine. Here's a message: you're right. I'm not a kid anymore. This isn't high school. So you can't boss me around. You can't put me on a time-out or ground me or order me to scrub toilets if I don't follow your bullshit rules. Those days are over. It's not me with the problem, it's you. It's *him*. So you go tell your boss that if he hopes to win a game in the next season, he better start treating me with respect and stop with his fucking ultimatums. Because you may be happy being his little errand boy. But I'm no one's bitch."

Definitely not my big brother's.

Not anymore.

And if he wants to take soccer away from me as a punishment, then so be it. I'm not fucking backing down like a coward.

"You're sick, you know that," Stellan bites, turning around and leaving.

And saving himself in the process.

Because that's the moment I let my anger free and paint the world red.

After which I only hear sounds and crashes.

Of things banging against the floor, booming against the walls.

Of me roaring and raging.

I'm not sure how long I keep at it but it feels like hours. When I'm tired and all burnt out, I slide down to the floor, my back against the wall, and sit like that for hours.

Until a beep sounds and my phone vibrates against my thigh.

Lately if I hear my phone, I ignore it. It's usually Gio or one of my brothers with an occasional text or a call from my teammates. In my time at New York City FC, I've hardly made any friends except a couple of guys who like to check up on me every now and then.

But for some reason, my phone chiming right now makes me go for it.

And when I see who it is a rush of calm washes over me.

I don't know how or why it happens but it's always been this way.

Since the beginning. Since she started calling and texting me.

I'd have a shitty day — maybe a fight with her brother or Conrad riding me hard during practice because he didn't think I was doing enough as the captain of the team — and my phone would beep with a random text from her and I'd take my first calm breath of the day.

Sometimes I wonder how is it that someone who's named Tempest and who's got a firecracker of a personality can be the one to give me peace.

But she did.

She gave me calm and in return, I gave her violence and pain.

My apology the other night doesn't even begin to cover the damage I've done. Both deliberately and by accident. Staying away won't fix things either.

I don't know what will though?

In any case, I open her text.

Feisty Firefly: I'm not your girl.

Feisty Firefly: You said that. When you came over to Callie's and my brother's house. But I'm not yours.

I can't help but smile as I let my bloody fingers type up an answer.

Me: You are.

Chapter Fourteen

HE CAME OVER FOR ME.

That night at my brother's and Callie's.

Something that Callie told me after he'd left. Not in so many words of course. Just that he'd known they'd be away and that I'd be there babysitting Halo. Which can only mean one thing: he'd come over to see me.

He'd come over to... apologize.

I mean I know. He did say that he was apologizing for being a douchebag to me at the bar and that he'd back off and let me live in peace from now on. But it was more than that. It was *bigger* than him doing the right thing.

It was his attempt at not only apologizing but also punishing himself in the process.

Right?

That was what that kiss was all about, wasn't it?

Holy mother of *God*, that kiss.

That my brother almost witnessed. That he *wanted* my brother to witness.

He'll give me what I deserve...

That's what he said.

I've been thinking about it and *thinking about it* for the last two days and that's the only conclusion I can come up with: he not only wanted to apologize but he also wanted to get punished. But I'm not going to do what I did before. I'm not going to assume things and blow them out of proportion in my head, no.

I'm going to ask him.

So sitting in the middle of my bed, my legs folded and my phone in my lap, I very reluctantly but also somehow eagerly pull up his name in my contact list and with a deep breath, type out a text.

Me: I'm not your girl.

Me: You said that. When you came over to Callie's and my brother's house. But I'm not yours.

I don't know why I started the conversation the way I had three years ago, when he'd found me behind the bushes, but I did. And now my heart's pounding in my chest with a fierceness that scares me. It also scares me that he might not reply.

Or worse, he'll reply and I'd be so overcome with stupid joy that I'd disgust myself.

That is not the purpose of this exercise, I remind myself.

My phone beeps with a text and it's him. In my haste to read what he said, I accidentally hit wrong apps twice before making it to the right place.

Beautiful Thorn: Yes, you are.

I narrow my eyes at his answer. Which if I'm being honest is totally expected because he's crazy that way, but still.

Me: No, I'm not. I never was.

Beautiful Thorn: Unless you've been crying over some other random asshole for the past year that I don't know about, you're mine.

I don't know how is it that I can practically hear him growling *mine* through the phone but I do. I've always been able to, even back then. And *back then*, it used to make me all kinds of restless and achy. It used to make me so desperate to be with him that when we were done, I'd... do things to myself.

While weeping in my pillow at the same time.

It was a weird combination, I'll say that. Being sad and horny, but that was what he made me feel.

Good thing I deleted all those messages from my phone after everything happened. I should've deleted his number as well, but I guess by this point it's a given that I'm pathetic enough to have memorized his number, so it wouldn't have helped.

Anyway.

Irritated, I stab at my screen to type out my reply.

Me: So what, I'm your heartbroken, lovelorn, pathetic girl?

Beautiful Thorn: No, you're my heartbroken, lovelorn, *feisty* Firefly.

Me: So what does that make you?

Beautiful Thorn: A cruel, sadistic, should-be-kicked-in-the-nuts asshole.

No.

You're my cruel, sadistic, beautiful Thorn.

Not that I'd ever say that to him.

Instead I say this: **Which my brother would've done that night.**
Me: No. Actually my brother would've killed you.
Beautiful Thorn: He would've tried, sure.
Me: And he would've been successful.
Beautiful Thorn: Maybe. Maybe not.
Beautiful Thorn: Either way it would've been fun.
Me: You're crazy, you know that, right?
Beautiful Thorn: Yeah?
Me: Only crazy people think that murder is fun. Especially theirs.
Beautiful Thorn: Again maybe. Maybe not.
Beautiful Thorn: Still better than being a cruel, sadistic, should be kicked in the nuts asshole though.
Me: And that's why you kissed me, didn't you?
Me: Because you wanted to get punished.
Me: So our first kiss was a revenge kiss and our second was your twisted attempt at punishment for the first.
Me: Good to know.

I'm breathing so hard and so fast as I finish firing off all the texts, one after the other. Making me realize how angry I am. How *furious* that he thinks he can touch me and kiss me and put his hands on me, all because he wants to.

All because of his ulterior motives.

For motives that have nothing to do with me.

And everything to do with what *he* wants in the moment.

I'm about to type out a very long text educating him in the art of respecting a girl's wishes and letting her make her own decisions when my phone starts to ring in my hand, flashing his name.

Or rather the nickname that I've given him.

I stare at it like it's a snake ready to bite me or a gun ready to fire a bullet, and knowing that, I still hasten to accept before it goes to voicemail. I open my mouth to tell him to fuck off when he growls, "Our first kiss was beautiful and our second was fucking phenomenal. Because it was my attempt at giving you something more than beautiful. Something beyond beautiful. That's what you deserve, you see. Not something *just* beautiful, something *beyond* that. Something out of this world. Something that doesn't exist but can only be created. But mostly it was my attempt at giving you something that you'll think about at night when you cry in your bed about me, when you think about how your first kiss was beautiful until I made it ugly, how it *wasn't* like the ones you read in your sappy love stories. So no, our second kiss wasn't an attempt at punishment, it was my attempt at giving you a kiss that you read about in your romance novels.

"Although I'm not gonna pretend and say that if it *had* been an attempt at punishment, I would have apologized about it. Because then I would've gotten what *I* deserve. Your brother giving me the ass-kicking of the century. Because what your brother did to my sister was an accident — although I'd still love to kick his ass about that — but what I did to you, I did deliberately. I did it with purpose and bad intentions. And if I had known before last week that you're still hurting over what I did a year ago, I would've made such attempts much earlier. I would've taken matters into my own hands a long time ago and provoked your brother into beating the crap out of me until I couldn't recognize my own face in the mirror. And as I said, I won't apologize for that. And neither will I apologize for any future attempts that I make. So you can save your hissy fit, all right?"

"What are you doing tomorrow night?" I blurt out.

And then drop down on the bed on my back and put a pillow over my head, cringing in embarrassment but still clutching the phone to my ear.

"What?"

Exactly.

What did I do? That was not the way I wanted to go about it.

First, I wanted to confirm if my suspicions were right. And if they were then I would've…

Although now that I think about it, I don't know how *else* I could have gone about it.

See, here's the thing: I've been thinking about it – I've been thinking about a lot of things – and I've come to a conclusion.

Which is that I'm not over him. Not yet.

Just look at the way I kissed him back the other night. Like a complete ho. Look at how he still affects me; how he can rile me up and provoke me and pulls reactions out of me that he shouldn't be able to.

But mostly, look at how every time I think about a baby, I think about him.

Every time I picture a baby in my arms, it looks like him.

So in short, I'm not over him. But I want to be.

And I have a plan for that. As to how to get over him. I just need his help.

Throwing the pillow away, I say, "Tomorrow night. What are you doing?"

"Why?"

"Because."

"Because what?"

I exhale a sharp breath. "Because I'd like you to meet me at the corner of Maple and Candle at six."

There's a silence that lasts for a few seconds where I'm cringing with embarrassment again. It sounds like I'm asking him out on a date. Something that I've done before — yes, I have, unfortunately — and he's always said no. And let me also say that he never made an excuse or said anything polite to let me down gently. He'd just say no. One word and topic over.

God, how come I kept calling him and running after him even after those things?

How come I had hope?

What kind of an idiot was I?

A giant one, that's what.

"Are you asking me out on a date?" he says.

I knife up on the bed at the shock. That not only did it sound exactly like I'm asking him out on a date, but that he had the same thought.

"No," I say, quickly and kinda loudly.

The silence that ensues feels laced with amusement.

On his part of course, not mine.

I clear my throat. "Of course not. Why would you even think that?"

"Because the corner of Maple and Candle is a Chinese restaurant."

"So?"

"So it's your favorite Chinese restaurant."

"How do you —"

"You told me, remember?"

Damn it.

I did.

Over one of my phone calls that apparently he remembers very well.

"You know, for someone who claimed to be *so* bored by my phone ramblings, you remember a lot of it."

"I remember all of it," he corrects.

"That's —"

"And the only reason I claimed to be bored by your ramblings was to discourage you from calling."

"I —"

"Which I think I've already explained."

He has.

It was because he was trying to protect me from himself.

And even though he ended up doing exactly what he was protecting me from, I can't hold on to my irritation with him in this moment.

Damn it.

Only he can both annoy me and make me melt in the same breath.

"Fine. Whatever," I mumble. "And it's not a date."

"So what is it then?"

I search for a term. Then, "A... meeting."

"A meeting."

"A *business* meeting," I say with sudden inspiration.

"A business meeting."

"Yes." I nod. "Think of it as two colleagues meeting for mouthwatering and amazing Chinese food."

"I'm not supposed to wear a tie or something, am I?"

I roll my eyes. "No, you're not."

"Or a jacket."

I roll my eyes again. "Not that either."

"Thank fuck."

"Mostly because I don't think they've made a jacket the size of the Incredible Hulk yet."

"That I am," he says. "The size of a monster. And I'm not just talking about my chest and shoulders."

I've been talking to him for *years*, I know how his mind works.

How he can make anything dirty and a dick joke.

And despite myself, I smile.

"You know it's a *green* monster, the Hulk, don't you? And no, I'm also not talking about your chest and shoulders," I quip, knowing exactly what he's talking about.

He chuckles. "Green or not, sounds like you've thought a lot about the heat I'm packing in my pants."

The sound of it shoots straight down to my belly, all deep and low, and I bite my lip. "I wouldn't call it heat. Rather an extraterrestrial thing."

"Well, that's a very high compliment then, isn't it?"

"Is it?"

"Uh-huh. Because it will make you see stars."

I shake my head at him even as my smile grows. "Can we give your ego a little rest please? For tonight. My mind is tired."

"Are you sure you're talking about your mind here and not something else?" he drawls, making another innuendo.

Which I immediately put a stop to. "No, I am definitely talking about my M. I. N. D. And not about something called P. U. S. S. Y." I roll my eyes for the third time. "Are you happy now? You made me say it."

He hums. "I would be. If we were in third grade or if Little Berry was around."

"You knew that word in the third grade?"

"I knew it in the first grade."

I gasp. "Shut up. You couldn't have."

"I could and I did."

"Holy shit." Then, "Do you think my brother knew?"

"I don't wanna talk about your brother right now," he growls.

"Yes, of course. Me neither. I don't know why I said that."

"So?"

"So what?"

"Are you gonna say it?"

I frown. "Say what?"

"The word that I knew in the first grade."

"You *want* me to say it?"

"I dare you to say it."

"You *dare* me."

"Uh-huh."

"How old are you?"

"Old enough to say it and not blush like you do."

"I do not blush."

"Yeah, you do."

"No, I don't."

"You're going to if I say pu —"

"Don't," I cut him off. "Do not say it."

He chuckles again and I swear I want to smack him.

And then bottle the sound of his chuckle and put it in my pocket. So I could fish it out and hear it whenever I wanted.

In any case, he's right.

I am blushing.

Which is the strangest thing.

I *never* blush. I have never blushed for another guy in my life.

Except him.

Not to mention, I've never blushed when talking about or reading about or thinking about sex. I read romance novels like it's my job, or at least I used to. I can give my girls advice on their love life *and* their sex life like it's nothing. Like I'm talking about the weather. I'm one of the most outgoing, out-there people there is.

Again, except for him.

When it comes to him and him saying dirty things, I turn into a tomato.

Like I did back in Callie's and my brother's house that night. Or even before, at the restaurant and at the bar.

And while it was okay before when I was obsessed with him, I hate it now.

Just another one of the reasons why I need to find closure and finally move on from him.

I let out a breath.

Quivering and shaky.

As I say, "As fascinating as all this is, you still haven't answered my question. Are you —"

"Yes."

"What?"

He exhales a breath. "I am free tomorrow night."

"Y-you are?"

"That's what I said."

I know he did.

I know that. But the thing is that this is a big deal for me.

Even though this isn't a date and I'm not asking him to meet me with any romantic intentions — my intentions are actually the opposite of that — it's still something that I've thought about a lot. It's still something that I wanted very, very badly. To be able to go out with him, share a meal at a restaurant like a normal couple. A couple whose life isn't as complicated as ours clearly was.

So I take a moment to absorb this.

That he said yes to give me something that I've always wanted.

But now have no use for.

"Okay," I say, clearing my throat, twisting the edges of my pillowcase.

"Okay."

"It's not a date though," I remind him, and of course myself.

"It's a business meeting."

"Yes. A business meeting."

"Noted."

"And I…"

"You what?"

I close my eyes for a second. Then, "I want you to promise me something."

"What?"

"I-I mean, obviously there's no reason for me to trust you or anything you say. You're not exactly a good guy."

"I'm not, no."

"And you do deserve to get beaten up by my brother."

"I do, yeah."

"But I…" I am twisting and twisting the pillowcase. "I don't want you to."

There's a prolonged silence then.

Followed by his quiet, "You don't want me to."

"No."

"Why?" he growls, almost angrily.

"Because that's not what I want from you. I don't want you to get beaten up by him. I don't…" I sigh. "What you did, you didn't do to him. You did it to *me*. You broke *my* heart. You made *me* cry. I'm your girl, aren't I? Your heartbroken, lovelorn, feisty Firefly."

"You are," he rasps.

It steals my breath for a second. "So I get to decide then. I get to decide what your punishment should be."

Exactly.

The plan that I have to get closure and move on with my life: this is it.

Punishment and revenge.

I'll exact revenge for what he did, punish him and finally, *finally* move on.

"You."

"Yes. Me. Not him, not even you. Do you understand that?"

"Yeah."

"Good. So then I don't want you to make any more of your attempts at punishment. I don't want you to involve him in something that's between you and me. So you have to *promise* to keep this between us. Our meeting tomorrow and whatever happens after. You have to promise to never, not *ever*, use it for your own purposes."

"I won't," he says immediately and God, *sincerely*.

Like he's being chastised and he doesn't even care about it. He's okay with whatever I choose to do to him.

It makes guilt pinch my chest a little but I ignore it.

At some point I have to do something for myself. I have to think about myself first. I've already given everything to him and he rejected it, didn't he? Not to mention, he didn't think twice before doing things for himself.

So why should *I* care?

I let out a relieved breath. "Okay then. Tomorrow at six."

"Tomorrow at six."

<hr>

TWENTY MINUTES BEFORE SIX, there comes a knock at my door.

It reverberates in my belly.

And between my thighs.

Like the beat of a drum.

Because I already know who it is.

Because I can feel him through the space. Through the door and through the living room and the hallway, all the way back to the bathroom where I'm standing in front of the mirror. If I close my eyes and let it, I know that I can also feel his heat, the way the very air parts itself to make room for him.

But I can't.

I *won't*.

I have to keep my wits about me.

Which have been scattered ever since I woke up this morning, unable to believe that I actually did it.

I actually set things into motion.

For my quest to un-break my heart.

And the fact that he's right outside my door instead of waiting for me in front of the restaurant like I told him to, is screwing up my carefully gathered courage and control.

Still I walk out of my bathroom, all calmly and coolly.

Instead of showing how freaked out I am, I paste a neutral expression on my face and open the door.

And all my attempts at keeping my wits about me vanish.

All my thoughts vanish too, chased away by that drumbeat between my legs.

Because it gets louder and more incessant. It's creating too much noise in my body, in my head, to hear or think anything except that he looks different.

Or rather he looks like he used to.

Before he came to my dorm room. Before, when I still thought he was a good guy.

And that's because his stubble is gone.

His jaw is clean-shaven.

For the first time in a year I can see his face clearly. I can see the hollows of his cheeks and the killer slant of his jawline. I can see the corners of his mouth, how curved they are and how really plush and pink his lips are.

And I realize that I missed seeing those lips.

I missed seeing his cresting cheekbones, his masculine jaw.

I *missed* seeing him.

Which is not good at all.

What's even worse is the fact that his clothes — although as usual, a t-shirt and jeans — look different too. His t-shirt isn't as faded as it usually is; it's still dark though and fits him very well. And his jeans aren't threadbare and washed out like that of a rockstar's. In fact they barely look worn at all.

And let's not forget that he's here.

At my door.

"You shaved," I say, looking up at him.

"It was about time."

"And you're wearing different clothes."

He looks down at himself. "I'm wearing what I usually wear."

"No, you're not." I grab the doorknob tightly. "Your t-shirt doesn't have an I'm-too-cool-for-this-world print and your jeans barely show the impression of your," I wave my free hand around, "package. Down there."

His eyes flash with amusement. "Well, I am too cool for this world and you *have* thought about my package then."

"It isn't funny."

"It's a little funny."

I breathe out sharply. "I told you this isn't a date."

"And?"

"And so what are you doing?" I squeak out. "Why are you all clean-shaven and put together and *what* are you doing at my apartment when I asked you to wait for me at the restaurant? Not to mention, you're early."

His eyes flick back and forth between mine, all relaxed and calm. "This is a business meeting, isn't it?"

"Yes. Yes, it is."

"So that's how I go to a business meeting."

"You —"

"Clean-shaven and put together. And early."

I glare at him then. "That still doesn't explain what you're doing at my apartment."

"It's on the way," he replies without missing a beat.

"No, it isn't. We live in totally opposite directions and —"

"I found a detour."

"A detour? That doesn't make —"

"Are you ready or not?"

"But —"

"Because I'm hungry as fuck and if you wanna argue, we can do it on the way," he cuts me off.

I bite my lip then.

Because I don't want to argue either. It defeats the whole purpose of this evening. If I want him to do what I want, then I need to be personable.

I sigh and nod. "Fine. Let me…" Then, completely switching gears when I catch sight of his hands, I go, "Oh my God, what happened here?" In fact I reach out and grab one and bring it closer to examine his knuckles. "What happened to your hand? Why does it look like…" I go for his other hand too. "Why do they both look like someone has run them over with their car?"

They do.

The knuckles are all torn up and scraped. The skin's all red and tender around them.

I mean, I have seen him with injuries before. He's a soccer player; of course he sustains injuries, big and small, almost every day. Plus he used to get into fights with my brother all the time. So of course I've seen him with bruises and cuts before.

And the reason that these ones worry me is because they didn't come from soccer and I know they didn't come from my brother either; he was fine yesterday when I saw him.

"Ran into a wall," he clips, taking his hands away from me and pushing them into his pockets.

"What?"

His face is all tight and blank as he clips again, "Let's go."

"What happened?" I ask, swallowing. "Did you get into a fight with someone?"

"Yes."

"With whom?"

"Don't know. Don't care."

"Why?"

His jaw clenches. "Why do you think I do anything?"

"I —"

"I'm the Angry Thorn, aren't I?" Another clench. "That's what I do. I get into fights. I beat people up."

For some reason his casual words don't sound so casual and my heart twists in my chest. "But that's not all who —"

"You're done," he says decisively, ready to turn around and leave.

"But Ledger —"

"Look," he begins, his jaw ticking. "We're making a stop along the way and as I already said, I'm hungry as fuck. So we're leaving."

"What stop?"

He breathes out, annoyed, and I hasten to say, "Doesn't matter. It's fine. Let me just get my purse."

Chapter Fifteen

THE STOP along the way was to my favorite place ever.

A bookstore in the heart of Bardstown: Burning the Midnight Candle.

When I asked him what we were doing there, he said, "I'm buying you romance novels."

"What, why?"

"Because you probably haven't bought them in over a year."

"Well, yeah, but I don't —"

"Just because you met a villain who broke your heart in real life doesn't mean you can't trust the heroes that live in the pages of your romance novels. It's not your fault that guys made of thunder and thorns exist in the world. It's mine for not being careful with a girl made of candies and cream."

I couldn't say anything after that.

I didn't know *what* to say after that.

I did end up buying a bunch of romance novels though. Which he paid for. At which point, I did say something but all he said was, "I said *I'm* buying you romance novels, didn't I? So this is what it looks like."

And again I fell silent, unable to comprehend what to say to him.

Which is how I spent the entire dinner AKA business meeting.

Not saying a single word.

He didn't say anything either. In fact, he looked kinda pissed off at times, which discouraged me further from saying anything. That and staring at me intensely.

And now we're a minute or so from my apartment.

I need to do something.

I need to find a way to start the conversation and get the ball rolling.

I can *see* my apartment building, for God's sake. There are the wide stairs that lead to the massive front door made of glass. And it's coming closer and closer and just as we're about to reach those stairs, I stumble.

Or I *make* myself stumble.

I also make myself gasp and exclaim on purpose, "Ow!"

And I was going to do more, to give a more convincing performance that I actually just hurt my ankle — I'm going with my right one; totally random — but I don't have to because he's already there.

To catch me.

And then he goes ahead and does me one better: making sure that I'm steady on my feet first, he lets go of my arm and bends down. He then puts his one arm behind my thighs and the other goes around my shoulders, and before I can even blink, he picks me up and I'm off the ground and in his arms.

And then he's bounding up the stairs and getting inside the building.

Meanwhile I'm still processing the fact that he just plucked me off the ground like I'm a fallen flower, like I weigh absolutely nothing at all, and now he's carrying me in his arms, striding across the polished floors, bridal style. All the while *still* carrying that heavy tote filled with books.

I mean this is insanity.

He is *insane.*

All I did was let out a little — and fake — painful squeak and he took that way too seriously.

Fisting his t-shirt at his chest and his shoulder — because really I don't know where to put my hands — I look up at him. "You didn't have to —"

He keeps looking ahead as he crosses the lobby. "Stay still."

I try to squirm instead to get free from his hold. "No, really. I'm fine. I —"

He squeezes his arms around me, pressing my body into his chest. "Stay. Still."

And I have to bite my lip at his harsh command.

At the *hard* contact with his body too.

Hard and heated.

Extra corded.

I think the latter is probably because he's carrying me and all his muscles are taut and flexed right now. Not that they usually aren't, but as I said, *extra* corded. But I stop admiring his muscles and how my curves fit against the arches of his pecs and insist again that I'm fine and he tells me to *stay the fuck still.*

Which is when I finally realize that me squirming the way I am is making things even more difficult for him.

So I keep my mouth shut and let him carry me.

I don't even make a peep when instead of taking the elevator, he takes the *stairs.* For the record, I live on the fourth floor, but by the time we reach my apartment, he's barely out of breath and hasn't even broken a sweat. In fact there's hardly any signs of exertion on him, and despite my guilt, I can't help but admire his strength. I can't help but press a little bit closer to him and rest my cheek on his chest and listen to his steadily beating heart.

Gosh, athletes are miraculous, aren't they?

Actually no, *he* is miraculous.

Him.

And no one else.

Oh my God, Tempest. Stop being a ho and focus.

Right.

Okay.

When we reach my door, I don't waste even a single second in retrieving my key and opening it. Because strong or not, he needs a break. I need one too. I need some physical distance from him so I can *think*.

However, I don't get that until we're well inside and in my kitchen.

Which is when he puts me down, or rather *sits* me down on the island.

He also sets down the tote he's been lugging around all evening, right by my side, and he does it carefully too. As if it's something precious.

I mean, it is.

To me.

And I can't help but think that maybe that's why it is for him as well. But I don't get the time to process that because as soon as he settles me on the island, he does something crazy — again — and goes down on his knees, wrapping his fingers around my right ankle.

"I was lying," I blurt out then, grabbing the edge of the island.

I did the same thing that I'd advised Echo to do. Why, I don't know but yeah.

He looks up at me.

And I continue, "I didn't... That was fake. I didn't hurt myself. I didn't —"

His fingers squeeze my ankles. "I know."

"What?"

"That you were lying."

My heart thuds. "So then why did you —"

"Because I didn't wanna take a chance if you were in fact telling the truth."

I try to extricate my foot from his hold. "But now you know that I wasn't, so you should —"

He tightens his hold on me. "Besides, three years ago, I made a promise to myself."

I go still, my nails digging into the island. "Y-you mean, three years ago when we... met for the first time?"

"Yeah, let's call it that."

I frown at his phrasing but go on. "What promise?"

He rubs my skin with his thumb, my delicate bones. "That night you fell on your knees. And you fell so hard that you were bleeding." His thumb presses into my skin then. "And the best that I could, that I *would* let myself do, was to follow you home. Like a pussy."

"But that's —"

"So I promised myself that if you ever got hurt because of me, I'd make sure to be there to take care of you."

So many things happen at once.

First, I can't believe he's bringing that night up. Not only that, he's bringing up that old injury. Something that I hardly ever think about. Something that I wouldn't ever think about, if he hadn't brought it up just now.

It was such a minor thing.

I'd actually almost forgotten about it.

And the fact that he remembers — well, I know he has a knack for remembering everything — and that he made a promise to himself based on something that I don't even think about, is… surreal.

It's something that I want to take a moment to absorb.

But he doesn't give me the space to do so.

Because I feel his fingers move.

I feel his fingers leave my ankle and go up my calves, both of them now. His rough calluses drag up and scrape against my smooth skin and my toes curl. Goosebumps rise over my skin and he watches it happen.

He watches his bronzed and bruised fingers trailing up my smooth and porcelain skin.

And I have to suck in a breath and bite my lip from letting out a whimper.

Because if this isn't the literal embodiment of who we are — a boy made of thunder and thorns and a girl made of candies and cream — then I don't know what is. And I don't think I've ever seen anything so heartbreaking and yet so erotic at the same time.

God, I have lost my mind, haven't I?

This has to be the most unique, the most original experience of my life.

And all he's doing is touching my legs.

When he reaches the backs of my knees, I whisper, "Is that… Is that why…"

He looks up, his eyes pitch black and glittering. "Is that why what?"

I lick my lips. "Is that why you'd get mad at me? When I, uh, would drive down to Bardstown for your games during a storm or when it was really dark. Because you thought I could get hurt and you didn't want me to."

He rubs his thumbs over my skin, making me squirm and breathe brokenly. Then, "Yeah."

"A-and that's why you also always insisted on me staying the night at your place when I..." Another swipe of his thumb, making it hard to speak. "...came to see Callie?"

"One of the reasons," he replies.

"What's the other —"

"Are you going to tell me?"

"T-tell you what?"

He watches me for a few seconds, his thumbs moving in circles over the tender skin around my knees and the inside of my thighs, before he stands up in one graceful motion. And then just like that I'm the one looking up at him and he's the one looking down, and the change is so jarring that I feel disoriented, as if the world has tilted itself, and my hands automatically go to grab his biceps for balance.

Settling himself in between my thighs that either fall open by themselves to make space for him or maybe he forced them to, I don't know, he says, "The agenda. For your business meeting tonight."

Oh.

Right.

"I'm guessing it's important," he continues, leaning over me with his arms on either side of my hips, making his sculpted shoulders look larger than life. "Given that you pretended to stumble for it. All so you could get me to come upstairs and into your apartment."

I pull at the sleeves of his t-shirt. "Well, to be fair —"

"A piece of advice though," he cuts me off, his eyes looking into mine. "Next time, you can just ask instead of going through all the trouble."

I blush, making his eyes flash. Then, "I never asked you to carry me up, first of all. And second of all, you could've taken the elevator up instead of —"

He pulls a face. "Elevators are for pussies."

"No, they're not. They're for sensible people."

"Well, no one ever accused me of being sensible."

I swallow. "I would've told you the agenda if you hadn't been so... angry at the restaurant."

His eyes narrow. "And I wouldn't have been so angry if you hadn't worn that dress."

"What?"

His eyes narrow further. "Because if you hadn't, then I would've been able to take at least one breath without wanting to strangle it out of someone."

I frown at him before looking down at my dress. "This dress?"

He growls in response.

I look up. "There's nothing wrong with this dress. It's modest."

It is.

I'm not even lying about that. It's a pumpkin colored dress with a square neckline that could've been really wide and exposing but is not. It hardly shows any cleavage and the sleeves go down to my elbows even. And the hem hits me just an inch above the knees and that's it.

I know exposing dresses — I own a lot of them — but this isn't one of them.

"Then why do I want to burn it?"

"Because you're crazy?"

"No," he states, his voice rough. "You are. If you think this is modest and that you haven't driven every single man at that restaurant crazy."

My frown thickens. "There were like, *four* men at that restaurant tonight. It's a school night, okay? And I think one of them was there with his family, a wife and two kids. And —"

"And why do you think he kept looking for the waiter every five seconds?"

"Uh, because he needed water and more fortune cookies, who cares?"

"No," he bites out, "because he wanted an excuse to stare at you. So he could solve the eternal mystery of how big your tits actually are and if he could fit his slimy hand down your cleavage. And that's only because his hand isn't *really* the thing he's interested in shoving down there."

"Ew, that's…" Then, biting my lip, "What's the real thing that he wants to shove down there though?"

His nostrils flare and I swear his chest expands so much that it looks like he's going to come out of his skin.

"Never mind," I say hastily. "That's not important. But I also don't think you're right. He was married."

"So?"

"With *two* kids."

"Yeah," he once again bites out angrily.

"So I don't think —"

"That's exactly why he's going to go home and fuck his wife while thinking about a wet dream of a girl in a tight-ass orange dress he saw at the restaurant tonight."

"Pumpkin," I correct him and his brows bunch up. "The color of my dress. It's a pumpkin colored dress."

His jaw tics for a second and I go to take it back, what I said, but he growls again, "That still doesn't change the fact that when he gets his nut off tonight, he'll be imagining he's doing it on your fucking face instead of inside his wife."

"That's very… ugh." I scrunch my nose. "Maybe it was a date night for him."

"With the kids."

"So what, some people like that," I tell him, swatting his arm. "And maybe he's f-fucking his wife because he's in a good mood. After the mouthwatering Chinese food that he's had."

"No, he's in a good mood because of your mouthwatering tits."

My chest heaves. "That's —"

"And the same thing can be said about that fucking teenager."

"What teenager?"

"The one who gave up all pretense on looking for the waiter and simply kept staring at you like a creepy fucking horndog."

"I don't —"

"The one who also nearly jizzed his pants while staring at your bouncy ass when you walked by to go to the restroom."

That rings a bell and I ask, "The one I smiled at when I walked back?"

"Yeah," he says with clenched teeth. "Which for the record probably pushed him over the edge and took him from nearly jizzing his pants to it being very fucking likely that tomorrow morning his mom will be putting a soiled pair of pants in the laundry."

"I —"

"And same goes for those two waiters, that bartender, a couple of delivery guys who walked in."

"But —"

"So yes," he declares. "I was angry. And if I wasn't in a hurry to get you out of there, I would've taken my time and beaten the shit out of them. And then I would've burned every dress in your fucking closet. In fact, I'd be burning them right now."

I gasp. "You're —"

"If I thought it would help."

My breaths are choppy now and I'm scratching at his skin. "You d-don't think it would?"

"No."

"Why not?"

"Because you could be wearing a burlap sack and people would still stare at you."

I lick my lips. "That's not true."

His eyes drop to my mouth. "So I guess it's not your fault, is it?"

"What isn't?"

"It's not your fault that you're the most beautiful girl to ever walk this earth."

My eyes go wide. "I'm not."

"And neither is it your problem that I want to kill every motherfucker out there who looks at you."

"I'm —"

"And wants to stare a little too long," he rasps, staring down at my lips.

"Ledger —"

"Wants to get a taste of your cotton candy mouth."

I lick my lips again, trembling.

His eyes flare. "Or wants to touch your creamy skin."

I don't know how I'm able to breathe right now.

Or how it is that I'm sitting still when all I feel is restless.

Antsy.

And God, so fucking turned on.

And he's still not done.

Not with staring at my lips and definitely not with his words.

"Or wants to trap you in a jar like the firefly you are. It's not your problem, is it? It's my problem. Mine. Every inch of it. It's *mine*." Then, a pause later, still staring and staring at my lips, "Mine. Mine. Mine. M —"

I do it then.

I grab his face and put my mouth on him.

And I do it all very hard.

In contrast to everything else up until now. Our whispers soft as roses and rasps like melted candy.

But then again, I don't think we're made for gentle things, him and me.

My cruel, sadistic, beautiful Thorn.

And his heartbroken, lovelorn, feisty Firefly.

I mean, look at what happened the first time we met: I cut my knees. And look at what happened what should've been the last time: he cut my heart.

We're violent and volatile.

We're the storm, him and me.

So maybe it's fitting that as soon as I touch his mouth with mine, all hell breaks loose.

Especially when his arms that were braced on the island on either side of me wrap themselves around me like ropes. No, like steel bands. All corded and unforgiving. One goes around my waist, thrusting me forward and making me crash against his torso, like he's angry at the micro inch of space between us. And the other goes into my hair, palming the back of my head, his fingers fisting and getting all tangled up in my strands.

And the growl that he emits sounds like thunder.

It goes straight down to my belly, making it all tight and achy.

Causing that place between my thighs — that's all pressed up against his hard stomach — to swell up.

And I emit a soft, satisfied sigh.

This is good.

This is great.

This is fucking phenomenal.

Our third kiss.

Actually it's even better than our first two kisses. Our kisses are aging like fine wine. The more we do it, the longer we do it, the better they become.

Not to mention his large hands and his brutal fingers.

They're fucking phenomenal too as they pull and tug at my hair. As they twist in my dress, crumpling the fabric, pinching the soft flesh beneath. And don't even get me started on his teeth. His sharp and nippy teeth that bite into my lips. Plus his dominating, cinnamon-y tongue that thrusts into my mouth and invades and conquers it.

Yeah, this is the best kiss of all.

And you know what else?

This is also the kiss that has no ulterior motive.

It's simply a kiss.

For the kiss's sake.

It's simply done because we both wanted to. Because he kept staring at my lips and I kept getting hypnotized by his words and thinking about what he tasted like. Not to mention, we'd just kissed. Like two days ago and so we wanted more and…

But wait a second.

I remember something.

I remember that it shouldn't have happened.

It shouldn't *be* happening.

This kiss.

This is our purest kiss.

This is the kiss with no *agenda*.

And I had one, remember?

I had an agenda when I asked him to dinner tonight. Not only was the kiss not on tonight's schedule, but also if I were to kiss him, I should've done it with carefully concealed passion. I should've done it with one goal in mind.

Closure.

And revenge.

My thoughts break when he pulls at me.

When both his hands go down to my waist and he slides me off the island. Squeaking, I clutch my thighs at his hips and my arms go around his neck. And in the next second, I'm off the island and his body is my only anchor in a world that's spinning and spinning and making me dizzy and drugged.

I feel him walking with me secure in his arms, going somewhere.

Still kissing, he strides out of the kitchen and I think he's crossing the hallway, all the way down to where my bedroom is.

I should ask him where we're going.

I should tell him to stop kissing me because I have an agenda.

Because I need to gather my thoughts and plan my next move.

And if he keeps kissing me the way he is right now, like he needs me more than air and more than food and maybe even more than the sun, the sky and fucking life itself, I won't be able to stop kissing him back the same way.

I won't be able to stop moving against him also.

Which is what I'm doing right now.

Aren't I?

I'm moving against him, rubbing my body, my tits and my pussy — there, I said it, or at least thought it in my head — against his muscles. Because I think I've got an itch.

My nipples need scratching.

And my pussy needs petting.

And I don't know what else to do or where to go to get that.

Plus I have a feeling that he isn't going to like it if I go somewhere else to get relief. *I* wouldn't like it either.

So he's my only option.

Not to mention, he keeps kneading my ass.

At some point during our ten-second journey to my bedroom, his arms have moved and now he's grabbing on to my ass, palming each cheek and massaging the flesh in such a way that I want him to do it without my stupid dress in the way. Maybe I should've asked him to burn all my clothes after all. So I'm forced to walk around naked all the time and he can touch my bare skin without all the nonsense in between.

That's my last thought until my world tilts and my back meets something soft and fluffy.

The sheets on my bed.

They should give me comfort.

I love my sheets.

But they don't.

Because I think as soon as he lays me down, he'll stop kissing me and, well, I don't want him to. Maybe we can talk about the agenda in a second, once I've had my fill of cinnamon and spice. So I tighten my thighs around his hips and palm his face to keep our mouths fused.

Plus if he stops, how will I see him naked?

Because that's what I want.

All of a sudden, I want to see him naked.

I want to see his bronzed skin, his body that he works so hard on. That freaking carried me and my stacks of romance novels four flights of stairs without even a hint of exertion.

The body that was on top of me, pressed up against me and into the same places, thirteen months ago.

I couldn't see him last time, see.

We never reached that part.

So I want to see him now.

Not to mention, I want to see his penis.

No wait, his dick.

That I've only ever seen as a light impression though his threadbare jeans. And from what I've seen, I bet it's huge.

It's a monster.

And I want it inside of me.

Right now.

Right the fuck now.

And I don't want any barriers either.

Nope.

No condoms for me. Not now, not ever.

Who even invented condoms? They're the worst thing in the world.

And when he breaks off the kiss to immediately latch onto my jaw, followed by the freckle on the side of my neck, I mumble, "No c-condoms."

I'm in the process of tilting my head to the side and baring my neck even more when he stops.

When I lose the sharp but delicious sting of his teeth.

What, why?!

Now I won't have his lovely teeth marks to look at in the mirror later.

Snapping my eyes open, I'm about to demand an answer when he grabs my jaw and turns my face himself so he can look down at me. When I'm lined up, he wraps his fingers around my throat — oh fuck, why do I love that so much — making me whimper and undulate my body against his, as he asks, "What was that?"

His voice is a thick growl that makes me whimper anew.

He increases the pressure around my throat, making me gasp in delight. "*What*. Was that?"

I blink a few times, trying to catch my breath.

Trying to focus on what he's asking me.

But if he keeps holding my throat like this, I probably won't be able to do any of that. "I don't... I'm not..."

"What the fuck did you mean," he growls, his eyes black and thunderous, "by no condoms?"

"N-no condoms," I breathe out.

He stares at me for a couple of seconds.

Then in a flash, he lets go of my throat and jerks away from me. He springs back to his feet, his hair all rumpled and messy, his t-shirt wrinkled and his plush mouth swollen and pinker.

All thanks to our kiss just now.

And I want him back so I can ruffle him some more.

But I don't think he's coming back.

Even all messy and tousled, he looks like his mind is on other things as he runs his eyes all over my body, a muscle jumping on his cheek.

Then, "Explain."

Chapter Sixteen

EXPLAIN.

It's one word and quite simple to understand.

Even so it takes me a little bit to gather myself and get things straight in my head. Quite possibly because I was so engrossed in the impromptu — also inadvisable — kiss, so drugged and so far gone, that now I have to carefully bring myself out of it all and come back to reality.

And reality is made of thorns and thunder, isn't it?

Not candies and cream.

So first, I sit up and straighten my dress. Which actually takes some work because the neck is all twisted up and pulled down, baring one of my shoulders. How he managed to do that I don't know, because it's a snug dress with very little give without undoing the zipper.

Then I work on the hem that's shoved all the way to the tops of my thighs, even giving a peek of my black panties. Again, how he managed to do that when my hem's as tight as my bust, I don't know. But I pull it down hastily and I'm about to fold my thighs so I can sit on them and look respectful when a growl comes from across the room.

"More."

He's standing all the way at the opposite wall.

Somewhere in the last however many seconds he moved away from the foot of my bed to the furthest wall from it. Like he needed some distance from me.

Which is just as well.

Because now that I'm slowly coming out of the fog, I decide it's for the best.

We both need some distance from each other.

"More what?" I ask, shifting under his scrutiny.

He stares at my face a second before flickering his eyes lower and staring at my thighs. "Your dress." That muscle on his cheek jumps again. "Pull it down more."

I look down at my lap before I look back up at him. "Why?"

"Because it's fucking with my head."

I look down at my dress again and again honestly, I can't see why. But I'm not going to argue with him about this and so I tell him the truth. "It's... I can't."

"Why the fuck not?"

"Because it won't stretch any more," I explain. "This is it."

His nostrils flare in displeasure. "Then fucking cover yourself up with something."

"I —"

"Don't want your wet fucking panties in my fucking face when I'm trying to be a saint here."

My heart skips a beat and I realize he's right.

They *are* wet.

And all sticky.

So I just do as he says and cover my thighs with a pillow. Which is when I notice that he exhales, some of the tautness leaving his frame.

Then, "Now, what the fuck did you mean by no condoms?"

I play with the tassels on the edge of my pillow as I reply, "It means exactly what it sounds like. No condoms."

I'm choosing a nonchalant tone because I think that's the best way to go.

To appear as casual as possible.

So he has no clue as to what's really going on inside of me.

So he has no clue about my secret revenge plan.

"And why is that?" he asks, his eyes sharp and pinned on me.

"Because," I say and raise my chin, "I don't want anything between us when we do it for the first time."

He waits a few seconds to answer.

And his answer is a repetition of my own words. "When we do it."

"Yes." I nod as calmly and as regally as possible.

"For the first time."

"Yup."

This time he doesn't say anything. He simply chooses to stare at me with an expressionless face and an intense stare.

So I'm compelled to add, "By that I mean sex."

Again he keeps silent.

And again I keep going, "With each other." Then, "Just so there's no confusion."

Finally he says, or more like murmurs, "That's where we were headed, were we?" A second later he adds, "And by that I mean sex. Just so there's no confusion."

I blush.

But I tell myself to be strong and reply, "Well, yeah. We were kissing."

"So?"

"So where does kissing lead, Ledger?"

"I don't know, you tell me, Firefly."

I give him a look. "It leads to doing it, okay? It leads to sex."

"It leads to *doing it* when both people involved can at least call it what it is: fucking."

I clench my teeth at his condescension.

Gosh, one of these days I'm going to learn to not blush when we're talking about stuff like this.

"Fine, whatever. Fucking. Kissing leads to *fucking*."

"Well congratulations, you said the F word."

"Why, thank you," I shoot back. "And I thought for someone as sophisticated as you, you'd know that."

"I do. Although I had no clue that you knew that."

"You're such a —"

"So was this your agenda then? For tonight's business meeting. Fucking."

I blush some more but reply, "Look, I realize that this is… sudden. And —"

"That's one way to put it."

I exhale a sharp breath at his interruption. "And that we should've talked about this. But as I said, you were all angry back there and —"

He folds his arms across his chest. "So let's talk now."

I take him in.

And swallow.

Or more like, gulp in nervousness.

"So," I clear my throat and begin. "As you already know, I loved you. Back then, I mean." I wrinkle my nose, embarrassment already creeping in, especially when he's staring at me with such intensity. "I ran after you. I chased you around and just did everything that I could to make you fall in love with me. Of course that never panned out and… you ended up breaking my heart thirteen months ago. Anyway, for the last year, all I did was try to forget you. I tried to put you out of my mind and live my life. I tried to move on. And I thought that I had. I *really* thought that I had." I take a deep breath. "But as it turns out, I haven't. I mean I have, but not completely. I'm only half moved on, if you will. I mean, exhibit A: the way I kiss you. I should be pushing you away and screaming murder or something but I…" I lick my lips, my cheeks burning something fierce. "But I latch on to you like a… like a ho, or a very enthusiastic environmentalist who hugs a tree in the park that's going to be cut down."

Oh God, why did I have to put it like that?

But moving on.

"Which is not flattering at all, and I don't like it. Actually I hate it. I really fucking hate it. So I've come up with a plan. And it's to find closure."

I stop here because, well, I need a break.

I need to breathe.

And I need for him to say something.

Anything.

And he does, with the same expression as he had before I started talking. "Closure."

Although I don't think it helped.

His one word and unchanged features.

In any case, I've come this far, haven't I? I might as well go all the way.

"Yes." I tuck my hair behind my ears. "I think I'm hung up on you because I haven't had any closure. Any sense of things being over between us. I mean, one minute I'm thinking that you're in my dorm room to confess your love for me and the next, I'm finally realizing the truth about you. I'm finally realizing that you'll never confess your love for me because you'll never see me as anything other than your rival's sister. So I..."

I pause because there's finally a movement on his frame.

He's moving his jaw back and forth, and his chest is undulating in big waves.

And for the first time I know that this is the face of his regret. The face of his anger directed at himself.

Which makes me waver once again.

It weakens my resolve a little.

Do I really need to do this? Revenge and all that.

Still I continue, "So when I said that I don't want you to get beaten up by my brother or try to punish yourself like that, I meant it. Because that's not what I need from you. I don't need you to break your bones. I don't need you to bleed for me. What I need from you is closure. So I can move on. So I don't have to think about you every single day. So you don't have the power to make me cry anymore. So I don't feel the pain anymore, the pain you caused. So I don't ache and feel lonely and feel like I'll never be happy again."

He waits a bit to answer me.

But I don't blame him. Because I don't think he's doing it on purpose.

It's just that I don't think he's capable of speaking right now.

I think for now, he needs to let his remorse and fury move through him. He needs to let these emotions run their course before he can speak.

Which he does a few seconds later.

He unhinges his tightly clamped jaw and says in a low, rough voice, "And how do you propose I give you that?"

"By f-fucking," I blurt out before I lose my courage.

"Fucking."

"Yes." I jerk out a nod. "I-I mean, it shouldn't be a hardship for you. Because it's not like you're immune to me either. You came on to me the other night. I know you said that you wanted to give me a better kiss than our first one. But you didn't have to. I never asked you to. You chose to kiss me. You wanted to kiss me. It was all you."

"It was, yeah," he replies instantly, without hesitation or any sarcastic comment.

Which kinda steals my breath for the next couple of seconds.

But I manage to find it and continue, "And if just the sight of my panties is fucking with your head, then you've got a problem too. You're into me. You may not have…" I fist the tassel I'm playing with, "loved me back then, but you wanted me. You still want me. So it's for both our benefits."

All true.

I don't think I've had to lie yet.

What are the chances that I won't have to? That he's forgotten about the whole condom incident and will now fall on me like a desperate, horny animal.

"That still doesn't explain the no condoms thing," he says, his eyes clear and alert.

Damn it.

Why's he so hung up on that?

I thought guys liked that. I thought convincing him to do it with me would be the hard part, not how it should happen.

But okay.

It's fine.

I can handle this.

I keep my eyes connected to his and try to keep my features neutral as I say, "I guess I was being hasty in that. In my defense, I just got caught up in the moment. And I apologize. No protection is a big deal in any situation, but if you add that to *our* history, it becomes an even bigger deal."

So far. So true.

"Meaning we should've talked about it. But since we didn't before, let's do it now." I clear my throat again. "Are you, uh, clean?"

Don't look away.

Do not look away from him.

Not only because I want to appear sophisticated, a girl capable of discussing these things — and I am by the way; it's just him who throws me — but also because I need to keep my feelings away from his.

This is business.

This is about me un-breaking my heart and getting my life back.

There is no place for emotions here. Especially emotions like jealousy.

I'm pretty sure while I was heartbroken and crying away for him these last thirteen months, he was having his fun. Yes, I know that he was remorseful for what he did but I also know that he's a guy. A very popular guy, a pro-soccer player that girls go crazy for. And there's no reason for him to have passed up opportunities that I'm sure he must've come across.

Actually, even when I *wasn't* heartbroken and crying away for him but rather running after him, he must've slept around.

Something that hadn't occurred to me until after the whole dorm room incident.

Mostly because I'd never seen him with a girl, in those two years. The only time I did see him with one was the night he used her as bait to draw me out from behind the bushes. But other than that, I never saw him paying attention to one, even though he'd get lots of attention from them.

In any case, that's not the point here.

The point is that I need to know if he's clean — I know he is — and if I can convince him to forgo protection.

Because if I can't, then there goes my whole closure/revenge/punishment plan.

"Clean," he repeats, as if he can't believe I'm asking him that.

"Yes." I swallow. "Are you?"

"Yeah," he replies, his voice all quiet and low.

See?

I knew it.

Because I know how he is.

He's a fiend when it comes to his body and his health. He always has been. The guy works out like three times a day or something. He would never take unnecessary risks when it comes to the body that he's worked so hard to build. Although I have to say that it still doesn't give me any idea about whether or not he slept with girls over the past few years.

And you don't want to know either, remember?

Focus, Tempest.

"Okay. Good." I nod. Then, putting a hand on my chest, I say, "I'm clean too. And —"

"Is that so?"

I frown. "What, you think I'm lying?"

"No, I definitely don't think you're lying."

"So then —"

"But I also don't think you've ever gotten dirty."

"What's —"

"Which you need to do in order to be clean." Then, "You know that, don't you?"

I study his both watchful and arrogant gaze.

As if he knows everything about me.

As if just by looking at me he can tell the state of my virginity.

That's what he's talking about, isn't he?

The jerk.

"Yes, I do. And I am. Clean, I mean. *After* I've gotten dirty."

It's such a childish way to put it. But *he* started it.

His eyes flash. "You have, have you?"

"Yes." I raise my chin. "Multiple times. With multiple guys." Then, just because I can't stop myself, "And they *all* had huge dicks. Massive dicks. Extraterrestrial dicks. Dicks that were out of this world. Dicks that made me see —"

"You've seen a dick," he goes, his jaw moving back and forth in anger.

Good.

How dare he?

"Yes. Lots of them."

"Where?" I open my mouth to answer but he doesn't let me. "And a porno doesn't count."

"I wasn't going to —"

"Or a flowery description of a man's appendage in your romance novels."

"You —"

"Not to mention, *when* did you see one?" he keeps going, his voice lashing. "When apparently you've been hung up on me for the past thirteen months."

I glare at him. "You're such an asshole."

"Better than being a liar, huh."

I come up on my knees. "I'm not —"

"And I'm not just talking about the status of your virginity."

My heart skips a beat.

Drops it.

Right to the bottom of my belly.

Because I know what he's talking about. I know that he can sense it.

That I'm hiding something from him.

"You know what I'm talking about, don't you?" Then, "Given our history."

At this, I don't even think my heart's ever going to pick up the lost beats.

I don't think my heart's ever going to start beating again.

I clutch at my dress, trying to play innocent. "I'm… I don't —"

"Either you tell me the truth or I'm walking out of here."

"Y-you'll… You'll seriously walk out of here even when I've told you what I want from you?"

His nostrils flare. "Because closure isn't the *only* thing that you want from me."

Yeah, that's not the only thing that I want from him.

As I've said before, in order to get closure and finally move on, I need revenge. I need to punish him. And telling him how I'm going to get revenge wasn't the plan.

Actually none of this was the plan at all. I wasn't supposed to kiss him tonight. I wasn't supposed to get him upstairs in the first place. I just wanted to talk. I just wanted to tell him what I wanted from him – only to the extent that he needed to know – and lay out the ground rules like, yes, a business meeting. This whole condom/no condom thing wasn't supposed to come up at all.

At least not tonight when I'm so frazzled.

I had a plan on how to handle it when we did, you know, do the deed. In about a week.

During my ovulation window.

God, why.

Why does he have to be so perceptive? Why can't he just let things go?

And I know he means it. He absolutely means to walk out of here if I don't tell him the truth.

If I don't tell him everything.

So I guess I have to, don't I?

Dread settles in my belly.

It's cold and hard.

And sharp.

Like him.

A thorn.

As I say, "Yes. Closure isn't the only thing that I want from you. I want… something else too."

He takes a deep breath, not only straining his chest with it, but also flexing his shoulders and his biceps. "And what is it that you want?"

I want to close my eyes, needing to hide.

But I also find that I can't.

Because I also need this connection with him and that need is stronger.

That need is the strongest of all, isn't it?

To be connected to him. To somehow have a piece of him, to keep, to cherish, to nurture and to love, so I can breathe. So I can move on and live my life.

I don't know why – especially after everything that he's done to me – but it is what it is.

And instead of fighting it like I've been doing so far, I'm going to embrace it and use it to get free.

"A baby," I whisper on an exhale.

"A baby."

I can't help but press a hand on my empty belly. "Yes."

His gaze still zeroes in on it. "My baby."

"Yours."

"*Mine.*"

At this, I do have to close my eyes.

Because I didn't think he could sound this possessive. This territorial.

And I *know* how territorial he can sound.

Especially when he says that word: mine.

When I open my eyes, I still find him staring at my belly, and words come out of me like a river. "The reason why I was so eager that night, why I went along with it, begging for it, begging for *you*, wasn't only because I was in love with you. It was also because…"

His eyes are pinned to me now, staring into my eyes, looking unfathomable as I say, "I have a secret. Well, it's not so much a secret, because a lot of people know about it or knew about it but… You didn't know. Because I never told you. And…"

God, enough rambling.

I lick my lips. "I've always wanted one. A baby."

No reaction from him.

At all.

He still keeps looking at me, staring with bottomless eyes and a cool face. A body that seems larger than the wall he's standing against. Larger than this room, my apartment, this building.

Maybe even the whole world, I don't know.

All I know is that he feels powerful in this moment.

He feels like he could crush everything that I ever wanted with one stomp of his foot. One snap of his fingers.

And he can, can't he?

He's done it before.

He can do it again.

But still, I have to keep going. "A husband. A family. A loving family. A loyal husband. Not that I'm asking any of those things from *you*. I want you to know that. That's not what this is about. I don't want to make a family with you or anything. And I'm sure you don't want to make one with me. We're not… right for each other. But you *can* give me a baby. And I want that. Although I realize how archaic it must sound to you, how unambitious and uninspired or whatever. I mean, girls want to rule the world, you know? They want to be queens and CEOs and whatnot and that's okay. All the more power to them. But I'm not like that. I never was.

"Mostly because I didn't have a loving family growing up. I didn't have a nurturing mom and a loving dad. I was alone. I mean, I had my brother but he was alone too. We were both alone and… Where I come from, that's normal. People aren't concerned about trivial things like going on family vacations or doing family dinners. They are, but it's not about the family per se but the status that it brings by vacationing in Paris or taking a private jet to the Bahamas. Or eating at the latest trendy restaurant that they can brag about to their friends. And I guess, I wanted my life to be different. I wanted more. And more in my world means real relationships. Love. Family and stuff like that. Stuff that makes you feel safe and secure. Happy.

"And to be honest, now that you know everything, I wanted all those things with you. I wanted to build a life with you." I chuckle then; can't help myself. "Oh my God, it sounds so… *stupid* right now. I mean, what was I thinking, right? Why did I ever think, even for a single second, that we could be together? I've read books with heroines that do really dumb shit and I guess I'm dumber than them. But anyway, that's not the point. The point is that it's my dream and I thought that if I ran after love, I'd catch it. I thought I'd put it in my pocket and keep it with me. But that's not true, is it? So now I have a slightly modified dream. And it's to have a baby. *Just* a baby though, nothing else."

I want to pause here and take a breath but if I don't get it all out now, I will never ever be able to say it, so I keep going. "And the reason I didn't tell you right away was because I was afraid. I was scared that if I told you the truth, the whole truth, you'd run away. I know you came to me a year ago to do the same thing that I'm asking you to do now but your reasons were different. You wanted revenge and you wanted to use me to get it. I'm not sure what your plan was if I had in fact gotten pregnant, but I'm sure it wasn't to live in holy matrimony, was it? I'm sure you would've found some way to contribute or whatever —"

"I would've stood by it. By you," he says then.

Low and rough.

In a voice that sounds unused, barely existent.

I hear him though and it clenches my heart. "You t-thought about it?"

Something flickers in his gaze, something that I don't understand but I think is super important to figure out for some reason. "Yeah."

I'm floored right now.

I'm absolutely fucking floored.

Because I thought that the only thing on his mind back then was revenge. The only thing that he could feel was blazing and burning anger.

It didn't even occur to me — not even as the remotest possibility — that he would've thought about anything else.

Especially about the consequences of his actions.

"It was going to be *my* baby," he says in a gruff, raspy voice. "Mine. Of course I would've taken care of it, of her."

"H-her?"

He jerks out a nod. A short but decisive one, an immediate nod like he doesn't care if I know. He *wants* me to, in fact. "Her."

Oh God.

Oh my God.

Is he saying that…

Is he *saying* that he even thought about the sex of the baby?

"I… I didn't…"

I don't know what to say.

But I realize it's a good thing. I don't need this right now.

I don't need to think about him in any terms other than the fact that he's the guy who broke my heart so he deserves what's coming to him.

I don't need to think about how in his head, it was a girl and how he'd already decided to take care of her.

"But again, that's not the point," I say, going against every grain of my instinct. "The point is that I want a baby. And I need to get over you. So I put two and two together. But I will understand if, knowing the whole truth, you don't want to do this. It was convenient for me, but I'm sure I can find someone who —"

"No."

"What?"

He finally unfolds his arms and fists them at his sides, his feet shoulder-width apart. "It's going to be me."

And finally, my heart starts to beat.

"Why?" I ask.

He mashes his teeth together, making the bones of his jaw and cheeks stand taut. Then, "Because you asked me for closure. You asked me to help you move on, and because I'm the one who broke your dream, I'm the one who hurt you, who crushed you, who gave you that ache in your chest... So I'm going to be the one to fix it. I'm going to be the one to give you what you want."

Oh God, he is.

He agreed. He's going to give me what I want.

I should be happy.

But I'm not. I'm devastated right now.

I'm all but destroyed.

Because he'll give me a baby.

And I'll give him revenge.

I'll use him to get pregnant and then I'll leave him behind.

As soon as I find out I'm pregnant, I'll cut all ties with him, and I'll take his baby — I'll take her — away from him.

And *that* is how I'll get my closure.

Chapter Seventeen

Her Beautiful Thorn

I HAVE A SECRET TOO.

Just like her.

No, it's not that I turn into a wolf during the full moon or I have powers that I use to save the world.

It's the fact that when I went to her that night, revenge wasn't the only thing in my mind.

There was something else too.

Something that I'd never felt before that night.

Actually, it's something that I'd never felt before I met her.

A need.

That only grew as soon as she opened the door in her white satin pajamas, looking all virginal and fuckable. And it kept growing and growing when I fell on her lips like an animal. Like I'd wanted to do since the first time I saw her on the hood of her brother's car. By the time I had her under me, naked and open, trusting, my need had grown a heart and ten heads.

My need had grown beastly.

And it had nothing to do with teaching her brother a lesson or exacting revenge, and everything to do with her.

My Firefly.

It had everything to do with trapping her in a jar.

To bind her.

To tie her to me so tightly and firmly, so *permanently*, that she never ever gets free.

That no one could ever take her away from me. Not the world. Not her brother.

Not even myself. Or soccer or my career, my goals and ambitions.

It was the need to mark her. From the inside. The need to fill her and pump her full of me.

Breed her.

It's the same need that rears its head when I see her with Halo. When I see her playing with Halo's chubby cheeks or fists; when I see her soothe Halo; strap Berry to her chest like she's really a mother.

Like this is what she was born to do.

To give, to nurture.

To soothe.

In fact it's gotten worse over the past year, this need. Maybe because I've already had a taste of it, of her. A taste of what her tight little body would look like, all swollen and ripe. Her creamy skin creamier. Her plump tits plumper. Her pink fucking pussy pinker.

My personal candy land.

All sugared up and juicy.

I wasn't lying when I said that yes, I have thought about it.

About getting her pregnant and taking care of her. Easing her pains as she grows. Holding her hand as she gives birth to our baby girl. Fucking staring at her as she feeds our baby with her tits and then falling on her myself to feed.

Fuck.

Fuck, fuck, *fuck.*

I don't need to think about that right now.

Not when I'm driving back and my boner's already hurting and pressing against my jeans. This is not the time to get into a fucking accident or worse, die.

When I'm so close to getting what I want.

So close to having all my dreams come true.

So I stop by the side of a deserted street and take out my dick.

I rub it and rub it, my cock already slippery from all the pre-cum that keeps dripping. It keeps dripping and dripping as I think about all the ways I'll get to play with her now, all the ways that I'll get to pump her full of me.

All the ways that I'll get to make her mine.

I come at the thought of squirting my load on her swollen belly as I squirt milk from her tits into my mouth.

And Jesus, I come like a fucking beast.

My cum soiling my hands, my jeans, spurting onto to the clenched shelf of my abs.

Once I'm done, I fall against the seat and breathe.

I close my eyes and try to get my raging, aggressive feelings under control. And *think.*

179

I need to think.

I can't get carried away. This isn't about me or what I want. It's about her. I've already taken a lot from her and I can't take this away from her too. I can't make it all about me.

I wanted a way to fix things, didn't I?

A way to make amends or at least begin to.

This is it.

Which means I can't keep her.

As much as I want to, I can't trap her in a jar. Not only because she doesn't want it — she just wants a baby — but also because I have my own bullshit, don't I?

Nothing has really changed from before.

I still have my career to think about, which apparently feels like it's in the gutter right now. But that doesn't mean that I don't have goals. That I won't do everything that I can — except bow down to my brothers — to revive it. To come out on fucking top and show them.

Meaning I can't be a romance novel hero.

And no matter how much the thought of her with another guy — fucking Ezra — fucks me up, I have to remember that this is about her and not me living out my fucked-up fantasy.

Even if she's lying to me.

She is, isn't she?

I could tell.

I know she still isn't telling me the whole truth. There's more going on in her scheming little brain.

I get it though. I get that I don't deserve the truth from her. I don't deserve her trust after all that I've done. But that doesn't mean that I'm going to let her get away with it either.

Or play me for a fool.

So if she wants to plot and scheme, I'll let her.

For now.

Because sooner or later, I'm going to find out the truth. I'm going to find out what she's hiding.

Part III

Chapter Eighteen

THE PHONE RINGS first thing in the morning and I scramble to pick it up.

The voice that comes from the other end makes me flinch. "Where the fuck have you been?"

I blink, confused. "Dad?"

"Why aren't you picking up my calls?" he thunders.

I swat my hair away from my face and try to focus. "I didn't... I didn't know you were calling. I just woke up. I —"

"Well, good fucking morning to you."

I flinch again but manage to sit up straight in my bed. "Okay, can you just stop yelling and let me open my eyes at least?"

Of course not.

Because his next statement is yelled out too. "You better be thankful that all I'm doing right now is fucking yelling at you."

I sigh.

Damn it.

This isn't what I needed right now. Not first thing in the morning.

I'm not a morning person at all. I need at least two to three cups of coffee before I can form a coherent thought and once I did that, I was going to call him. I knew I had to and I also knew that he wasn't going to be happy with what I had to tell him.

But he got there first and now I have to do damage control, half-asleep. "Dad, listen —"

"Don't you fucking 'Dad' me, you bitch," he seethes. "You owe me something and despite being very, very clear, you still haven't delivered."

I clench my eyes shut.

He's right.

I owe him a wedding date, or rather a preponed wedding date, and no, I haven't been able to deliver. Turns out, Ezra and I couldn't connect at all over the last week like he'd told me we would. I couldn't even get him on the phone, and I did try. Every time I'd call he'd be busy, and truth be told, I understood that.

I mean the guy is busy with an international merger and this huge hotel project that he's going to oversee. Of course he's busy. Plus it's not as if we are BFFs and we talk every day. Our marriage is a business arrangement, and not being able to get ahold of each other is not that uncommon.

In fact that's exactly what happens in all the marriages that I've ever known. My mom and dad go weeks, sometimes months, without talking to each other or knowing what the other is doing.

Although I also understand that my situation is different.

Not only is this a business arrangement, but I have a little something that I need to tell him too. Something that I'm not very sure how he'd react to because we never got to finish our discussion that day at the restaurant, but he still needs to know.

He still needs to be on the same page with me.

And frankly, like I told him at our dinner date the other night, I think this is a good thing.

Not only for me but also for him. For his image. For keeping his father and other people like his father off his back.

But now he is gone.

He left yesterday for Korea and I'm certainly not breaking the news to him over the phone. I'm also not going to harass him about the wedding date over a phone call either.

Which means everything will have to wait until he gets back.

Which could be in a couple of months — optimistically — but it could also be longer. It all depends on how things go for him over there. The longer his return gets delayed though, the more I'm going to get anxious about telling him.

But that's still fine. The bigger problem is my father.

He's bound to get pissed, the longer Ezra's return takes.

And that does not bode well for me *or* my brother. So I have to somehow convince my father to keep a lid on it.

Meaning I can't get angry and/or sarcastic with him. "Yes, about that. I think —"

"I need that wedding date, you understand," he tells me again, his voice growling. "I need this merger to happen. I *need* that fucking money and if you think for one second that you can sleep on the job, I will make it so that you can never sleep for the rest of your sorry life. Do you hear me? I'll make it so that every time you close your eyes, you see your brother's ugly mug —"

"Shut up," I snap, losing all my patience with him.

There's a couple of seconds of silence. Then, "What'd you say to me?"

I clutch the phone tightly to my ear and with a pounding heart, I repeat, "I said shut the fuck up."

"You think you're so brave, huh? Telling your father to shut up over the phone," he growls. "Why don't you —"

"Because I'm done with your threats," I cut him off and keep going. "Do you hear *me*? I'm fucking done. You want to screw up Reed's life, you go ahead and do that. And then let's see how fast *you* get dead when you don't see even a single cent of the money that the Vandekamps have promised you. Now I've already told you that I'm doing this, that I'll do this, so give me some credit, all right? You want me to do a job, let me do it. My way. Not yours.

"Ezra isn't a dog that I can train to do as he's told. He loves his company. He loves his job. And he has a mind of his own. If we keep putting pressure on him, he's going to get suspicious. You want that money, you'll get it. But you'll have to be patient. You'll have to let me run the show a little bit. Because as much as you like to remind me how powerless I am against you, you need me too. You need me to do your dirty work so you're still breathing next year and the year after that and the year after that. So back the fuck off."

And surprisingly, he does.

I wasn't expecting that of him but I'm glad he did.

I'm fucking relieved.

Not only because my calling his bluff — very risky move by the way — worked but also because I can't worry about my father when I've got other things to worry about. And I'm not just talking about telling my future husband about this little decision I've made.

It's the decision in itself.

The fact that I'm going to have a baby.

Well, I'm going to *try* to have a baby.

And I'm going to start tomorrow.

It's not me; it's science.

My ovulation window starts tomorrow and from what I've read it lasts about two to four days.

So yeah, if everything goes right, I may end up pregnant on the other side of my ovulation window. And as scary as that is — getting pregnant — it's still not as scary as *whose baby* I'm getting pregnant with.

And as usual, every time this thought enters my mind, I do the same thing that I've been doing for the past week. Ever since the night of the Chinese restaurant. I shove it down.

I thrust it away.

I distract myself.

And tonight the distraction comes in the form of baking with my BFF.

"Why would you agree to bake all of these by yourself?" I ask as I work on the frosting.

By all these I mean two hundred and fifty cupcakes.

Pink-cheeked and her blonde hair all fluttery and framing her face, she sighs sharply. "Because I'm an idiot and I wanted to contribute more."

"You already do a lot for them," I remind her.

"Not enough though," she says, pouring the cupcake batter in the tin. "I only work there part-time. Sometimes I cancel without much notice and they don't mind. They know I have a new baby at home. They try to work around my schedule. And this is my way of both contributing more and paying them back."

Callie works at a ballet studio in town and they're having a bake sale this coming weekend. A ballerina herself, she teaches ballet to little girls and loves it. Although this is only temporary. Until she starts school at Juilliard next year. She had to defer her admission a year because she got pregnant with Halo.

Who, as usual, is strapped to my chest as I work.

I look down at her; she's cooing and playing peacefully with her fishy rattle toy. "Your mommy is crazy, Little Berry. You know that, don't you? But it's okay. You still lucked out. Because your aunt is extremely smart and intelligent."

She jiggles her toy. "Gah. Gah. Gaaaah."

I look at Callie, smiling. "See? She agrees with me."

She's rolling her eyes however. Then, "Since when do you call her Little Berry?"

"What?"

"Only Ledger calls her that," she tells me.

I can feel her gaze on me but I keep my focus on the frosting and try to sound as causal as I can. "Oh, does he? Maybe I heard it from him."

I can still feel her stare on me.

Making me feel like she isn't buying it.

So to put her off the scent and also because I really am dying to talk about this, I ask, "Can I ask you something?"

She takes a few seconds to answer but then she turns back to her task and replies, "Sure."

I blow out a quiet breath and, rubbing Halo's dark curls, I ask, "When you, uh, told my brother that you were pregnant, what was his reaction?"

Again she takes a few seconds to answer but this time it's because she has a small smile on her lips. "Well, he already knew."

"What?"

"He already knew something was up before I ever told him."

"Really? You never told me that."

She shrugs. "Yeah, he already knew. And he somehow also knew that I was freaking out and I was. I had half a mind to never tell him and just run away."

"You did not." I completely turn toward her then. "Really?"

"Yup." She chuckles. "I wanted to keep it a secret, you know. I wanted to, I don't know, punish him for everything that he had done. I mean, I hated him so much back then and it wasn't supposed to happen. So I thought I'd just never tell him."

So maybe I'm not that crazy after all.

Maybe my need for revenge — as ugly as it is — isn't so unjustified.

"So then," I try to keep my voice calm and not show my enthusiasm at this, "what made you change your mind?"

Finally, she turns to me, her blue eyes full of emotions and love. "He did."

"What?"

"I just… I could sense it, see. Just the way he knew that I was freaking out even though I still wanted her," she glances down at Halo, "I knew that he wanted her too. He wanted her badly. In fact he wasn't even freaking out. He was so sure since day one. About everything. About being there for me, for her. Doing everything that he could to make things okay for me — us — and she wasn't even born yet. And I… I didn't think that I could do it. I didn't think that I could take that away from him. He just had so much to give, something that I never could've expected until I got pregnant with our baby girl. So yeah, as much as I wanted to hate him and punish him and teach him a lesson, I just couldn't do it this way. I couldn't take his baby girl away from him."

My eyes sting.

Silent tears are running down my cheeks and my heart is aching.

In fact my heart is aching more than it's been for the past week.

Because that's exactly how *he* is, isn't he?

For all his flaws and all his mistakes and all the ways that we're wrong for each other, he's perfect for *her*. His baby girl. In fact that was one of the things that attracted me to him at the very beginning, wasn't it? That he helped raise his baby sister. That he was there for her, so protective over her, so safe and secure.

And I know he's going to do the same, *be* the same, with our baby.

If I ever told him about it.

Which I'm not going to.

It's something that I've been going back and forth on this entire week.

My initial plan was just to start an affair with him and once, unbeknownst to him, I'd accomplished my goal, I would've broken up with him and simply left. It wouldn't be hard; I'm getting married soon anyway, and I was going to pass the baby off as Ezra's.

Now that he knows what we're doing, it still doesn't mean that my plan has changed. I can still not tell him and cut things off when I get pregnant and go live the rest of my life with Ezra.

It's cruel and immoral and *God*, it makes me sick every time I think about it.

But I need to do it.

For myself.

I'm extremely happy for Callie and my brother, but they're an exception. I'm not. *We* are not. So I need to do everything that I can to exact my revenge and move on. So for now, I'm only focusing on one thing and one day at a time.

Meaning: I need to bake, bake, bake.

Or rather frost, frost, frost.

And I think I'm doing a good job of it until I hear Callie's gasp. "Don't. Stop it, Ledger. These are not for you."

I don't even think about. I whirl around.

And somehow there he is.

Standing at the island. His dark eyes on me.

On my hands specifically. One on Halo's diapered bottom and the other on her sweet-smelling head.

This is the first time I'm seeing him since that night and for some reason, he still looks so large. Like he did in my room, standing by the wall, demanding truth from me. *Demanding* that I give him everything.

And it was so tempting to do that.

So tempting to give in to the urge and lay everything at his feet.

And that urge has only grown stronger and more incessant as the days passed. Probably because even though we haven't seen each other in a week, we have talked.

Over the phone.

On the calls that *he* made.

How surreal is that, huh? I waited for years for him to make one phone call, just one, and he never did. While I know why now, it still hurt back then. It still made me cry. But this entire last week, he called me every single night. Just before going to sleep. And *every single night*, he demanded that I tell him a story. That I tell him what book I was reading and give him a point-by-point description of what's happening.

And I did.

Maybe because all my badassery was used up in keeping this huge secret from him.

Whatever it is, I'm still glad that I'm holding strong.

That I'm keeping a piece of me to myself and thinking about me for a change.

Although as I said, it's hard. And seeing him here, unexpectedly, isn't helping anything.

And neither is it helping that he keeps staring at me and staring at me.

At how I'm holding Halo. At how I'm rubbing her back and just naturally rocking her in my arms.

When he looks up though, I have to take a step back.

Because his gaze, pitch black and burning, is a force of its own. It has its own impact and energy, and I know, I can feel it down to my marrow, what he's thinking.

I know exactly what he's imagining.

Me with our baby girl.

His baby girl.

And gosh, my womb clenches so hard at that, so fucking hard, that it takes everything in me to not press my hand on my belly. It takes everything in me to not press my thighs together and rub the hurt that he's causing between my legs.

"Ledger," Callie says. "Are you listening to me? Put down the cupcake."

At my best friend's voice, I remember that we're not alone — of course we're not — and I jerk my eyes away from him.

Even though I'm not looking at him, I can still feel his eyes on me and I blush.

God, please don't let Callie see this.

I sigh in relief when I feel him turn away from me and focus on his sister. Instead of doing what she asked him to, he takes off the liner and pops the whole thing in his mouth as a response.

"You're going to pay for that," she snaps at him.

Again, his response is to swallow the cupcake down and throw her a smirk.

Which only makes her angrier. "Stay away from the cupcakes, okay? These are not for you."

Shrugging, he goes, "Might as well, I guess. Didn't feel it."

"Didn't feel what?"

"The cupcake."

"What?"

"You're losing your touch."

She puts a hand on her hips. "I'm not."

"Being married to that motherfu —" Then, "*brother pucker* is making you worse by the day."

Callie glares at him. "First of all, good job on reining yourself in. But that still doesn't mean you can call my husband names. And second, get out, okay? If you hate my cupcakes so much, you're not allowed to be in this room."

But Callie's baby girl has other plans.

Because by now she's caught on that her favorite uncle is here and she's creating a ruckus.

"I think she wants me."

At his voice, I *have* to focus on him.

And I can't believe he's still looking at me in the same way.

He's still looking at me like I'm… already pregnant. Or if I'm not then he can't wait to get me that way.

He can't wait to put his baby in me and watch me play with her one day.

Thankfully Callie still doesn't catch anything because she goes, "Yeah, she goes crazy when Ledge comes around. You'd better just give her to him and he can take care of her. So we can focus on the baking."

After her rant, Callie goes back to her mixing bowl and starts working on another batch of cupcakes. While I abandon mine and walk over to him. Something that shouldn't be so difficult, putting one foot in front of the other, but it is because he's tracking my movements.

When I finally reach him, I have to look away so I don't tremble as much as I'm doing while loosening the sling from around my body. Once it's loosened enough, I hand still-squirming Halo over to him. Last time when we did that, our fingers had hardly touched and now I know it was because he was deliberately keeping himself away from me.

Not so much now.

Now he touches not only my fingers but also my forearms, the underside of my elbow.

He even goes so far as to graze his fingers across my waist and my hips, and while you could say that it's perfectly normal to touch those parts of my body while I'm handing a really wiggly baby over to him, in this case it was completely unnecessary. Because Halo is already secure in his arms.

I take a step back then.

But only because his sister is here.

If we were alone, I'd probably be forgetting everything about the ovulation window and falling on him.

Like I did that night.

Totally inadvisable.

I'm about to take a step back when Ledger, keeping his eyes on me, addresses Callie. "Are there any that you didn't make?"

I feel Callie whirl around but thankfully my back is to her so she can't see how furiously I'm blushing right now. I widen my eyes at him and his response is to twitch his lips.

"You're such a douche —"

Looking away, he shakes his head. "You can't curse in front of Little Berry, remember?"

I know she's glaring at him. "Why are you still here?"

He's rubbing Halo's back who's smacking her palms on his jaw. Clean-shaven by the way, just like last week. "Because you still haven't answered my question."

I can feel the anger radiating out of Callie and I speak up. "These ones."

He turns back to me, that smirk still lingering on his lips but his eyes are a lot more intense than they were when they were on his sister. Slowly, he glances down to where I'm pointing: to the tray full of frosted cupcakes. Then, looking up, "You baked them?"

"Yes."

He stares at me a beat before he grabs it. "They're mine then."

"Ledger!" Callie snaps.

But his focus is on me and my shocked eyes. "All of them."

"I swear to God, Ledger, I —"

He doesn't stand around to listen to her rant and simply leaves with Halo and my cupcakes.

Well, his.

According to him.

It takes me a bit to get Callie to calm down but we manage to finish her big project. And when I get back home after that, I'm the one calling him.

As soon as he picks up, I go, "What was that?"

I hear him sigh. "What was what?"

Standing at the foot of my bed, I say, "About the cupcakes."

"What about the cupcakes?"

I frown. "There was nothing wrong with Callie's cupcakes."

"There was."

"No, there wasn't. They were —"

"They weren't made by you," he says.

My mouth was already open, ready with a retort, but now I don't know what to say. I don't know how to be mad at him. So I plop down on the bed and say, "You didn't have to eat almost the whole tray. And bring the leftovers home."

Which is what he ended up doing.

Much to Callie's displeasure.

And when Callie's displeased, my brother is displeased as well. Which means it made for a fun — not — dinner.

He sighs as if in pleasure though. "I had to."

"No, you —"

"Because they were mine. And they were delicious as fuck."

Again, I lose all my steam and say, "You're crazy, you know that."

He hums. "Better than being a pussy who barely gets to taste the cupcakes his girl made just because she said so." Then, "Like your brother."

Again, that's exactly what happened.

Reed came home from work, saw cupcakes scattered all over the kitchen island, and grabbed a couple. But Callie got mad and so he left it at that. Despite the fact that Ledger was snickering at him and eating cupcakes from his tray. Which I'd like to point out that he did not share with Reed.

"You could've at least shared one with my brother," I grumble.

"Absolutely fucking not."

"It would've been the polite thing to do."

"Fuck polite," he retorts.

"Seriously, Ledger, you guys need to —"

"He would've done the same thing."

"No, he wouldn't have," I lie.

"You *know* he would have."

I open my mouth to retort but then close it. Because he's right.

My brother would've done the same thing. Just because he appears slightly tamed after marrying Callie and having his baby girl, he's every bit of an asshole like Ledger. And I know; he's *my* brother.

So shaking my head, all I say is, "Fine. He would have. But it still wasn't right."

He grunts in response.

"And why were you staring at me?" I ask then, lying down on the bed. "In front of your sister no less."

"Because it's my turn now."

"Your turn at what?"

"At staring at you," he says, his voice sounding low. "You've stared at me plenty, remember? Given that you were my pretty little stalker."

I was playing with the button on my dress but at his words, I stop.

And I blush.

Which he somehow knows. "Are you blushing?"

"No."

"You're blushing."

"Shut up."

Which makes him chuckle.

Biting my lip, I say, "So what, you're my stalker now?"

"No," he says. "I don't think staring and wanting from afar is my forte."

"So then what is?"

"*Taking* the thing I want." Then, "So no, I'm not your stalker, Firefly. I'm your neighborhood's friendly kidnapper. I take what I want."

A shiver rolls down my spine. "That's wrong on so many levels."

"Maybe."

Another shiver at his cavalier attitude. "It's actually criminal."

"So then when you get off the phone with me, you should call the cops."

"Maybe I will."

"And lock your doors."

I press my thighs together. "Maybe I will do that too."

"Although I do have to warn you."

"About what?"

"If I want to get to you, there isn't a door in existence that would keep me out."

I swallow, my throat going dry. "You're scaring me."

"Yeah, but you like it."

Yes.

God, yes. I do.

And I hate that he knows that.

Switching gears, I say, "It was obscene. The way you were staring at me."

"Was it?"

"Yes. It was like…"

"Like what?"

"Like you were imagining things."

"What things?"

I lick my lips. "Me…"

"You."

"Pregnant."

"Pregnant."

"W-with your baby."

"With my baby."

As always whenever he says that I have to clench my eyes shut and really tighten my belly. Against the onslaught of emotions that run through me. And good thing I'm lying down because I also have to contend with getting weak in the knees and a pulse in between my legs.

Opening my eyes, I somehow ask, "Were you?"

His voice is raspy as he replies, "I was."

I swallow then.

Trying to keep breathlessness away from my tone. Trying to keep the need to see him buried.

This is business.

Just business.

And revenge.

God, I hate revenge. I hate that I'm doing this.

"Well, I'm not pregnant yet."

"No, not yet," he agrees.

"So then —"

"Soon though."

He says it like a promise that sounds like a threat.

An even bigger threat than him claiming to be a criminal kidnapper.

"Well, we don't know that," I tell him. "I mean, we're just trying and —"

"No, we know that."

"We know that?"

"Yes, we do."

I frown. "How?"

"Because it's me."

"So?"

"And I've got a superior dick."

That completely gives me a pause. "What?"

"So you lucked out," he says and the thing that is still giving me pause is the fact that he sounds serious.

Absolutely.

"You're serious."

"Do I sound like I'm joking?"

"You actually think you have a superior dick."

"I'm a better soccer player than most. Arguably the best. Always have been. I've got a better body than most, always did. Of course my dick's superior."

Oh my God, he's really crazy, isn't he?

I don't know whether to laugh or smack his arrogant face.

Or just kiss the fuck out of him.

But wait, that's not even the worst part, is it?

"And *I* lucked out?"

"Well, I don't like to brag but —"

I prop myself up on my elbows. "*You* don't like to brag?"

He exhales sharply and completes his sentence. "But yeah, you lucked out."

"I can't believe how arrogant you are. That's such a guy thing to say."

"I'm a guy, aren't I? And I'm not ashamed to admit that I've got a phenomenal dick."

I roll my eyes. "Oh please."

"But of course, it's not just me, is it? It's you too."

"Oh, I'm so glad you realize that."

"And I know you've got a super fertile pussy."

At this, I completely sit up. "What?"

"I've seen it, remember?"

"I don't —"

"All pink and ripe." Then, "Juicy."

"Oh my God, can we not talk about my p-pussy?"

"I know it gets wet. Just like that. But I bet it's super tight too."

"Well, thank you very much but —"

"Yeah, you should thank me," he says in a growly voice, as if he's mad at me.

For having a tight pussy.

"You —"

"Because I'm the one who's going to put a baby in your belly, and trust me, there's going to be one. But I'm also the one who's going to make sure you like it."

"L-like what?"

"Your first time."

"My f-first time?" I whisper.

As if I don't know.

As if it didn't occur to me.

But honestly it didn't. I mean I knew it was going to be my first time, but I've been so focused on everything else, my plan and revenge and a *baby* — *his* baby — that I hadn't made the connection. I hadn't thought about how along with so many other significant things that are happening, there's yet another thing as significant as the rest of them.

My first time.

I'll be losing my virginity.

To him.

Like I'd dreamed about ever since I saw him.

"Yeah," he rasps. "Which I hear is hard on a girl. And a girl your size, it's going to be ten times harder."

It makes me clench my thighs but this time, there's a little fear involved too. "Y-you don't know that."

"Fuck yeah I know that."

"But I…" I fist the sheet, clenching and unclenching my thighs. "I still have a day left."

I told him about my ovulation window and strangely, he agreed to let me run the show and wait.

"Look at the clock, Firefly," he drawls and my eyes fly over to the digital clock sitting on my nightstand. "It's midnight. Meaning your time's up."

My heartbeats jack up and I blurt out, "B-but I… I can still back out."

"No you can't."

I don't mean it. Not at all.

But still I say it, "I can. I still get a choice."

"No, you don't."

"But —"

"You *had* a choice. A week ago. But you blew it."

"I-I don't understand."

"You *chose* to tell me about your dream."

"And?"

"And now that I know what you want, what you dream of, you're getting it. And I'm the one giving it to you. I'm the one who will *make sure* to give it to you. I'll move the sky and stop the earth; I'll tear down the ground and part the seas to give you what your heart desires. So you had a choice, Firefly, but you don't anymore. Now in a few hours, you'll pack a bag and you'll come with me. And I'm going to make your dreams come true."

Chapter Nineteen

IT'S something out of a romance novel.

The place that he takes me to.

For the ovulation window.

For the record, I didn't want to go anywhere. I thought he could come to my apartment and we could commence the 'trying.' And I also would like to go on the record and say that my idea totally sucked.

Yes, I still want to keep boundaries and treat this like a business arrangement.

But oh my gosh, this place is fucking phenomenal.

First, it's in the middle of the woods.

And when I say 'in the middle,' I actually mean that.

It's so deep into the woods that surround the Bardstown Highway that you can't see anything for miles and miles except for thick and sprawling trees. The ground is covered in dead, crunchy leaves and I bet during summer and spring, the sky is barely visible through the canopy of the leaves up above.

As it is, it's winter creeping on fall and so the branches are naked and bare and you can see endless gray skies.

And second, there's a cabin here.

A little wooden cabin with a sloping roof and a chimney; two windows in the front and a curved door.

Plus — oh my God, the wonders are never-ending — there's a shimmering lake. It's not very large; I can see the ends of it, but it looks so pretty. All surrounded by shrubs and beautiful rocks, all peaceful looking and private.

As soon as he stops his truck, I jump out of it and actually run toward the cabin before stopping and spinning around, taking it all in. This has to be the most beautiful place I've ever seen.

I stop when I hear the truck door slamming shut, see him approach me.

Slowly.

As if prowling.

His eyes on me.

All intense and full of purpose.

He's got both our bags slung over his shoulder and I can't help but notice his beautiful taut veins running up and down his forearms.

Not to mention the afternoon sun.

When it hits him, his bronzed skin and his wavy hair, it makes him look dipped in gold.

Not the bright kind of gold, the sunny kind, but the kind of gold that has darker, more sensual undertones.

More dangerous and threatening undertones.

When he reaches me, I ask, "You're not kidnapping me, are you?"

He runs his eyes up and down my body, as slowly as his prowl. "Are you planning on running away?"

Biting my lip, I shake my head. "No."

"So then you're safe."

Safe.

The thing I always feel around him.

Even when I shouldn't.

Even when being here, in the middle of the woods and all alone with him, should be a scary thing. But somehow it's not. Somehow every mile he put between Bardstown and us made me feel lighter. It made me feel freer. Probably because he was driving me away from my complicated life and bringing me closer to my dream.

"You always made me feel that," I tell him.

His eyes flick back and forth between mine. "Feel what?"

"Safe." I swallow, unsure why I'm telling him this. "In fact, that's one of the first things I felt when I saw you. I thought you'd keep me safe. Like no one else had ever had."

His features ripple with something as he replies, "I didn't though."

I shake my head, my heart aching. "But you tried."

"I did."

"So that's —"

"But it wasn't enough, was it?"

I take a step closer to him, my neck tilting back. "But it's —"

He does his thing with his body, his shoulders, where he bridges the gap between us so I don't have to make the effort and says, "I'm going to though. Now."

I know I shouldn't trust him.

I *know* that.

But somehow I can't help but whisper, "I'm scared."

About so many things.

The secrets that I'm keeping from him. My father, my complicated life.

The baby.

Our baby.

But somehow most of all, I'm scared about the fact that I'm going to lose my virginity tonight. I know it's silly, given that not only do I have so many things to be worried about, but also it's not a big deal. Every girl loses her virginity at some point. And yes, it hurts, but they survive, don't they?

Not to mention, I've thought about it for so long.

Read about it in so many romance novels and always replaced the hero with him and heroine with myself.

So I don't know why I'm feeling so shaky.

But I am and he knows that.

And I see things flashing in his eyes, regret and hunger and impatience and torment. As if he wants it but he regrets it. He regrets how much he wants it.

"I know," he whispers.

"Will you..." I lick my lips and grab his t-shirt. "Will you stop? If it hurts too much."

He shakes his head slowly. "No."

I twist his t-shirt. "But you —"

"You know I can't."

All I can do is breathe haphazardly then.

And he cradles my cheek with his free hand. "Don't you?"

The gentle touch of his rough fingers calms me down a little. "Y-yes."

Because if he did stop, then I won't get what I want.

He rubs the apple of my cheek. "But I'll make it better."

I burrow my face in his palm. "Promise?"

"Promise."

I swallow again and nod, absolutely and irrevocably believing him that he'd do that. That he'd do everything to make it better for me. I'm ready to step away from him and check out the cabin when he tightens his hold on my jaw and stops me. "You don't have any more red dresses, do you?"

I'm thrown by his out of the blue question and look down at my red dress for a second. Just for the record, this one's really modest, even more modest that the one I wore at the restaurant last week, with a boatneck and cap sleeves and an empire waist that hardly shows off my ass or my legs.

Then, looking up at him, I reply, "Of course I do. Although I didn't bring any here."

He looks thoughtful for a second before throwing me a short nod and moving away. "Good."

"Why?"

"Because," he says, his voice low, his eyes sweeping across my body one more time as if he can't help himself, "red is the color that provokes the bull."

"So?"

"So turns out it's not the only thing it provokes." My breath hitches and he keeps going, "And I don't want to hurt you any more than I have to."

⸺

"Is this a date?" I ask hours and hours later.

That passed, believe it or not, in the blink of an eye.

As soon as I entered the cabin, I became fascinated with this place. It has a real wood-burning fireplace, dark leather couches, plush rugs covering the floors. With an open floor plan, you can see the kitchen from the living room and there's a hallway that leads to the bedroom in the back.

Like the living room, the bedroom also has a fireplace and it screams coziness. There's a chest of drawers against the wall by the door where I put all my stuff that I brought in my overnight bag; a giant window overlooking the lake and the fall foliage; a plush armchair by the window that looks super masculine but still I can picture myself in it, huddled under a blanket with my knees drawn up and a romance novel in my hand.

But that wasn't the thing I was interested in.

I was interested in the main thing.

That took up almost all the room in this bedroom.

The king-sized bed.

With white sheets and wooden slats as the headboard.

I don't know why I became so fascinated with them, the slats, but I did. I even went so far as to touch them, wrap my fingers around them to see how sturdy they were. And then I got in the bed, probably because the mattress looked super high and super comfortable and the sheets looked brand new and made of the softest fabric.

And then the next thing I knew, it was dark outside and dinnertime.

Now here we are.

At dinner.

Or rather, after dinner but still at the table. A small thing made of dark wood like the rest of the cabin, seating no more than four people. We're sitting on opposite sides and these are the first words either of us have spoken, much like the Chinese restaurant; although I'm glad he isn't angry.

He's watchful though.

And staring.

While I'm once again speechless at the fact that he not only took the time to make dinner — lasagna, which was delicious by the way — but also decorate the place with candles and fairy lights.

It sounds surreal, doesn't it?

That he did that.

That he took the time to string lights along the walls and light up actual real candles.

Hence my question.

He puts down the tumbler of whiskey he's been nursing — oh yeah, he's been drinking all through dinner too; just the one tumbler with possibly two fingers of scotch but still — and says, "No. A business meeting."

"You decorated the place."

"That's what I do for a business meeting."

I don't know why his words make me squirm in my seat and blush like crazy. Actually I think I haven't stopped blushing ever since last week, but still.

Taking a sip of my water, I ask, "What is this place?"

"My dad's cabin."

My eyes go wide. "Your dad's cabin."

"Yeah."

"I didn't…" I shake my head, sitting up straight in the chair. "I didn't know your dad had a cabin. As in, Callie never said anything about that."

"Because she doesn't know."

"What?"

For the first time since we sat down to eat, he takes his eyes off me and looks at the whiskey. "It's not something we talk about. The cabin in the woods that belong to our piece-of-shit father. One of the rules that Con laid out a long time ago."

"Rules?"

He looks up. "Rules."

Even though he's only repeated my one word, something about his tone makes me go even more alert. "Does your brother have a lot of them?"

"You've met him, haven't you?"

"Yes."

"So you already know."

I think I do.

I'm not close with any of his brothers by any means. I don't even think I've talked to them for more than five minutes. Well, except for that one time when I flirted with Shepard to piss Ledger off. But I definitely know that I haven't spoken more than two sentences to their oldest brother, Conrad. Even though he also happens to be the boyfriend of one of my St. Mary's friends, Wyn. Still, I've always been able to tell that he's a man you shouldn't mess with.

Apart from being the oldest Thorne and former guardian of all his siblings, he's also one of the most authoritative men I've ever met. One of the most domineering, and that's saying something, given that Reed is my brother and Ledger used to be the love of my life. But while Conrad's vibe is controlled and disciplined and maybe even leashed, his youngest brother's vibe is dangerous, untamed and ready to snap at any given moment.

In any case, I can totally see Conrad laying down rules for his siblings. "What are some of his other rules?" I ask before I can stop myself.

He'd gone back to watching the last of the amber liquid in the tumbler but at my question, he comes back to me again. "Don't go to the cabin."

"But…" I clear my throat. "We're here."

He throws out a casual shrug. "He didn't want any of us to have to do anything with our father. And despite what it looks like, I don't disagree with him. In fact for the longest time I'd been on onboard with his plan of letting this place sit and rot."

"So then what changed?" I ask, sitting at the edge of my seat.

Staring at him so intensely, straining my ears so that I don't miss anything.

This is the first time he's said anything about his family to me. And despite my decision to keep this arrangement as formal as possible, I'm not going to refuse what he's giving me.

I'm not going to refuse a chance to get a glimpse at his life.

The very thing that attracted me to him in the first place.

"I grew up," he clips.

"I don't —"

"Realized I didn't like rules very much and that I could make up my own mind," he cuts me off, his eyes going back to the whiskey, as if he's looking into the past. "But people don't like it when you try to exert independence. Especially when they're your family and especially when to them, you've always been the youngest. So one day I got fed up. Of all the bullshit and rules and whatever the fuck they came up with when it came to me, and ran away. I was twelve I think. Eleven? Can't remember. But the first thing that I did after gaining my so-called freedom in the middle of the night was to go to the cabin. Something that was completely forbidden. I walked. Stole someone's bike when I got tired of walking and somehow I got here. It was pretty spooky, this place. All abandoned, in the middle of the woods. No one had been here in ages I think. Definitely not my siblings and *definitely* not my piece-of-shit father. I think the last time any of us were here was when both our parents were with us. Although I don't remember any of that because I was just a kid.

"Anyway, I spent the night here. Slept on the floor. Woke up with sun in my face. Swam in the lake. Slept under a tree when I got tired. It was the most beautiful, peaceful day I'd ever spent. Despite the fact that I was hungry as fuck. But by afternoon I realized that I needed go back."

"Why?" I whisper.

Again, he lifts his eyes and I notice they're swimming with a thousand things and I want to take the time to sift through every single one of them.

I don't get that though.

Because they all vanish in an instant and his eyes turn harsh, his jaw clenching. "For my sister. For them, my brothers. Because as fed up as I was with my so-called family, they needed me. My brothers needed me to have their backs and my sister needed me to take care of her. But the funny thing is that they hadn't even noticed. That I was gone, that I'd been gone for hours. Maybe the possibility didn't even occur to them, that I could abandon them. All I remember is Stellan telling me to pick up the slack and do the dishes. And Conrad giving me the weekly grocery list because it was my turn that week to make the grocery run." Then, sighing, "Anyway since then I like to come here whenever I need to get away for a while. And since I don't care for sleeping on the floor or going hungry, I keep it stocked."

So this is his fortress.

Of solitude. Of peace.

Where he goes to be by himself.

Where he goes to be away from his family.

His *broken* family.

Because it is that, isn't it?

While I always knew that our stories are similar – no parents and only siblings to rely on – I never thought of his family as broken before.

Probably because they all look so in sync with each other with Conrad being the authority and the rest of them following his rules and order. They always look so united and *together*. In fact, sometimes it's hard to distinguish between them. Not because of their looks but the way they carry them-selves. Their demeanor, their aura, their dominating presence.

But maybe that's the problem, isn't it?

That they're so similar to each other.

They're all confident and authoritative. Protective and super masculine.

They're used to getting what they want.

Except maybe when they're with each other.

And since he's the youngest, I can see why he'd get the brunt of all that.

Which makes me think of something else. And before I can process it fully, I blurt out, "Is that why you're taking a break from soccer? Because of your brothers."

Maybe I shouldn't have asked him this.

Or at least not so abruptly as I did.

His features become tight and sharp, closed off.

He picks up the tumbler with jutting out knuckles, drains the last of his drink, and stands up as if on wooden legs and clips, "You done?"

I know he's referring to my empty plate, but it could also be in the context of this conversation, my probing. Before I can answer him though, he picks up my plate, stacks it on top of his and strides over to the sink. While I sit there with my mind whirling.

That's the reason, isn't it?

His brothers.

Even though he hasn't said anything, his silence is answer enough.

That's why he's taking a break from something he loves. Because of

Conrad and his rules. Because all his brothers — older than him — are once again in the same place, probably binding him in rules and caging him with orders. As soon as I work it all out in my head, I spring up from my seat and go to him.

He's standing at the sink, rinsing the dishes, his profile still tight, and I want to lean into him. Wrap my arms around him and just… hold him.

Hold the little boy he used to be.

The man that he's become.

One that puts his family above all else.

But I know he'll reject it, my sympathy, my tenderness. This fierce rush of feelings that even *I* know I shouldn't feel but I don't care. And since I have to do something, *say* something — it's imperative that I do — I go with this:

"I love it."

He doesn't respond.

In fact, it looks as if he hasn't even heard. As if he's unaware of my presence at his side even.

I'm not going to be deterred though.

"The cabin," I tell him. "I loved it as soon as I saw it."

Again no response from him but I keep going.

"And I love all the things that you put in here."

At this, finally I get a reaction.

A clench of his jaw.

I know it's not a lot, but it is something, isn't it?

"I also loved the food," I say, almost fiercely as if I want him to understand the depth of my feelings, the things I'm not able to say. "Thank you for cooking. You didn't have to though. I could —"

At last, he looks at me.

He pierces me with his angry gaze, halting my words mid-speech. "What is this?"

"What?"

Turning toward me completely, he growls, "Is this pity?"

"What, no. I —"

Apparently he's not happy with simply growling and snapping at me. Because with his next words, he advances on me as well. "Are you fucking *pitying* me?"

I have no choice but to step back, accommodate his muscular bulk and his mounting anger as I shake my head. "No. Ledger, I'm not —"

"Because let me tell you," he cuts me off, forcing me backward with every step that he takes. "I don't like it. I don't fucking like anyone pitying me. Least of all you. So —"

I stop him then.

At least his words.

By putting a hand on his mouth.

God, it's so soft and plush and instead of my hand, I want to put my mouth on his.

But I stop myself, and looking into his dark and narrowed eyes, I say, "I'm not pitying you. I've *never* pitied you. Not even before. The reason you made me feel safe was because of this. It was because of how you've always cared for your family. For your sister. The reason I wanted to build a life with you was because of this. Because..." His warm, cinnamon-y breath wafts over my palm and I have to swallow. "I-I wanted that for myself. I... My brother has always been the one to protect me and I mean, he had to, right? He's family. And as grateful as I've always been to him, I guess I just wanted someone to protect me not because they have to but because they want to, and..."

Maybe you want the same thing too.

I don't know where the thought came from, but now that it's here, it won't leave.

And after everything that he's told me tonight, is it any wonder that it's there in the first place?

Since our stories are so similar, what if...

What if he wants the same things as me?

What if he wants a family too? A wife, a baby. Someone to share his life with, someone who understands him and protects him and keeps him safe and...

No.

Absolutely not.

I absolutely cannot think this way.

I can't get all hopeful and romantic and forget why I'm here to begin with.

I'm here for myself.

Not for him or anyone else.

Besides, even if he does want these things, he never said he wanted them from me. Plus I can't be the one to give them to him anyway. I can't be the one to give him anything at all.

My life isn't my own, remember?

So just as abruptly as I put my hand on his mouth, I take it off and fist it at my side. "This is not pity. I genuinely like the cabin." And then just because he's staring down at me, with so much focus and intensity like he was during dinner, I keep going. "I like the fireplace. And the couches. Although I'd put at least a little pink or purple in the room. It's all very black and brown. And I love your armchair in the bedroom, by the window. I can sit there for hours and read. Plus your bed is amazing. It's feels like a fluffy cloud, and even though those slats are super old-fashioned, I think I like them too. I don't know why. I even touched them and —"

"You liked the slats," he says.

"Yes."

He doesn't respond to that, choosing to simply watch me. So licking my lips, I continue, "Wouldn't be my first choice at a store, I mean. B-but they looked strong and sturdy and —"

"That's because they are," he tells me.

I lick my lips again. "Okay. Well, good."

"Is it?"

My heart's started to race now. At his stare, his mysterious tone. "Yes. I-I mean, I'm sure you enjoy that bed."

"More or less."

"*I* fell asleep in it the moment my head hit the pillow so I'm sure you love sleeping there too."

"Love's a strong word."

"Plus you bought it."

"I did."

"So great and —"

"For you."

I draw back. "What?"

Which is the moment I realize that I'm trapped.

Between him and the wall.

Because at my sudden movement, my head scrapes against the wall and I know that I have nowhere to go. And while he's still a few feet away, it still feels like being captured.

"Well, with the thought of you in my head," he says.

I press my spine into the wall as I clarify, "Y-you bought your bed with me in your head."

He shakes his head slowly. "No, I bought my bed *with slats*. With you in my head."

"What does that…" I breathe first. "Mean?"

He inches closer. "You know what slats can be used for, don't you?"

I press myself even further into the wall. Although it doesn't make any difference; I'm not actually going anywhere. "Uh, to be able to hold on. If there's an earthquake?"

He takes another step toward me. "Close but no."

"Uh, to be able to hold on if the bed is *shaking*."

"Try again."

My heart is going and going right now. I bet he can see it, on the side of my neck, my freckle dancing with the beat. Although he still hasn't looked away from my eyes. "I…" Then suddenly it occurs to me and makes me go heated and flushed from the top to bottom. "To t-tie someone up."

That's when he looks.

At the side of my neck, I mean.

That's when he stares at my jumping pulse and dancing freckle.

And with a satisfied, wicked-looking glint in his eyes, he murmurs, "Yeah."

"I don't —"

"Although not someone, just you."

"Me?" I squeak.

"Because as I said, I bought my bed *with slats* with you in my mind."

Finally he's here, where I can't draw a breath without the threat of my breasts scraping against his chest, slamming the door of the cage that he's made for me.

Truly trapping me between the wall and his body.

"But I don't… When did you…"

"A few months after I saw you."

"But that was three years ago."

"Yeah, let's say it was."

"Are you…" I hiccup and clear my throat. "Are you saying that you wanted to tie me up back then?"

"Yeah."

My breaths whoosh out of me. "Y-you did?"

"Yes."

"Why?"

"Why do you think?"

At his question, my heart slows down. My knees tremble.

And even though I'm stuck to the wall and I've got support, I still need more.

So I go for him.

For his t-shirt and fist it.

It's crazy, my actions, when I've figured out the answer to his question. Crazy, inadvisable, dangerous. But maybe this is what they call Stockholm syndrome. Where you seek comfort from your tormentor. And isn't every brokenhearted and lovelorn love story a classic example of Stockholm syndrome?

Where you seek to un-break your heart from the very person who broke it in the first place?

So maybe it's all fitting.

It's all how it should be.

Me seeking safety from him.

"To use me to hurt my brother," I whisper, my breaths choppy.

Remorse flashes through his features, tightening them up, making them sharper. "Yeah."

Making his body sharp as well.

Hardening his muscles, turning him more than muscles and bones.

And I splay my fingers on his chest, trying to bring him back. Trying to inject him with life again as I ask, "Is that one of the things that you imagined? Before. When you were trying to keep me safe."

His jaw clenches. "Yes."

Oh.

He wanted to tie me up then.

No, he wanted to bring me here, in the middle of nowhere that I know no one would be able to find, not if they didn't know where they were going, and tie me to his bed.

The bed that he got with me in mind.

I know it's wrong. It's despicable, what he thought, what he imagined. And I should be horrified. But all I can think about is him wanting to bring me to his safe place. To a place where he goes to escape. To be by himself.

Oh God, I'm crazy, aren't I?

This is beyond Stockholm syndrome.

This is… absolute insanity.

But even so, I can't help but feel a flutter in my tummy. A thrum in my thighs.

In my pussy.

At the thought of being tied up in his bed.

"What… What did you imagine?" I ask then, pressing my palms on his chest, feeling the thuds of his heart.

Which is slowing down, I think, at my question.

And it's as if now he's the one needing support to be able to stand.

Because he puts his hand on the wall by my head and leans over.

As he rasps, his eyes all stormy and dark, "How you would've let me, if I had wanted that."

I don't know why I deny the truth — he already knows this about me; I've already confessed my feelings to him — but I do as I reply, "I wouldn't have."

"Yeah, you would have."

"No."

"Yes."

"I —"

"If I looked at you and crooked my finger once, you would've come running to me."

I don't know why that's so arousing, the opposite of what it should be: demeaning and condescending. But it is. It makes my skin shiver, my body pulse as I imagine him doing just that.

Not only back then but now.

Crooking his finger at me, telling me to follow him wherever he goes.

It's all the whiskey, I'm sure. That I watched him drink and somehow got drunk myself.

Even so, I shake my head. "That's not… That's not true."

He ignores that thought and continues, "And if I told you to get in my truck, you would've already been halfway inside before I even finished my sentence."

"No, I would've asked."

"Asked what?"

207

"W-where we were going."

"Like you did today," he says in a flat tone.

I didn't actually.

I did exactly what he's describing. Got in his truck before he'd opened the door halfway. Mostly because I'd always wanted to ride in it. I'd always wanted to see the inside of it, feel it, smell it, be in it.

"Today was…" I shift restlessly against the wall, "different."

"No it wasn't."

"It was," I insist for some reason.

Which he yet again ignores, as he puts his other hand on the wall too. As if to make his point, to scream his point at me. Although I don't understand what his point is. I don't understand what my point is either.

I don't understand what's happening right now.

Except that I want him to both stop and keep going; I can't decide which.

He decides for me though as he says, his gaze dark like the night, "And then I would've driven you out of town, without saying a single word, and you would've looked at me like I was taking you to heaven."

I shake my head again. "No."

"I would've brought you here, to the cabin and I would've shown you the bedroom and you would've loved the bed just as much as you did today. In fact I wouldn't even have to tell you to get into it, you would've done that yourself. But I don't think you would've fallen asleep."

"I would —"

"Because you'd be too excited."

"I —"

"To be here. To be with me. Finally. Because not only had I spared you a glance, which I never did before, I put you in my truck and drove you out here. I took you to this beautiful place with a beautiful cabin, a beautiful bed with slats, and you would've thought that this was the best day of your life. The most beautiful day. The day your dreams came true just because the guy you were in love with paid you a little bit of attention." Then, "Wouldn't you?"

"Yes," I blurt out, my fingers pulling at his t-shirt. "I would have. I would have thought that this was the best day of my life and I would've been stupid and —"

"Brave."

"What?"

His eyes flash with an emotion that I don't get right away as he says, "You would've been brave. You *were* brave. To put yourself out there. To want something and go for it. To dream of something and do everything you can to make it come true. You had courage. You had guts. You did what your heart told you to do, without any reservations, without any regrets. You believed. You had faith. You did what others can only dream of. What others write about and read about. So you were brave, Firefly. Not stupid. You're the girl in your romance novels. The girl made of candies and cream."

Only when he finishes do I realize the look in his eyes.

Admiration.

Pure and blatant.

He thinks I'm admirable. To have done what I did.

Brave for putting myself out there and for exposing my heart, my nerve endings. To have faith.

It doesn't make sense.

Right?

I should be embarrassed for all the things that I did. Which is why I was denying the truth back there, wasn't I? Because I'm embarrassed. Because I'm ashamed of all the things that I've done in the name of running after him, in the name of love.

So yeah, it doesn't make sense.

But then…

Doesn't it?

Because isn't that what people do with God as well? They don't know — not really — if He exists. They don't know if what they believe in is true or can be proven. But they still worship him. They still follow His word. They still follow scriptures and religion without being ashamed.

So why should what I felt for him be different?

Why should love be any different than worship?

As soon as the truth of it settles into my brain, my heart, into the crevices of my body, I know what I have to do. I know that I have to tell him.

The truth.

The whole truth this time.

Because I can't do it.

I can't do this to him. I can't exact revenge on someone who's not only made me realize something this important, this life-changing about myself but also who's already remorseful for what he did.

So we can't do this.

We need to stop.

I should leave and…

"And I wanted to tie her up in my bed," he says, bringing me back to the moment.

Urgently, I grab his t-shirt and say, "Ledger, I —"

"But do you wanna hear the worst part?" he asks, his eyes somehow both glazed over and alert.

"No, it doesn't matter. You —"

"The worst part is that even though I knew, right from the beginning, right from the day that I saw you, that you were the girl they write books about, I still would've done it. I still would've tied you up. I would've looked into your gray-blue eyes, into your *trusting* eyes, and I still would've wrapped your hands with a rope and tied you to my bed."

"No, Ledger —"

"And then," he licks his lips, "I would've asked you to smile for the camera."

"C-camera?"

"Yeah," he rasps. "I would've asked you to pose for it. Pose for *me*. And we both know that you would've done it. In a heartbeat."

"I would have," I tell him without hesitation, without any shame.

And it's amazing.

It's glorious.

It makes me wonder why I didn't do this before.

"And then I would've sent those pictures to your brother," he continues.

I expect myself to flinch.

I expect to feel anger, which is what I'd normally feel, or rather have felt for the past year.

But I don't.

It's not there. The anger. The fury.

Instead, I want to... soothe him.

I want to cup his ticking jaw — clean-shaven and sharp — and tell him that it's okay. It's okay if he wanted to do it because the important thing is that he didn't. Which I realize is stupid, because although he didn't do what he's describing, he did do *something*, right? He did act upon his revenge fantasy.

But then so what?

Honestly.

So he did come to my dorm room with the intention of using me to hurt my brother. He was angry and rightfully so; my brother had knocked up his sister and of course he was angry. I never blamed him for that, just for the record. I never blamed him for being angry. I only blamed him for not being able to control it and taking it out on me.

And while him being not being able to control his anger is an issue in and of itself that I'm not going to touch right now, maybe that night he just made a mistake. A bad judgement call and everyone deserves a second chance, right?

I mean, look at what I was going to do.

What I almost did.

So I let go of his t-shirt and go for his face. I cup his cheeks and open my mouth to tell him that it's okay. But he speaks first. "And then of course you would've realized what I'd done and you'd be heartbroken. You'd probably be crying. You'd ask me to let you go. You'd even beg and struggle, scream, kick. But I wouldn't. I wouldn't because..."

"Because what?"

He presses his palms on the wall, thereby pressing his body into mine, pressing his ribs into my tits. "Because I'm not done with you yet."

My breaths drag my nipple along his muscles. "You aren't?"

"No. That was for your brother, what I did. For the rivalry, for revenge. For *winning*. But now it's my turn. Now what I'm going to do is for me. For *my* eyes. No one else's. Even though like a motherfucker, I'd capture it on camera too."

"Capture what?"

"You."

"Me."

"Painted."

"P-painted?"

"With my cum."

I jerk then, a current running through my entire body.

From top to bottom.

Tingling my hair, tickling my throat. Scratching my tits and nipples, making my tummy clench. All the way down to my pussy and thighs and toes, all pulsing and throbbing.

"It's not the norm, you see," he says, his eyes looking into mine, "making a girl suck your dick the very first time you're together. Something my brothers used to say. Be patient, they'd tell me. Be mindful of what she wants. Go gentle. And as much as I hated being told what to do, I understood why. Girls are delicate, aren't they? They're fragile and vulnerable."

He sweeps his eyes all over my features, taking in my parted lips, my flushed cheeks.

Then, "And you're the most fragile of all. The most delicate. All silky soft, spun from sugar. Made of candies and cream. My Firefly. But I still would've stuck my dick down your throat and fucked it like it was my last moments on this earth. And I still would've come on your face, blown all over it like you were a whore."

I jerk again.

This time more violently than before.

And he notices.

His brows furrow and his body presses even closer to me. "But I don't want you to be afraid, Firefly. It's not because I think you're a whore, no. It's not because I don't value you, you understand. It's because I value you too much. It's because I treasure you too much. It's because I don't think I've ever wanted a girl to suck my dick the way I want *you* to. Like if you didn't wrap your lips around my cock, I'd die. Like if I didn't push my cock into your mouth and keep pushing it and pushing it until I reach the back of your throat, stretching not only your lips in the process but also your delicate throat, I'd die right here, right now. That's why. Tell me you understand that."

I nod.

Because I can't *not* nod my head.

Because it looks like he depends on my answer. His sanity depends on it. His very life depends on me understanding that even though he wants me to suck his dick like a whore, he still cherishes me.

And God, I already knew that.

I already knew that that's why he *has* to make me suck his cock like a whore.

Because he cherishes me too much.

Because when my Beautiful Thorn cherishes someone the way he does his Lovelorn Firefly, there's nothing left to do *but* treat her like the whore that I am for him anyway.

It's the purest form of cherishing.

The highest form of treasuring.

So I not only nod but also whisper, "I do. I do understand that."

"Good." He lets out a breath, swallowing thickly. "That's good. Because I wouldn't be able to take it. I wouldn't be able to take if you thought I was doing this because of anything other than that. If you thought me treating you like a whore is anything other than because I want to. And Jesus, I do. I fucking *do*. So fucking much. I want to hang your head over the edge of the bed. Just so it's easier to slide my dick all the way down your throat. Not only that, I also want to watch. I also want to *see* it happen. See how your slim throat swells up with my fat dick in it. I want to see how your heartbeat jacks up, how your freckle dances over your pulse as I choke you with my dick."

I'm struggling to breathe now.

And his dick is nowhere near my mouth.

Which I think is a travesty.

I think it's a gross miscarriage of justice and fairness.

Not only because he wants my mouth so much but also because I want to give it to him, my mouth, my throat.

My breaths.

"And that's because I've always wanted to choke you," he informs me. "I've always wanted to make you gag. I'm a guy, aren't I? I like messy blow jobs. I like it when a girl drools around my dick. I like it when it drips down her chin and pools in the triangle of her throat, in her cleavage. And you've got a fantastic cleavage, haven't you? So yeah, I've thought about it, your slim throat swelling up with dick and your saliva pooling in between your fat tits. But the main reason why I want you to struggle to breathe is because I've always thought it would be peaceful. Your choking sounds. Your whimpers and moans. I've always thought if I could control your breaths, control the air that goes into your body, control the beats of your cotton candy heart, it would give me peace. It would calm me down."

I want to tell him that he's already doing that.

He's already in control of me, my body, my heart and my breaths.

"So that's what I would do. Make you choke a little, maybe a lot. Make you gag on my cock, ruin your mascara, wreck your lipstick before I painted your pretty face with my cum. And when I'm done I'll ask you to look at the camera and stick your tongue out. So I can capture you. Your beauty. To keep forever. To carry with me everywhere I go. And all of this because I want to. No agendas. No ulterior motives. Just you and me."

Just him and me.

I want that too.

I want it so much that when he comes for my mouth, I don't stop him.

Even though I should.

Even though I should tell him that I do have an ulterior motive. I do have an agenda.

Or at least I did.

But with our mouths fused, when he picks me up and carries me over to his bedroom, I find that the only thing I'm capable of doing is letting him and kissing him back.

Chapter Twenty

I SHOULD TELL HIM NOW.

I know that.

Especially because we're in the bedroom and we're not kissing anymore. I'm in bed and he's standing at the foot of it. This is the perfect opportunity to say something, to tell him the truth and put a stop to this. Ask him to take me back to Bardstown because this was a mistake.

"I have..."

I trail off because he chooses this very moment to shed his t-shirt.

With his dark eyes pinned on me, he reaches back and snags his t-shirt. He yanks it up and over his head in one go and then I'm staring at his massive chest.

Massive and muscular.

Massive and muscular and *naked*.

Massive, muscular, naked and fucking beautiful.

It's more beautiful than I remember. More gorgeous than it was thirteen months ago, and trust me, it was plenty gorgeous back then. But it looks like he's bulked up even more over the last year. Which I did have a suspicion about, of course. I could sense that through his t-shirt, but here's the proof.

He *has* bulked up.

His shoulders have grown more corded and rounded. And his chest has grown more arched and wider so when it tapers down to his slim waist, the effect is more dramatic. The effect is fucking mind-blowing.

Not to mention, he has an eight-pack now.

Eight.

Not just six.

As if a six-pack is for losers and since he's such a soccer god, he needs to have eight.

And they need to be all tight and ridged and ladder-like.

Like I could put my dainty feet on them and use them to climb up his body. I could actually hold them in my hands, those dense and muscular bumps, like steel pipes or something.

This is not real.

No one has a body like that.

Not even him.

I mean just look at him. The guy not only has a perfect freaking body, he also has that glorious V that every girl goes crazy for. And well, I've always been one of those girls and now I can say that I always will be, because those grooves and indentations have only deepened and sharpened over the last year.

And as much as I don't want to look away from his beautifully built torso, I do.

Because if I'm following that V, I'm also following that trail of dark hair.

That starts at his tight belly button and disappears down his jeans.

Which then brings me to that bulge in his jeans.

Yes, the bulge.

Because he's hard.

Already.

Although I can't blame him because I'm wet too. Already. So I guess we're in the same boat. And then I feel a drop of wetness trickle down my core, wetting my already messy panties because his sexy, veined, dusted-with-dark-hair forearms go to his jeans and my eyes fly up to his to find him still watching me.

"W-what are you doing?" I ask stupidly.

Isn't it obvious what he's doing?

"Giving you your turn," he replies, his voice abraded.

"My turn at what?"

"Last time it was me. Who got to see you naked." My heart thuds and shudders as he keeps going. "But you never got to see me. So now it's your turn."

Tell him.

Tell. Him.

Now.

For the love of God, tell him now, Tempest, before he takes his pants off and totally fries your brain.

But I don't. I don't even open my mouth, or at least I don't open my mouth to form words. I open it for other things though. Such as for gasping and breathing out, "Holy fuck."

Because he's done it.

He's unbuttoned his jeans and he's pushed them down, and no.

Just no.

Absolutely not.

That is definitely, definitely not real.

What I'm seeing is not real at all.

It can't be.

His penis cannot be that big.

In fact I can't even call it a penis. As in, I know that's what a guy's thing is called but *his thing* can't be called that. His thing needs to be called a dick. A cock. A hammer or a baseball bat.

Because yes, it's long. So long that it could actually touch his belly button.

But that's not the worst part — or the best? The worst part is that it's thick.

It's so very thick.

That it's actually being pulled down by its own weight. So it sticks out from the thatch of dark hair, looking all ruddy and angry. Or maybe it's not the weight of his dick itself.

It's the weight of the other things.

That his dick is decorated with.

Like those piercings.

Or more like the horizontal bar-type thingies, three of them that look like a ladder.

I've seen dicks before, though yes, I've only seen them in porn as he so easily figured out the other night. And I will admit that I'm a fair porn enthusiast, but in all the years of me venturing into it, I don't think I've ever seen a pierced dick.

"W-what…" I clear my throat and realize that at some point in the last ten seconds of staring at his piercings and his baseball bat of a dick, I've moved closer to him. "What is that?"

"Jacob's ladder."

His voice is hoarse, as if he's having difficulty talking, but I don't care right now.

I'm more interested in the shiny, silvery things that I'm still staring at with wide eyes. "Have you… Have you always had it?"

"No."

"Did you have it, uh, last time?"

"No."

My hand reaches out on its own but I stop short of touching it.

I get super close though and I *think* I see it move, his dick.

"So when did you…"

"After that."

I move ever so slightly closer still and I definitely know that it jerked this time.

A tiny drop of something white oozes out of the head too and slides down the length of his hard rod.

It's cum, Tempest. Or pre-cum. Just call it what it is.

I know I'm just freaking out right now. At how fascinating this is. How beautiful his dick is with shiny little studs on it.

"Why?" I whisper, and I'm not even ashamed that it sounds reverential.

"Because I knew it would hurt."

My eyes fly up to his then.

And God, he's changed.

His features, his body.

His eyes.

They're black and yes, I've seen them grow dark this way but I've never seen them fraught with what I can only call so much lust and so much pain. And his cheekbones that are sharper and higher than ever. Plus his chest is rising and falling rapidly, like he can't get enough air.

And he's all sweaty.

Drops of sweat bead his forehead. I see another sliding down the side of his corded neck.

"Hurt?"

He nods but barely, as if that too is hard for him. "After what I did to you."

My wide eyes grow even wider. "What?"

"The guy gave me a couple of options. And I tried to pick the one that I thought would hurt the most."

"You did this on purpose?" I ask with hitched breaths.

Breaths just like his.

Fast and noisy.

"Had to. Getting beaten up in the boxing ring wasn't doing anything for me."

"You got beaten up?" Now my breaths are even louder than his. "On *purpose?*"

"Yeah." Another drop of sweat falls down the side of his face. "A few times."

"That's…"

"But as I said, they did nothing. And then I heard a couple of guys talking about it in the locker room and thought, why not." Then, shrugging tightly, "It hurt for a few seconds but… I don't think it helped either."

I study him then.

His severe and sweaty and flushed features. His dark eyes.

The body that's made of slabs of strained, almost vibrating muscles.

His power, his strength.

"You're crazy," I whisper.

His nostrils flare. "Better than being the asshole who made you cry and did nothing about it." Then, "Even if it was bare minimum."

I close my eyes. Then, "Ledger?"

He frowns slightly. "Yeah?"

Opening them, I say, very seriously and sternly so he knows that I mean it, "Choke me with your cock. *Now*."

He stares at me for a second before his features relax slightly and his lips twitch.

Which I think is a complete waste of time and the opposite of *now*. So I close the gap between us and attack him myself. And thank God, he's ready for me. Thank God, he captures my mouth, conquers it just the way I like it.

No, actually. *Thank God* that he doesn't stop there.

He doesn't stop at just kissing me.

He gets busy with other things too. Like pulling and tugging at my red dress, taking it off my body and throwing it away somewhere, followed by my annoying bra and my even more annoying panties. All the while only breaking the kiss for a few seconds here and there.

But that's not all.

Just like he's dominating my mouth with a hot and a wet kiss, complete with his tongue and teeth, he also dominates my now naked body. He fists my hair. He bends my neck. He bends my spine. He pushes me down on the bed and then he's rubbing himself on me.

Or is that me?

Am I the one rubbing myself on him? Am I the one going up and down and side to side and rubbing my heaving tits and my trembling belly on his naked body, my bare wet pussy against his dick?

I think so.

It's me.

I'm the one being slutty here. Whore-ish.

But I don't think he minds.

He did say that he wanted me to suck his dick like a whore.

But oh no, wait.

Didn't I just ask him to choke me with his cock? This doesn't feel like choking. This feels like we're heading toward the other thing. Fucking. With how I'm rocking under him and how he's settled between my thighs with his cock right there, pressed up against my hot wet pussy.

So I go about reminding him.

But in order to do that, we need to break the kiss first. Which is no easy task because he doesn't let me.

Every time I try to move away, he gives me more of his weight. He gives me more of his tongue and his sucks become harder, hungrier. So I have no choice but to push at him, his shoulders. I have no choice but to buck under him, which accomplishes the exact opposite because it fuses us together even more.

So finally, I take drastic measures and bite his lip.

He hisses and rears back, and I take my shot at getting away.

At which he growls and grabs my neck. "Stop trying to get away from me."

But I'm not getting away from him. Instead of telling him that, I get waylaid by the drop of blood on his lip. "You're... You're bleeding."

"It pisses me the fuck off," he growls again, his face dipped in anger.

My hands on his shoulders go to his face. "B-but I didn't mean to bite so hard. I —"

He tightens his grip on my neck. "Do you understand?"

I arch my neck up as I pant, "I-I'm sorry."

"Fuck your sorry and fuck that blood," he grunts, the drop of blood oozing down his lips. "Just tell me you won't try to get away from me."

I lick my lips in lieu of licking that drop off. "I wasn't." He growls again and I press my hands on his cheek. "I was just... I just wanted to say that you forgot to do something."

"Do what?"

I rock under him, feeling extremely shy and horny at the same time. "T-tie me to the bed."

He jerks over me, his muscles going taut. "What?"

"And make me suck your d-dick."

He stares down at me for a few seconds. Then, "Is that what I said I'd do? Make you suck my dick?"

I swallow under his grip. "N-no."

"So then what'd I say?"

"That you'd fuck my throat."

His fingers flex around my neck. "Exactly."

I rub my thighs on his hips, restless. "So —"

"And as eager as you are, tonight's not about that, is it?"

"But —"

Another flex of his fingers, his power over me. "Is it?"

"No."

"What is tonight about?"

"F-fucking."

His jaw clenches, that drop of blood down to his chin now. "No. Tonight's about me taking your tight little cherry."

I jerk under him, my pussy rubbing against his cock, making him grunt again. "O-okay."

"And leaving you with my cum in your freshly popped pussy."

"Ledger —"

"Tell me why."

I swallow again. "Because I... I want a baby."

His narrow slightly. "Yeah. Because you want a baby and I'm the guy who's going to put it in your trim little tummy."

He is.

I know that.

But the thing is that he still doesn't know everything and I should tell him. But then again if I did tell him, he might — definitely — will get angry and put a stop to this. And over the course of however many minutes since I decided that I should tell him to now, I've realized that… I want to do this.

I want to have sex with Ledger.

At least once.

Simply because I want to. No agendas. No ulterior motives. Nothing but me and him.

And we can do that tonight, right?

At least for one night we can be together without the past, without any history and definitely without the future.

So I let it go.

For now.

I nod. "Yes."

"So who am I then?"

"What?"

"Who *the fuck*," he insists, "am I, Firefly?"

My heart's banging in my chest as I say, "The guy who'll put a baby in my trim little tummy and m-make my dream come true."

"I am, aren't I? So I'm the one who's going to run the show now, you understand?" He pushes my head into the pillow some more, arching my neck up. "*I'm* the one who's going to decide where my big dick is going to go. Whether I choke your throat with it or use it to cream pie that pussy. All you have to do is stay where I put you and let me fuck the hole I want to, okay?"

"Okay."

Although I rock under him, breaking my word the very next second.

At which he narrows his eyes and I blurt out, "Can I please kiss you though?"

His jaw clenches again as if in irritation but a second later he lets me do it.

He lets me kiss him and lick his mouth. Lick his jaw and that drop of blood that he had to shed because of me. I know he doesn't care, I know he wants to hurt because of what he did to me, but I can't let him take another bite of pain.

Not anymore.

So we're kissing and licking and touching, sliding against each other.

Until I feel him right there.

Right at my entrance.

I look down and see him in position, those silver studs looking all shiny and wet with his pre-cum, maybe even my own juices that I realize are smeared all over my thighs. My thighs are sprawled and folded at the knees. And since they're on the bed, I wrap my legs around his tapered waist and settle my hands that were clutching the sheets on his biceps.

"It's time," he whispers.

"Okay," I whisper back.

"I'll go slow," he adds, frowning, fresh drops of sweat beading his forehead.

My hand goes up and I swipe those drops off, caressing his skin. "You don't have to."

His eyelids flutter closed and he clenches his jaw.

But I think that clench is strangely a sign of relief.

At my touch, my care.

Then, swallowing, he says, "People say it's better to do it quickly. Like ripping off a band-aid." He winces as if he knows how that feels, and he probably does from playing soccer all his life. "But after that."

"Okay."

"But I…"

"You what?"

"I won't stop."

"I know."

"If it hurts too much." Still frowning and dripping sweat, he says, "I don't think I'd be able to."

And still rubbing his frown away and caressing his forehead, I say, "It's okay."

He swallows thickly. "No, you don't understand. I… I haven't…"

"You haven't what?"

His biceps strain. As if from the effort it takes for him to stay up and detached from me. But given that he can carry me up four flights of stairs, I know it's something else. It's something more.

"What is it, Ledger?" I ask, my heart clenching in my chest.

"I haven't done this," he says, the veins standing up on his neck.

"What?"

"In three years."

"In th-three years?"

He grunts in response. As if that's all he had in himself. To give right now.

But I'm sorry to say I want more. I *demand* more.

"What do you mean," I ask urgently. "That you haven't done this in three years? You haven't had sex in three years?"

His chest shakes with his breath and all he manages to say, his words slurred, "Didn't think I deserved any pleasure," a breath puffs out of him, his dick lurching against my pussy, dripping pre-cum, "after how I kept treating you."

I shudder then.

My chest heaving, my belly hollowing out.

My thighs tightening around him.

"Do it," I tell him.

Not the most beautiful and dressed up words. Especially after what he told me. After what he's just revealed. The mind-boggling answer to all the questions I've had about whether or not he'd been with other girls. When I was running after him.

And honestly all of that seems so trivial now.

So petty and small.

In the face of this.

Him.

Hovering over me, barely able to hold on, shaking with need.

I writhe my hips under him, rubbing my pussy against his dick. "Put it inside me. It's because of me, isn't it, that you waited. It's because of me that you hurt yourself. And I know it couldn't have been easy. Not the pain but also the waiting. Especially since I kept throwing myself at you back then. How I wore all those tight dresses without any care, without any thought about you. I'd flaunt my tits, my ass, making you angry and horny. And today I wore red and tortured you the whole way here. Because it doesn't just provoke the bull, does it? It provokes you too. So do it. Fuck me. Now."

His nostrils flare.

His jaw clenches.

And with a growl and one powerful thrust of his hips, he does it.

He tears his way in. Forces and rips and lodges himself inside of me.

And I scream, throwing my head back, my body feeling like it's been set on fire.

I know I bleed as well.

There's no question about it.

I can feel it.

I can feel his dick — all thick and hard, studded with bars — puncturing my soft and slick and *tight* flesh, bruising it. And somehow setting it free in the same breath. Making me *somehow* gush blood and my cum in the same breath too.

Because nothing has ever been more painful and more beautiful than this.

Than his forced invasion.

It's strange, pain and beauty going together, but maybe not really. Nothing beautiful is ever made without enduring some pain first, isn't it? Whether it be the making of a star or a diamond. Whether it be birth of a new life or death of a girl's innocence.

So I'm happy.

I'm happy that it hurts and God, it hurts so bad that I know whatever it is we're making is going to be the most beautiful thing ever.

But he doesn't seem to think so.

Because there's agony on his face. Agony in every inch of his body. His breaths are shattered. His arms are shaking.

And his eyes are frantic.

His eyes are agitated and panic-stricken and he's chanting, "Fuck, fuck, fuck. I'm sorry. I'm sorry. I'm so fucking sorry, baby. I... My dick... My... Fuck, fuck, fuck..."

He would've gone on if I hadn't raised my head up and kissed the words out of him. Then, against his parted mouth, I whisper, "Don't be s-sorry."

His trembling hands are framing my face, wiping off my tears that I didn't even know I was shedding. "It hurts, doesn't it?"

My belly clenches as a fresh wave of pain washes over me. But all I say is, "But it's beautiful."

He presses his fingers on my cheeks. "It's fucking ugly. I-I made it ugly. I —"

"It's the most beautiful thing ever."

He stares at me for a few beats before shaking his head. "I'm pulling out."

"No, you're not. You're —"

I gasp when he tries to slide out and the pain flares once again, making my body tighten as a fresh batch of tears spills out.

Which makes him clench his teeth in anger. But I can see that there's pleasure too.

Because I guess it feels good to him.

The tightness of my pussy. The slick walls.

But he ignores it all to take care of me. To lick my tears off and whisper apologies all over my skin.

Closing my eyes, I whimper, feeling his dick throb inside of me, "You said you won't stop."

His chest heaves. "Because I'm an asshole. I didn't know what I was talking about."

"You did. You do. I don't want you to go a-away," I whisper, clutching his hair now.

"I guess I can't anyway," he says in between kisses. "You're fucking stuck on my dick."

I am.

Stuck and pinned.

Trapped.

And while I feel another wave of pain coming in, I still can't help but smile through my tears. "It's because I'm a Firefly."

He looks up, his tormented eyes flashing with possession, his dick throbbing even harder inside of me. "Yeah, you are."

"Your Lovelorn Firefly."

"My Lovelorn Firefly."

"And you're my Beautiful Thorn."

"I am."

"So then," I adjust my lower body, trying to ease up the pain, "m-make it fit."

His hand immediately goes down to my hips to stop me. "I will."

"Promise?"

"Promise."

He dips down to kiss me and then he sets about doing that.

He sets about making it fit, making us fit.

The Beautiful Thorn and his Firefly. Which at first glance may seem impossible, unnatural, us fitting together.

But it's not.

Not when he kisses me with his wet and hungry and hot mouth. Not when that kiss almost makes me forget that I've got a giant dick inside my tiny hole, stretching it out, putting pressure on my pelvis and making it burn.

And when he touches me, my clit, with his magical fingers, my almost-forgetting becomes complete.

It's like he's sucking the pain out of me.

Sucking the poison out not only with his mouth but also draining it out with his expert fingers.

And slowly I become delirious.

I become euphoric.

I become barely aware.

Of what I'm doing, of the things around me.

All I know is that I'm tasting cinnamon on my tongue. I'm breathing cinnamon too. I'm also scratching my nails along something smooth and long, muscular and arched, his back maybe or his obliques. My heels are running along something coarse, probably the backs of his hair-dusted thighs.

But most of all, I'm aware of this need.

This intense and potent need to move.

To grind and writhe under him.

I think this need has replaced my pain. Actually it hasn't just replaced it, it's grown bigger than the pain ever was.

So much bigger and incessant and urgent.

So I do.

I move and holy fuck, I think I see stars.

And so I move again and there it is once more: a flash of stars and bright light.

I guess he was right then. His dick is magic. It's out of this world.

And God, the friction.

There's a friction too, down there, that I haven't felt before. That makes me moan into his mouth, and I wonder if it's those studs. Those ladder-like beautiful studs that he got to punish himself for hurting me.

That are now giving me this otherworldly experience.

This immense pleasure.

Poetic pleasure even.

His pain turning into my pleasure.

And oh my God, I want more.

I want more of his poetry. I want more of his artistry, his beauty that he created for me.

So I keep moving. I keep undulating and writhing. And it's so easy too. So *easy* to move under him.

So effortless.

It's almost like we're sliding against each other. Gliding and slipping.

As if we're in a dream.

And in this dream, not only has he made it so that his dick fits in my pussy but he's also somehow made our bodies fit too. His hips fitting into the juncture of my thighs, his pelvis grinding into mine. My heavy breasts and tight nipples sliding into place just under his arched pecs. My thighs settling in the nook of his tapering waist and my heels digging into his muscular, flexing ass.

And before I know it, something starts to build in my belly.

Especially where my belly button is.

Something tight and swollen.

Something that can be called an orgasm.

Only this isn't mild like the orgasms that I've given myself in the past. Or ordinary.

This is something else.

A thunderstorm. A hurricane.

A bright flash of falling stars.

At which point, my eyes pop open and I come back to the world, and I realize that none of what's happening is a dream.

We *do* fit together. It *is* easy to move against him. It is easy to push back against his relentless strokes. And holy God, his dick is hitting spots inside of me that my small fingers never did. My vibrator never did, even, and this is definitely the work of those ladder-like studs.

Definitely.

Not to mention, he's stopped kissing me now.

Instead, he's watching me.

And he's doing that with a ferocity that matches this thing that's swirling in my belly.

This thing that feels scary.

So much so that I hold onto him tighter. Especially when his thrusts become just as ferocious and the scariness of this all ratchets up ten-fold.

"L-Ledger…" I gasp, my eyes wide. "I think I…"

A drop of sweat from his hard-working body plops down in between my breasts. "Do it."

I shake my head frantically. "I d-don't… I can't."

"Squirt on my dick, Firefly."

Squirt?

I can't squirt. I've never squirted before.

I keep shaking my head. "I'm scared. I'm…"

Still thrusting inside of me, he comes even closer and whispers against my parted lips, "I'm here."

"I —"

"I'll keep you safe."

So that's when I do it.

I come on his dick.

No, I squirt.

Because he said he'd keep me safe.

My cum bursts out of me as that pressure in my belly pops. And it's brutal. Violent. It's like an exorcism that makes me throw my head back and scream up to the ceiling, up to the sky. It makes my back arch up too. Plus I think my legs are shaking. My belly is pulled tight like a drum, but even so I can't stop my pelvis from rocking and thrusting and God, coming.

I can't stop coming.

Or holding on to him, his shoulders, clutching them and clawing at them.

And he's holding on to me back.

He's keeping me grounded with a hand on my hips and the other around my neck.

Safe.

I'm so safe like this. Under his domination. His relentless thrusts.

It's the most ferocious experience of my life. Most thunderous experience.

And no wonder he's the one giving it to me.

The thunder itself.

My Thorn.

Who in the next second, comes as well.

With hard but erratic thrusts and his head thrown back, he comes inside of me.

His cock throbs and pulses inside my slick and swollen channel.

As it fills me with his cum.

Fills me and fills me with his life-giving cum.

Fills me to the point that I feel it overflowing, smearing my thighs, the sheets. And I close my eyes and pray. I pray that despite everything, it takes root. It latches on inside of me and gives me a piece of him.

Of the guy made of thorns and thunder.

Of the guy I used to love.

It's the most selfish thing that I've ever done, that I've ever wished for, but I can't help it.

I can't help it that when he comes down from his high, I kiss him back with everything that I am.

And when he finishes kissing me and goes down my body to lap up the sprinkled juices, I can't help but moan and let him. I can't help but let him suck on my tits and my soft belly. I can't help but think that maybe he's doing more than that. He's sucking on my juices, drinking them from my belly button, but he's also imagining and praying for things like me.

For his seed to take root in my womb and give him a little piece of me.

Chapter Twenty-One

Her Beautiful Thorn

SHE'S SLEEPING.

Completely dead to the world.

I guess I tired her out.

Both by the animalistic way I fucked her and then by the bath I drew for her.

To soothe her aches and soreness.

I'm not going to lie, I've always been proud of my dick, its size and its girth. And I mean that in a very vain and immature way. In a way where you strut around the locker room looking self-important because you're an arrogant asshole. And when I got it pierced, somewhere in the back of my mind I had this very hypothetical idea of giving her pleasure at the cost of my pain.

And yes, I felt proud about that too.

Proud that I could take the pain — although it turned out to be extremely underwhelming — and that if I ever got a chance, if I ever got *lucky enough*, to get near her sweet pussy, I'd blow her mind.

Although I think she blew *my* mind.

With how tight she was. How small and soft.

Like velvet.

And even if I could've imagined her tightness on the account of being untouched, I never ever would've imagined that she'd be a squirter.

I groan, raking a hand over my face, still watching her sleep.

I need that again. I have to have that again.

Her cum spilled all over me, her body both tight and shaking uncontrollably.

Her screams filling up my head, giving me peace.

And that's what makes you an asshole, doesn't it?

Because look at what I'm doing right now.

She's sleeping on her back, her freshly dried hair sprawled over the pillow, her eyelashes casting shadows over her pale cheeks. I didn't let her wear clothes after her bath and she was so out of it that she didn't argue. So there's a blanket covering her body from my eyes, which I don't like much but it's okay.

She looks so trusting right now, her fingers lightly curled, one hand by her cheek and the other on her tight but soft belly.

I shouldn't do this.

I shouldn't take the hand by her cheek and raise the arm up. I shouldn't loop the rope I brought around her wrist and the slat like I told her I've wanted to. I definitely shouldn't do the same to her other arm as well.

Thinking about it hypothetically and doing it are two different things.

When her arms are secure by the knot that's not too tight so as to dig into her wrists while she sleeps and has enough give that she can move her arms without getting free, I straighten away from her.

I watch her for a few seconds all because I can't take my eyes off of her.

In my bed. Tied up and naked.

How many times have I imagined that over the years?

A million times probably.

But this isn't for that. I'm not tying her up for myself. Not doing it for some sick fantasy.

Where I keep her locked up in the bedroom, tied and naked, and fill her with my cum whenever I want to. Where I watch her and care for her as she grows swollen with my baby. And when she pushes one baby out, I put another in her belly. And I keep doing it and doing it until we grow old together.

Jesus.

Don't think about that. Do not think about that right now, you sick fuck.

I'm doing this because she's lying to me.

She's hiding something from me.

I'm doing this to force the truth out of her.

To scare her a little. To intimidate her into telling me what the fuck is really going on. And because I feel like she's going to run away. Maybe I'm being paranoid but I need to know, and so far she hasn't volunteered the information on her own.

So this is a quick fix.

I'm not kidnapping her or keeping her here as a prisoner.

There's no keeping her, period.

She isn't mine to keep.

Never was. Never will be.

So yeah.

I climb into the bed with her then, naked and hard. Not going to do anything of course; not after the pounding her pussy took only an hour ago. Just want to hold her and sleep.

Just want to put my hand in her belly, settle it where her belly button is.

Her womb.

And when I do that, I close my eyes and hope.

I hope that even though there can't be anything between us, I want this.

I want a baby.

I want to leave a little piece of me inside her. So I can get a little piece of her.

To care for and cherish forever.

Chapter Twenty-Two

THE FIRST THING I see when I wake up is the expanse of his chest.

Gently moving up and down with his breaths.

All smooth and rippling flesh.

Sleepy flesh.

I think he looks darker first thing in the morning, all flushed with heat and slumber.

I also think that I can't *believe* the way I fell asleep last night that I didn't even realize that he was sleeping beside me. I didn't even realize — until now — that his heavy arm is thrown around my waist and our heads are so close together that we're sharing one pillow, with me on my back and him turned toward me.

His lower half is covered with the blanket, the same one that I've got on. But I can see a slight peek of his happy trail, that fucking amazing V and oh my God, the tight globe of his ass. You know how when a guy's ass is so muscular and tight that it has dips on the sides?

Yeah, I think he definitely has that.

And it makes me swallow and move my thighs restlessly against each other.

Which in turn makes the soreness between my legs flare up and I wince.

"You hurting still?"

The question is asked in a deeply hoarse voice and my eyes fly up to find that his are open and clear.

Meaning he's been up for a while.

"You're up," I whisper, taking in his features.

Even though it looks like he's been awake a while, his features are still relaxed and flushed with sleep. His hair's all messy — messier than usual —

waves falling over his forehead with abandon. His mouth is softer than it's ever looked before.

God, he's beautiful.

"Thank you for the bath last night," I whisper shyly, looking down to his throat. "I was so completely out of it that I didn't get to —"

"Tell me how much."

I lift my eyes then, noticing a frown marring his relaxed features. "It's not —"

"Tell me how much it hurts."

I know he isn't going to like that answer.

But I also know that he isn't going to let his go so I reply, going down to his throat again, "A little."

His arm over me squeezes my waist in a silent command to look up. "How much is a little?"

I do look up but it's not easy. "Not a lot."

His jaw clenches. "Tempest."

Now I frown. "Hey, you never call me by my name."

"What?"

"You always call me Firefly," I tell him.

"And?"

I keep frowning. "You calling me Tempest like that, all low and growly. Is that your way of telling me that I'm in trouble?"

His arm squeezes my waist again. "That's my way of telling you to answer the fucking question."

"I don't think I appreciate your tone, Ledger," I say, just to be difficult.

"I don't give a fuck."

"You should if I'm going to be…"

The breath gets knocked out of me at what I was going to say.

The mother of your child.

I was going to say that.

And I have no right to, right?

I mean I still haven't told him the truth. And I had so many opportunities last night to spill my guts. But I chose to hold my silence. All because I wanted to have sex with him. All because I knew that if I told him, he was going to put a stop it and quite possibly hate me forever.

And despite all that, I prayed for a baby last night.

I prayed that his seed will take root and that I do get to have a piece of him.

God, I'm so selfish.

He moves his arm from around my waist and slides it down to my stomach.

He settles his palm on my lower belly and splays his fingers wide, pressing the heel into my pelvis, making me arch up. Then, moving up on his elbow so he can lean over me, making himself my entire vision, "And you should tell me the truth if I'm going to be the father of your baby." I flinch but he keeps going, "Which is going to happen, *Tempest*, isn't it? I'm going to put a baby in your belly." He digs his heel even more deeply into my soft flesh and my spine bows even more. "Right here. In this spot. This is where your womb is, isn't it?"

"L-Ledger, I…"

Without easing the pressure, he rubs it, my pelvis, and oh my God, why does that make me all swollen down there?

Why does it make me rock my hips and press my thighs together?

"You know how big my dick is now, don't you? Really. You know that if I put my mind to it, if I really fucking work for it, I can get it this high up. I can fucking get it this deep, right at your womb. And I can fill it up. I can fill it up with so much cum, Tempest, that you won't be able to hold it. Like last night, I'll run out of you like a river, smearing your thighs, pooling on the sheets. But it won't matter, will it? Because whatever escapes, I'll just put it back in. So I can still leave you full of me. Full of my dick, my cum, my fucking baby. So you better tell me the truth."

I'm undulating at his words.

Rocking my hips up and down, twisting them side to side, even though I feel all sore and achy.

My arousal for him is bigger than any little discomfort lingering from last night.

My arousal seems even bigger than the problem at hand.

The truth.

I know he isn't asking about the big bombshell of a truth that I'm hiding from him — he can't, can he? — but it still feels like it. But instead of being smart and brave, like he told me last night I was, I whisper, "It… I hurt. Down there. It's not as bad as it was last night but I do feel it. When I move too much."

He watches me for a few seconds, something unreadable on his face.

Unreadable but harsh that makes him breathe out sharply.

It also makes his jaw all firm and set in stone almost.

Then, he gives me a sharp nod. "So then you're not going to move."

With that, he gets up from the bed.

All naked.

His tight, muscular ass with those dips on the sides — yes, he has them — on full display. In addition to his back and shoulder blades. They're rippling, moving, twitching and all he's doing is walking to the bathroom.

I keep lying down and simply raise my head a little to try to see him as I ask, "What are you doing?"

The door to the bathroom is partially open but I can't see him.

I hear him though.

The sound of him peeing, and I have to press my thighs together again. Because I'm hit by how intimate this is: him peeing with the door half open. So intimate that I don't think even girlfriends and boyfriends do this. At least not in the beginning of a relationship. I think this is reserved for married couples, or couples who have been together for years and years.

The fact that he's doing it now, all shamelessly, fills me with something very akin to joy.

Also lust.

Which is not good because I need to focus.

And tell him.

I hear the flush then and the tap comes on. Which is when he says, "You'll eat. You'll take meds and then you'll go to back to sleep."

I frown. "Why?"

He doesn't answer for a couple of minutes. Probably because he's brushing his teeth, freshening up or whatever. Again, something so normal and so intimate. Something that makes me move restlessly under the sheets despite the soreness.

Then, appearing at the door, he declares, "Because you need to rest."

"Oh."

That comes out breathy and totally without thought.

Because he's still naked. And because I'm busy staring at the front of him. Not his chest or his arms though. I mean, they're beautiful and all but I've seen them plenty of times.

I'm more focused on his dick.

Holy fuck.

In the light of day, I think it looks even more intimidating. It looks like a tree trunk, so heavy and ruddy and veiny. No wonder I'm so sore. Even half hard and resting against his thigh, it looks so large and powerful. Plus those ladder-patterned studs. They make it more rugged but beautiful.

"Stop fucking staring at it," he snaps, still standing at the threshold.

My eyes jump up to look at his face. "It's so big."

His eyes narrow. "If you don't stop staring at it, it's gonna get bigger."

"Like, huge."

He sighs in response and walks further into the room. I turn my head on the pillow to watch him go to the chest and open a drawer.

"Has it always been this way?" I ask out of curiosity as he retrieves a pair of gray sweatpants. When he silently starts to put them on, I continue, "I mean like, were you born this way, with a larger than average sized penis?" He's done putting his pants on but still hasn't said a word. As he slams the drawer shut, I ask, "Is it heavy? Does it like, move around when you walk? Can you hold it with one hand? Do you need *both* your hands to hold it?"

He turns to face me. "No, but you would."

"I would what?"

"Need both your *baby* hands to hold it."

I ignore his condescending comment and ask, "Do they make condoms your size?"

"We don't need to worry about condoms now, do we?"

"Do you think if they did, they'd name it quadruple X or something? For measurement purposes, of course."

"How about we find that out by sticking it in your mouth and measuring it against your gag reflex."

"That's why you're always bragging about your dick, isn't it?"

"If it keeps hurting you every time I stick it in your pussy, then I don't think I've got anything to brag about."

Swallowing, I bite my lip. "It's just that I've never seen a dick this big."

"You've never seen a dick other than mine, period."

"Not even in porn."

"Fuck porn. You don't need porn now that you've got me."

"Do you think every guy —"

"You're not allowed to think about other guys."

My belly flip-flops. "And the girls? They —"

"I have no interest in thinking about other girls."

My belly flip-flops harder. "Were you serious?"

"About what?"

"That you hadn't slept with anyone for three years."

His jaw tics. "What do you think?"

"I can't believe you did that."

His jaw tics again.

"No one does that."

"I do it," he says then.

"It doesn't even happen in romance books."

"Then maybe you should read different books."

I open my mouth to say something.

But my words seem to have gotten stuck on the tip of my tongue. And there are two reasons for it.

One, I realize that I'm naked. Something that I should've clued in to way before this, but I guess I had lust-colored glasses on. And the reason I realize this now is because I make my first attempt to sit up ever since I woke up, causing my cozy little blanket to slide down my body. And when I go to catch it, I run into the second reason.

This being that I can't.

Catch it I mean.

Or at least not as easily as I would've liked.

Because my arm is stuck. Both my arms are stuck.

And while they're stuck with enough of a give that I do manage to solve my blanket predicament, my main problem still remains: both my arms are stuck to the bed.

No, they're *tied* to the bed.

With a rope.

Looped around my wrists and those slats that we were talking about last night.

I stare down at them for a couple of seconds. Trying to make sense of what I'm seeing. Trying to determine whether or not this is real.

Even after attempting to understand it though, I don't.

I have no clue as to why I'm seeing what I'm seeing.

So I look up at him in confusion. "What... What is this?"

He, on the other hand, looks calm. He looks completely unaffected, the opposite of confused. He even goes so far as to lean his hips against the dresser, crossing his arms across his muscular chest as he replies, "A rope."

The fact that he's so blasé about everything is making me even more confused.

And scared.

Then twisting my tied-up wrists that I can only bring forward slightly, I ask, "Why is it tied around my wrists?"

"You shouldn't do that," he says.

"Shouldn't do what?"

He jerks his lightly stubbled jaw to point to my wrist. "Twist your wrists like that. The knot's loose enough not to leave any marks but you shouldn't push your luck."

Right.

Okay, so he's giving me advice about the rope.

It makes me even more scared.

Because I don't think...

Oh God, let me breathe for a second.

I don't think this is an accident or a joke or done without purpose.

"My luck," I murmur, dread squeezing my heart.

"Yes."

"Can you explain to me though, how I pushed my luck anyway so that I ended up tied to your bed?"

Something menacing flashes through his eyes. "You ended up tied to my bed because I don't want you to go anywhere."

"And where is it you think I'm going to go that you had to tie me up?"

"That's what I intend to find out."

Okay.

Okay, just relax.

I'm sure there's a good explanation for this.

Although so far he hasn't given me any.

But it's okay. It's fine.

Just stay calm, I tell myself.

Then, clutching the sheet tightly under my arms, "Ledger, what *the fuck* is going on?"

Needless to say that didn't sound very calm just now.

But I don't really care.

I need him to give me a straight answer or I'm going to lose my mind.

"Sucks, doesn't it?" he murmurs then, his voice soft. "Not knowing."

"What are you talking about?"

His jaw clenches, his biceps flexing. "I'm talking about the truth."

"What?"

"That you still haven't given me."

I flinch.

Then deflate.

As if with his words, he'd popped a balloon inside of me and all my anger fizzes out.

The only thing that remains is the guilt.

Which I think is easy for him to notice on my face. Because he says, "You haven't, have you?"

I swallow and shake my head. "No."

He moves his jaw back and forth, watching me and watching me. Then, "So let's hear it then."

So this is it.

The time is here to tell him the truth, and I realize that the guilt is not the only thing that is inside of me.

There's also sadness.

Abject misery.

A deep, dark well of it.

Because once I tell him, this will be over.

This thing between us.

Because he's going to hate me, isn't he?

I'm the girl who was going to use him.

I was going to make a fool out of him and leave him behind when my purpose was over. And even though I'd already decided not to do that, I still should've told him before we had sex.

I got selfish and greedy and God, I deserve his wrath and hatred and whatever else he chooses to give me.

My heart twisting in my chest, I begin, "Well, you already know that I want a baby. You know that I want to move on and live my life. Free of you, I mean. Free of heartbreak and sadness and… and all that. But I… I wasn't going to tell you if and when I got pregnant. I wasn't going to tell you that there's a baby. Ever."

Pin drop silence meets my confession.

Which isn't what I was expecting at all.

I don't know *what* I was expecting exactly, but him watching me with a blank expression was not it. It's as if he didn't hear me at all. Or maybe he did but didn't really grasp the meaning of what I'm telling him.

So I go on, insisting, "I was going to lie to you. The second I found out that I was pregnant, I was going to break off our relationship and leave. And never ever, *not ever*, tell you that we made a baby together. I-I was going to disappear for a while and come back when I had the baby. And I was going to…" I'm cringing, *absolutely fucking cringing*, on the inside, "pass it off as another man's."

Yes, that was exactly what I was going to do.

And when I did come back, I would've come back married and telling everyone that the baby belonged to my new husband Ezra.

Although that's not my immediate concern right now.

My stupid, naive, revenge plans.

I'm more concerned about the fact that he still hasn't shown any reaction. He still hasn't moved or twitched or flexed a single muscle in his body.

"And I wanted to do that, I wanted to lie to you and use you and leave you, because I wanted revenge. I wanted to teach you a lesson. I wanted you to know what it felt like when someone dupes you and uses you for their own purposes. I guess I thought if I did to you what you did to me, I'd finally get closure. I'd finally stop feeling so foolish and stupid for the way I ran after you. I'd finally… move on.

"But then I realized something. Actually *you* made me realize it. Last night. You made me realize that I have nothing to be ashamed of. I have nothing to feel stupid for. Because all I did was listen to my heart. All I did was go after something — someone — that I loved. And I was brave to do that. I was brave to put myself out there, to go for what I want, to love you to the point of recklessness. And bravery does require that, doesn't it? Recklessness and thoughtlessness. If we always listen to our survival instinct, no one would ever scale a mountain or dive into an ocean. If we always kept protecting ourselves, we'd never venture into the unknown. No one would ever change the world, either their own or someone else's. No one would ever create something, invent something, discover something. No one would ever fall in love. And I don't think I want to live in a world like that. A world without the romantics and the dreamers, the poets, the storytellers. Anyway, I needed that. I needed to hear that. *That's* what I needed. To be able to move on. To get closure. To… get my life back, and you did that for me, Ledger. You…"

I sigh, my eyes stinging. "I used to think that what you did was unforgivable. That it was the most horrible thing that anyone had ever done to me. And that may be true, but I also think that you're not alone. In acting out your anger. I'm the same. And I've been angry for so long, you see. I've been angry and bitter and just *miserable*. For so so long. And I don't want to be angry anymore. I don't want to hate you anymore. I'm *done* hating you. I'm done looking back. I'm done.

"I guess I put you on a pedestal. Back then. I thought you were this perfect guy and I thought you could do no wrong, but that's not fair to you. You're human. You make mistakes just like the rest of us. And so I forgive you. For whatever you did. For however you treated me. Not only that night but before that too. I forgive you for everything, Ledger."

Until I said it all out loud, I hadn't realized how true each word is.

I did put him on a pedestal. I did expect too much from him. I expected him to give up his lifelong issues for me, his anger, his ego. His rivalry with my brother. I expected him to choose me over his forever dream of soccer. And while anger is never a good thing and revenge and rivalry will only hurt you in the end, I had no right to expect him to change all of that for me.

If he ever wants to change, he needs to do it for himself.

Not for anyone else.

So I guess it's time to put the past to rest. It's time to grow up and accept that I was too young for him back then and he was too angry for me. And that it's for the best that we never came together.

Some stories are just not meant to be love stories. And our story is one of them.

But our story doesn't have to be a hate story either.

Although it may not be in my hands anymore. After what I just told him, there's no way that he doesn't hate me or isn't angry with me.

I don't know what he's thinking right now though.

I don't know what's going through his head.

"Anyway it's not about that. It's not about the past. Not anymore at least. I know I should've told you all this, last night. Before we had sex, and I was going to but… But I got scared. And selfish. I wanted to have one night with you. Where it was just you and me and nothing else. But I guess I was wrong. Because we did have something else in between and I put it there: my lie. And all I can say is that…" I pause to take a shaking breath in. "I'm sorry. I'm so fucking sorry, Ledger. I know it's not enough and I don't expect you to accept my apology. When I didn't accept yours. But I wish I hadn't done what I did or what I was planning to do. I guess I got too caught up in revenge and hate and I twisted it all up in my head. It's not an excuse but it's all I have. I think it would be best if I just left. I shouldn't have come here in the first place. I shouldn't have —"

"No."

"What?"

Finally I see a movement on him: his feet shifting and his spine going even straighter.

It's hardly anything but I'm glad that it's there.

I'm glad that he's responding.

For some reason it's better than his absolute silence so far.

"You're not going anywhere."

I blink. "But… But I just told you that —"

"I know what you told me," he cuts me off. "That still doesn't change the fact that you're not going anywhere."

"I don't —"

"Just because you wanted to punish me doesn't mean that you shouldn't get what you want," he states, his voice sounding determined. "What you've always wanted."

All I can do is breathe in this moment.

Breathe and blink at him.

Because I wasn't... I definitely wasn't expecting that.

He stares at me for a few seconds as if collecting his thoughts before saying, "I don't blame you for wanting revenge. I *get* revenge. Revenge is the only thing I get and I admire you for wanting that. I admire the fuck out of you for wanting to put me in my place. So no, you're not going anywhere because I intend to keep my promise. I *intend* to give you your dream." Then, "I broke your dream once, I'm not going to do that again."

That finally gets me speaking. "But my dream wasn't your responsibility. I just told you that. I just told you that I put you on a pedestal and Ledger, you don't have to —"

"I have to and it is," he says, determination lined not only in his voice but also on his features, all over his hard body. "My responsibility. My job."

I watch him for a few seconds because I don't know what else to do.

I don't know what I can do except memorize his sun-drenched features, the shadows and grooves of his bare chest, the exact shade of his bronzed skin, those gray sweatpants both loose but still somehow molded against his strong thighs. That messy, crazy hair. Those dark eyes.

He's too beautiful to be true.

What he's saying is too beautiful to be true as well.

"So then..." I swallow. "We're... We're doing this?"

"We are."

I'm still stunned.

I'm still in quite possibly the biggest shock of my life but I have enough life left in me, enough hope, that I start to smile.

Until he says, "Was it going to be him?"

"What, who?"

He unfolds his arms and brings them down to his sides, his fingers immediately fisting. The veins running up and down his forearms immediately standing taut and tight. Threateningly.

How veins can be threatening, I don't know.

But his are.

And so are his fierce eyes, his clamped jaw.

As if he was waiting for everything else to be settled first, the truth, his promise, before getting to this. To whatever it is that he's asking me.

Which I understand when those fierce eyes of his drop down to my belly.

Looking up a second later, he goes, "Was it going to be that fuckface from the restaurant?"

Fear curdles in my belly. "L-Ledger —"

"It was, wasn't it?"

I shake my head. "It doesn't —"

His jaw clenches and clenches. "The guy you were going to pass off as the baby's father."

"I —"

"*My* baby's father."

Shit.

Shit, shit, shit.

Jesus fucking shit.

How does he know?

How does he fucking know?

And God, God, I can feel it. I can feel the air turning. I can feel it buzzing and growing heavy.

With his anger.

With his fury that appears to be mounting and mounting.

And I try get up on my knees, which is also when I realize that I'm still tied up. But thrusting that away, I hasten to explain, "But it doesn't matter. It doesn't matter who it was going to be or... or anything like that. I'm not going to do that, Ledger. I'm not going to keep your baby away from you. I won't *ever* keep her away from you. I won't —"

My words come to a screeching halt when he pushes away from the dresser.

When he takes me in, my flushed face, my heaving form, my tied-up hand, as if for the last time before leaving the room.

Before leaving *me* here.

"What are you doing?" I ask, frantic. "W-where are you going?"

My words don't stop him from turning and heading toward the door and my voice becomes even louder and shriller. "Ledger, where the fuck are you going? Where —"

He stops at the threshold. "I'm going to get you breakfast. And some pain meds."

It sounds so bizarre.

So crazy in the face of everything that's happened. In the face of his anger that I can still detect on his features.

In the air.

Not to mention, the fact that I'm still tied up.

"What... You're..."

"As I said, you're going to eat and then rest. Save your strength."

"Save my strength for what?"

"For the things I've got planned for you —"

"You're being crazy."

"And your ovulation window," he finishes his sentence that sounds more like a threat.

Dread has permanently made a home in me now. In my chest. My belly.

And I can't help but pull at the rope. Twist my wrists, trying to break free.

His response to that, in a very matter of fact tone, only makes it worse. "I told you not to do that."

"You told me? You…" I take a deep breath. "Untie me. Now."

"No."

"Ledger," I tell him, my entire body shaking. "Untie me *right now*." When he simply keeps staring at me, I continue, "You can't *leave*. You can't —"

"While I appreciate the spirit of revenge and deserve every bit of it from you, I'm also not going to let you fuck me over."

"But I just told you I'm not—"

"Yeah, I'm having a little trouble believing you."

"God, Ledger. Please, okay?" I pull at the rope again. "Let's talk about this. Let's —"

"As much as I enjoy bantering with you and your constant babbling, I think I'm going to pass. Because I don't think we've got anything to talk about. We —"

"That's not true," I burst out, straining against the rope. "That's not… We do have things to talk about. We —"

"Because what we came here to do doesn't involve a lot of talking, does it? It does involve your mouth though. But only to the extent where I tell you to open it so I can stick my dick in and throat-fuck you like the treasured, cherished whore you are." I go to say something but he gets there first. "But I don't want you to worry, yeah? I'll still nut where I'm supposed to. Can't waste my load down your throat when I'm saving it for your fertile little pussy, can I?"

I try to speak but again, he gets there first. "But if you interrupt me again while I'm talking, I may have to change tactics and come down your throat after all. Just to teach you a lesson. Which can start right now if you like. Instead of breakfast and soothing your hurting cunt, I can give you a belly full of my cum and a sore fucking throat. And since you're tied up, you won't be able to do anything about it. So I suggest you shut your fucking mouth, keep the talking to a minimum and be a good girl for me. Or you won't get my cum where you really want it."

Chapter Twenty-Three

Her Beautiful Thorn

I SHOULDN'T HAVE DONE that.

I shouldn't have tied her up in the first place and then left her there, screaming and crying.

It takes running about seventeen laps around the woods and chopping enough wood to last through this winter, if not the next, for my anger to calm down.

I knew it.

I *knew* before she even told me that she'd been hiding something similar. I knew that whatever it was, it would make her run. Take her away from me. Not that she's mine to keep, but yeah. And I wasn't lying when I said that I understand her need for revenge. I even admire that she tried to put me in my place.

I deserve nothing less.

What I *don't* deserve is her forgiveness.

Especially when she doesn't even know what my true crime is. She doesn't even know that I had something far worse than revenge on my mind that night. That I wanted to trap her. Wanted to entwine her life with mine, tie her to my selfish, sorry ass. Despite *knowing* that I've got nothing to give in return.

But that's not important right now.

What's important is that she'd go to him. She'd all but admitted that.

If she left here, she'd go to that little shitstain from the restaurant.

Someone *better* than me.

Someone who hasn't hurt her the way I have. Someone who knows how to take care of her, who knows how to love her the way she wants to be loved, the way she wants to be cherished. Someone better to give her the dream that she's been harboring all her life. Someone whose life, whose career isn't such a mess.

And I can't let her do that.

I can't let her go to him.

Not yet.

One day, yes. But not now.

Not until I give her her dream.

And hopefully by then, I will have figured out a way to let her go. But yeah, not now.

And speaking of career, I need to do something.

It's something that I've been thinking about ever since I brought her here.

Actually even before that.

Maybe the night she told me about her dreams and I decided that I'd be the one to give them to her.

Standing under the afternoon sun, sweat dripping down my neck and my bare chest, I whip out my cell phone from my running pants and dial the number that I've dialed countless times before but never thought I'd be dialing it again so soon.

Especially after avoiding his calls and texts for weeks.

He picks up after one ring as if he's been waiting for my call all this time.

"Ledger," he says by way of greeting. "Is everything okay?"

I grit my teeth.

Both at hearing his voice after weeks and weeks, and the concern in his tone.

My oldest brother Conrad and I have never gone this long without talking before. Even when our mother was alive and he was away at college, he'd call home every two to three days to check up on us. Mostly because our mom was sick during those months, but also because that's who he is.

He's responsible.

He's a caretaker. A guardian.

And he'd make it a point to talk to each one of us.

And then when we all scattered around and went away for college, he'd still carried on that ritual and called up individually every week. All his calls always started with 'is everything okay?' As if some invisible danger always lurks around us Thornes. Although when he asks me this question, he usually means, 'is everyone *around me* okay?' Or have I broken any new bones lately.

Ignoring the twinge of longing at his voice and my irritation at his age-old question, I say, "Yes, everything is okay." Then, "*Everyone* around me is fine too."

I hear him sigh.

Something else that he does a lot when I'm around.

Sighing and breathing deep.

Sometimes praying for patience. Other times irritated and annoyed.

This one's irritated as he says, "I've been calling you. We all have been."

"Yeah, I know. Stellan told me when he showed up at the house last week. I'll tell you the same thing that I told him."

"Which is what?"

"I lost my phone."

Another sharp, *irritated* breath. "You think this is a joke?"

"Holy shit. He said the same thing." I let out a humorless chuckle. "Well, then I told him —"

"Enough."

I grit my teeth at his tone.

I grit my teeth harder when he speaks. "I don't fucking need a blow by blow of your conversation with Stellan. I already know what happened and what a dumb little shit you are who isn't done fucking around yet." And then maybe because he can't stop himself, he keeps going. "You do understand that everything you've worked for is hanging by a thread right now? That the board isn't happy with you? You're losing endorsements left and right and the press is going nuts about that. Pretty soon, no amount of PR damage control is going to help you. The team's going to drop you to save their own asses and you'll be left with nothing. Everything that you've worked for, everything that we fought so hard to give you, me, Stellan, Shep, all of it is going to go away. Just because you can't get your head out of your ass. And —"

"Yeah I know," I cut him off then. "And like you, I don't need a blow by fucking blow of what Stellan already told me."

The familiar burning starts up in my gut.

The familiar tightness. The itch.

That threatens to take over everything and color my vision red.

The silence on the line stretches for a few seconds before he clips, "Well, at least you were listening."

"I was," I tell him, my muscles tight. "So if you don't mind, I'd like to get to the point."

"By all means then, let's get to the fucking point."

"I'll do it."

"Do what?"

"Go to," *fucking*, "therapy."

It was hard to push those words out.

It was hard to push any words out except 'fuck off.' To him and by extension to my other two brothers too.

That I'm done with this. I'm done being beholden to them. I'm done being their hotheaded little brother that they can all boss around and keep in line.

I can do this on my own.

But that's the thing, isn't it? My reputation precedes me. Something my agent likes to remind me every other day.

It doesn't matter how good of a player I am, how valuable to the team. They will drop me and if it gets out why then no team in their right mind would take me on. And if it was just me, I wouldn't care. It would hurt, yes, that my dream of being the best, going to the European League would be destroyed but I'd live with it.

If it meant finally breaking free of my family.

But it's not just me anymore.

It's her too.

The girl I left in my bedroom with the door locked. Even though she's still tied up and can't go anywhere.

You're a fucking psycho, aren't you?

Yeah, only for her.

My Firefly and *her* as well.

That tiny baby girl in her belly.

I don't know if she's there yet or not. But I know that I'm doing this for her too.

Because I'm the one who's providing for her.

No matter what happens in the future, where or who — the anger jumps in my veins at the thought — my Firefly ends up with, I will always provide for her and our baby girl. I'm not going to be like our father who abandoned everything, every responsibility and left us to struggle in his wake. I'm not going to ever, *not ever*, abandon them.

And if I have to go to therapy and have my brain analyzed because of my fucking issues, in order to do that, I will.

I'll do anything for her.

For them.

Because I finally have something worth fighting for.

I finally have something bigger than soccer, my ambitions.

Them.

"You will."

I clench and clench my teeth for a second or two. "Yes."

"What changed?"

"That's none of your business."

"It is. Because I'm not only your brother, I'm your coach. And I need to know if I can trust this sudden change of heart or not."

"You can."

"I still —"

"No, you don't get to hear why or how. All you need to know, as my coach, is that I'll do it. I'll do my time and then I'm coming back and taking my fucking place on the team."

He doesn't utter a word but I can feel him grinding his teeth.

I can feel how much he hates not being obeyed.

At least there's some satisfaction in that.

But it only lasts a few seconds before he speaks. "Fine. If you want things to be that way, it's up to you. But now as your brother, let me tell you something: I don't trust you. I've never trusted you. Not with this thing inside of you. This boiling anger, this *heated* rage. Your hotheadedness. And I've tried my very best to stamp it out of you. I've tried to do everything that I can to erase that from your system and get you to straighten the fuck out. And for a little while I thought that you had. I thought that you'd found something to keep your anger in check. Soccer. I thought soccer could finally fix you, make you better, make you responsible, help you to grow the fuck up so I don't have to get a call every other day that my little brother is starting shit again. That my little brother is the bane of everyone's existence, including mine. But apparently not. Apparently, you haven't changed. You're still my little brother who kept me up at night sitting by the phone expecting bad news and who fucking embarrassed the shit out of me wherever I went. And as your brother I have to tell you that I'd hoped better for you. I'd hoped that you wouldn't still be fucking around. And as your coach, if I find out that you're not holding up your end of the bargain or are a liability to the team, I'll cut you loose so fast that you'd think twice about playing games with me."

There's a sting in my eyes.

A burn.

It's different from my anger that's always lurking under the surface.

It's more devastating and painful than that.

And it's something that I've only felt around him: sadness and loneliness.

"Don't worry, Coach, the only game I intend to play is the one I was born for," I say. "And as your brother, let me tell you that you don't have to worry about me ever again. You're off the hook and relieved of all your brotherly fucking duties."

Chapter Twenty-Four

HE'S SLEEPING.

With his arm thrown over my waist and his front molded to my back.

Or rather my back molded to his front.

He's too hard and unforgiving to bend to someone else's shape or will.

And if there was ever any doubt about that, it was cleared today. Especially when not only did he leave me tied up in his bed this morning, causing me to childishly decide that I'd never speak to him or look at him again, but also when he made me break that promise only a few minutes later.

I did look at him and speak to him, mostly to hurl insults and threats.

Like, "Get out of my sight, you motherfucker."

And, "I don't want your stupid food or your stupid meds," when he brought breakfast and painkillers.

"I don't need to go to the bathroom. I can hold it. Don't show mercy on my account when we both know what a monster you are," when he came over with the intention of untying me and letting me use the facilities.

"I pray that we never have a baby. I pray that your dick falls off."

"If you bring that Godzilla of a thing anywhere close to my pussy, I will fuck it up."

"If you think I'll forget about this, then you're wrong. Do you get that? I'll never forget about this, Ledger. Never. And trust me, my brother will hear about this. My brother and your sister. And the cops. Because I'm dragging you to court, asshole. I'm done protecting you. You just watch and wait."

Not once did he say anything back to me.

And yes, I ended up doing all the things that he wanted me to anyway: eat, go to the bathroom, take medication and all that.

But of course *he* didn't do what I wanted him to do.

Untie me and let me go.

So I sat there, naked and tied up and angry.

Although my anger turned into frustration and despair real soon. So after sitting on my ass for a couple of hours, I curled into myself and started crying into the pillow. At which point, he came into the room but I didn't give him a chance to state his intentions. I threw a pillow at him and told him to get the fuck out. And then I somehow went to sleep.

I think I slept — on and off; when I was off I could sense him coming into the room to check on me but I pretended to be asleep — until dinner-time when he came over again with the food and by then I was so tired that I didn't say a word and simply ate what he gave me.

Even though I hated how tasty it was: lasagna.

I hated that he also gave me dessert: cotton candy ice cream, my favorite that he must've bought for me specifically when we drove to the cabin.

But more than that I hated that after a while, coming in and out of slumber, I couldn't hold on to my anger. I couldn't hold on to my ire and outrage and the sense of unfairness and blame. Because well I did lie to him, knowing that it was wrong. That it was extremely fucking unethical and of course as unethical as his actions from last year. Which was the whole point but still.

So I deserved his anger and his wrath.

However that came about.

But.

That doesn't mean that I'm not going to take advantage of this opportunity.

This opportunity being: I'm untied.

I woke up about ten minutes ago and realized that I'm finally, *finally* untied and God, I have to get out of here. I *have* to run. I can't stay here all tied up until he's done with his anger. Not to mention, how ballistic he got when he assumed — rightfully — that it was Ezra that I was going to go to after I got pregnant.

Which I'm still going to do, aren't I?

I have to.

It's not like I have a choice.

So yeah, I need to run. I need to leave because we can't do this.

We can't make a baby.

So with bated breath, I move his heavy arm off my body and ignore how I instantly miss his heat, the weight of his corded muscles. Somehow it was keeping me grounded and safe.

I clench my eyes shut at the thought.

I don't want to think about that. I don't want to think that this was the first time since I got forcibly engaged that I'd felt safe somewhere. Actually this was the first time I'd felt safe ever since he left me in that dorm room over a year ago.

I need to focus.

Once his arm is off and I'm sure that he's still sleeping, I slowly creep out of bed and put my feet on the floor, hoping for no loose floorboards. But the threat of a creaking floor isn't enough to stop me from making my attempt. And neither is the fact that I notice something around my wrist.

It shines in the darkness. Under the pearly moonlight streaming through the window.

A stark white bandage.

He's taped up my wrists that were bound the whole day. Probably because I kept twisting and twisting them, trying to get free but mostly trying to rebel against what he'd told me. I push away all the angsty, tender feelings at the thought of him taking care of me and tiptoe around — thankfully, no loose floorboards so far — and hunt for something to put on. I pick up the first thing I encounter, his discarded t-shirt, lying on the floor at the foot of the bed. I put it on and once again ignore the cozy warmth that slides over my skin and how soft his t-shirts are.

Once I'm dressed, it's go time.

I realize that not only is it the middle of the night but we're also in the middle of the woods. I have no idea where I'm going or how to get out of here. But I don't care; I need to leave. Taking a deep but quiet breath, I walk toward the bedroom door, which is thankfully open.

But before I step out of it, I pause and look at him.

I study his slumbering form for a second, trying to commit it to memory. He's lying on his side just like he was yesterday when I woke up, all lusty and warm. He's got his one arm under the pillow and the other that I removed from my body lies right beside it.

I'm momentarily entranced by how the moonlight dances over the ridges and curves of his muscles, creating shadows and patterns. How his hair's all messy and almost fanning out on the pillow, his soft lips relaxed and parted. How even in his sleep, he doesn't lose even a drop of his power, his beauty.

But most of all I notice how peaceful he looks.

Usually when he's awake and going, there's always something tight and strained about him. Either there's a light frown on his brows or his jaw is clenched. Or maybe the slant of his shoulders is too severe or the line of his back is too straight.

The only time I've seen him completely at peace is right now, while sleeping.

Or when he's with Halo, and I can't help but put a hand on my belly, flat and empty.

My heart clenches and I hesitate once more.

Probably because when he finds out that I left him in the middle of the night, his hard-won peace is going to evaporate.

Not to mention, I'm leaving him alone and hasn't he always been alone? *It's not your responsibility, Tempest. You need to leave.*

Now.

Fisting my fingers at my sides, I cast a last look at him and turn away, heading for the front door. I open it without any issues and then I'm out. Into the night that seems bright even through the canopy of the trees, the moonlight and the stars lighting up my path.

Thanking the universe that at least one thing is going in my favor right now, I take off.

I run in the direction that I think we came in. Although honestly every direction looks the same to me right now, and my only goal is to get as far away from the cabin as possible. So I keep going, my bare feet crunching the leaves, stepping on stray branches and rocks, stumbling every now and then.

But it's okay.

I'm not going to give up that easily.

Nothing can stop me.

That's what I think until I hear a huge bellow that rends the air, cutting it in half and halting me in my tracks.

At first I think it's an animal. A wild feral animal, something that I didn't think about before but should have; we're in the middle of the woods. But then that animalistic roar calls out my name and I realize that it's worse than an animal.

It's him.

And along with being wild and feral, he has a one-track mind.

To come after me.

To hunt me down and trap me.

So like the frightened prey that I am, I start running again. I run harder this time, stepping onto jagged things that I'm sure are cutting into my skin and making me bleed. But I can't afford to care about that in this moment. Tears make my vision blurry and my heart pounds so fast and so hard in my chest that I know it's going to burst right out of my body any second now.

But I don't stop.

Until I step on something too sharp and I stumble. And this time, I do it so hard that there's no way I can save myself from falling. When something stops my rapid descent.

A large hand wrapped around my bicep that jerks me back.

And I go crashing into a heated and sculpted — *safe* — wall of muscles that easily takes the brunt of my body and the speed with which I was running. He not only takes the brunt of it but gives me a soft — again safe — landing as we both meet the ground.

With him below me, cradling my back and keeping me securely tucked against his chest.

I ignore the security and safety and all the cozy things that he provides though and start struggling against him. I kick out my legs, claw at his arms that are now wrapped around my chest and my waist, trying to subdue me as I scream and scream and wiggle and twist my body, trying to get free.

If anything, his hold on me tightens up and somehow he rolls us in a way that I end up underneath him, his powerful body in a position of dominance, jammed up between my spread thighs with his heavy torso pinning me to the ground. My arms are still free though, and until he takes them as prisoners, I fight.

I hit him and punch him and keep clawing at whatever I can get my hands on.

His shoulders and neck and face. His hair.

All the while chanting: "Let me go. Let me go. *Let me go.*"

He responds to my assault with heavy grunts and growls and giving more of his weight to my small body. Not that I care. He can suffocate me with his muscles and bury me in the ground but I'm not going to stop. Until he manages to get both my hands locked down on either side of my head, stopping my assault.

"Enough," he growls then, his face somehow both shadowed and clear, jacking up his dangerous aura.

Panting, I still try to buck him off, twisting and rolling my torso. "Let me go."

He growls at my attempts and presses my arms into the ground. "No."

"You're such a —"

"Not until you calm down."

I don't.

I fight him harder, kicking at his thighs with my heels, rolling my hips. "Fuck your calm down. Fuck you. Fuck —"

"*Jesus Christ,*" he snaps. "Calm the fuck down or you'll hurt yourself."

I open my mouth to tell him that he'll be the one ending up hurt at the end of this when his torso slams down so hard on me that I lose my breath. Making me think that up until now he wasn't really trying to subdue me. He wasn't really trying to pin me under him like the firefly I am.

But he is now.

And I have no choice but to lay still under him.

Still and panting and *hating.*

When he knows he has me under his control, he loosens his grip from around my wrists. Not enough for me to be able to do something about it but still loose enough that he isn't cutting off my blood supply.

He's panting too.

But I think it's more because of the agitation, the absolute concern that I see on his face.

"Are you insane?" he asks, his voice rough and raspy.

"No, you are. If you think you can keep me here."

"Are you *fucking* insane?" His face drops closer to mine, his voice rough but now rising in volume.

I get up in his face too. "Let me go."

He narrows his eyes. "What the fuck do you think you're doing? Where *the fuck* do you think you're going?"

"Where do you think, asshole?" I buck my hips again, or rather try to but of course get nowhere. "Away from you."

"Did you, for one second," he goes on, slowly, kinda menacingly, "stop to think how dangerous it is to be out in the woods in the middle of the night?"

"No." I clench my teeth and fist my fingers. "Because I'm willing to take my chances out here rather than be in there with you."

A muscle jumps in his cheek. Jumps and jumps and he gets so close to me that the tip of our noses brush against each other with every breath we take.

"Especially," he rumbles roughly, "when you could be pregnant."

I swallow.

And suck in my belly. Because I feel a twinge, a tug in my womb.

But more than that I *swear* he can feel it.

He can feel that pull in my belly because in response, he presses back with his stomach.

"*Especially* when you could've gotten hurt out here." Then, "You and *her*."

I swallow again.

I also steel myself against him, against his concern, his very obvious distress that I've been ignoring ever since I got a glimpse of his face.

It's becoming harder though.

Much harder as the seconds pass and as I wonder if what he's saying could be true.

What if she is in there and all this running and stumbling has hurt her?

I know all of this is irrational and crazy and just a figment of our imaginations. I read online that it could take up to five to fifteen days for the implantation to occur or whatever it's called but... But just the idea of hurting her is abhorrent to me. Just the idea that maybe she's trying to work her way to us inside of me right this second makes me want to kick myself for being so reckless.

"N-nothing has happened to her," I tell him.

He clenches his jaw. "You don't know that."

"Well, you don't know if I'm pregnant yet."

"You fucking *could* be."

"I'm not," I insist, even though I'd like nothing more. And just because I'd like nothing more, I add, "And I hope I'm not. Not with y-your baby."

A sting pierces my heart.

And it's so vicious that I flinch.

He flinches too I think.

But I can't be sure.

"Don't you fucking *understand?*" he says then, his voice sounding even rougher than before.

More sanded down, more guttural.

"Understand what?"

"You could've…"

"I could've *what?*"

He doesn't reply right away.

First, he swallows. Thickly and jerkily.

Then, his eyes rove over my features, my throat, down to my chest, and I think it's not without purpose. I *think* he's trying to check me out, determine whether I'm okay or not.

"When I woke up and didn't find you in the bed, I thought…" Another jerky, awkward swallow. "I thought I'd never see you again. I thought I'd… I thought you ran away and something happened to you. Something… bad. Something awful. These woods, they're not… You can't wander through them if you have no idea where you're going. You can't…" Then, with his fingers squeezing my wrists, "You were about to fall."

"I was fine," I tell him, struck by how he's stumbling and tripping over his words.

He mashes his teeth before he attempts to speak again. "You could've… You could've twisted your ankle. You could've broken your leg, hit your head on the ground. You could've been…" He clenches his jaw again. "*Bleeding.* In pain, and it could've taken hours for me to find you. Hours for me to get to you and come to your rescue and if something had happened during that time. If something —"

"But nothing happened. I'm fine," I blurt out, unable to stop myself.

Finally unable to ignore his concern.

His chest presses into me with another one of his erratic breaths, as he says, "If something had happened to you out here, if you'd gotten *hurt*, I would've lost my fucking mind. I would've…" Another clench of his teeth. "I would've lost my fucking sanity if you and *her*… If I lost my family. Again. I would've —"

"Your f-family," I breathe out.

He flinches again.

As if he hadn't realized that he'd said it. Out loud.

As if he hadn't realized that he'd exposed a particularly vulnerable nerve in his body. A secret vein in his rapidly beating heart. As if he hadn't realized that without me having to lift my finger, he's made it so that I'm touching his pulse.

And I knew it, didn't I?

I knew his secret wish and that's why he looks so undone. That's why he looks so crazy and animalistic.

Beastly and primal.

Under the moonlight.

Because he thought his family was hurt.

"You think I'm your…" I begin but have to take a moment to myself. "I'm your family?"

His chest crashes against mine with the feral breaths he's taking. "I think that you could be pregnant with my baby and you shouldn't be running around in the middle of the fucking night when you could injure yourself or get hurt."

I shake my head, adamant on talking about this. "No, but you j-just said that I'm, that *we* are —"

He flexes his grip on my wrists again. "If you're so fucking good at listening to me, then I want you to listen to this: don't you ever, not fucking ever, do what you did tonight. Don't you fucking ever put yourself in danger like this." He stares down at me for a second, then, "Is that fucking clear or do I have to *make* it clear? And trust me, you're not gonna like how I do it."

I should be annoyed at him.

Angry.

For being so high-handed. So dominating and controlling, especially after how I spent the entire day today.

Being tied to his bed.

But I'm not.

What I am though is sad.

So fucking sad because he's right. To do this I mean.

He's right to sweep this whole thing under the rug. Because for a moment, I'd forgotten.

I'd forgotten that I can't be his family.

In fact, I can't be anything to him.

Not only because I'm going to be someone else's soon, but also I don't want to.

Right?

I mean he's the guy who broke my heart, and while I've forgiven him, I haven't forgotten. I still haven't forgotten that he has things in his life that are more important to him than me. His ego, his anger, his career. His hatred of my brother still. Just because he's regretful of how he treated me and because he's agreed to help me with my dream, doesn't mean that all of the other things have vanished from between us.

No, they're still there.

So there's no use talking about what he's just revealed.

Actually we should talk about something else. Something even more important.

So fisting my hands, I focus. "Why, is it going to involve ropes again?"

His jaw tics.

"Are you going to tie me up to the bed and keep me here? Against my will."

Another tic. But then he replies, "Shouldn't have done that."

"What?"

His chest crashes with mine again as he breathes deep. "Shouldn't have tied you up. Shouldn't have left you there. I was —"

"Jealous," I complete the sentence for him, trying to sound stern even though a little steam has left my body at such an easy acknowledgment.

"Yes."

"Because you thought Ezra —"

"Don't," he growls, tightening his grip, thrusting his torso into mine "Don't fucking say his name."

Despite it being inadvisable, I can't help but arch my back under him. "I will. If I want to."

This time his growl comes from the center of his chest, a mean, threatening sound, unaccompanied by words.

"And it's none of your business."

"I swear to fucking God, Firefly, if you —"

"No," I cut him off and even though I hate what I'm going to say next, I still do because it's the right thing. It's the *only* thing to do in the face of his crazy jealousy. The only thing that will get me out of here and away from him. I can't have him complicating my already complicated life.

"Don't you see? You can't get jealous. You have no right to get jealous, Ledger. I'm not your girlfriend. I'm not your wife. I'm nothing to you." My throat feels filled with sharp glass. "And after what you did today, I'm also not the mother of your baby. Because we're not having a baby together. Just because you keep calling me yours doesn't mean that I am. And I'm allowed to say his name if —"

"Don't say it," he warns.

And I'm thankful for it. For his warning, for him cutting me off.

Because it was getting painful. To say those things.

It was getting physically impossible to push the words out. They were making me bleed.

They were scraping my tongue, banging against my teeth.

So I needed a break, a pause for a couple of seconds before resuming and doing the right thing.

I open my mouth to continue what I was saying but then I whisper, "Ezra."

Fuck.

Fuck, fuck, *fuck*.

Why would I do that? Why would I provoke him like this?

And I *have* provoked him.

Because as soon as I say it, his nostrils flare.

His entire body tightens up over me, thrumming.

And I don't know why but I say it again. "Ezra." And this time I keep going, "Ezra. Ezra. Ezra. Ezra. Ez —"
And then I find I can't anymore.
Because his mouth slams down on mine.
Hard.
Capturing my words, kissing the breath out of me under the moonlight.

Chapter Twenty-Five

THIS IS CRAZY.

This is insane. This isn't supposed to happen.

We're not supposed to do this.

I'm not supposed to do this. I'm not supposed to provoke him further, egg him on like this. I shouldn't open my mouth quite so much and let him plunder inside. I shouldn't be giving him my tongue so he can suck on it. God, and I shouldn't be biting his lip so he bites mine back.

No, I should push him away.

I can't be giving him mixed signals.

So somehow, *somehow*, I start to do that. Now that my hands are free — he let my wrists go so he could thrust his long mean fingers in my hair and maneuver my face the way he wants to — I start to tug at his hair. I pull at the messy strands. I scratch the side of his neck. I dig my nails in his shoulders, rake them across his back, along his dense biceps.

I rock under him.

Buck and roll my hips. Twist them.

All in the hope of getting him off me. All in the hope that he'll stop kissing me and I can tell him to let me go. To take me back.

But what happens is the opposite.

What happens is that he's groaning and grunting at the sting of my nails. And he's thrusting back, matching the rhythm of my hips, thrusting and pushing against that place in between my thighs.

That sore and hurt-y place.

And oh gosh, I realize that I'm not wearing any panties.

Which of course I knew; I didn't have the time to put on any when I ran away.

But what I hadn't realized or let myself realize until now is that he's bare as well. At least he's bare-chested and now my naked pussy is rubbing against his naked and ridged abdomen, painting his skin with my arousal, making it slippery and sticky and all messy. Like he's always wanted to paint mine with his.

And that's only making things worse.

It's arousing me like nothing has ever aroused me before, and instead of trying to get him off of me, I'm only bringing him closer. I'm only kissing him and kissing him back.

Just when I think I'll run out of air though, he breaks the kiss and I take my chance.

"Let me... g-go," I tell him as his mouth moves down to my neck. "Let me go, Ledger."

He doesn't.

He bears down on me and goes for my freckle.

He sucks on it and sucks on it, definitely leaving his teeth marks.

I pull at his hair again. "Stop kissing me, you asshole. I don't... I don't want this. I don't..."

I have to stop on account of a gasp I emit because he chooses that moment to really dig his teeth into my skin, possibly as a punishment to what I'm saying. And my whole body arches and rocks under him as if electrocuted.

That psycho.

I start slapping him then. His shoulders, his arms, his jaw, whatever I can get my hands on.

And he does it more.

He bites me more and God, why does that feel so good?

Why does everything that he's doing feel so good?

Every bite, every lick, every suck, every push of his hips is making me crazier and crazier and fucking crazier.

"You can't tell me what to do. You can't... Not after you tied me up," I say, still going at him with my nails. "You f-fucking tied me up. And you left me there. You just left. I was so... s-scared and afraid and so mad. I wanted to hit you. I wanted to punch your face. I wanted... I wanted you... God, I wanted you so much."

In the midst of my rant, I realize something.

I realize that his bites and hard thrusts have become soothing sucks and gentle rocking. And his growls and grunts have reduced to guttural chants of *I'm sorry.*

His fingers that were fisting my hair are now cradling my cheeks and oh my God, his lips are moving now. They're leaving my throat and are making their way up, stopping to suck at my jaw, lick at my skin, and I realize that I'm crying. My tears are streaming down my cheeks and he's drinking them up, licking them off as he repeats the same thing over and over and over.

Which is when it happens.

Which is when I lose all sense of rationality, I think.

I lose all my resistance.

Not that there was a lot of it before. I was barely hanging on by a thread. But I still had some concept of right and wrong. I still had some concept that we shouldn't do this.

But all of it is gone now.

Along with licking my tears off, he's robbed me of all sanity.

And I grab his face and whisper my own apologies.

"I'm sorry, okay? I'm sorry for lying to you. For keeping the truth from you. I don't... I can't... I can't believe that I was going to do that. That I was going to take h-her away from you." I dig my fingers in his cheeks while he rubs his open mouth all over the side of my face. "She's yours. Just yours. And I'm sorry for provoking you. For saying his name." He jerks over me, his own fingers tightening over jaw, my chin. "I-I was trying to make you jealous. I was trying to... I don't know why I do that. I don't know why I want you to suffer like you make me suffer. I don't... I don't know... You should make it so that I never do that. You should —"

He shuts me up with another kiss and this one I return without any reservations.

Like I wanted to do with his last one.

But it's over all too soon and suddenly I find myself looking up at his dark eyes, darker than the night. Suddenly, I find my wrists trapped just like before and I want to get free. Not because I want to run away but because I want to touch him. I want to go back to feeling his dense and solid muscles, his smooth skin.

But I won't fight him.

I won't.

I don't want to fight. I just want him.

"I should," he rasps, his lips hovering over mine.

I lift my head, trying to capture them. "Yes."

He keeps them out of reach though, as he says, "And how do you think I should do that?"

"I don't... I don't know. I don't know what..."

"I do."

"H-how?"

"With my dick."

"Yes." I nod eagerly, rolling my hips under him. "Just p-put it in me."

"Tell me where."

This, I definitely know the answer to. "In my mouth."

"Yeah?"

"Yes," I reply eagerly.

Coming down again, he rasps against my lips, "Tell me why."

Again, I try to capture his mouth but fail to. "Because..."

"Because what?"

I'm breathing harshly, restlessly as I look up at him. "Because I said his name."

His jaw clenches and a ripple goes through his body. "You did."

I try again to reach him, his lips but to no avail. "Y-yes."

"And just the fact that I had to kiss you on that same mouth to shut you up is pissing me off."

"I-I know and I'm sorry. I —"

Another tic of his jaw. "Sorry doesn't cut it though, does it?"

Swallowing, I shake my head. "No."

"Sorry doesn't make it okay that you said his name when I specifically asked you not to."

"I know. I —"

"So then you're right. I need to make it so that you don't ever do it again. I need to make it so that no one else's name comes out of that mouth other than mine."

"Yes."

"And there's only way to do that, isn't there?"

"Uh-huh."

"It's to make you gag on my cock."

I swallow again, nodding. "Yes."

His fingers tighten on my face. "It's to make you fucking choke on it."

"Yes. God, please."

"The only way to get the taste of that motherfucker's name off your mouth is to wash it out with my cum."

I twist my wrists in his grip, my thighs clenching around him. "Yes. The only way."

"And that's because you're my whore, aren't you?"

I jerk under him. "I am."

"My fucking whore," he bites out. "My *fucking* property."

"I-I am."

"And no matter what you say, no matter how much you deny it, it still doesn't change the fact that you're my Firefly. *Mine.*"

I know he's throwing my own words from earlier back at me.

I know I pissed him off by saying those things.

And I also know that I should argue with him about it right now. But as I said, my concept of right and wrong has completely cracked down the middle. I've gone as crazy as him in this moment and I don't care if it's toxic or poisonous or a train wreck.

I want him and I want him to do to me whatever he likes.

"O-okay."

He grinds his jaw then, looking menacing as ever.

"So let's go then," he says. "Let's get to fucking work. Let's baptize that cotton candy mouth with my dick so it's fit to be called mine again."

With that, he gets up and away from my body.

He comes up to his knees between my spread thighs. Spread and wet and smeared with my juices.

So wet that my skin shines in the moonlight.

His skin does too.

His abs, that little happy trail, all drenched in my cum and so shiny looking.

As beautiful as the sight is though, I can't waste my time on it. Not right now when I'm being punished for saying someone else's name and my focus should be on the tool of my punishment.

On the heavy bulge in his gray sweatpants.

Heavy and throbbing.

I swear I can see it pulsing through the fabric.

But more than that I think I see a wet spot on it. Making me realize that he's dripping.

And God, I can't let it go to waste.

When it belongs in my mouth so I can be a good whore again.

His whore again.

So under his intense scrutiny, I raise myself up from my prone position and come down to my hands and knees.

I see his muscles shudder, his chest heaving and his abdomen flexing. And then I start to crawl toward him, causing his eyes to narrow down to slits and his jaw to turn to granite. It's not a long distance of course; he's right here. But the couple of steps that I do have to take seem longer than usual.

Probably because of the way he's watching me.

With hunger and desperation.

Impatience too.

Because when I do get there, in between his spread thighs, and go for his waistband, his arm strikes out of nowhere and his fingers bury themselves in my hair, fisting the strands. He gives them a jerk then, pulling me up and tugging me toward his body.

"You didn't think I'd forget though, did you?" he rasps.

My hands go to his sides and hold on. "Forget what?"

"That you aren't the only one who needs baptizing."

"I don't understand."

Tightening his fist in my hair, he jerks me closer. "I fucked up too, didn't I? I tied you up, left you alone. All because I was jealous and angry. All because the moment you said his name, it fucked me up. And it fucked me up so bad that all I could see was red. For hours and hours after that."

"You don't —"

"So," he tugs my head back, "while you choke on my dick, I'm going to drown in your cunt. While you drool over me, I'm going to drink every drop of your juices. And while you struggle to fit me inside your mouth, I'm going to jam my tongue inside your tight little pussy that I'm pretty sure has by now snapped back to its original pinprick size, even though I stretched it out last night, and fuck it until you gush all over my face and turn me into a new man. A *man*," he bites out, "worthy of calling you his whore."

He doesn't give me a chance to respond to that because he starts putting me in position and re-arranging my body.

First, he lies down on the ground with me draped over him, my thighs straddling his hard stomach. Then in all his athletic grace and glory, he spins me around and settles me back down but this time, facing away from him. And then he goes for my t-shirt. Or rather his t-shirt, and takes it off.

He throws it to the side, baring my body to the moonlight and the woods.

And honestly I'm so turned on and so hungry and so ready for it that I don't object. I don't make a sound. I simply let him pull me back to where I'm straddling his face while mine is where his throbbing dick is. All the while pulling his sweatpants down to reveal the thick and veiny and bejeweled cock.

And I fall on him then.

I wrap my lips around his head and moan at the first taste of him. Making him tighten up, his abs bunching under me, while he lets out a long sigh as if he's home now. As if all the trauma of tonight, of finding me gone from his bed and saving me from falling is finally, *finally* draining out of him.

It's finally leaving his body and I couldn't be happier.

I couldn't be more relieved myself, at that.

But only for a second or two because after that his mouth takes the first taste of my pussy and I'm in shambles. I'm ruined, my body falling apart just like that. And I could've put myself back together if he hadn't gone for that second lick and third and fourth and then completely latching onto my pussy, drinking from it as he'd said.

And he likes what he's drinking too.

Because he's grunting and groaning and slurping, making noises that are hitting me right at the center of my belly.

It's so intimate, God.

It's so fucking intimate, him licking my pussy.

For some reason, fucking it with his cock — as amazing and earth-shattering as that was — doesn't sound as intense as him sucking on my pussy. And oh my God, that was my clit, wasn't it? He's sucking on my clit now and I think... I think it has to be the most intimate thing anyone has ever done to me.

Anyone could *ever* do to anyone.

And —

I hear it first rather than feel it.

His palm smacking me on the ass.

Did he just... spank me?

263

Before I can adjust to the sudden turn of events and the burn on my ass cheek, he growls, "This is a lesson, remember? You wanna be a good whore for me, Firefly, then get to fucking work. I'm not letting this pussy come until I'm touching the back of your throat and all you can breathe is me."

He finishes that with another smack, and despite the burn and minor annoyance, I do get to work.

Because I can't be selfish.

Although I don't know if sucking his dick is much of a lesson or even a punishment. Because again as soon as I lick the tip, I moan. His cinnamon-y flavor explodes on my tongue and this time without getting distracted, I crack my jaw wide open and envelop him with my lips. And when I do that, I get to touch those ladder-like studs and yeah, not a punishment at all.

More like a reward.

For me and for him as well.

He got them to hurt himself, didn't he? To punish himself for that night.

So tonight I reward him.

I make him feel good as I lick them and flick them with my tongue, feeling the delicious weight of the metal on my tongue. Their delicious taste mixed in with his cinnamon flavor. And I think I do a little too well because not only does his body jump and twitch under me, but his mouth on my cunt falters.

It makes me smile.

And suck on him harder.

Grip him with both hands — he was right though; I do need both hands to hold him — and just go crazy over his beautiful cock.

Although I'm not sure how he knows that I'm reveling in making him lose control but he does. Because he smacks my ass again, making me jump and undulate my hips, and he uses those rough large hands of his to part my cheeks and *really* go to town on my completely exposed pussy.

After that, it becomes a contest I think.

We're both licking and sucking and rubbing.

I'm riding his face while he's riding my mouth.

I dance over him, my hips writhing, and he shakes under me, his thighs straining and jumping.

I'm opening my mouth as far as it will go, uncaring of the pain, the soreness that's starting to creep in and will be in full swing tomorrow, and taking him in deep, choking with my tries, gagging and making a mess on his dick and his balls. And he's sucking on my pussy lips, nudging my super sensitive clit with his nose, and gosh, I can feel it. I can feel my juices gushing out and him drinking them as fast as they come.

Transforming him.

Making him reborn.

Making *me* even more determined to make it good for him.

The best he's ever had.

So I don't give up.

I keep trying to take him in as much as I can, going up and down on his length that's probably as slippery with my drool now as my dripping pussy. All the while feeling something swirl and tighten up in my belly, rocking my hips over his tongue, riding his face.

I think I have it all under control though.

I think I'm going to last until I make him touch the back of my throat.

But all my plans are derailed when I feel a pinch.

Down there.

It's not from his fingers or his lips.

It's from his teeth.

From the little nip he doles out to my clit and all my focus, my hard-won control and dedication to worship his dick goes down the drain and I come. His length slips out of my mouth and I arch my back, moaning and shaking, and thinking that this will never stop.

This earthquake in my body, in my pussy.

Especially if he doesn't stop sucking on it.

The more he sucks and drinks me down, the more I drip and gush and the more my thighs shake.

At one point I think I pass out, even though my body is still jerking and writhing. Because the next thing I know I'm on my hands and knees and he's behind me. I have no clue as to how that happened. How he managed to get away from under me and position me without me knowing anything at all.

All I know now is that he's lining up his saliva-drenched cock with my still clenching pussy, ready to enter.

And I say, wiping my the drool off my mouth, "W-wait."

He looks up, his chest all shiny from sweat and my juices, his mouth shiny as well, his chest heaving so rapidly like a hurtling train.

"You haven't…" I can't quite catch my breath but I persevere. "You didn't come and —"

My words end in a startled gasp and a shocked, high-pitched moan that's almost a scream.

Because he chooses that moment to thrust inside of me.

And I would've fallen face down on the ground with the force, the slight pain of his invasion, if he didn't have a hand gripping my hips and his arm around my trembling belly. As it is, all I do is scream and shake with his dick throbbing inside of me as he pulls me up, my spine bowing and my head resting on his chest.

"Again," he growls in my ear, "you didn't think I'd forget, did you?"

He's pumping inside of me, prolonging my orgasm from before so it's hard to focus. But I still say, "F-forget what?"

"That my load's supposed to end up in your womb, not down your throat."

He finishes that with a violent thrust of his hips and my hands fly back and hold on to his rippling obliques. I don't know where the flash of clarity is coming from but I do remind him, "B-but I don't want —"

"You do." Another jerk of his hips as one of his hands leaves my hip and clutches my throat. "You *fucking do* want my baby."

Arching my back, I revel in his control as I insist for no reason at all, "N-no."

He tightens his hold around my neck, pulls my head back some more so I'm looking at him upside down. Then, "You know what these are for, right?"

He squeezes a part of my body, hips, that makes me jerk against him and moan.

But that's the only thing I can do.

He doesn't seem to need an answer from me anyway because he gives it himself, "These. Soft. Meaty. Hips." Each word is punctuated by the slam of his cock and each slam of his cock is punctuated by my whimpers and moans. "These soft, meaty hips are not only something for me to hold on to when I fuck you like this, and trust me, there's going to be a lot of times when I pound this pussy from behind like I'm an animal and you're my bitch in heat." He squeezes my hip again, making me bite my lip at the pleasure/pain of it. "These are also for when I give you a baby. These are what they call child-bearing hips, Firefly, and you've got them in spades. You've fucking got them for days and if you think I'm going to let them go to waste, then you better think again, yeah?"

I'm panting and whimpering and my eyes are about to flutter closed but he squeezes my throat, making me pop them right open and I gasp again.

"Eyes on me," he growls with clenched teeth, "when I'm fucking educating you about birds and bees."

I shiver at his tone, my pussy spasming over his rod, gushing cum that not only drenches him but also my thighs. And God, he doesn't stop. He doesn't stop pumping inside of me and now there are noises. There are squelching noises with every thrust he delivers.

Still I hear him though.

I hear what he says.

"And these," leaving my hip, he goes up to my breasts and squeezes one, "haven't you ever wondered why these are so plump and ripe? Why your nipples look like juicy cherries," he rolls one between his thumb and finger, making me go *uh*, "and why when you walk, these titties jiggle under your dress as if dying to pop out and find a hungry fucking mouth that can latch on to them." He squeezes my flesh something fierce at this and goes, "The only hungry mouth you need to worry about right now though, is mine. Just FYI. Don't get any fucking ideas in your head, yeah? These. Are. *Mine.*"

Again, he punctuates his words with harsh slams of his hips and again, I go *uh, uh, uh.* "And for the baby that I'm going to give you. Because these are what they call milkmaid tits, Firefly. These are tits made for milking, for suckling, for fucking drinking from, and again, if you think I'm going to let them go to fucking waste, then maybe you're not as smart as you think are."

He looks like a beast right now.

Dipped in silvery moonlight, his eyes jet black and his features tight and flushed.

And I can't help but wonder how it is that I got caught up with someone like him. How it is that he's got me so in his clutches that I don't want to leave. That I never ever want to leave. That I always want to live here, in his violent arms and his animal heart.

"And then," he rasps, his thrusts slowing down a bit, letting me catch my breath, "there's this pussy." His hand that was grasping my tit, after smacking it once and making me moan, travels down to my pussy. "Why do you think it's so tight, baby, huh? Why do you think God gave you such a tiny fucking pussy that's not only so hard to get in but also to get out of. Why do you think God made it so that not only does your pussy get wet like no one's business but also so clingy that when you do try to get out, it won't let you go. It won't let you leave so you have to stay in. You have to pump, pump, pump into it and before you know or can even think about maybe pulling out and doing the right thing by leaving you unbred, you're already dumping your load in it. You're already filling that tight fucking snatch to the brim like a motherfucking teenager who's never pumped into anything except his fist."

I have no clue what he's saying.

I have absolutely no clue at all as I roll my head back and forth on his chest and whimper and jerk and twist my hips. Because he's not just whispering these things into my ear but also rubbing my clit at the same time, and he's right. He's so fucking right that my pussy gets wet like no one's business.

Because those squelching noises have jacked up.

I can hear myself getting wetter and wetter. I can *hear* myself juicing up.

"So yes," he whispers again, "you do want a baby. Because that's your purpose, Firefly. That's why you were put on this godforsaken earth with a body like that. With hips so fleshy that you can't help but smack them until they turn red. With tits so milky that you can't help but bite into them and a pussy so tight that you can't help but come inside of it. *That's why.* Do you understand? That's why you've got such tight curves and a body made to fuck and breed. And who's going to breed you, baby?"

"Y-you," I whisper back even though I have no idea how I did that.

How I formed a word and how I knew when to say it.

"Exactly." He keeps rubbing his fingers on my pussy as his dick pumps in and out of me at a slow and a lazy pace. "Me. And why is that?"

My vision is going in and out of focus. "B-because I'm your Firefly."

"Uh-huh. And because I'm your Thorn, aren't I?"

"You are."

"Good." He presses a soft kiss in my hair. "So then no more fighting, okay? No more arguments about whether you want my baby or not. Because we both know that you do. And we both know that I'm going to give it to you."

Drugged and hypnotized, I nod. "Okay."

"Although," he breathes on my forehead for a second as if it's getting real hard for him to keep up a conversation now that everything's settled and the pleasure is getting unbearable, "I do have to say that maybe you were right to run from me." I stiffen then but he keeps going, "Because with a body like that, I'm gonna wanna breed you over and over again. I'm going to want to put my baby in you as soon as your tummy goes back to being all tight and trim. So a piece of advice, okay? Don't let me catch you like that, don't let me catch you without a baby in your belly because if I do, I'm going to hold you down wherever I find you and stick my cock in your tight hole and fuck you until I breed you again, yeah? And with your fertile pussy and my superior dick, you know I'd do it."

And thankfully I'm not required to answer that because that's the moment he not only smacks my pussy like he'd smacked my ass and then my tits, but I also come. And I come like a hurricane, this orgasm even more intense than my last. Although to be honest I've been coming ever since he started licking my pussy and then whispered filthy things in my ear.

Although this time I'm at least aware of when he pushes me down, making me go on my hands and knees, and resumes his pumping at a break-neck speed. He fucks me like he just said he would, by holding me down, his hand now wrapped around the back of my neck, and his hips slapping against my ass.

I wish I could turn my head and watch him though.

I didn't realize it but that was one of the highlights for me. Along with his dirty but erotic words and of course his cock inside of me.

But not only is he keeping me leashed with his hand, but I also don't have the strength to do anything but take whatever he gives me, my body jiggling and my hair flying around my face with his brutal thrusts.

Oh, and coming.

Because I haven't stopped doing that yet.

Not even when I feel him reach climax and come himself.

In fact my never-ending orgasm becomes even stronger as I feel his dick jumping and pulsing inside of me, dumping his load. That I know I will want over and over and over again. Even when he gives me a baby and all of this is done. Because if my pussy is made to breed, then his is the cock that's made to breed me.

And the thought is so dangerous and so sure — like the sun rising every morning — I think I see stars.

I think I see pieces of them falling all around us and I smile, still feeling his dick throbbing inside of me, still coming myself.

But then I realize these are not stars.

These are fireflies.

Tons and tons of them, surrounding us, lighting up the night for us. And they're so magical.

Magical and majestic.

Beautiful.

They're the most beautiful thing I've ever seen.

And a few minutes later, when Ledger's done and he pulls himself out of my body only to pick me up in his arms bridal style, they still stay and frolic around us and I can't help but whisper, "Fireflies."

Holding me in his arms, he begins to walk. "Yeah."

I look up at his face, illuminated by these tiny creatures and the mighty moon. "Is that why you call me Firefly? Because they light up your favorite woods."

His eyes glitter. "I call you Firefly because you light up my life."

My heart races even though it hadn't calmed down much after our mind-blowing sex. "They're beautiful."

He doesn't move his eyes from me as he says, "Yeah."

And I think instead of the fireflies, he's talking about me.

I'm also talking about him when my heart whispers, *you beautiful thing, you.*

Chapter Twenty-Six

"WHY DO YOU WANT A GIRL?" I ask him an hour later.

When we're back at the cabin and in the bath.

It's steamy and hot and absolutely perfect.

I hadn't realized how exhausted I was after a day of crying and being angry and then running and yes, the epic sex in the woods. And apparently, he's exhausted too because he takes a little bit of time answering me.

And it's kinda adorable.

Him waking up now after having almost fallen asleep.

The way he blinks his eyes open, his brows bunching up slightly in confusion. And the way he breathes all sleepily, his warm chest moving beneath my cheek. Not to mention, his arms that were around me like he couldn't bear to let me go jerk slightly before tightening up.

"Hi," I whisper, looking up at him.

Finally he dips his face, focusing on me. "Because I like the idea of a little girl with blue-gray eyes and dark hair. Who'll love cotton candy and have a tinkling laugh like wind chimes."

I blink. Then, "Y-you think I have a tinkling laugh like wind chimes?"

His gaze roves over my face. "Yeah."

"You've…" I lick my lips. "You've never said that before."

He gazes down at my lips. "I've also never said that your voice is loud."

I gasp. "How dare you?"

"But I find it peaceful."

My eyes are wide. "P-peaceful?"

"Yeah." Then, "Why else do you think I ask you to tell me stories at night?"

"Because…" I can't believe I'm saying this. "I give you peace."

"Sure," he says, his voice strangely sounding amused. "And put me to sleep."

I open my mouth to say something but then realize what *he* said. Swatting his chest, I say, "You're such a jerk. I'm never telling you a story ever again."

He chuckles lightly. "You will."

"I won't."

"Only so you can torture me."

That gives me a pause. "Actually, that's not a bad idea."

He smirks. "That's my bloodthirsty girl."

I blush then.

For more reasons than one. Not only is he right about my bloodthirsty and revenge-thirsty ways — something that I didn't know I had until I met him honestly — but also because I did draw literal blood tonight with all my scratching and digging my nails.

He's got scratches all over his back, his sides, his neck.

Something that so totally horrified me when I saw them in the bathroom's mirror. But all he did was smirk and said, with pride even, "My girl's got mean nails."

"I'm so sorry," I'd whispered in distress.

"It's okay though. I've got a mean dick. We're even."

God, he's crazy, isn't he?

Despite blushing, I raise my eyebrows. "Well given what a firecracker I am, are you sure you'll be able to handle not one but two of me?"

His amusement increases. "I think I'll be fine. Given that I'm the Thorn and I'm the only one who knows how to handle my Firefly."

I shiver at his affectionate but also determined tone as I tell him, "And what if she turns out to be a hopeless romantic like me?"

"I hope she's a hopeless romantic."

"She may even read romance novels."

"I hope she reads romance novels." Then, "In fact, I'll buy her one when it's time."

"And what about high heels?"

"What about them?"

"What if like me, she likes high heels?"

"If she does then I'll make sure she never falls."

"What if she does fall?"

"Then I'll be there to catch her."

Damn it.

I hate when he does that.

I hate when he's sweet like that; I can't be mad at him or annoyed with him.

Shaking my head, I whisper, "She'll drive you crazy."

"It's her God-given right to drive me crazy."

"*And* the guy she falls in love with."

That gives him a pause. Then, with a light frown between his brows. "The guy she falls in love with."

"Or a girl," I tell him. "You know, someone special in her life."

His frown thickens. "No."

"What?"

"I don't know."

I frown too. "You don't know what?"

"If there will be someone special in her life."

"I don't —"

"Besides me."

I blink silently. Then, "You."

"Yeah."

I open my mouth to respond but then close it. I do this for a couple of times before I ask, "Are you saying that you don't want there to be someone special in her life?"

"No," he explains with a deep frown. "I'm saying that there's no need for someone special in her life when she's already got me."

I look at him then.

At his angry frown. The stubborn jut of his chin. His arrogant brows.

Yup, he's crazy.

And yeah, I think it's adorable.

"That's very," I search for a word that won't offend him, "sweet."

Although I don't think I was successful because his frown only grows.

I keep going though, "But Ledger, I think you need to prepare yourself for the eventuality that she's going to have someone else in her life —"

"I don't need to prepare for anything."

I press my lips together to stop the burst of laughter. "I mean, of course you're going to be her first love but —"

"And her last. There's no but."

Okay, he's making it real hard for me to keep my laughter at bay. But somehow I manage to stay sober. "But there's going to come a time when she'll find someone," he opens his mouth but I speak over him, "who'll, I don't know, take her to prom or the homecoming dance. Or like, on dates or —"

"I'll take her to prom and homecoming."

"I —"

"They're extremely overrated, by the way, but yeah, if she wants to go, I'll take her. And she doesn't need an asshole boy to take her out on dates. I'll do that too. In fact, I'll teach her how every guy she'll ever meet is never going to be good enough for her and so she'd better stay away from all of them." Then, "Oh, or *a girl*. No girl is good enough for her either. But it doesn't matter because as I said, she already has someone special in her life."

"You, you mean?"

"Yes."

"You sound completely insane, you know that, right?"

"Better than being a loser dad who lets his baby girl go out on dates with douchebags."

I go speechless after that.

Only able to study his damp hair, his wet eyelashes, the droplets all over his flushed, bronzed skin.

Dad.

He's going to be a dad.

Isn't he?

I don't know why it's hitting me like this. Or more than that, the fact that if he's going to be a daddy, then I'm going to be a mommy. Which is equally if not more life-changing, but…

All I can think about right now is that he already is more of a daddy to our little girl who may or may not be there yet than our fathers ever were to us. His abandoned him and his siblings the moment he could, and mine, while present all my life, is more of an evil presence.

How could I have ever thought of *keeping* her from him?

Keeping his family away from him.

"I want to stay here," I blurt out with no finesse whatsoever.

His arms around me flex. "What?"

I know it's a shock to him.

It's a shock to me too. Before I said the words out loud, I didn't know that I was going to say them. I didn't know how badly I want to stay here. At the place that gives him peace. Because apparently it gives me peace too. After months and months of living in fear and on the edge because of my father, I want something… calm and simple.

I want something that gives me joy. And being here with him — despite what happened today — has been the most joyous thing that's happened to me since last year.

I know it is the same for him too.

This is his favorite place, his place of solitude, and I know something is going on with his brothers and soccer. Maybe if we stay here, I can figure it all out and help him. Like he's helping me.

So fuck the ovulation window. Fuck reality.

Fuck everything for now.

And live in paradise.

"A-at the cabin." His frown is back and I explain, "I don't want to leave tomorrow. Like we'd planned, but…"

"But what?"

I turn toward him a little more. Because this is important. This is something that needs to be said and decided before we both say goodbye to real life for a while.

"You have to promise me that you won't do what you did today. You have to *promise me* that you won't get jealous." I watch his jaw clench but I keep going, "I know you don't like to hear this and it might piss you off. But Ledger, it's the truth, okay? You can't be jealous. You have no right to get jealous. He's just a family friend. He's —"

"A family friend."

"Yes," I tell him firmly. "There can never be anything between us. Not like that."

He stares at me for a few seconds and I hope that he buys it.

I know I have twisted around my words a little. Because there *is* something between us. But even though we're engaged, there never *can* be anything between us because he's gay.

When he keeps his silence and doesn't catch me out on my sort-of lie, I continue, "I'm not yours. Not really. I never was and I never will be. And I'm sorry. God I'm so so sorry that I even thought about keeping her from you. But I promise that I won't. I will never ever keep this baby from you, Ledger."

And I promise to myself that I will find a way to make it happen.

No matter what my future holds and where I go, I will make sure that Ledger is never away from her.

Because just like we're his family, he's *ours.*

He's *mine.*

And I will stand by him. As much as I can. I know it's not going to be ideal, my life is more complicated than anybody realizes, but I'm nothing if not resourceful. I'm nothing if not a fighter.

I'm brave; he told me that.

And I will find a way.

But I need him to promise me that he can't do what he did today.

I reach for his face and cradle it with my palms. "I meant it when I said that that's all I want from you. A baby. And nothing else. I don't want…" My heart clenches in my chest. "An us. There is no us. So I need you to promise that you won't get jealous and territorial because —"

He straightens up then and for the second time tonight, works his athletic magic to position my body. He picks me up by the waist and turns me around so rather than sitting between his thighs like I was up until now, I'm straddling his hips.

Bringing his hands down to my butt cheeks, he goes, "Because my dick's the only thing you want."

I flinch, my hands settling on his shoulders. "I-I mean when you put it like that, it does sound very crass, but —"

He squeezes my butt cheeks. "No other way to put it, Firefly."

I blush. "No, it's not… I mean yes. I realize that, but it's not really like that. I only said that because I just don't want there to be any confusion between us and —"

"Confusion."

"Yes. I just…" I squirm on his lap and he squeezes my butt cheeks again, stopping me. "Listen, this is coming out all wrong. What I meant was that we both need a break from reality, you and me. I know you haven't said anything but I can guess. There's something going on with you and your brothers and it's affecting your game. And I… I just want to help and —"

"Don't need your help."

"But I —"

"What I really need to know though," he cuts me off, "is what's your reality?"

"Nothing," I say quickly and unconvincingly, tensing up.

"I'm guessing your asshole dad."

"That's not important." I try to push away from him. "That's not what I was saying. I was saying that —"

He doesn't let me go, keeping his hold on me firm and tight. "That all you want from me is my dick."

I wince again. "Look, I didn't mean that. I meant —"

"You should have," he says then. "Because I don't have anything else to give you anyway."

"That's not true. That's —"

Determination lurks in his features as he goes back to the topic I've been trying to avoid. "Are you going to tell me what your piece of shit father is doing to you?"

I regard him silently, cursing my own mouth for leading me down this path. Then, "No."

A muscle jumps in his cheek, his eyes dark and displeased.

"Because as I said, it's not important and I don't want to talk about him. Or anything related to real life," I tell him resolutely. "I just need you to promise me that you won't act out like you did today because you're jealous, and that y-you'll let me leave when I want to."

Still, he remains silent and displeased.

And I have to whisper, "Please, Ledger. Promise me."

"Are you going to run out on me like you did tonight?" he asks at last.

I shake my head. "I-I won't. I won't run. I promise."

"You promise."

"Yes. I won't worry you like this."

His eyes rake over my features. "Fine then. We can stay here, at the cabin. And you can leave whenever you want to. But when I find out what your father is doing, I don't want you to blame me for what I do to him in return."

His threatening tone sends shivers down my spine.

And warms me from the inside out.

Even though I will make every effort so he never finds out.

Because like my brother, he will lose his shit too. He'll lose it bigger than my brother, actually.

But I'm not going to think about that now, when I've gotten what I wanted.

So smiling, I whisper, "We're staying here then."

"Yes."

"I can't believe it." I grin. "I'm so happy."

He rakes his eyes over my features. "I can see that."

"I'm going to go swim in the lake every day," I say happily. "And we can have a picnic by the water. We can look at fall leaves and —"

"I think you need to shut up now."

I jerk back, offended. "What?"

"Because I think if I let you talk any longer, you're going to put me to sleep." I gasp but he keeps going, "And then this big fat boner that I've had ever since we sat down in the tub would just go to waste."

"That's very —"

"And then where will your poor little cum-hungry pussy be?"

"I hate —"

He puts a hand on my mouth. "Shh. So less talking and more fucking, okay?" With his other hand, he smacks my ass. "Come on, if I'm going to be stuck here with you, you might as well make yourself useful. Because my dick isn't going to fuck itself now, is it?"

Ugh.

He's so so arrogant.

But I love, love, love it anyway.

Chapter Twenty-Seven

EVERY NIGHT STARTS THE SAME.

He takes a shower before bed and, when he's finished, appears at the threshold all naked. I'm already under the covers by then and at the sight of him, I feel a quickening start up in my belly.

He starts to prowl toward the bed, his eyes pinned on me in a way that I can only call predatory. And my grip on the sheets tightens the closer he gets to the bed. I don't mean to do it, clutching my sheet to my chest as if I'm trying to protect myself from him, but it's something that happens every night.

Maybe because he looks so large and threatening.

A beast really. A creature of these woods with no clothes to tame his bursting muscles.

No cover of civility to hide just how powerful and strong and *raw* he is.

Plus his dick is right there.

All hard and studded with twinkling jewelry and pulsing with every step that he takes toward me. It makes my thighs thrum and my core clench. That trunk of flesh, rising from a thatch of dark hair. And I can't wait for it to get here. I can't wait until he puts it in me. Which is why it always surprises me that when he does reach me, I try to lean away from him.

Not that I go anywhere.

His hand strikes out like a rattlesnake and grabs me by the throat. My pulse flares under his grip, jumping and leaping under my skin. He uses his hold on me to bring me back where I belong — close to him — and up on my knees. It only takes a few seconds but by the time I get where he wants me to go, I'm halfway to breathless heaven.

Where he controls the air that goes into my lungs.

And doles out only a handful of heartbeats per minute.

Making everything slow and sluggish and sticky.

"Let go," he growls softly, referring to the sheet.

I blink and do what he asks me to.

He looks down at my nightie then, with a displeased frown.

Keeping me pinned in place with his hand around my neck, he uses his other to pull and snap the delicate spaghetti straps of my peach-colored nightie. I jerk each time it gives in to his superior strength, and each jerk of mine makes his dark eyes darker. It makes him press his thumb on my freckle, my pulse, as if impressing upon me once again that he's in control. He's the one who decides when I breathe and when my heart takes a beat.

"What number is this?" he asks then.

"S-seven."

"And you still don't learn."

"Because you like it."

"I like what?"

"Tearing them."

He pulls at my neck, bringing us even closer. "I do, huh."

My hands automatically go to settle on his heated abs, tracing the ridges, the rungs of his damp muscles. "Y-yes. I think you secretly like tearing my nighties. That's why I wear them."

And good thing that he stopped by my apartment a few days ago and got me a ton of extra ones now that we're staying here for a while.

He hums. "Maybe."

"Because you like proving that nothing can stop you from h-having me."

He licks his lips, with both satisfaction and hunger. "And no one can, can they?"

I press my thighs together at his gesture. "No."

"So maybe you are learning after all."

I nod, biting my lip.

Which is when he comes at me with a kiss.

And I latch on to it with all that I am.

But like always, his kiss comes to an end all too soon because he pushes me down and gets between my thighs. Lowering himself on the bed and putting his mouth right there.

On my pussy.

When he doles out the first swipe of his tongue, I come off the bed, my back arching up, my thighs spreading wider than before. But they're never wide enough that he can fit easily between them. He still has to put his hands on my limbs to open them more, to make the gap wider.

Not to mention, I have the tendency to snap them closed when he covers my entire core in his mouth, sucking at my slick lips and jiggling my tight little clit against the roof of his mouth. Like he's doing right now. So he has to keep his hands there, his large fingers dimpling my flesh and pinning me to the bed.

Which of course I love.

I love being pinned down by him like the firefly I am.

I also love it when he pins me down with his dick in my mouth.

You know the sixty-nine we did, back in the woods?

It's been over a week since then and now it's become my favorite thing in the world. Well, apart from him actually fucking me. And he knows that. He knows how much I love being choked by his cock while he's eating my pussy and how much I like it when he does it in the way that I can't move at all. With my head hanging over the edge of the bed and him bent over my shaking body to get to my cunt.

And yes, he does it while I'm tied up.

I never had a problem with the rope. My only problem was that he wouldn't let me leave, so I love it when he does that.

I love it when he ties me up and fucks my mouth, taking away my control. Something about his dominant position, with him stabbing his dick in my throat over and over as he lashes his tongue on my clit, covering my pale body with his tanned one, makes me come so fast and so hard that I don't stop for ages.

But sometimes he likes to simply spread my thighs and eat me out.

He likes to slurp at my pussy, growling and grunting at my taste. He likes to move his head side to side as if bathing his mouth, his jaw in my juices. And trust me, there's always a lot of it, my juices, my cum that keeps rushing out of me continuously. Streaming down my thighs, soaking the bedsheet but mostly ending up in his mouth.

Soon I'm grabbing his damp hair and getting him to come closer, my thighs coming to bend at my knees, my heels pushing against his shoulders, beating at them. Which I guess is a signal to him that I'm close and then it's up to him whether he wants to take me there or take his time with it, driving me even crazier and hungrier.

Tonight however, he takes mercy on me, and so when he notices my tell-tale signs, he pushes his tongue inside, spearing my little hole with it and giving me a hint of the electric pain to come, and bites at my clit. And as soon as he does that, gives me the hurt that I've come to love, I break apart.

It's always a revelation, the way I come for him.

My legs shaking uncontrollably, my pelvis contracting and my wet-as-fuck pussy clenching and clenching, squirting without my say-so. The way my body gives away all that I am and completely empties itself out for him.

The way I never ever came for myself.

And why wouldn't I?

I mean look at him.

Look at him rising from between my thighs, his mouth wet, his throat glistening.

Even his heaving chest and contracting abs are drenched.

My cum clinging to his hot bronzed skin and dense muscles like little raindrops.

That he then rubs into his skin.

Like some kind of an animal, bathing himself in his mate, making himself smell like me.

And every time I watch him do that, a mini orgasm runs through me.

Even so, I want his cock now.

Instead of him pumping it in his fist, I want him to pump it in my hungry pussy. Plus it looks so hard and ruddy and so *so* thick right now.

Thicker than ever.

Meaning he's hornier than ever.

Which doesn't bode well for me and my tiny pussy.

Which *in turn* means I'm going to fucking love that.

He runs his eyes up and down my bare body and I arch my back, thrusting my tits up, shaking them just the way he likes, and open my wet thighs some more for him. I even go so far as to touch my pussy, run my fingers through the center of my messy, sloppy core as I watch him back.

And like always when I do that, his eyes narrow to become slits and his jaw clenches so hard that I almost stop tormenting him. Growling, he knocks my hand away from my pussy like only he has the right to touch it, not even me. And motions with his finger for me to turn around.

It's such an arrogant gesture, bordering on rude.

Like he can't even be bothered to use his words or be civilized about it. And I love that so much that even though I'm still shaking, I do what I'm commanded to. I turn around and get on my hands and knees for him.

And then he's there.

Where I need him the most, right behind me and thrusting inside before I can even blink. And I'm dead to the world and alive only for him.

The very first thing I feel is the pain.

It's always there no matter how many times he's fucked me in the last week.

The struggle to get inside at first, his frustrated groans, my pained and horny moans. My own attempts to get away from him that he thwarts very easily when he grabs my meaty, child-bearing hips and pulls me back. But after five or six strokes, my pussy has no choice but to give in and bend to his will, stretching itself open to make space for his hard and thrusting, *mean* cock.

So the pain eases but the sharper edges of pleasure still remain.

And I think it's because like this, he touches places inside of me that I don't think are possible in any other position. I don't think those ladder-like studs of his can rub against these places, stroke these intimate parts of me any other way.

So even the pleasure becomes something that I have to suffer through.

With broken moans and clenched teeth and teary eyes.

As I push *backbackback* into his powerful thrusts.

But.

As addictive and earth-shattering as all of this is, the best is yet to come and I'm hoping and *praying* that it does tonight.

It starts with his thumb on my ass.

Right where my second tiny hole is.

My entire pelvis contracts including my slick channel, making him groan and pound into me harder for the next few seconds. Then with his other arm, he reaches out and grabs my hair in his fist, pulling me up, making me arch against his chest. It also makes his thumb push itself into my hole — only a tiny bit though.

But it's enough to make me whine, "No."

Slowing down his thrusts, he grabs my throat then so he can look at me upside down; his favorite way to look at me, I've found. "No?"

Reaching back to grab his thighs, I whisper, "No, please."

A muscle jumps in his cheek as he challenges, "Why not?"

"B-because."

"Because what?"

"It'll hurt."

"Yeah," he squeezes my throat and delivers a hard thrust, making my milkmaid tits jiggle, "For you."

"Yes."

"But it'll feel like a dream to me."

"B-but you can't be selfish."

"Yeah, why not?"

"Because I'm…" I have to stop here to go *uh, uh, uh* because he delivers three thrusts in a row, hard and fast, "I'm going to h-have your baby."

We don't know that yet.

But I'm really hoping that it happens soon.

He chuckles cruelly, harshly. "All the more reason to use your other hole now that I've used up your pussy."

It sends firecrackers rushing through my veins.

His threatening words. His threatening tone.

Just the fact that I know he can do it but he won't. Not without making it good for me.

So I whisper like I always do, "Just one stroke?"

And as always, he scoffs. "You know I won't stop at one."

"But I won't be able to sit down for a w-week."

Another sharp thrust that makes my teeth clatter. "Your problem, isn't it? Not mine."

"Or walk straight."

"Again. Not my problem."

I dig my nails in the backs of his thighs, my core clenching around his length. "But what if someone asks?"

He watches me with horny, narrowed eyes. "Asks what?"

I lick my lips. "Why I'm walking funny."

"You can lie, can't you? You're good at that," he taunts in a raspy whisper.

I shake my head. "I can't. I promised you that I won't lie."

"Are you saying you're a good girl now?"

"Yes."

"So what's a good girl going to say if someone asks why she's walking funny?"

"I'll..." My breaths jar out of me when he pounds into me again, his torso smacking against my ass. "I'll have to t-tell them that you did it. You put your dick in my asshole and it was so big. It wouldn't fit. But you didn't..."

"Care," he completes my sentence.

"No. You still put it in there."

"Yeah, I still put it in there."

"And it hurt."

"Poor baby," he murmurs, coming down to kiss my forehead as he flicks my back hole with his thumb once again.

I jerk and squeeze his length with my pussy. "And you were so mean to me."

"I was."

"I didn't want it."

"Yeah, you kept saying no, didn't you?"

"Yes."

"But I wouldn't listen to that either."

"I told you to stop it. That I don't l-like it."

"But I told you that I fucking love it and so you need to suck it up."

"Yes."

"Because ass-fucking is for the guys, not the girls, isn't it, baby?"

"Yes."

"Plus it's going to be over soon anyway."

"It is."

"But of course I lied."

"You always do when you're fucking me there."

"Tell me why."

"Because you always say..." My breaths are stuttering now like they always do when I'm spinning this dirty, filthy tale, driving him and myself all crazy and horny. "That my ass feels like heaven."

"Yeah, it does," he says, his mouth rubbing over my forehead, his thumb almost inside my ass and his lazy thrusts giving me life. "Your asshole feels like I've died and gone to heaven. And I know it's a mistake. I shouldn't be in heaven when my name's probably been written all over hell since the beginning of time."

"I don't—"

"But then, I'm not going be that dumb motherfucker who misses out on the opportunity, am I? I'm going to stay here, fuck the tight asshole of an angel who made the mistake of bending over in front of me until they tear me apart from her and put me where I belong."

I try to warn him then.

I try to tell him that I can't play this game anymore. The game where I'm a Powerless Firefly and he's my Selfish Thorn. The game where it seems like he's the only one winning but in reality we both win.

That I'm going to come.

But I guess he already knows that.

Because he pushes me over the edge with his next words: "So how about we make a deal then? How about if I make you come right now, I get to fuck your asshole. Because if you come, it means you like it, don't you? No matter how many times you say no. Because if you come, you can tell them that even though I fucked your ass without your consent and made you hurt, you still came all over me. Like a good little whore."

At this, the orgasm that overcomes me is even bigger than the orgasm that came before.

It's so massive and painful and *electric* that it sends me into a whole other stratosphere altogether. Where I don't know who I am or where I begin. Or what's happening around me, but I do know when he comes. When he fills me to the brim with his cum.

His seed.

And then like always, he picks me up and runs a bath for me. Where I instantly fall asleep as he washes my hair and soothes my still-trembling body.

So yeah, that's how our nights go.

Our mornings have a routine too though.

He's always the first to wake up and God, he wakes up at a really ungodly hour like 5AM every morning. But instead of getting annoyed by it, I like to enjoy the show.

After his morning ritual, he comes out as he does after his shower: naked. Dropping his towel on the floor and going to the dresser to pull out his running clothes.

With the sheet wrapped around my chest, I prop myself up on my elbow, watching him put on his running pants. "You do know that you don't have a magical cleaning fairy who cleans up after you, don't you?"

He turns toward me then, his chest still bare and his pants sitting low on his hips, displaying his V, looking all daisy-fresh and ready to go for the day. "But I do have a Firefly who does it for me."

"Oh you do, do you?"

He nods slowly, his eyes taking me in from top to bottom. "Yeah. And I'd say she's pretty magical herself."

My heart skips a beat. "Pick up your towel, Ledger."

"And deprive you of the pleasure of doing so yourself?" he deadpans. "Not even in my dreams."

"I do not get *pleasure* in cleaning up after you."

It's a total lie but whatever.

He smirks, folding his arms across his chest, flexing all his muscles and making himself look even more appealing. "Yeah, is that why you almost have an orgasm every time I leave my dirty laundry on the floor?"

I sit up, offended, still clutching my sheet. "I do not almost have an orgasm."

"Fine, a mini-orgasm then."

"You're such a jerk, okay? You can —"

"*I* do though."

I swipe my hair off my face, glaring at him. "You do what?"

"Almost blow in my pants when you bend down to pick up my towel."

"Ha ha." I stab a finger at him. "Very offensive and such a cliché in the porny-housemaid genre."

Unfolding his arms, he approaches the bed. "*And* when you run around the kitchen, your cheeks all flushed from the heat, your tits jiggling, to get me my cookies or cupcakes in time for dinner every night."

"Again, cliché."

"But mostly," he reaches the bed and, putting a hand on it, he bends down, "I'm this close to creaming all over myself when you write out your lists for me."

Okay, that's a new one.

I blink a couple of times. "The g-grocery list?"

"Yeah," he says, his eyes flicking back and forth. "Because it makes me feel like you depend on me. For things. That if you want something, I'll be the one to give it to you. *You know* that I'll be the one to give it to you."

My heart is banging in my chest now and I say breathily, "For the third time, cliché." Then, I add, "Although this one's in the uber masculine-caveman genre."

Amusement runs through his eyes and he murmurs, "Well, it's a cliché for a reason, isn't it?"

"I —"

His eyes rove over my face. "Because if I'm ready to blow in my pants right now, you're dripping onto the sheets."

My core clenches. "I am not."

"I can smell you."

"You can't smell me. That's absurd."

"But true."

"You know what, you should go."

"Yeah?"

"Yes. You're getting late for your stupid workout."

"That also gives you a mini-orgasm."

I roll my eyes even though he's right. "You really should leave now. The wood won't chop itself if you stand here all day staring at me."

Because that's what he does: he chops wood and then he runs laps and laps on end around this place.

While I lounge around in bed, watching him through the window.

And yes, having mini-orgasms.

"No, it won't," he agrees.

"So then —"

"I think if I stand here staring at you all day, no power on this earth can chop this wood, let alone me."

I nod sagely. "Exactly." Then, confused, "What? What wood?"

His mouth pulls up in a smirk. "Why don't you think on it while I do this?"

"Do wh —"

His hand shoots out and grabs the back of my neck, pulling me toward him. At which point, he kisses the breath out of me and when he's finished, he straightens up and, grabbing a t-shirt, leaves.

He's almost to the door when I gasp. "I just got it," I say to his retreating back. "Your stupid, immature wood joke."

Then before I can think about it, I grab a pillow from beside me and throw it at him, making him chuckle.

With a sigh, I settle back against the pillows and I do it smiling.

As always though I fall back to sleep after watching him wield the axe and his hypnotic, rhythmic movements. Only to wake up an hour or so later — which is still early for me — to start my day. Which usually includes prepping breakfast before he comes back, all sweaty and panting.

All delicious.

So I guess he was right; I *do* run around the kitchen, trying to get everything ready on time.

Whatever.

Anyway, where we eat that breakfast depends on what the weather's like.

Sometimes when it's sunshiny, we go out and have a picnic by the lake like I told him I wanted. We swim in the lake; we take walks and whatnot.

But sometimes when it's cloudy and raining, we stay home and after finishing our breakfast, we hang out in the living room. Especially by the big window that overlooks the pretty rain and the woods. We usually end up on the cozy rug with me sitting propped up against the couch and him — believe it or not — with his head in my lap while I read him my favorite romance novels.

Which of course he makes fun of.

If he doesn't fall asleep after a while.

285

Which I don't mind at all because he looks so peaceful like that.

But sometimes he stays awake and that usually happens when the book is super angsty. And I can't believe I'm saying this, but he is a big chicken when it comes to angst.

"What the fuck?"

I stop reading. "What?"

"They're about to fuck in his office," he states like I don't know.

"Well, yeah. So?"

"So." He frowns, the lines around his mouth pulled tight. "They're going to get caught, aren't they?"

I close the book and set it aside as I answer, "I'm not going to tell you that. I'm not going to spoil it for you."

His jaw clenches. "I don't care. We're not reading that shit."

"Why not?"

"Because it's bullshit," he goes, that frown thickening between his brows. "Because they're idiots. Because why the fuck would they take that risk, fucking in his goddamn office. And because if they're going to fucking do that, be stupid like that, I'm not going to waste my time reading about it. Take your fucking pick."

Just for context: I'm reading a particular favorite of mine where the hero's a poetry professor and the heroine is his student who gets obsessed with him and stalks him. And I've hit the part where the hero and the heroine are about to do it in his office.

I purse my lips together lest I burst out laughing.

Although I don't think I'm doing a very good job of it because his frown thickens even more and he glares up at me.

Somehow I do get control of my amusement and say, running my fingers over his forehead, "You do know this is just fiction, right?"

"I don't care."

"And it's romance. They are going to get together in the end, just so you know."

"I don't fucking care if they get together at the end. I'm still not wasting my time reading their dumb story."

I trace my fingers along the side of his face, his high cheekbones and the slant of his jaw. "I think you do care."

"No, I don't."

This time I can't stop my smile as I reply, "*I* think that big bad Ledger Thorne AKA my Beautiful Thorn that everyone is afraid of, is a teeny-tiny bit of afraid of angsty romance novels."

His eyes narrow. "Is that so?"

"Yup." I nod, grinning like a fool. "I think you're a big bad *baby* when it comes to even a little bit of drama in love stories."

His jaw tics for a bit before he murmurs, "And that's funny, huh?"

I chuckle. "A little bit, yes."

And then I lean over and kiss his displeased frown. But then I think maybe I should kiss him some more, a lot more, so I place kisses all over his face. From his sharp cheekbones to the tip of his arrogant nose. From one side of his sculpted jawline to the other before coming back and pecking him on his downturned mouth.

He lets me do it for a bit, probably for half a minute or so, before he comes for me.

Before his arms shoot out and he grabs the back of my neck with one and my hair that was making a curtain around us with the other. Fisting my strands and pulling me back toward his lips, he gives me a proper kiss.

A kiss the way that he likes it.

Wet and thorough.

That I like as well.

Not for long though.

Because pretty soon he breaks away and then he's tackling me to the floor. He's sitting up but bringing me down on the rug, maneuvering my body under him, rolling it on the cozy rug and going for the attack.

By that I mean not the sexy kind but the other kind.

The ticklish kind.

And I can't stop squealing and writhing and laughing and screaming for him.

I can't stop pushing him away and going breathless when it doesn't work. I even warn him that I'm going to pee if he doesn't stop torturing me, but of course he's not afraid. Just when I think though that I'm either going to pass out or *really* going to pee, he stops and stares down at me, panting and all flushed.

I'm flushed too.

Probably more than him.

I'm definitely panting more than him for sure.

"Y-you're…" I swallow, tightening my fists on his shoulders. "You're a jerk."

His own hands, which have somehow ended up framing my face with his fingers buried in my hair, tighten. "Better than being an asshole who doesn't make you laugh."

I don't know how it's possible but my rapidly beating heart squeezes. "That's —"

"You're beautiful, you know that," he rasps, his eyes glittering, swimming with things.

"I —"

"The most beautiful girl I've ever seen."

"You —"

"Sometimes I don't know whether to wrap you up in the softest silk and feed you cotton candy while you sit in my lap."

"I think you need to stop talking."

"Or burn all of your clothes so I can keep you naked 24/7."

"Stop *talking*, Ledger."

"And choke you with my cock when the mood strikes."

I blink my eyes. "Okay, I'm gonna cry now."

He rubs his thumbs over my cheeks. "Yeah?"

"Yes." I hike my open thighs up his body and wrap them around his hips. "You can't be all poetic and filthy and expect me to keep my cool."

His lips twitch. "Well if you cry, I'm here to wipe your tears."

I sniff. "With your dick?"

"If I want to."

"I don't get a choice?"

He hikes my thighs even higher then. "When have you ever gotten a choice?"

My eyes almost glaze over. "Oh, good point."

And he does.

Wipe my tears with his dick.

Well, first he makes me shed them while I'm on my knees, struggling to fit his big cock in my mouth, but yeah, he totally gives me what I want.

Which is how all our breakfasts and romance storytellings go.

Sometimes I don't want it to end, my time here.

I don't want to go back to reality. Back to Bardstown, where everything is bleak and hopeless. That's why I also keep my texts and phone calls with my friends short and sweet. I've met them a couple of times but not as frequently as I used to before. They got a little worried in the beginning but I assured them that everything was fine so they've backed off now. Which is great.

But I guess you don't always get what you want, do you?

Because reality comes knocking when I get my period.

I've been watching the calendar as the days pass and for a little while it looked like I got my wish. My period was late and given that I've always been fairly regular, I couldn't help but hope. But all my hopes are dashed when one morning, after days of being late, I wake up with telltale signs of the time of the month. And since my period is always bad, I have bloody thighs and excruciating pain in my belly.

So much so that this becomes the first morning where I wake up before him.

In fact I jump up from the bed and run to the bathroom when, along with waves of pain in my pelvis, I also feel a surge of nausea. While I'm throwing up in the toilet, Ledger rushes in and I wave my hands at him, telling him silently — while puking — to go away.

But he comes even closer and, dropping down to his knees, he holds my shivering, shaking body in his arms. He pulls my hair back as I empty my stomach. When I'm done, he helps me flush the toilet and stand up on trembling legs. He opens the tap at the sink and I throw water in my face and brush my teeth.

All the while slowly dying inside.

And all the while he stands behind me, rubbing my back, majorly concerned — I can feel the tightness in his body — but patient to what I need in the moment. I wipe my face with the towel that he hands me and I think that I'm okay now. I think I can calmly tell him what's going on but when our eyes meet in the mirror, I can't stop it.

I can't stop the tears or the sob that bursts out of my mouth.

And he spins me around and plasters me to his chest.

He cages me in his warm embrace and I sob and shake against his sturdy frame as I tell him in broken and sputtering words that I just got my period. I don't know how I was expecting him to react to this news but all he does is rub my back some more while chanting, "It's okay. It's okay. I've got you. I've got you, baby."

I dig my nails in his bare chest and sputter, "S-she's…"

That's all I manage to get out but he doesn't mind. He keeps doing what he's been doing, rubbing my back, squeezing my body to his, lending me all his warmth while making shushing noises.

But I try again, looking up. "She's not… She's not h-here."

His jaw clenches and it makes me sob even more.

He's disappointed, isn't he?

Of course he is.

He wanted this as much as me, but all he does is wipe my tears and says, "It's okay. We'll —"

"No, it's n-not," I snap, or rather try to while also hiccuping. "She's not here, Ledger. I'm not pregnant. I-I thought I was when I didn't get my p-period but it was just late and it's here and she's n-not and I…" I look up at him with pleading, begging eyes. "What if… What if there's something wrong with me?"

It has occurred to me in the dead of the night, see.

That even though I want this badly — and I've always wanted this badly — there are no guarantees. And what if something *is* actually wrong. What if…

He squeezes my body, breaking my thoughts. "There is *nothing* wrong with you."

And he means it.

I can tell.

What I thought was disappointment on his face is actually determination. He's firm in making this happen. In fact, he has absolute faith that it will happen.

And I want to melt then.

I want to melt into his chest, his warmth. His words.

I want to let him reassure me and then carry me back to bed and keep me in his arms forever.

But I can't do that.

I have to say something to him. I have to tell him something.

"Listen," I say, getting my misery under control and putting my hands on his harsh jaw. "I know you want this. I know you want *her*. But…" I take a deep, shaky breath and forge ahead. "If I can't, for some reason, for *any* reason, give her to you then I want you to go find s-someone else, do you understand? I want you to go out there and find it with… some other girl. Who could —"

I don't get the words out because he swoops down and captures my mouth in a kiss, effectively shutting me up.

Which is both good and bad.

Because I don't want to talk about him building something with another girl. I don't want to even *think* about that. And I know how selfish that sounds, given that I can't build anything with him.

Because my period isn't the only reality that we have to face, isn't it?

We have other things coming and soon.

———

My period is late again.

And I wake up with slight nausea for the third day in a row.

After last month, I know what it could mean but I also know what it couldn't. There's one way to find out but I've been afraid.

What if it's not what I'm thinking?

What if all my hopes are for nothing?

Even so, I can't hide under the covers forever, can I?

So I make myself climb off the bed and go to the bathroom. I open the medicine cabinet and get out the simple test that'll tell me the truth — well, 99% of the time: a pregnancy test. Something Ledger bought tons and tons of without me ever putting it on the list.

I quickly take the test and then wait the appropriate two minutes as directed.

Which turn out to be the longest two minutes of my life.

When the time's here, I grip the stick tightly as I check my fate.

At first, I can't believe it. I think I'm seeing things.

But somehow it registers.

And when it does the knowledge hits me in my belly.

Right in my womb.

Before I can give it a conscious thought, I'm running out of the bathroom. I'm dashing down the hallway, throwing the front door open, hurrying to get to him. I know he's doing his workout thingy — chopping wood; I could see him through the window before I went to do the test.

Plus I can hear him.

The hypnotic thwack that I always fall asleep to.

Even through the noise though, he hears me coming.

Which is a good thing because as soon as he turns around and spots me, his forehead bunching into a frown, I jump into his arms. But thanks to his fiendish workout schedule, he hardly gets jarred.

I wind my arms around his neck and for the first couple of seconds, all I do is breathe his musky, cinnamon-y scent. And I think he does the same with his palms under my ass, clutching my panty-covered cheeks and his nose buried in my neck, our chests moving in a rhythm.

Then, I whisper, panting, "I think you should get your tux ready."

"What?"

"Because it looks like you're going to the prom."

He doesn't respond to it but I know he heard me.

But more than that I know he understood me.

Because his fingers on my ass squeeze tightly.

But still I don't want there to be any confusion so I continue, "Daddy."

At this, he goes completely still.

His wildly breathing chest freezes and I don't detect even a single twitch on his body that I'm plastered to. Squeezing my thighs around his naked hips, I'm about to break away from him but he does it himself.

One of his hands snaps up to my hair and he yanks my head back.

Which is when I realize that all his emotions, all the life in his body has been reflected in his beautiful dark eyes.

"What'd you say to me?" he rasps, barely able to get the words, his voice even, out.

My lips pull into a smile. "I'm pregnant."

"Pregnant."

"With your baby."

"My baby."

My smile blooms into a grin then even as my eyes tear up. "She's here. She's coming. We did it."

Finally a shudder goes through him.

A tremor.

Bigger than ever.

Bigger than the jolt that had hit me when I saw the test myself.

So I slide my hands up to his face and cradle his cheeks and ask him what he asks me every day. "Are you happy?"

With his eyes looking liquid and flickering with a thousand emotions, he rasps, "Fuck yeah."

At which, my tears spill out and he comes down to lick them away before sealing our lips in a sweet, sweet kiss.

Chapter Twenty-Eight

Her Beautiful Thorn

THERE ARE certain moments in your life that you remember forever.

That you *know* you'll remember forever.

Not because these are happy memories — most of them aren't — but because these are the memories that have shaped your life.

The day your father left and your mother wouldn't stop crying. The day it *really* sank in that he wasn't coming back. The first time you punched someone and it felt so fucking good. The day your mother died. The first time you wanted to run away from home; it was either that or kill your own big brother and his rules. The first time you held a soccer ball in your hand. The very first goal you scored.

The day you saw her for the very first time, sitting on the hood of her brother's car.

The first time she came to your soccer game. The first time she smiled at you.

The day you broke her heart and left her crying in her dorm room.

And then there's the day when she tells you she's pregnant.

With your baby.

And immediately after telling you that and changing your whole fucking life and making you the happiest son of a bitch on this planet, she texts a guy named Ezra.

Ezra Vandekamp, that's his full name.

He's a real estate mogul and the heir to the Vandekamp empire. Currently in Korea for a big-ass merger and the groundbreaking for a construction project of a hotel building. They're calling it the next masterpiece of architecture and him a genius for managing both the business side and the design side of it. They're also saying that he may be what the Vandekamp empire needs to keep pace with the changing architecture and real estate markets.

There's a whole interview on him in *Architectural Digest* and *Forbes*; I looked it up online.

I'm not into reading so I didn't read the whole thing. Plus I didn't think that I could. Not after reading her texts, or rather a couple of them. For the record, I hadn't gone snooping on her phone. It was right there, on the nightstand, opened on the texting app. She'd just gone to take a shower after I'd fucked her against the tree right after she told me the news. I found that I couldn't stop myself from making that connection with her.

Even though what we'd set out to do had been done.

Turns out she didn't mind it either, so I fucked her like an animal and then carried her back into the cabin where she fiddled with her phone for a bit — I remember that specifically — before going for a shower, and I'd been hunting for a fresh pair of pants.

Which is when I saw it.

The texts.

Her: Can't wait until you get back. We have so much to talk about.

Him: Still trying to wrap things up here. Will keep you updated on my return.

That was a week ago.

In the week that has followed, I've tried to put it out of my mind. I've tried to ignore it. Every time she picks up her phone, I've tried to not focus on it and wonder who she's texting now. Why is there a fucking smile on her face? Has he *updated* her on his fucking return? Are they fucking making plans to meet with each other?

Mostly, what are they going to do when they do meet?

Is she going to smile at him, just the way she had back at that restaurant when I saw them together? Is *he* going to try to touch her? Because if he is, I'm going to fucking break every bone in every finger that makes contact with her creamy skin. Actually I'm going to break his every finger period.

And his toes.

He may be a real estate mogul approved by her daddy but I'm the Angry Thorn; I can break him into two if he so much as looks at her.

Because he is that, isn't he? Approved by her daddy.

No, I haven't forgotten about that. About what she'd told me at the restaurant a few weeks back, about her piece of shit father wanting her to get together with him, wanting her to *mingle* with him. And neither have I forgotten about the fact that she wants to stay here to escape reality, that I already know has something to do with her father.

So what, is he fucking *forcing* her to marry Ezra?

Is she saying no and her father is not letting it go?

Would he hurt her, hurt the baby growing inside of her, if she didn't agree to his demands?

What is it?

What *the fuck* is it?

If I don't know then how can I protect her?

So as I said, in the week that has followed, I've tried to not think about it but ended up obsessing over it anyway.

Which is why I'm doing this.

On the surface it may appear criminal — and yeah, it is; breaking and entering into someone's apartment and stealing important documents is criminal — and it may also appear that I'm breaking my promise to her.

The promise that I gave her weeks ago.

About not getting jealous and letting her leave when she wants to.

But I'm not.

I want to be very clear about that. That this is not me breaking the promise.

This is me specifically taking measures to *not* break it.

This is me putting my obsession over this piece of shit Ezra, my jealousy — that she specifically asked me to not feel — to rest. And of course, trying to protect her from whatever danger is waiting for her in the real world. I have no intention of ever holding her to what's about to happen here.

Why would I?

She doesn't want anything from me — except a baby, which we've made — and I've got nothing to give her.

Even though I'm going to regular therapy sessions — with an old woman called Dr. Mayberry who watches me far too closely for my liking — I still haven't been allowed to go back to practice. Apparently it will happen when I've completed a certain number of mandatory sessions.

Meaning my career is still a mess.

And frankly it's going to remain so until I get out from under my brothers' thumbs.

And while taking care of her and our baby girl has become my priority now rather than soccer or European league, I'm still the same guy who hurt her.

I'm still the same guy who hardly knows anything about love or softer emotions or tenderness. I still can't give her a romance novel life.

So all of this is to protect her and get my rage under control.

Could it all turn out badly? Fuck yeah.

Could she see it as me betraying her? Also fuck yeah.

But I don't care about that right now.

Right now, I need to do this. I need to calm the beast, clear my head, my vision that's been painted red ever since I saw those texts. So I don't make it worse. I don't break the promise that she specifically asked me to make and kill Ezra.

And maybe, just maybe, I can protect her from her father in the process too.

"I need you to sign these," I hear myself say to her.

Sitting at the dining table, she barely lifts her head from the grocery list she's making. "Sign what?"

Standing over her, I clench my teeth. "These papers."

"What papers?" she asks. Then, to her herself, "Wait, do we have that tomato sauce you like? Or are we all out?"

"I —"

"You know what, let me go check and —"

She's about to get up from the table when I stop her, my voice more severe than I want it to be. "You can check later. Just sign the fucking papers."

She finally looks up, her frown in place. "That was very rude. I'm doing it for you. Because if I use a different kind of tomato sauce for the pasta, you get all snippy and fussy."

I do not get snippy and fussy.

For anything.

Ever.

But I don't want to argue with her right now when I'm already on edge and shaking with impatience. "It'll take two seconds. Then you can go back to making all the fucking lists you want."

Her frown only grows. "What are these papers exactly?"

"Insurance."

"What?"

I exhale sharply. "I want you on it. On my medical insurance. So I had my manager get the paperwork started. And he needs your signature before filing it."

I hate that I'm lying to her.

Or rather, not telling her the whole truth. Because there are indeed insurance papers in the bundle that I've given her. It's just that there's something else in there too.

Her face softens and she presses a hand on her still flat belly. "For her?"

Fuck.

Fuck.

Why does she have to be so goddamn beautiful?

So *heartbreakingly* beautiful.

Her blue-gray eyes are shining and there's a rosy flush on her cheeks. Her dark hair is tied up in a messy knot like it usually is by dinnertime with a few tendrils of hair teasing her neck.

And I don't see any other way. I don't see how my anger can be abated if I don't do this.

I don't see any other way to protect her either.

Glancing at her small hand on her tummy, my chest tightens and I rasp, "Yes."

If possible, her face grows even softer. "Fine. Gimme."

Before she can change her mind, I slide the papers toward her. She picks up her pen and signs on every page where I tell her to. And then it's done.

Since I already roped in a couple of bought witnesses to sign the papers before, with her signature, the deed is fucking done.

She gets up from her chair then and flits over to the fridge, once again mumbling something about the sauce that I like. But I don't hear her over the roar in my blood.

The thunder in my heart.

The ringing in my ears.

I can actually feel my restlessness, my jealously abating. The red leaches from my vision and I can finally see the world clearly. I can finally *breathe*.

The first free breath I've taken since I saw those texts.

Mine.

She's mine.

Even though that's not what this is about, I can't help but feel a rush of satisfaction coursing through me. At the thought that Ezra can't take her away from me. *Her father* can't take her away from me. No one can.

No power on this earth or the sky.

Because now I'm standing between them and her and our baby.

Me.

Her husband.

And she's my wife.

Part IV

Chapter Twenty-Nine

"ARE YOU OKAY?" I ask the dark interior as soon as the truck comes to a stop.

He doesn't answer me however. He keeps gripping the wheel just as tightly as he's been doing for the past hour, while driving all the way from the cabin to my brother's house.

I don't take offense at his silence though. I know there are various reasons for it.

First because I didn't want him here in the first place.

We had an argument about it too, which he won obviously. And even though I'm secretly happy that he'll be here with me — I'm going to need all the moral support that I can get tonight — I still think it would've been better if he'd stayed away.

For his sake I mean.

Because I'm going to tell my brother.

That I'm pregnant.

With the baby of the guy he's hated for years.

Not to mention, this also means that by extension I will be telling my best friend as well. Who may or may not have a clue about my history of obsession with her brother.

Well, if she didn't know before, she'll know after tonight.

My brother will as well.

Because time has come to spill all my secrets when it comes to his high school rival.

Who still hasn't spoken so I try again. "Ledger —"

He gets out of the truck then, cutting my words off. And I want to jump out as well but I know that will only piss him off — these days he gets really

299

mad when I do things by myself, including putting away groceries or opening my own doors — so I wait for him to round the vehicle so he can do it for me.

And I climb out.

Slowly.

Again something he gets really mad about. When I do things at my pre-pregnancy speed.

I don't know whether to be mad at his craziness or simply laugh at it because it's cute, yes, but totally unnecessary.

Especially at this stage.

When I'm only seven weeks pregnant.

Which is still surreal to me, that it's been seven weeks already, when it feels like it was only yesterday when I found out about my pregnancy. We even got the confirmation from the doctor yesterday. We wanted to go sooner — as soon as we'd found out a few weeks ago — but the people at the clinic advised to wait some. Because sometimes it's hard to detect a heartbeat that early.

So yeah, seven weeks.

Which means the time has come to tell my brother and my best friend that we're having a baby.

And that's the second reason why he's so quiet and stressed.

At the fact that I'm telling them anything at all.

He doesn't think they need to know. He doesn't think it's any of their business, what we do, what happens between us, what happens to this little secret in my belly. Something that is very ironic because once upon a time he was all about bragging and exacting revenge. Which only goes to show that we've come so far, he and I. And I do agree with him to some extent.

That this isn't any of their business.

We're both adults and we both made a decision.

But they're still a part of our lives, so they should know. So when it looks like after closing the door he's about to walk away from me, I grab his arm to stop him. "It's going to be fine."

He looks down at me, his eyes hard, the lines of his beautiful face firm.

Still silent. Still displeased.

So I put my hand to his face, rubbing the muscle that's jumping on his cheek. "He's my brother, okay? He doesn't run my life, but he has a right to know."

That muscle beats under my touch for a couple of seconds. Then, "I want you to know that if he says something to you, if he makes you even little upset, I'm going to —"

"No, you won't," I tell him with a firm but a calm tone. "You won't do anything. You'll let me handle it."

"I —"

"Like I asked you to, remember?"

I did ask him to do that.

Before we drove over, I asked him to let me take the lead on this. To let me handle whatever happens tonight. He didn't like it but he also couldn't say no to me. Another thing that has happened over the past weeks; he can't say no to me. For anything.

It's amusing actually.

The way he pampers me and takes care of me like I'm the most precious thing to him in the world.

But right now, he grinds his jaw because as I said, he hates this.

"Look," I throw him a small smile and caress his harsh jaw, "I know you hate this. I know you hated it when I asked you to promise me that you'd let me handle it. But trust me when I say that I know him, okay? I know how to handle him. He's my brother and —"

"And you're my wi —"

His words come to a screeching halt.

Which is strange.

What's stranger is that he looks like he's been stunned. All color leaches out from his face and he goes stark white.

And I don't understand.

What just happened? What was he going to say?

Worried, I step closer to him. "Ledger? What happened? What's —"

His trance breaks then and he looks just as angry as he did before.

Like nothing ever happened.

"I don't care if you know him or if he's your brother. I won't allow anyone, and by that I mean *any-fucking-one*, to upset you right now."

I sigh at his unforgiving expression. "He may get mad in the beginning, sure. But he'll come around when he sees how happy I am."

At least that's what I'm hoping.

That he'll see the smile on my face that I can't seem to contain these days. The hope in my eyes, the way I walk on clouds, the way I can't stop touching my still-flat belly waiting, *just waiting*, for it to grow and swell.

"And are you?" he asks like he's taken to asking ever since we found out about the pregnancy.

And he always does it with a strangely intense look in his eyes.

Like everything depends on my answer.

His entire life depends on it. His world. His very existence.

Like he won't be able to bear it if I'm not happy.

It's crazy and so very sweet.

And gosh, it makes me want things that I shouldn't want.

Like the fact that I never want to leave. Our cabin. Our little dreamland. Our paradise.

The fact that I want to stay here with him forever.

Smiling, I nod. "More than anything."

His jaw clenches with emotion. Things swirl in his gaze and I do what

I've taken to doing these days. I grab his hand and bring it to my belly. As soon as his fingers touch me, he breathes out a long breath.

A long peaceful breath.

That makes me think that all his worries just left his body and all he cares about is this.

What's in my belly.

"And they are too," I add.

His fingers flex and his chest shudders. "They."

I bite my lip, looking into his wonder-filled eyes. "Uh-huh. Both of them."

He swallows, speechless.

I'm kinda speechless too.

Not in a million years could I have expected that when we went to the doctor's office and the technician pulled out her wand, that we'd hear not one but two heartbeats. One after the other, totally unrhythmic but the sweetest music to ever exist. Ledger was so shocked that for a few moments he was frozen. And when he did come out of his stupor, I noticed that his eyes appeared the prettiest that they've ever been.

Because they were glistening.

Before I could point that out though, he whipped out his cell phone and proceeded to grab the video.

Which he watches and listens to every night before going to sleep.

"I don't know how you're going to decide," I whisper then, getting my emotions under control and pressing my own hand over his.

"Decide what?"

"Which one to take to prom."

He frowns slightly. "I'm not going to."

"No?"

"Fuck no," he says, digging his fingers harder. "I'm taking both."

I shake my head at this. "You're such a girl dad, you know that?"

"What's a girl dad?"

"Someone like you. Someone extremely protective and possessive. Super tough on the outside but a *big* softie like..." Then, "Hey, a big softie like cotton candy on the inside."

"Cotton candy."

"Yup. All sugary sweet soul and a glittery pink heart." He narrows his eyes but I don't get deterred. "And look, now you'll have two princesses to spoil."

"Are you done?"

I press a hand to my chest. "Aww, how sweet."

"You're done."

I widen my eyes in mock horror and say in a sing-songy voice, "Ooh, I'm so scared, big daddy."

I would've laughed at my own joke.

But somehow it doesn't feel like one. Not when he's staring at me like that.

At the D word I mean.

With a heightened intensity and something dark — darker than the early winter evening around us; darker than his pitch black eyes — lurking in his gaze.

It makes my heart beat faster. It makes a pulse start up between my thighs.

Making them shake and tremble.

And just when I think I'll explode with it, with the awareness and his potent gaze, he breaks it.

He steps back, taking his hand off my body. "Let's just get this over with."

He's right.

There are more important things to think about right now.

Than the way he looks at me and makes me feel.

But before I could obey him, he says, "And it's three."

"Three what?"

His features are blank but his voice ripples with meaning when he answers, "Three princesses. Not two."

It's only when I'm halfway up to my brother's house that I get it.

I get what he meant.

He doesn't just have two princesses to spoil, he has three. And the third is me.

Isn't it?

A smile blooms on my lips as I reach my brother's house.

Alone for now.

The plan is for me to get there first and then for Ledger to follow me a few minutes later. So as to look like we didn't arrive here together. I even asked Ledger to park out of sight from the house. He can bring his truck with him when it's time for him to make his entry.

Only because I want to ease them into the news, not break it like an explosion. So first we're going to have dinner — which was how I proposed tonight's plan to Callie: let's have dinner together — and then when it's over, I'm going to ask Reed if we can talk in private, which is when I will break the news.

When I knock at the door, a tired looking Reed — messy dark hair and bloodshot eyes — opens it with a sleepy Halo in his arms.

"Hey, bro," I greet with sympathy. Then I turn to the lethargic baby, rubbing her soft curls. "How are we doing?"

Callie told me over the phone that Halo's having a hard time with teething and her schedule is out of whack right now. Meaning both their schedules are out of whack and they haven't gotten much sleep.

Reed steps to the side, letting me enter as he says, "Well, we barely slept last night and haven't stopped screaming and crying all day long. So," he rubs his palm on her back, soothing her, "pretty fucking good."

I give him a look at his F word.

He pulls a face. "Oh, for fuck's sake. My baby girl's suffering. That's pretty much all the torture that I can take right now."

Callie emerges from the kitchen, looking pretty as ever but also the exhausted mom of a sick baby. "It's true. I'm letting him get away with it."

Before I can respond, there comes a knock at the door and both Callie and Reed frown.

Reed longer and harder than Callie.

Because they can see who it is through the glass door.

My brother's hated enemy and my best friend's beloved older brother.

With curt movements, Reed opens the door. "What the fuck are you doing here?"

I flinch at my brother's rude tone.

And then I flinch at the clench in Ledger's jaw.

Not because I think he's going to break his promise to me. But because I know he won't.

I know he's trying to control his temper right now and I know he's doing it for me.

"I was in the area," he says finally, proving me right.

"In the area," Reed repeats.

"That's what I said."

"I live in the middle of nowhere, asshole. There's no such thing as being in the same area."

Ledger shifts on his feet. "Well what can I say, I like taking walks in the middle of nowhere."

Reed fumes. "You have five seconds to tell me exactly what the fuck you're doing here or I'm shutting this door in your face."

And I've had it.

"Reed," I snap. "Enough. Let him in. His sister lives here. And his niece."

Reed glares at me for a few seconds before turning to Callie, who's shaking her head at him. Her disapproval is what makes my brother budge and he steps away from the door, letting Ledger in. I close my eyes in relief but then snap them open when I feel *his* gaze on me.

He looks me up and down, takes me in, as if checking to make sure that I'm okay.

Even though I left him only like ten minutes ago.

As ill-advised as it is, to stare at each other in front of our siblings, I can't fault him for it.

Because I can't take my eyes off him either.

I can't help but want to go to him and put my arms around him.

Wanting to soothe. Wanting to make his strain go away. God, I fucking hate reality. I hate the world. I hate all the people in it.

I just want us to go back to our little paradise in the middle of a forest and never leave.

"This is the third time."

Reed's voice makes me flinch and I break my gaze away from Ledger to look at my brother.

His words are clearly addressed to Ledger so he focuses back on Reed. "Third time what?"

"Third time I've found you here, sniffing around my sister." My heart skips a beat as Reed keeps going, "If I find out that there's a reason for that, no one, not even *your* sister, can stop me from feeding you your own teeth, you got that?"

Ledger's jaw tics for a few suspended moments.

Then, "I wouldn't expect anything less."

Not completely satisfied because Ledger is going to stay, Reed reluctantly still jerks up his chin at him and turns away, heading for the couch where I think he was sitting, keeping Halo company and looking after her, before we came. And Callie heads for her brother, wrapping her arms around his torso and face-planting on his chest in exhaustion.

Great.

Just *great*, isn't it?

Everything is going super well.

Not.

———

ACTUALLY, I take it back.

Everything is going well, if not super well.

After the initial tension between Reed and Ledger, things seemed to mellow out. Quite possibly because of Halo. Because both of them are trying to cheer her up and make her smile.

So many times over the past couple of hours, I wanted to touch my own belly and imagine how Ledger will play with our two little girls; how he'll take care of them; carry them in his thick and sculpted arms; put them to sleep in his burly chest. How they'll call him dada; how, like Halo, they'll get excited to see him too; they'll babble and coo and play with his crazy hair; they'll crawl or wobble or run on their chubby feet to get to the man who'll be their best champion for the rest of their lives.

God, I can't wait.

I absolutely *cannot* wait to see my baby girls play with their daddy.

And their daddy being a total pushover for them.

But I refrain. From touching my belly, I mean. Because if that's not a dead giveaway of the secret that I'm carrying, then I don't know what is. And this is not the way that I want my best friend to find out the truth.

But anyway, as I said, things have been going well.

So it never occurs to me that I'll be the one to blow it all to hell.

I am though.

And the stupid culprit is the carrot cake that Callie has baked for dessert. The spices in it and their normally very appealing scent.

Honestly, I was kind of afraid of this.

Dinner triggering my nausea.

But I've been fairly symptom-free so far. I do get mild nausea here and there but other than that I've been okay. But then again I'm only seven weeks, which the doctor told us is fairly early for any major symptoms to kick in. I tuned out during her whole explanation about hormones and whatnot but from what I understood, the next few weeks could be brutal. If they are, there's nothing to worry about because my body is simply doing its job.

Besides, I figured if I want to ask questions later, I can always go to Ledger.

Because, believe it or not, the man was taking notes.

And asking questions.

About what, I don't know. I did hear something about how to relieve the symptoms if they do show up and if a twin pregnancy is different than a single pregnancy, and if that's likely to cause me more stress and severe symptoms.

But anyway, the fact that my nausea is at its worst right now and every breath I take seems to make it worse is not what I need right now. I can't even swallow; everything feels heavy and sticky in my mouth. In my tummy and my chest.

I don't want to make anyone suspicious though.

Not before I tell them.

So I have no choice but to take bites out of this giant piece of carrot cake.

"You okay?" Callie asks, concern a thick frown between her brows.

"Uh-huh," I say, pursing my lips and making a very difficult swallow.

"You don't look so good," Callie goes on still.

"No, I'm…" I exhale slowly. "Fine."

"Why do you look like you're going to be sick?"

That's Reed.

Both with his big brotherly concern and disgust. And that spooks me more, because being my big brother and my only caretaker all my life, he does know what my 'sick' face looks like. Instantly I shake my head, trying to deny it; which turns out to be a mistake.

"If you're going to throw up, Pest," Reed goes on, "you better —"

"Can you leave her the fuck alone?" Ledger snaps. "Let her breathe, for God's sake."

I glance at him then.

I've been trying to avoid looking at him all throughout dinner even though I felt his eyes on me from time to time. Looking at him now helps a little, makes me feel safer and that things are going to be okay.

"Yeah, what do you know about it, asshole? Who the fuck are you to tell me how to talk to my sister?" Reed growls.

"Can we please keep it down," Callie chimes in. "Halo's sleeping down the hall and…"

I'm pretty sure she's saying something more.

But I can't hear her because in the next second, I'm shooting out of the chair and running out of the dining room. I burst through the bathroom door down the hall and my legs give out, sending me down on the floor and in front of the toilet where I finally throw up.

God.

I've never felt such relief in my life like I do now.

Although it only lasts a second or *maybe* two. Because first, when I stop gagging and can breathe, I hear noises behind me: scraping of chairs across the floor, thuds of footsteps, raised voices — mostly masculine. And second, when I think it's over, my urge to throw up, and I can run out of the bathroom to see what the hell is going on, it comes right back.

And it comes with a vengeance.

That makes me keep throwing up until I have nothing left in my body but my muscles are still contracting in a major way.

When I think I might pass out, I feel a hand on my back.

A soothing, cool hand.

To match the soothing, cool voice of my BFF. "You okay?"

Panting, I hug the toilet. "I… I don't…"

"It's okay," she coos, rubbing my back as if I'm her distressed baby girl. "It'll pass. I promise."

I shake my head. "What's… What's happening out t-there?"

"You don't have to worry about that now," she says, pulling my hair back and away from my face. "You just take a few deep breaths."

I try to pull myself up and straight. "No, I think I'm… fine now. I —"

"Just give it a minute," she advises, still rubbing my back. "Sometimes it feels that way. But then it hits you out of nowhere and —"

She gets cut off because she's right.

Just when I thought it was over, it comes right back again and then for the next however many minutes, I'm still throwing up in the toilet. When I'm done and my muscles are all sore, Callie reaches out from behind and flushes the toilet. She helps me stand up and walk to the sink where she opens the tap for me and I proceed to rinse my mouth and clean up.

She's holding me throughout all this and I'm thankful for it because it doesn't look like I can stand on my own.

"So how far along are you?"

At her question, I jerk my eyes up and meet hers in the mirror.

They're knowing.

She *knows*.

Maybe because like touching your belly, throwing up from a random food — something you really liked pre-pregnancy — is another dead giveaway. Plus she's been through all this herself.

So even if I wanted to, I wouldn't be able to deny it to her.

And honestly I don't want to anyway and I whisper, "Seven weeks."

"It's his, isn't it?" she asks next, her eyes frank and her tone clear. "My brother's."

I swallow, trying to gauge her mood, but I get nothing.

Besides, again it's the truth, so I nod. "Yes." Then, "Just don't tell —" I hear the door slamming against the wall then and I straighten up from the sink, throwing the towel away. "He knows too, doesn't he? My brother."

Callie grimaces. "Well, there was no way to hide it. When you were throwing up in here and Ledger was going crazy out there, trying to get to you, he kinda figured it out."

Now I'm feeling nauseated for another reason altogether. "I need to go out there. I need —"

"No," Callie stops me. "What you need is to gather your strength. You need to relax and maybe lie down."

"I can't lie down," I say frantically, turning away from the mirror and facing her. "They're out there and I'm pretty sure Reed is trying to commit murder right now."

Callie is still unbothered. "Well, if he is then I can assure you that Ledger can take care of himself. They've done this before, remember? They both know how to handle themselves. *Your* health is more important right now, especially when it's only going to get rougher after this."

"No, they haven't."

"What?"

I can't believe I'm standing here, explaining things to her when Ledger is out there, going through God knows what.

But the sooner we finish chit-chatting, the sooner I can go out there. "Listen, the reason I came here tonight was to tell you guys. You and my brother. I was going to explain everything to you guys and somehow, someway, diffuse the situation enough so my brother doesn't end up killing *your* brother."

"But —"

"And he can do it, okay? Reed *can* and *will* kill Ledger if I don't go out there and interfere. Because in my stupid infinite wisdom, I told Ledger to behave."

Callie is still confused. "You told him to behave."

"Yes," I say frantically, my dread mounting by the second. "I told him to not antagonize Reed. I made him promise, so we need to get out of here and save his fucking life."

She still doesn't move. "You made him promise."

"Yes," I say exasperatedly. "Why is that such a big deal?"

"Because," she replies slowly. "No one can make my brother promise anything. He's a hothead, remember? Completely unpredictable and —"

"You know what." I fold my arms across my chest, still feeling weak but not too weak to make my point. "I find it very offensive that you'd talk about your brother like that. He's not a hothead." Then, "Okay, maybe he is. But that's not all that he is. There's more to him than just being the Angry Thorn. So yes, he's done some unpredictable crap in the past and made some mistakes. But who hasn't? Are you saying that *you're* so perfect that you've never made a mistake? He cares about people, okay? Maybe he doesn't show it all the time but he does and yes, I made him promise and he agreed to it and —"

"Okay, I get it," Callie says, her face lined with something very akin to amusement. "My brother is a saint."

"I never —"

She reaches out and squeezes my shoulder. "Hey, I'm glad. I'm actually pretty thrilled. About all this."

"Y-you are?"

"Yes." She smiles. "Not only because we get to be double sisters now but also that my brother has found someone who finally understands him. Ledger has always been different, you know. From the rest of my brothers. Well, he's the same in so many ways but he's … his own person. His personality is different and I always wondered, growing up, if we ever understood him completely. And the fact that you get that, that you can actually see beneath the surface is the most wonderful news ever." Then she grins. "Plus you guys are having a baby together. This is amazing. This is like, the *best* news I've heard ever since my studio told me they're opening up an on-site daycare center." Then, even more excitedly, "Oh my God, I need to decide what to wear to your wedding!" Gasping, she goes on, "Can Halo be your flower girl? Please, I'll train her."

She looks so happy right now.

Something that I didn't expect.

Not right away at least.

I thought I'd have to do more convincing, and I never thought I'd say it, but this is worse.

This is worse than the worst.

Because I'm not marrying Ledger. We're not even *together* together. Yes, we will raise our babies together, but from a distance. It's going to be a harmonious co-parenting situation.

Right?

Well, it has to be. Because there's no other option.

"Listen, Callie, the thing is that —"

She slaps a hand to her forehead. "Oh my God, what are we doing? We need to get out there before my husband kills your future husband."

Holy shit, yes.

And so we both rush out of there and by the time we get outside, I'm relieved to see that Ledger is alive but distressed at the fact that he looks wrecked.

His eyes are already swollen and there are bruises all over his jaw.

Plus his lips are bleeding.

And he's pinned against his truck with Reed at his throat.

I rush down the front steps as I snap, "Reed, stop it."

My plan is to physically separate my brother from Ledger if I have to. But it falls apart because Ledger snaps his eyes over to me and thrusts his hand out. "Stay back."

I come to a halt with Callie at my side. "Ledger, you —"

"Stay the fuck back, Tempest," he pants out, his chest heaving.

"But —"

My protests come to a halt when Reed pulls at Ledger's t-shirt, jerking him away from the truck, before slamming him right back. Hard, making Ledger grimace slightly and me gasp.

Then, "Answer me, motherfucker. Is it because of what I did to Fae? Is this your idea of payback for getting your sister pregnant?"

"Roman, let him —"

Reed snaps his eyes over to Callie, his gaze full of venom. "Don't."

Callie bites her lip and stands down.

And I hate that I'm coming in between them. Reed never — not ever — denies Callie anything. He'll walk through broken glass if it means he can watch Callie smile. So for him to say no to her makes my heart squeeze.

Painfully.

"Reed, please," I implore then. "Let him go. Let him —"

"No," Ledger says then, replying back to Reed's question.

Ignoring me and Callie, Reed turns back to him. Then as if I hadn't spoken, he tightens his grip on Ledger's t-shirt and goes, "So what, you wanted to do it?"

Ledger licks his bloody lip. "Yeah."

It's the wrong answer because Reed decks Ledger under the jaw, making his head snap to the side.

I scream again for Reed to stop. Callie does it too.

But he doesn't listen.

He doesn't even turn away from Ledger. "Are you saying that you wanted this? That you did this to her on purpose. You *knocked my sister up* on fucking purpose."

Ledger faces Reed again, wiping the dripping blood from his mouth. "Yeah. I wanted to knock your sister up on purpose. So I did."

Again, it's the wrong answer.

Actually it's probably the wrongest answer in the moment because it sends Reed into a rage. And when he starts raining down punches on Ledger, he doesn't stop. He keeps going and going and I don't know what to do.

I don't know how to make my brother stop.

Except to shout at the top of my lungs, "It was me, okay? I asked him to."

I even try to ignore Ledger's command from before and rush over to the pair of them. But this time, it's Callie who stops me. She shakes her head at me as she whispers, "You can't. Not in your condition."

So helpless, I try again. "Reed, please. Stop it. Let him go. I told him to do it. It was me. My decision."

Something about what I said penetrates through the fog and Reed finally stops.

Thank God.

Although if Ledger was wrecked before, he's completely destroyed right now. His t-shirt is torn. There's blood everywhere. Bruises and cuts are blooming left and right on his face. And not once during all this did he try to fight back.

Actually, not once did he try to defend himself even.

Not once did he try to dodge my brother's wrath or protect himself in any way.

All because he made me a promise.

All because he's my Beautiful Thorn and I'm his Lovelorn Firefly. And I stand here, watching him with all the misery and all the sorrow in my eyes, while he stares back with all the concern in his. Because of the bout of nausea that I went through and all the stress that I'm going through now in my condition.

Finally, I give in and put my hand on my belly. To tell him that they're okay.

We're okay.

"Your decision," Reed says, still keeping a hold of Ledger but now focused on me.

I sniffle and wipe the silent tears off my cheek. "Yes, it was me."

My brother's jaw clenches. "Why?"

I rub my belly in short strokes. "B-because I always wanted a baby."

At this, my brother's gaze goes to my belly. Then, looking up, "Why him?"

Before I can say anything to my brother, Ledger growls, "Leave her alone."

Reed ignores him though as he repeats, "Why him, Tempest?"

Because once upon a time, I loved him. And I loved him like crazy and all the dreams that I'd ever had became attached to him. And even though things are different now — I'm not in love anymore and he will never be; plus both our lives are messy — I still wanted a piece of him. I still wanted something to remember him by.

Because for the life of me, I can't imagine not having that.

I can't imagine not being connected to him in some way.

It started out as revenge, an effort for me to move on but it has become so much more now. We have become so much more than who we were to each other.

We are a family.

And guess what, he ended up giving me so much more than a baby too.

He gave me my self back.

For the past year, I've been living in shame.

Shame for falling in love with him. Shame for pursuing him. Shame for being stupid enough to think that there could be something between us. But he taught me different. He made me realize that I'm brave.

And so tonight, I'm also going to let go the shame that I've harbored even before this last year.

The shame of falling for my brother's enemy. The guilt for betraying him.

Because I wasn't. I was just following my heart.

And doing that can never be wrong.

Could I possibly hurt my brother with this news that I'm about to give him, yes. And I'm sorry for that. I'll always be sorry for whatever hurt I'm about to dole out to him in this moment. But I'm not going to feel sorry for wanting who I wanted before and for taking him in whatever capacity that I could now.

So steeling my spine, I reply, "Because he and I, we have history."

"History," my brother says in a flat voice.

"Yes." I nod, still keeping a hand on my stomach proudly. "I know this will come as a shock to you because I never told you. And that's on me. I should've told you. I should've said something. Way before this. But for the longest time I thought I was betraying you. I was betraying your trust for... wanting the guy you hated so much. Because I did. I did want him. I more than wanted him. I loved him and... And the truth is that I don't want to be ashamed anymore. Of the past and who I wanted. Or of the fact that I chose to do this. Because being ashamed of that would mean being ashamed of myself and I'm not. I'm not ashamed of myself or what I want. In fact, I'm brave. For wanting these things and going after them. Even if they seem unconventional to others."

I press a hand on my belly. "And I know it may look unconventional to you. Maybe even a mistake. But it's not. It's my decision. A very adult decision. Something that I've thought about really long and hard. And if you just let him go and forget your anger for a second, I'll tell you everything. About the past. About why I chose to do this, okay? Just please, I —"

"How long?" Reed asks.

"What?"

"How *long* is your fucking history?"

Before I can answer him though, Ledger goes, "Leave her the fuck alone."

Something about Ledger's voice registers with Reed and he turns back to him. "Or what?"

"Or it's time that I show you…" for the first time tonight, he goes for my brother's fists in his t-shirt and shakes them loose, "…how to really lay down a punch."

"Yeah, what was stopping you before?"

Ledger's ticking jaw is his only answer.

"I'm guessing my sister, huh. Who's apparently your girlfriend. Well, your *knocked up* girlfriend. Who just told me she's been betraying me all this time."

I flinch at Reed's angry tone.

And I know Ledger notices because his tone gets eerily soft. "You wanna be pissy about that, be my fucking guest. But if you upset her in this condition, *after* she puked her guts out in your bathroom, I will make you swallow your own teeth, you understand? Before you can ever come for mine."

"Is that so?"

"Fuck yeah," Ledger bites out. "And you don't want to test me on that because if we're giving each other high school labels now, then let me tell you that she's not my fucking girlfriend. She's the girl I'd burn down the world for. The girl I'd kill for. And then die a thousand fucking deaths for. And yes, I knocked her up. Not with one but two babies. Which means I don't have just two but three people to protect now. I'd fucking bury you in the ground without so much as a thought while your wife and your sister watch. So I suggest you think really long and hard before opening your mouth."

For the longest time all I can hear are my breaths.

Frantic and heavy and needy.

So freaking needy for him.

To go to him.

To hug him, to touch him. To kiss him.

But then Reed speaks. "Well that was a nice fucking speech, wasn't it?"

Ledger growls; I swear I hear it.

"Color me impressed," he goes on. "And completely on board with this fucking craziness you two have got going on. Except," a muscle beats in his cheek, "you tell her yet?"

Ledger stiffens at that.

313

"You haven't, have you?" Reed continues with a smirk. "The girl you'd burn down the world for. You haven't told her the truth."

My heart slams in my chest.

It slams even harder when I feel tension radiating out of Ledger's body.

"Reed," I call out, not being able to stop the tremor in my voice.

My brother turns to me then, his face hard and his eyes — so much like mine — appearing angry. "You're an adult, aren't you? You've thought this through. Well, congratu-fucking-lations for hitching your wagon to a guy who's not only wrecked his career but apparently, is also a liar. And hasn't said a word about it to you. But hey, send me the wedding invitation, won't you? And save me a piece of cake because I'd love to watch this train wreck happen in real time."

Chapter Thirty

"OKAY, THAT SHOULD DO IT," I say, finishing tending to the last of his cuts.

In *our* bathroom. Not at my brother's and Callie's.

Because we're back at the cabin.

After the fight, my brother left us all out there and went for a drive. Callie tried to make us stay — and I wanted to, because Halo's sick and she could use all the help — but given that Reed literally left the place because Ledger and I were there, it was best just to leave.

"Although I still think we should go to an ER because I don't like the look of your nose. I'm worried it may be broken."

Not the first time I've said this tonight but so far, he's completely refused.

All because I threw up a little tonight. Well, a lot, but still.

It's the norm though, isn't it?

You're pregnant, you throw up.

But nope, leave it to him to make a big deal out of something that happens to every pregnant woman.

When he chooses to remain silent, which basically means no again, I shake my head and pack up the first-aid kit, ready to put it away, when he grabs my arm and pulls me back.

And I have no choice but to look into his eyes.

I wasn't until now.

I haven't, ever since we left Callie and Reed's house.

Not because I'm mad at him. Or I believe what my brother said about him lying. But I knew that if I looked at him, I'd break down and ask him. I'd beg him to tell me what the hell is going on with him.

And his brothers.

And why and how is it affecting his soccer.

So far in the past weeks I haven't. Mostly because we both have been trying to avoid reality and living inside our own bubble. Plus I understand keeping things to yourself. Now more than ever, when he himself suspects that I'm hiding things from him and he has respected my wishes to not poke and prod.

But now that I'm finally looking at him, looking into his eyes, I'm finding it so much harder to resist.

So much harder to simply stand here and not do something.

Something like hug him and soothe him while at the same time, somehow fight against the whole world for him.

For his bloodshot and agonized eyes.

As if someone is tearing him apart on the inside and he's bleeding.

And the fact that his face is more purple and swollen than not is making it even worse.

"Ledger," I begin, "What my bro —"

"I've been suspended," he says, his voice hoarse but firm.

"What?"

His chest moves with a breath. "From the team."

My heart thuds. "Why?"

At this, his chest moves even more, his breath longer and noisier. I leave the stupid first-aid kit and grab his bare waist. Somehow knowing that he needs the support for what he's going to say next. And the fact that he puts his hands on my waist in return, as if he's thankful that I'm there, is only making me want to weep more.

But I can't.

Not right now when he needs me to be strong.

"Because I punched someone."

"What, who?"

He clenches his jaw for a second before replying, "Another player. From the opposite team. And I did it at the game, *during* the game."

"O-on live television?"

Another clench but he nods. "Yeah." Then, "And he... pressed charges."

I step closer to him. "What?"

"I spent a night in jail."

"Oh my God, I... I didn't —"

"That's not important though," he cuts me off. "My team pulled a lot of strings to get me out in twenty-four hours, which got them a lot of bad publicity. The press kept saying that instead of punishing the player that went rogue on the field, they were trying to save his ass. So they suspended me for the foreseeable future." Then, "And well, forced me to take anger management therapy. So until a therapist deems me fit to return, I can't play. I can't set foot on the premises. I can't go to practice. I can't do anything."

"Anger management therapy?"

He stares down at me with harsh eyes and his torn lips twist into a bitter smile. "I'm the Angry Thorn, aren't I? The hothead. The unpredictable player. Who knows what I'd do if left unchecked."

"But that's not all of who you are. Yes, you have your moments but —"

"To them I am."

"Who are they?"

This is the question he doesn't reply to but he doesn't need to.

I already know.

"Your brothers," I whisper.

Anger ripples through his features before he says, his voice low, "Well, they do know me better than anyone else."

They don't.

They absolutely do not know him better than most.

I don't think *anyone* knows him. Not the real him at least.

Not the layers and layers that make him who he is.

That's what Callie said tonight, didn't she?

That no one has ever understood him, understood what's inside of him.

"Why did you punch him?" I ask, my hands on his chest now, stroking his hot and smooth flesh, trying to soothe him.

His brows bunch together. "What?"

"Why did you punch him? This guy," I explain. "What did he do?"

His eyes look back and forth between mine. "No one's ever asked me that."

And oh my God, I could start crying right here.

I could start bawling my eyes out at how *sad* and *lonely* and *fucking heartbreaking* that statement sounds. How it completely shatters my heart and seals my belief that no one, absolutely no one, knows who he is.

My arms go up and clutch his shoulders then, my fingers dig into his skin and my body automatically comes even closer to his, my curves molding themselves around his unforgiving parts so I can touch him everywhere.

So I can seep into him and give him peace.

"*I'm* asking," I whisper, craning my neck up and looking at him intently.

His arms do the same, going around my waist, fisting my dress. "Because he was running his mouth. And not for the first time."

"Running his mouth about what?"

His grip on my dress tightens and he takes a few seconds before he answers, "The truth."

I bring my hands even higher and grip the side of his neck, pressing my thumb over his pulse. Like he does mine. Not in a dominating way, no. But in *my* way, my gentle way, trying to calm his heartbeats as I ask, "What truth?"

He licks his torn lips. "About how I never could've made it on the team. Not without my brother's help."

"What?"

"I was the last draft pick," he says, his eyes intent and staring. "If Shep hadn't stepped in, I never would've made it onto the team, let alone *any* team. I never would've scored an agent and such a highly regarded one at that. Shep was the one who convinced everybody at New York FC to let me come aboard. He gave them reassurances, guarantees. He vouched for me and told them that even though my reputation precedes me and I'm considered a wildcard, I'm his brother. I'm talented and hard-working and I'd never let them down."

Shaking his head, he continues, "I hated that. I fucking *hated* how he had to come to my rescue. How he had to save me yet again. Save his hothead of a younger brother. Just like he used to back when we were kids. Not only that, Stellan stepped in too. He vouched for me as well. He told them that as the Assistant Coach he'd keep me in line. He'd make sure that I behaved. And then Conrad came on. The star coach everyone's always wanted on their team and of course, management was pretty fucking happy not only to snag him but also because he knew how to handle me. He knew what to do, what rules to make, how to fucking push me to do my best and keep me reined in. Which is why they went to him when I fucked up."

He chuckles harshly. "They went to him when they didn't know how to save their asses after what I'd done. And instead of having my back, my own brother threw me under the bus. It was his idea to have me benched. To send me to therapy. To fucking treat me like a liability. Like he's always done."

The air around us has changed.

It feels heavy and swollen.

Like before a thunderstorm.

And I realize two things in this moment.

One, that I haven't felt this in a long time. This change in the air that he causes, that his *anger* causes. I didn't even feel it back at my brother's and Callie's house. And I think it's because he's been so at peace for the past weeks. He's been calm and happy even.

And second, his anger isn't anger at all.

His anger that he's *so* famous for, that he's known for far and wide — so much so that yes, his reputation does precede him — isn't anger in the first place.

It's pain.

It's hurt and anguish. It's torment and trauma.

He's not angry at his brothers, he's hurt at their actions. He's hurt that they don't give him the benefit of the doubt. Probably never did. That *no one* ever gives him the benefit of the doubt. He's hurt that they design rules and build cages and pass judgement to rein him in, instead of actually listening to him.

Instead of actually understanding him.

And when you're that isolated, that misunderstood, your pain comes out as anger.

Anger that hurts other people.

But also him, doesn't it?

I mean, I don't have to look further than myself for this. Just imagining how tormented he's been over what he did to me. Not only a little over a year ago but since the day we met. He's been punishing himself all this time for hurting me, for taking his anger out on me.

And I'm about to tell him that.

I'm about to tell him that his anger isn't anger at all.

That his nickname — the stupid fucking nickname — is a myth. Everything about him is a big giant myth.

When he says, urgently, "And I want you to know something. I want you to *know* that yes, I fucking hated the idea of anger management and I still do but I'm doing it."

"What?"

Determination ripples across his bruised yet still beautiful face. "If it's the only way to get back on the team, then I'll do it. I'll go to therapy."

"Y-you will?"

"Yeah. I'll do it for you."

My chest heaves. "For me?"

So is that where he goes?

Is that where he's been going for the past few weeks when he isn't going for grocery runs? To therapy. I never asked him because again, I didn't want to seem nosy but I've wondered.

His gaze bores into mine and his fingers on my waist unfurl and splay, touching my tummy from one end to the other. "And for them." He digs his thumbs into my belly button and I arch up. "I'll do it because for the first time in my life, I have a purpose. A bigger purpose. A purpose bigger than soccer or trophies or championships. A bigger purpose than my ego, revenge, rivalries. And it's to provide for them. It's to take care of them. And you. I'm not going to let you down. I'm not going to let *them* down. I know I didn't tell you the truth before tonight. I know I kept this big secret from you and I... I'm sorry for that. I'm so fucking sorry. The only excuse I've got is that I didn't want you, *not for a single second*, to think that I'm incapable. That I'm incapable of taking care of you and of them. Because I'm not. I'm not like my father. I'm not like your father. I want you to know that. I won't ever do anything to make you or them feel unsafe or not provided for or —"

I press my trembling hand on his lips to make him stop. "I trust you."

His eyes flare slightly in response.

But I don't move my hand from his mouth until I've said my piece. "I do. I don't care that you hid this from me. I've hidden a lot of things from you too." *I still am.* "And neither do I care what my brother said. What he did tonight, how he reacted, it hurt me, and in a way I understand where he's coming from. I don't know if he'll ever be able to forgive me for keeping the truth from him. But I don't care what he thinks. Not about this. About us. About you."

Then putting a hand on my tummy, where he's gripping me, I continue, "While I don't need you to take care of me, Ledger, I know you'll do everything in your power to take care of them. You'll do everything that you can to provide for them, to always be there for them. You already *are* doing it. You already are the best daddy in the world. But I want you to listen to me, okay? I want you to know and understand that this is for you. Your career. Your therapy. *Especially* your therapy. But Ledger, if you're doing it, you need to do it for you. For yourself. Not because of me or our babies. Or anyone else. And I know you're hurt by what they've done, your brothers, but I think you've been unhappy without them, haven't you? Just like you've been unhappy without soccer. And I think you should at least talk to them or —"

Suddenly, he goes for my wrist.

He grips it and takes my hand off his mouth, his fingers strangely tight, mashing into my pulse as if he wants to kill it. Or maybe absorb it into his skin like a kiss, I don't know.

All I know is that I'm breathless at the sudden intensity in his gaze.

And in his voice when he says, "You trust me."

My answer is thoughtless and effortless, like a muscle memory. "More than anyone."

And I'm not ashamed to say that.

I'm not ashamed to admit that the guy who broke my trust over a year ago is the guy I trust the most in the world.

Because the girl whose heart he broke, I'm not that girl anymore.

I've grown up.

My rose-colored glasses are gone. I know he's flawed. I know he's capable of doing bad things but I also know that he's capable of doing good things. Things so precious that they make me weep.

Things so beautiful that no one has ever imagined them.

Like these two babies in my belly.

So yeah, I trust him.

Although I don't understand his reaction.

I don't get why his frame seems to shake a little before going stone still. And why the look in his eyes is stricken before going harsh. Meanwhile those fingers of his around my wrist have really managed to kill my pulse or at least slow it down.

Then as if he knows that I'm on the verge of passing out, he steps back.

He abruptly lets me go and I want to tell him that this is what may kill me, his sudden abandonment, not his brutal grip.

"I'm going for a run," he says before leaving the bathroom.

Leaving me stunned in his wake.

Leaving me to wonder what just happened.

But maybe I shouldn't. Maybe I should be used to it by now because this isn't the first time he's gone for a run at night.

This isn't the second or the third time either.

He's been doing it for weeks now.

Ever since we found out that I'm pregnant.

Just like his intensity and his need to pamper me have grown and changed, his routine has changed as well. In addition to going to therapy I mean.

We still sleep in the same bed and he still spoons me the entire night — in fact his arm around me sometimes feels too tight, too caging; not that I mind but I've noticed the difference — and he still wakes up before me to go exercising.

But there's no playful early morning banter like before. Or after even.

He exercises for longer these days. Our breakfasts — that we still have together — are quieter. The storytelling times are somber as well. His grocery runs are longer and after dinner, he usually disappears for another round of workouts.

But the biggest, most epic change is that we don't have sex anymore.

He hardly ever touches me except during the night when we cuddle together. Or rather he cuddles me because by the time he hits the bed, I'm already asleep. And while I've been trying to be patient with him, I'm wondering if this drastic change is because… of me.

Because he doesn't want me anymore.

As in, you know, sexually.

What if now that he's given me my dream, his dream too by the way, he thinks there is no need for physical intimacy between us.

On wooden legs, I walk out of the bathroom and find him opening and shutting drawers. He's already changed out of his jeans and into his gray sweatpants and now he's in the process of deftly putting on a t-shirt that I personally think is even more lethal than his sweatpants; it's white and extremely soft-looking and has big armholes instead of sleeves.

So big that you can see his ribs and obliques and the way they ripple when he moves.

God.

Why?

Why does he have to be so sexy and why do I have to be so freaking obsessed with his body when I'm beginning to think that maybe he isn't with mine.

Not anymore.

"I…"

He doesn't turn around at my hesitant voice, still busy with picking up his cell phone and his keys and shoving them down the pockets of his sweatpants. When he's done, he turns around but doesn't even spare me a glance as he strides toward the door, every line on his bruised face severe and sharp.

He's just about to cross over the threshold when I try again, "I think we should —"

"Don't wait up."

With my heart racing, I follow him out into the hallway, his lunging steps taking him further and further away from me. In desperation, I plead to his back, "I-I think we should talk." Then, "Now that I'm pregnant."

Finally, he comes to a halt.

And I watch the broad planes of his back lift up and down with his breath.

I'm not sure what kind of a breath it is. A fortifying breath or a breath that says *finally*. Like he was waiting for me to bring it up, this talk thing. So we could...

We could go our separate ways.

I mean that's what's going to happen eventually, right?

I'm going to leave pretty soon.

As soon as Ezra comes back.

I've been in constant contact with him this whole time, mostly texting and a couple of phone calls here and there. I usually make sure that Ledger isn't around when that happens. I don't want him to get suspicious or agitated, especially when in a way there's nothing to get agitated about.

Yes, I am going to marry him but no, there isn't anything between us nor there ever will ever be.

But anyway, so far things haven't gone well for him in Korea and he's had to extend his trip. Which to be honest, I'm actually very thrilled about. I'm not looking forward to resuming duping him once he does come back. Plus now I have something else to tell him as well and I have no idea how he's going to react to my happy news.

I've decided to stress about all that later though.

The only good thing in all of this is that my dad can't say the same.

A couple of times that I have talked to him these past few weeks, he's sounded angry and agitated. And for once, not at me but at Ezra's father. Who apparently is insisting on hiring a third-party appraiser of his choice. Turns out, when one company buys another company, the buyer brings in an appraiser to evaluate the value of the company they're buying. Which of course makes sense, but since my dad's company is in shambles, he'd very cunningly convinced Mr. Vandekamp to use the appraiser of my dad's choice who was going to spin the whole thing in my dad's favor. But now Mr. Vandekamp is having second thoughts.

Go Mr. Vandekamp! Even though he's a homophobic piece of shit.

So anyway, my dad's dealing with that and for once, the heat's off my back.

But all that still doesn't mean that I get to stay here.

In my safe space.

With the guy who makes me feel safe.

I'm not sure how visible they are, my frantic thoughts and my active imagination, on my face. But I still try to school my features when he turns around. Then in a wooden tone, he asks, "Talk about what."

"A-are you sure you want to go on a run?" I ask instead. "I-I mean, you're all banged up and —"

"What's there to talk about?"

Damn it.

Now that I've broached the subject, I don't know where to begin.

How to phrase the question, *have you gotten bored of me?*

"Tempest," he prods/warns when I go minutes without saying anything.

I get myself together and go, "Right. We should talk about things. Now that I'm pregnant."

"You said that already."

"Yes, I have," I agree with him.

He narrows his eyes in response.

"Okay so, I-I know that I wanted us to stay here. Back when we were trying…"

I leave my sentence hanging because I'm hoping that he'll fill the silence.

But then again, when has he ever filled silences?

He's pretty content simply standing there and regarding me in brooding silence. So I have to keep going, "But we are not trying anymore."

"No, we're not," he says at last.

I can't read his tone but I also can't waste any more time trying to go over things in my head. I need to let it out. "And well, all we've done for the past couple of months is, uh, try."

"Yes." Then, "All we've done for the past couple of months is fuck."

I suck my belly in at his 'fuck.'

Not the most shocking thing he's ever said, but something about him saying it in this moment when we're having a serious discussion does things to me.

"Yes, we have," I say somehow. "So I was just wondering, now that I'm pregnant," *God, please stop saying that,* "and we even had our first appointment and everything, if, uh, I should still stay here or…"

"Or."

"Uh," I let out another breath, "g-go back."

"Go back."

"Yes, back to B-Bardstown."

As soon as I say it, a pain so piercing stabs my chest that it's a wonder I haven't gasped out loud.

Not to mention it becomes even more of a miracle for me to stay still and not tremble when he repeats my words once again in a wooden, emotionless tone. "You want to go back to Bardstown."

I shake my head. "N-no... I mean, yes. As in, if you think I should. If you want me to."

"Because we aren't fucking anymore."

I swallow. "Yes, and if you want to..."

Fuck someone else.

This time, I do gasp and go for the wall beside me, propping against it because my knees are shaking.

Just at the thought of him going for someone else.

Somehow it feels like both: a big thing, a giant thing and a thing so silly that I could start laughing until I cry.

After everything that we've been through, all the ways we've grown and come closer, the fact that I'm carrying his babies, the fact that we're a family — an unconventional one but a family nonetheless — him going for another girl seems so trivial. It seems like I shouldn't even be concerned with things like that.

But of course I should be.

Just because I think we've come so far doesn't mean *he* thinks that.

Just because he's going to be a daddy doesn't mean his life should stop. Plus he'd been celibate for the last three years because of me, shouldn't he get to live his life now?

"Look," I take a deep breath, "you haven't even touched me. In days. Well, if we're being honest about it, it's been weeks. Like ever since we found out that I'm pregnant." Then, thinking about it, "Actually, that's not true. I think it happened around the time when you made me sign those stupid insurance papers. Which was very sweet, by the way. While all I could do was watch baby videos, you had practical, real things on your mind. But maybe... maybe you want to live your life now. Just because I know you'll be there for the babies and you know, be a good dad, doesn't mean you should stop yourself from..."

"From what?"

I still can't read his tone but I reply anyway, "From living your life. I mean, there's no reason for you to not go out there and... be with s-someone. And maybe I'm in your way now and honestly I'm no slouch either. I have guys salivating over me as well. And just because I'm pregnant doesn't mean that I can't —"

His sudden flurry of movements bring my words to a screeching halt.

Which is a good thing to be honest.

Because I was doing what I always do: trying to make him jealous, and I really need to change that about myself. It's not healthy and serves no purpose whatsoever when we have no future together. Not to mention, I've *specifically* asked him and made him promise to not get jealous.

But in any case, I have other things to think about in this moment.

Like the fact that he's here, where I am, and he's pinning me to the wall.

With his hands splayed wide on either side of my head, making a cage, and his bruised face dipped toward me.

Good.

I like that.

I like being trapped in the cages that he makes for me.

In fact I like it so much that I grab onto him, to his sleek muscles and whisper, "What are you doing?"

"You can't what?" he rasps.

Confused, I ask, "I can't… what?"

"Yeah." His eyes flash. "You can't *what*. Just because you are pregnant."

Oh, right.

I was saying something to that effect.

I stroke his hot skin. "I-I don't… remember."

"No?"

"No."

His eyes flash again. "How about I remind you."

"Okay."

I think I would say okay to just about anything in this moment.

I'm so under his spell that I don't even care if it's pathetic.

I don't care that it's easy for him to fool me.

To shake me and thrill me, hurt me and mold me in whatever shape he wants.

"Do you know who you are?" he asks.

"Who I am?"

"To me," he qualifies.

"To you."

"Yeah," he nods. "Who are you to me?"

"I… I don't…"

"Are you my girlfriend?"

"No."

"Then who are you?"

At his tone, his specific use of the word *girlfriend*, something teases the back of my mind. "The girl you…"

"The girl I what?"

"The girl you'd burn down the world for," I repeat his words to him from earlier, the ones he said to my brother.

"What else?"

My heart pounds in my chest. "The girl you'd kill for."

"I would, wouldn't I?"

"Yes."

"Now tell me." His skin vibrates under my fingers, thrums heated and smooth. "Who put those babies in your belly?"

My womb pulses. "Y-you did."

"I did."

"Yes."

"Me, yeah?"

"Yeah."

"Not those guys who salivate over you."

"Not them, no."

"*Me*, Ledger."

"Yes."

"Now I want you to put two and two together, okay?"

I swallow. "Okay."

"If Ledger," he begins, his eyes all black, "put those babies in your belly, the babies who are going to grow and make it round and swell, who're going to change your body and make it even more ripe and soft. And if Ledger would burn down the whole world for you. What do you think he'd do to the guys who dare to look at you let alone salivate over you and your pregnant-as-fuck body?"

I scratch his skin, rubbing my thighs together. "Ledger, I was just—"

"Tell me."

"K-kill them."

"Yeah. And I'd make it hurt. I'd fucking make it excruciating."

"You —"

"So what do you think you should do?"

"Not look at other guys?"

"No."

"I'm —"

"You shouldn't even think about them."

"Oh."

"You shouldn't *be* where they are."

"But —"

"What you *should* do, if you want to prevent mass murder and keep me from being sent to death row for it, is to stay locked up. It's to stay the fuck here. Where no motherfucker can ever look at you or get to you. Do you understand?"

"Yes," I say, trembling and weak in the knees.

"Good."

"I was just trying to make you jealous."

"I know."

"So then why did you —"

"Because you don't want other guys to salivate over you."

"No, I don't."

"You want me."

"Yes."

"So here I am, baby," he says with a threatening tone. "Salivating over you. Sniffing around your skirts like an animal. Beating at my chest and snapping my teeth at any asshole that comes near you. But remember what I told you about animals, about bulls?"

"Yes," I lick my lips, "You told me that I shouldn't p-provoke them."

"Exactly. Because I'm already half a beast for you, an angry bull, and if you keep provoking me, I'm going to be worse than any animal you've ever known."

My panties are wet.

My pussy is flooded.

And I don't think I can take another second of being separated from him. "So then why won't you —"

"Now," he says, stepping away from me. "I want you to go to sleep because you've had enough fucking excitement for one night and I need to go for a run until I can't fucking think."

"But you —"

This time, I can't speak because I'm bent halfway down and throwing up all over the floor.

Which is what I keep doing for the next several weeks.

Chapter Thirty-One

Her Beautiful Thorn

MY WIFE.

She's my wife.

And it's getting harder and harder to stay away from her.

Harder and *harder* to not touch her. To not make her mine, not only on paper but in life too.

To not do that one act that will dry the ink on paper and seal the deal in every sense.

Every day that passes I remind myself of the reasons why I need to keep my distance:

1. I'm not the guy for her.
2. I wouldn't even *know* how to be the guy for her. The guy who can give her all the things she wants and make her happy.
3. She doesn't want anything from me anyway.
4. And she shouldn't because I'm lying to her.
5. I tricked her into marrying me.

Yes, it was necessary at the time. To keep my anger in check. To keep my jealousy at bay. Although I can't say making her my wife has changed much of anything. I get still as angry, as jealous at the thought of Ezra fucking Vandekamp, as I used to before she signed those papers.

Actually it's worse now.

Mostly because she's my wife and I can't tell anyone. I can't shout it off the rooftops like I want to. I can't write it on the walls and carve it into the ground. I can't spray paint it on every building I pass.

My wife. My wife. My *wife*.

Which once again makes me think that my anger may really be a problem.

That my anger may destroy everything, if I'm not careful.

That maybe, just *maybe*, I should open up and talk to Dr. Mayberry. I have to see her anyway, right? Might as well talk to her and use her legendary wisdom that everyone keeps telling me about. Especially now that I'm allowed back into practice.

Maybe the good doctor can give me some pointers.

How to tell your wife that she's your wife now? And how to stop her from running away from me?

Because when she finds out she's going to run; I know that.

She's going to take our babies away from me and I don't think I could blame her.

She's already going to leave one day — and yes, I still remember my promise of letting her go when she does — and this will only send her away faster.

So not touching her, not taking this one last thing from her is my puny effort to do the right thing. Not that it's going to matter but when you do the wrong thing — the wrongest thing that anyone could ever do to someone — doing the right thing kinda becomes your only choice.

Besides, I'm not going to take advantage of her when she's like this.

Sick and weak.

This first trimester is hard for her. She's throwing up all the time, barely able to keep any food in her. She's lost weight. She's pale and lethargic. Her boobs hurt, she says. She can't stand the smell of her once-favorite foods. She cries at the drop of a hat. Which I think is not only hormonal. I think it's also because her asshole of a brother hasn't come around yet and I could fucking kill him for that. For putting her through such a hard time in her condition.

Not to mention, she hates cotton candy with a passion.

The only thing that remotely gives her relief is smelling orange peels.

She keeps them on her nightstand and every time she gets a bout of nausea, she sniffs them like a junkie. So I've filled our cabin with oranges. She also likes evening walks in crisp air, so I make sure to be home after practice in time to take her on one. I make sure to hold her hand and support her when she gets dizzy and shaky. Which is also happening a lot these days.

Apparently these are all hormones and she has a lot of them because of the twin pregnancy. But there's apparently nothing to worry about because the worse you are, the better your pregnancy is going.

Her doctor's words, not mine.

Fuck her.

Fuck all the doctors.

In fact, fuck anyone who said pregnancy is a joyous thing.

It's not. It's fucking torture.

And the worst part is that it's not even a torture to me. It's torture for her and I can't do anything other than rub her back, buy her oranges and hold her hair when she empties her stomach.

I've been so angry about all this that when they tell us — at our week ten appointment — that if we want we can know the sex of our babies with a simple blood test, I refuse.

I tell them I don't want to, much to my Firefly's shock.

Because sometimes I feel like I'm angry at them too. At our babies. For making their mommy so sick.

It's fucking irrational; I know that.

I don't mean it either.

Because as soon as the thought crosses my mind, I'm left with crippling guilt and remorse.

But the thing is that I can't see her like this. I can't see my wife dimmed and dulled out.

Hurting.

Which I know is ironic because when she finds out that she indeed is my wife and her own husband is lying to her, she's going to get hurt worse than any pregnancy hormones.

Chapter Thirty-Two

I'M fifteen weeks pregnant today.

And today's the day I'm going to tell my fiancé that I'm having a baby.

Two babies, actually.

Two girls.

Although it hasn't been confirmed yet. Because we're choosing not to know.

Well, *he* is choosing not to know.

The daddy.

Why, I don't know. When I asked all he said was it doesn't matter. Which confused me but then later I realized that he was right. It actually doesn't matter what we're having because I'll love them no matter what.

He will too.

In fact I think it's more fun this way.

We'll have something good to look forward to in the future. Well, apart from the whole meeting the babies thing. Because we have plenty of bad things happening in the future already.

Or at least I do.

Including this meeting.

A few days ago I got the text that I've been dreading for weeks now. It was from Ezra, telling me that he was finally, after months, heading back. And that if I had some time this week, we should meet.

Of course I said yes.

And of course immediately after, my father called me and told me that he was counting on me to bring it home.

So that's what I'm here to do.

To bring it home at this swanky restaurant in midtown Manhattan. And tell him that what we'd talked about before he left for Korea is actually coming true. Meaning I'm pregnant and we could definitely spin this in his favor and get everyone, including his father, off his back about his sexuality.

That the father of *my* babies is also going to be involved down the line is not something that I'm going to tell him today. I also understand that there will be press coverage for this, our wedding and my pregnancy etc. But we will figure it all out later and well, that's why we have PR people, don't we? I need to first secure my father's plan and thereby my brother's future before I rock the boat again.

So with bated breath, I wait for him to arrive.

Only he doesn't.

At first I think he's stood me up. But then in a very strange turn of events, there's a very no-nonsense brunette who seems to have approached my table and taken a seat right across from me before I can even realize what's happening. In her tight bun and glasses, along with her very formal satchel that she sets down at the table and fishes out a thick file from before putting it on the floor, she looks like someone's secretary.

A very efficient and capable secretary.

I open my mouth to ask her who she is when she looks up and gives me a curt smile. "Hi, I'm Alice. Mr. Vandekamp's assistant."

So bingo.

She is an assistant.

I blink a couple of times before remembering my manners. "Um, hi."

Before I can even think to ask her what she's doing here, she tells me, "Mr. Vandekamp has had something urgent come up so he won't be able to make it. He sends his regrets. But he didn't want to break the date with you, his fiancée," she throws me a small formal smile, "so he sent me instead."

Double bingo.

She is efficient.

I mean, she explained everything to me without me even having to ask.

The only problem is what we're going to talk about when Ezra is not here.

"Okay," I say, confused. "I'm not really sure what we're going to... do though."

"We can discuss logistics, of course," she says as if it should be obvious to me.

I clear my throat. "Discuss logistics of what?"

She inches up her glasses. "Of the wedding. Which is what he sent me here to do." I open my mouth to respond but she's already opening the thick file and uncapping a pen that I hadn't even seen her take out of her satchel. "Now, first things first: How's April twentieth for you?"

"I'm sorry?"

She looks up for a second. "For the wedding date." She goes back down to her file then. "That's the earliest that I can do. And then the next date is," she flips a few pages, "all the way into the summer. Which Mr. Vandekamp knows that you don't like as much, since you always wanted a spring wedding." Again she looks up. "So, shall I?"

It takes me a second to respond to her.

And even then all I can say is, "April twentieth?"

"Yes." She nods. "Shall I put you down for that?"

"That's," I lick my lips and swallow, "only six weeks away."

"Correct."

"I'm…"

"If you're worried about all the arrangements and things like that, please don't give it another thought. I'm really good at my job. Once we nail down the date and a wedding venue you'd like, I will fix your meeting with a wedding planner and I'll make sure that everything happens to your taste."

It's a good thing that my nausea passed last week or I'd be throwing up all over the table.

April twentieth.

My wedding day.

I will be twenty-one weeks then. My babies will be the size of a large banana, more or less; I've been Googling week by week baby development for the past few weeks. The only thing that seemed to give me joy when I felt sick twenty-four seven. That and orange peels and walks in woods.

But the latter is because I took those walks with him.

While holding his hand.

While feeling safe and warm by his side.

Which won't be for much longer now, will it?

I've only got six weeks left.

And I want to blame Ezra for that. I want to be angry at him for springing this on me without any discussion or even deigning to come to see me. But I can't. Because the arrangement that we have doesn't require him to see me. In fact, even if we were going to have a real marriage, we wouldn't have to see each other at all, not until our wedding day. And he *was* listening to me, the last time we'd met. When again, he didn't have to; not in a fake or a real marriage.

Actually I think this whole thing, his assistant showing up with the specific instructions to take notes on what I want, is his way of being nice to me. To show me that he cares about me even though we're not really going to be married.

So I should be ecstatic.

That despite my father choosing a man for me, I ended up with someone considerate.

Plus I brought it home and I didn't even have to do anything.

I have a wedding date that my dad's going to be very happy about.

But all I want to do is break down and sob. All I want to do is curl up in a ball on the floor and never ever get up. Never ever face reality. Because I don't want to do this.

I *don't* want to marry him.

I don't.

I never did.

And now instead of something vague, a summer wedding, we have a wedding *date*. An actual fucking wedding date that's only six weeks away and...

Just the idea of leaving that cabin, leaving *him* for the rest of my life is making me want to vomit and Ezra doesn't even know about the pregnancy yet and I...

"Miss Jackson?"

Alice's voice breaks into my thoughts and my reply comes bursting forth before I've had time to think about it all. "Yes, it works."

"The date?"

"Yes."

She smiles. "Perfect."

While she makes a note of it in her file, I say, "And my mother will be happy to co-ordinate with you regarding any wedding plans."

Her smile widens as she makes a note of that too.

"And, uh," I try to take a deep breath but fail to, "please thank Ezra for me. For arranging all of this. And thank you for coming to meet with me and being so competent."

"Of course. I'm just doing my job."

"Right, okay." I throw her a shaky smile. "I'm just going to... go."

Her smile wavers slightly. "Okay. But are you all right? You don't —"

"I'm fine. I'm absolutely fine. I think I just need a little fresh air."

With that, I stand up and walk out of there.

⸻

HE'S BEAUTIFUL.

The most beautiful man I've ever seen.

His crazy hair whipping in the wind. His bronzed skin flushed. His strong body hurtling across the field. His legs always keeping the ball in his possession, mostly through his dexterous leg work and other times with his sheer force of will. Whatever the case may be it's hard to take the ball away from him once he's got it in his possession.

And if he takes a shot with it, you know he's going to score.

I've seen him at practice and at games countless times to know that.

And I have to say that I missed it.

Watching him play.

I missed the electric feeling that I'd get, that I'd gotten the very first time that I'd seen him play at Bardstown High. The euphoria, the thrill. The awe that I'm in the presence of something great, something otherworldly and majestic.

That I'm in the presence of the Angry Thorn.

Only he never was and never will be that to me.

To me, he's my Beautiful Thorn.

And I can't take my eyes off him.

But I have to when a couple of minutes later I hear someone say, "He's good, isn't he?"

Startled, I turn and find that the voice belongs to Conrad Thorne.

The oldest Thorne brother and the head coach of New York City FC.

When I'd left the restaurant, all I wanted to do was take a walk through the city. A slow and leisurely walk. Even though I wanted to run and run and never stop. But these days I get dizzy so quickly and since I'm prone to falling, I took it easy. Because I'm not alone anymore, am I? I have these two little birdies inside of me, these two little butterflies, my cute companions.

I have them to think about.

And I have him.

He'd lose his shit if something happened to me or to them. So much so that I've quit wearing heels. Just for his peace of mind and mine.

But anyway, I took slow and measured paces before flagging down a cab and ended up here.

At New York City FC's stadium.

Where I knew I'd find him, practicing for his comeback game next week. Something he's been really hard at work for. Although I forgot that there may be a chance that I might run into his brother. Not Shepard or Stellan, both of whom I can see through this wall-to-wall window that I'm standing at, Shepard running on the field and Stellan on the sidelines, directing the players.

But him.

Con, their oldest brother.

"He's more than good," I say to him. "He's fantastic."

His eyes, blue and completely different than Ledger's dark ones, take me in and his lips stretch up into a very faint smile. "He is." Then turning to look at the game, he adds, "And he always has been. Pure and unadulterated talent. Better and stronger than anyone else I've come across."

I turn back to the game as well.

Completely in agreement with him.

Stellan blows on his whistle and calls a halt before going to Ledger and another guy, whose jersey says Rivera, and having a chat with them. I watch Ledger listening to Stellan but at one point his jaw clenches and I know whatever he's hearing is not something he likes.

I can see the annoyance flickering on his features and for a second or two I think he's going to snap at Stellan.

But then he gives him a curt nod and the game resumes.

I breathe out a quiet sigh of relief.

Not because I think he's his namesake, Angry Thorn, but because if he had gotten angry, people would think he was.

His brothers would think he was, and he's so much more than that.

I hear Conrad shift on his feet then. "But he's his own enemy."

I snap my gaze back at him. "Excuse me?"

Again, he turns away from the window and thrusts his hands down his pockets. "How are you?"

Abandoning the game once again, I turn to him as well.

Because I think this — whatever it is that's going to happen now — requires my full attention. "How am I?"

He glances down at my belly and I palm it in a blatantly possessive gesture.

I'm not showing a lot yet; although my old dresses, because they were so tight, don't fit me anymore and so I've taken to wearing things that are slightly looser in the waist. But I do feel the expanded curve when I touch my stomach.

"Yes. I hear you've been having a hard time. I apologize that I haven't come to see you or talk to you directly. I know that you've been friends with Callie for a long time and of course, you're family. Because of Reed, and now... this. It's just that..." He sighs then, rubbing the back of his neck. "It's been a shock. Which is not an excuse, but I want you to know that I'm here for you. I know we haven't had much of a chance to interact in the past but if the need should arise, you can count on the fact that I'll be —"

"It won't," I cut him off.

He looks at me for a second, and even though with his dirty blond hair and blue eyes he looks nothing like my dark-haired and dark-eyed Ledger, I can still see the similarities in them. I can still see that they have the same body language, the same demeanor, the same dominating aura.

Especially when he's regarding me silently.

But I'm not going to get intimated. "Because Ledger is taking good care of me. So you don't have to apologize or offer your help. I'm covered, thank you."

I'm speaking the truth.

I *am* covered.

Not only because Ledger has taken such good care of me these last few weeks when I thought I was going to die and probably never make it to my second trimester, let alone the third *or* my due date, but also because I've got such good friends.

First there's Callie, my BFF and my sister-in-law.

Who, after we broke the news to her and my brother, came right over to the cabin that very week, as soon as Halo had started to feel better. She was definitely surprised at our choice of home, especially when I told her who it belonged to. Since Ledger wasn't going to, I also explained its significance to him. Which brought tears to her eyes before she told me, yet again, how happy she was that we'd finally gotten together.

Apparently, she had all the clues that there was something going on between us. I guess we didn't fool her with our intense looks at each other and friction and whatnot over the past few years. So at that point I had to burst her bubble and say that we aren't. I didn't go into a lot of detail but simply said that we weren't meant to be and so far she's accepted the idea — although reluctantly — and hasn't questioned me or anything.

In any case I know she's happy that we're having a baby. And not one but two.

"So you mean like, Stellan and Shepard?" she said excitedly the day she'd come over.

Ledger had just returned from his second workout of the day and had replied, "Fuck no. Not like Stellan and Shepard."

"What, of course like them. They're the twins."

"They're Satan's spawn."

"Well, that's true. Shep definitely is."

"My baby girls are nothing like Stellan and Shep." Then, with a slight dopey look on his face, "They're my two little fireflies."

Callie smiled. "Oooh, I like that. Two little fireflies." Then, "Oh my God, I just got this amazing idea for mittens that I want to knit for them."

After which she went on a tangent about all the stuff she's going to knit for them while all I could do was stare at him and blush.

But anyway, she also told me that Conrad and all her brothers were having a hard time with the news. Something they found out from Ledger and something Ledger and I had a fight over, because I had no idea that he was going to tell them. If I had, I would've liked to be there when that happened to support him.

Like he had when I'd told Reed.

Who still hasn't come around, by the way.

I haven't talked to my brother in weeks and it hurts the same way it did the night I told him about the pregnancy. And again, Callie told me to give him time. Although I'm not sure if time's going to be able to work its magic this time around.

Anyway, apart from Callie, I've got my other friends as well.

Who all showed up one weekend or another over the last few weeks. Jupiter, Echo, Poe, even Wyn — Con's girlfriend, Salem over FaceTime because she's in California with her pro-soccer player boyfriend, Arrow Carlisle. Who by the way is flying over with him next week for his game against New York City FC.

But that's neither here nor there.

The point is that Conrad doesn't need to worry about me.

I've got my people.

And I've got *him*.

The most wonderful and misunderstood guy in the world.

I'm about to put an end to this conversation with Conrad and turn back to watch the practice when he begins, "I'm glad. That you're covered and he's taking good care of you. And I hope that it lasts. But," he shifts on his feet and thinks over things for a second before saying, "if it doesn't, I want you to know that we will stand by you. Not only me but all of us. Stellan, Shep, Callie. The whole family."

My spine was already straight and I was already prepared for him to say something that might make me angry as soon as he started talking. But I still wasn't prepared for the hot rush of anger that goes through me at his words.

The whole family.

That somehow doesn't include Ledger.

Fisting my hands at my sides, I raise my chin. "As I said, you don't have to worry about that. *My* family is already standing by me."

Again he regards me silently and again I'm struck by how similar they are to each other, the oldest and the youngest brother. God, even their heights are similar and now that I don't wear heels, I'm feeling the impact of it so much more.

"I'm glad that that's true," he says, his eyes full of meaning. "And it's admirable that you trust him so much. But I'd be doing you a great disservice if I didn't tell you that it's tricky with him. He's loyal and hard-working, yes. He's a good brother. But I don't know if you could particularly trust him. I don't know if you could particularly trust his unpredictable behavior. He does things that end up hurting him and people around him and I want you to be prepared for that. I want —"

"I know," I tell him just so I can put a stop to what he's saying. "I know what he's capable of."

He frowns. "And yet here you are saying that you trust him."

"Yes, because I do," I say proudly. "Because I know he's flawed. I know he has his issues. I *know* that he's made of things that are ugly. And I'm not afraid of them, those things. I'm not afraid to take them on and stare them down. Because I also know that he's made of beautiful things too. Like the rest of us. Like you and like me. Like the rest of your family that shockingly didn't include your own brother."

I step closer to him then.

Fuck his height and fuck his intimidating aura.

I will stand by Ledger now and till the end of time.

He's my family, *our* family.

"And let me tell you something else too, sometimes people who know us the most and the longest are the very people who don't really see us. They are the ones who don't really appreciate what we have to offer. They don't really appreciate the subtle nuances in us. Actually, screw the subtle nuances. They're the ones who are *completely* blind to everything that makes us *us*. I know you love your brother. I know you've made sacrifices for him. I know you care about him. But I wish that you understood him too. I wish you took the time to look closer and see for yourself how completely amazing he is. How every part of him, the good and the bad, the beautiful and the ugly, makes him *him*. And all he needs from you is for you to see him. Just once."

I'm not sure if me saying these things would make a difference. Or if Ledger would even like that I talked to his brother and poked my nose in their business behind his back. But I'm glad that I did. Someone had to say it. *Someone* had to have his back and tell these people to stop perpetually judging him and judging him solely based on his mistakes and errors and...

Just then I hear a door slamming shut, reverberating all throughout the blue-painted hallway that we're standing in. One side of it is lined with office doors and cases made of glass displaying trophies and years' worth of photos. But the other is almost completely wall-to-wall windows and everything from trophy cases to photographs to windows shake with the impact.

And then I see him emerge from the corner, all sweaty and heated and well, angry.

Not at me though.

At his brother from the looks of it, because his dark eyes are pinned on him as he strides over.

"What the fuck?" he mutters as he gets closer.

And I try to run interference. "Ledger —"

"What'd you say to her?" Ledger asks his brother.

Who looks completely unaffected or bothered by Ledger's sudden appearance and his aggressive demeanor. Shaking his head, he says in a calm voice, "I didn't —"

"What the fuck did you say to her?" he asks again, now coming to a halt directly in front of Conrad.

I step between them and try to placate Ledger again. "Ledger, no. He didn't say anything. He —"

His eyes are still on his brother. "Answer me. Are you fucking upsetting her?"

"You need to calm down, Ledger," Conrad says from behind me.

And Ledger advances on him. But thankfully I'm here to stop him.

I'm here to put my hands on his body and push him back.

Even so, it's hard to make him stand down as he growls, "Or what? You're gonna kick me out? For good this time." He leans forward. "Because let me tell you something, I don't give a fuck. I don't fucking give a *fuck*. You can take your soccer and shove it up your ass. If I find out that you've upset her, all bets are off. I don't care about playing for you or for any other team. Now and always."

"Ledger." With a pounding heart, I go for his face and try to turn his focus on me. "Seriously. He didn't say anything. He didn't upset me, okay? We were just having a conversation, I swear. I'm fine."

It takes him a couple of seconds to look away from his brother and finally focus on me.

Thank God.

"You need to calm down," I tell him again, looking into his angry eyes.

He remains silent though.

Silent and staring. Breathing harshly.

Which is fine.

As long as he's not doing anything rash because of me. Because he thinks he needs to protect me from some unseen grave danger.

And God, how is it possible that people can't see that?

That people can't see how protective he is. How loyal and *safe*.

I'm so engrossed in watching him and thumbing his cheek, focusing on his calming breaths, that I don't realize we're surrounded by people. Not until Conrad says, "It's fine. Everything's under control."

Which is when I look away from Ledger — who I don't think has a clue that we're not alone anymore — and find that the entire team, including some of the coaches and staff members, are flooding the hallway.

Shit.

Are they going to think that he's causing problems again?

"Hit the showers," Conrad says, emerging from behind me. Then, to Stellan who cuts through the crowd to stand in the front, "Now."

Stellan nods and gestures for the team to clear out the space.

Which they do except for the third Thorne brother, Shepard. He stands there with a frown — God, Stellan and Shepard look exactly alike, don't they? It's so hard to find a difference between their eerily identical faces, dark eyes and dark hair — watching Ledger and Conrad.

"Shep." Conrad jerks his chin at him. "Now."

He doesn't like it; I can see it on his face but he eventually does it and leaves. And with a final look at Ledger and me, Stellan leaves too, leaving the hallway empty once again.

I breathe out a sigh of relief and Conrad says, "You can use my office."

At that, Ledger glances at his brother and a rough tone, he says, "You've got something to say, you say it to me. Not to her. Not in her condition."

Conrad stares at his brother for a few seconds before jerking out a nod. Then, to me, "It was nice talking to you, Tempest. Take care of yourself."

Breathing out, I nod. "Thanks. You too."

And then, he leaves, strides down the hallway much as his youngest brother had done only a few minutes before. Reminding me once again about the similarities between them.

But then I don't have the time to think about these things because stepping away from me, Ledger is grabbing my hand and pulling me in the opposite direction, quite possibly to Conrad's office. When we get there, he pulls me inside and closes the door, pinning me to it.

All impatient-like.

Then, putting his hands on the wood as if he's going to do a push-up, he looks me over. From the top of my head to the bottom of my flats, and I let him do it. Because I know from experience that he isn't going to be satisfied if he hasn't made sure, on his own, that I'm really and truly okay.

Just one of the things that he does ever since he started going to practice.

Probably because he isn't with me all day and he thinks that not watching me like a hawk 24/7 may bring harm upon me.

So yeah, if he was bad when we'd just found out about my pregnancy, he's even worse now. With his constant worrying and treating me like I'm made of silk and feathers.

Of course I let him do it all, because arguing with him is futile. Plus I really want to tell him this.

"You shouldn't have done that, Ledger," I tell him. "You shouldn't have had an argument with Conrad like that. Now everyone's going to think that your therapy isn't working and what if they really kick you off the team? What —"

"Fuck therapy."

"Ledger —"

"You okay?" he asks with a frown.

"You need to take it seriously, Ledger. Your therapy, your game. Your *career*. I know you said you're only doing it for us but it needs —"

"Are you," he enunciates every word, "*fucking* okay?"

I watch his impatient face, lined with agitation.

With worry.

About me and the babies.

I know when he's like this, I can't get him to listen to anything. I can't get him to see my point.

And God, I want to.

So badly.

I want him to understand that as much as I love that he's taking his responsibilities seriously, there's certain things that are just for him. Certain areas in life that he's allowed to be selfish about, especially if it's related to his dream: soccer, his career, the European League.

I know he hates therapy. It's pretty clear every time he comes home from his sessions. He's more agitated and angry than he usually is after spending a day with his brothers. And I want him to understand that it doesn't have to be this way. He doesn't have to treat his sessions like chores, something to simply keep his job. I know they're mandatory but he really can make use of them. Maybe it can help repair his issues with his brothers.

In any case, as I said, I can't make him see anything right now.

So I give up for the time being and answer him, "Yes. I'm not upset, Ledger. Your brother wasn't —"

"I'll deal with my brother later."

"There's nothing to deal with."

"What are you doing here?" he asks, the residual tension still lining his features.

Which reminds me that I did have a purpose in coming here; I just wanted to see him. And why exactly I wanted to do that. It actually all comes rushing back, jarring into me and stealing all my breaths.

Stealing all the hope from my chest.

Six weeks.

I only have six more weeks with him.

Schooling my features to remain calm, I whisper, "I just wanted to see you."

He studies me carefully and I hope I don't give anything away.

I don't want to stress him out before his comeback game. Not to mention when I do tell him, I'm obviously not going to disclose the truth. That I'm getting married to the man he doesn't even want me saying the name of.

Which means I'm going to have to lie.

And I'm not looking forward to that.

As much as I hate the game I'm playing with practically everyone in my life at this point, I'm still okay with it. What I'm not okay with and absolutely do not want to do is lie to *him*.

Just the thought of it makes my chest tight.

But I don't have any other choice.

If I want to keep my brother and his family safe, I have to do this.

So I will but I don't have to do anything *right this second*, do I?

Meaning I'm going to have to keep a lid on my emotions right now.

"You feeling sick?" he asks then.

"No." I shake my head, trying for a smile. "Not at all. I'm fine. My nausea's gone now, remember? It's been gone for days now. You know that."

"Yeah, but pregnancy is fucking weird."

This time I don't have to try; my smile is genuine and amused. "It's not."

"It fucking is."

"I love being pregnant," I say truthfully.

Even the nausea part.

Crazily or maybe not so crazily, it makes me think that my body is doing its job. That they're safe in there. They're growing and healthy and if I have to suffer for a few weeks, then so be it.

Of course Ledger has different opinions and he hasn't hesitated in sharing them.

Not so much with words though. But with his body language.

That would get all tight and agitated every time I threw up what I ate.

In fact he even scared the nurse one time. I was on the scale and she made an innocent comment about the weight that I'd lost. Which was only three pounds by the way. And God, she nearly pissed her pants when Ledger pierced her with his angry gaze. As if it was her fault that I was losing weight.

My guy is crazy.

And beautiful.

And I don't know what I'll do when the six weeks are up and I have to leave him.

"Well, I'm really fucking glad," he bites out.

His anger only manages to amuse me more. "You don't like me pregnant?"

"I don't like you throwing up."

"It's just the hormones."

"If I have to hear hormones one more time, I'm going to punch a hole in this wall."

"And twins, remember? So double the hormones."

"You just said the magic word, Firefly."

I chuckle. "Besides, who knew you had such super fertile sperm."

He pulls a face. "We knew."

I roll my eyes. "So it's all your fault anyway."

He comes closer, his biceps bunching. "I know."

All my amusement vanishes then, and rubbing his corded and vibrating biceps, I say, "Remember what the doctor said? It's all normal and I'm healthy. So you can relax."

His jaw clenches and he says in a raspy tone, "I can't."

"Why not?"

"Because someone upset you."

"No one —"

"Who was it?"

"Ledger —"

He comes even closer, his arms vibrating with the effort. "Who upset you?"

My heart is pounding in my chest and with choppy breaths, I lie, "No one."

"Was it your father?"

"No."

"It was, wasn't it?"

I swallow thickly. "It wasn't."

"You know I'm going to fuck him up, don't you?"

My heart races even more at his violent tone. "I don't need you to."

"Yeah, I know." Then, "That's why I haven't done anything."

"And you won't."

"*Yet*," he qualifies.

We stare at each other for a few seconds. I look at his violent eyes and harsh features and he's probably noticing my rapid breaths and pink cheeks. I don't know what he's thinking but I know what *I'm* thinking.

It's the same thing that I think every time I look at him these days. Every time I see his concerned frown when he watches me struggle with my pregnancy symptoms or watch him come back home — God, *home* — all stressed and agitated after a long day of practice or his therapy sessions.

The same thing that I think when he slides into bed with me and wraps me up in his arms and lets me burrow into his chest. And when he slides out of bed in the morning, I think that very same thing again.

So far I haven't been able to do much about it.

With my symptoms and his crazy schedule, I haven't pursued this line of conversation. Plus I thought he needed to adjust to working with his brothers again, going to therapy that he still hates and never talks about.

But I can't wait anymore.

I only have six weeks left with him.

I need to make every day count.

So when it looks like he's going to step away from me, I hold onto him. "Actually, I do need something from you."

I watch him go into his provider mode. "What?"

Watching a drop of sweat trailing down the side of his neck, I whisper, "I want you to kiss me."

He flinches.

And tries to step back anyway.

I don't let him go though; I latch onto his biceps with my fingers and lick my lips. "Until I can't breathe."

His nostrils flare. "You —"

"And then I want you to kiss me some more."

"Tempest."

"And keep kissing me until I'm dizzy with the lack of air."

"Shut up," he growls, trying to back away again.

But I go with him. "And I also need you to touch my belly."

He shudders at that.

"Because you haven't," I keep going, feeling the flutters in my tummy. "And that's not good, Ledger."

"Shut the fuck up," he manages to say and takes a small step back.

Again I follow him right back. "You need to touch it so our babies know their daddy's touch. People say that it helps with bonding."

His chest heaves. "Get away from me."

"And I want that too."

"Tempest, I —"

"I want you to touch me. It's been so long, Ledger. It's been weeks and months and I don't know if I can bear it anymore."

"I swear if you don't stop talking, I'm —"

"And I've been very patient with you," I tell him, again following him when he steps back. "I've given you time and not bothered you about this.

Even though I have no clue why you're being this way. I don't know why you don't touch me anymore."

"Stop," he growls, his jaw ticking, "*talking.*"

"I mean, initially I thought that maybe you wanted other girls," he growls this time without words, making me pause, "but I don't think you do. I also don't think that you're bored of me. And —"

"What?"

I bite my lip. "It's a valid concern. What if all the, uh, 'trying' that we did made you feel bored with me and —"

"Well, it *didn't*," he says with clenched teeth.

"Okay."

"In fact it did the opposite," he mutters as if to himself.

"What's the opposite?"

My question makes him realize that he's said it out loud and he shakes his head once. "Doesn't fucking matter."

"But —"

"Now I want you to stop following me and let me go."

"Can't," I tell him. "I'm your pretty little stalker, remember?"

I feel him making fists at his sides. "I don't want to use force because —"

"I'm pregnant."

His eyes narrow. "So you really need to —"

"And you'd die before you let something happen to me or to them."

He leans over me then. "You know, I *hate* being interrupted and —"

"Oh, I know that."

He grinds his jaw for a second before saying, "And if you don't stop doing that, I'm going to have to take the kind of measures to shut your mouth that you may not find as enjoyable."

I bite my lip. "I'm counting on that."

He exhales sharply.

Going up on my tiptoes, I whisper, "But I think by now you should know that there are quite a lot of things that I find enjoyable. Including the kind of measures you take to shut my mouth."

Another sharp breath.

Followed by a second and a third.

Before his mouth swoops down over mine and he does what I asked him to do.

Kisses the breath out of me.

Chapter Thirty-Three

THE TRUCK COMES to a screeching halt and I thank God for it.

Because I don't know how long I could've borne it for.

In fact the seconds it's taking him rounding the truck to get to me seem much longer than they are. And then he's snapping the door open and before I can make a move to climb out, he's already picking me up and carrying me over to the cabin.

I know it could be his impatience — I mean, *I am* impatient as well — but somehow when he crosses the threshold with me in his arms, bridal style, it seems significant.

It seems like a big moment.

Which is ridiculous because he's done this once before. The night I was running away from him and he caught me in the woods. The only difference is that that night I was so out of it, I barely knew what was happening. But today, *right now*, I'm very aware of everything.

His strong hold on me, his heat, my side pressed up against his chest.

His eyes.

That are not only locked with mine but are also dark and full of some unfathomable but intense emotions.

Like he's thinking the same thing as me.

That this is significant.

Him carrying me over the threshold.

But as we come closer to the bedroom, I wave these silly thoughts away and focus on the now.

On this moment.

That I thought would never come. Especially seeing how it's been over an hour since the kiss in his brother's office. The time that's been filled with meeting with his teammates. Apparently they were lurking around the hallway, and as soon as we came out of the office, several of them made their approach.

At first I was a little overwhelmed. Only because my mind had been on other things, such as how fast we could go back to touching each other again. But slowly I relaxed because they were all very nice to me, smiling and polite, congratulating me on the babies.

Soon I figured out that Ledger is close to only a couple of guys: A guy named Riot Rivera, the same guy that was with him when Stellan had called a halt to practice to I assume give them some pointers; and this other guy named Vlad Pavlov. While Vlad was talkative and charming, Riot was on the reserved side but of course polite. I have to say that between Riot and Vlad, I liked Riot more. Only because he has a little girl of three named Sophia and he sounded totally enamored while talking about her.

Kinda like Ledger.

I also got to meet or at least say hi to both Stellan and Shep. Despite my impatience to be alone with Ledger, I would've liked to talk to his brothers more, just because they're family and to reassure them that what they had witnessed with Conrad was a total misunderstanding and they shouldn't blame Ledger.

But the guy in question wasn't having it.

He let me say hi to them and then he practically dragged me away, leaving the building altogether. He put me in his truck, drove back to our cabin and now here we are.

Me on the bed after he deposited me there, and him standing in the middle of the room, watching me.

Thinking about something.

Which I don't like; I don't want him thinking about anything.

I don't want him to back out, not now. Not when we both have waited and waited for this. And I *know* he has. If that kiss proved anything, then it was that he's been waiting too.

He's been waiting to touch me.

To fuck me.

I still don't know why he's been holding back all this time; he probably thinks pregnancy has made me fragile or something. But I'm not letting him get inside his head and ruin this.

So I say the first thing that comes to me. "How did they all know?"

He blinks, jerking a little as if he was so engrossed in watching me and in his thoughts that he'd forgotten everything. Good thing I woke him up then.

"Know what?"

His tone is all scratchy and low, rough, turned on. And it turns *me* on and changes my voice too as I ask, "Who I was. Your teammates." Then, I explain, "Even when I got there. The security guard knew who I was and also the guy at reception. They all seemed to know that I…"

I trail off on the account of searching for a better word.

"They all seemed to know that you what?"

I swallow, thinking that perhaps there's no better word than the one that I already have. "That I… belong to you."

"Because you do."

My heart races as I cradle my slightly-swollen belly. "And that I'm having your babies."

"Because you are."

I rub my belly in circles. "Well, they all seemed really nice."

He fists his fingers, watching my movements for a second and I wonder if I'm doing this for myself or for him. If I'm taunting him to come get me, to come touch my belly that I know he wants to.

Looking up, he says, his voice even lower, "They're not."

"What?"

"*Nice*," he bites out.

"But they all —"

"What they are, are a bunch of fucking horndogs."

My hand comes to a halt and I frown. "What? That's not —"

"Who couldn't keep their eyes off of you."

"I don't think that's true."

"Even though they knew," he clenches his teeth, "that you belong to me."

"I —"

"And that you're carrying my babies."

I shake my head. "I think you're overreacting, as usual. There is —"

"Although," his expression is flickering with possession and something else, "I shouldn't be surprised now, should I?"

"I'm sorry?"

"It's always been the case."

"Y-your teammates looking at me?"

"Even back then."

"You mean when I came to your practice in high school?" I ask, figuring out that the other thing in his eyes is nostalgia.

He's remembering things from before as he says, "They'd stare at you then too."

I frown, trying to think back also, "I don't… remember that."

"That's because you couldn't take your eyes off of me," he tells me. "So you had no clue what was going around you."

I blush but I have no shame in admitting the truth, not anymore. So I agree. "I couldn't, no. But I still don't think that they stared at me like you're saying."

He gives me a look then.

Like I've lost my mind.

Then, "You were the only girl in the bleachers who didn't go to our school *and* you put the cheerleading squad to shame with the way you'd jump up and down and bounce on the seat every time I scored a goal. So yeah, they'd stare at you."

"That is not true," I tell him. "I did not jump up and down and bounce around when you scored a goal. My brother was there too, remember? He would've killed me if I cheered for his enemy."

"I could see your perky tits trembling with joy in your fucking dress every time I scored a goal," he tells me back. "So yes, you would jump and bounce *and* clap while smiling as bright as the sun, fucking blinding half the school with your happiness."

I bite my lip then.

I would smile, yes. Because that was the only thing I *could* do. Because as I said, my brother was there, and he used to get super annoyed that I'd show up to practice and his games when he'd always asked me not to. But now I'm rethinking things.

Even so, I maintain my position. "Again, I think you're overreacting. You think every guy looks at me and —"

"Why do you think I'd score so many goals?" he asks.

"What?"

His eyes are narrowed, giving him a threatening look. "Why do you think I'd fight your brother so hard for the ball?"

I blink.

"Why do you *think*," he keeps going, "I'd fight your brother not only for the ball but for every little thing that I could think of?"

"For me," I breathe out.

"Because you were watching," he says, his eyes boring into mine. "Because I wanted you to know that I was stronger. Than him. Better than him. I wanted to show you that I could crush him with my bare hands if I wanted to. And then take you away from him while he lay there broken and bleeding to death."

A tic has started up in his jaw, making him look ten times more aggressive.

More violent now.

And the fact that I can see the outline of his dick through his workout pants — he's still in his practice clothes from before, all deliciously sweaty and male — all hard and big and so fucking ferocious, makes me throb with lust.

Makes my pussy all slick and juiced up.

"But mostly," he goes on, his hand going to his dick now, pressing it over his sweatpants as if soothing the ache, "I wanted to take you away from my asshole teammates who would pant over you like a bunch of dogs and give you what you'd been asking for."

I'm rhythmically pressing my thighs together as well.

I may even be rocking and subtly humping the air but I can't be sure.

All I know is that I want him here, not over there, and I want *me* to rub that cock, to soothe it, to pet it and lick it, not him. Licking my own lips because I can't lick his yet, I ask, "Asking for what?"

His eyes drop down my body, to my chest specifically. "For a titty fuck."

His words hit me with force, right in the center of my belly, and I have to do what he's doing. I have to massage my lower tummy like he's massaging his dick.

I also want to massage my tits with my other hand because I think he's right.

I think I did want that.

Maybe that's why — subconsciously — I would shake and bounce on those bleachers even though I knew it was dangerous to do that with my brother present.

"You were, weren't you?" he asks.

And even though he already knows the answer, I nod. "Yes."

He licks his lips then.

As if like me, he wants to lick something else right now, maybe my tits. But because he can't, he has to make do with his own mouth.

Still massaging himself, he goes, "And I would. But I wouldn't do it behind closed doors, no."

"W-what?"

He lifts his eyes then and I know he's speaking the truth.

I know every word that's coming out of his mouth is God's honest truth. Because he's so gone, see. His lust has overtaken him, every part of his body, every inch of his brain and every thread in his soul. He doesn't have it in him to lie right now. To make stuff up.

And that just gets me more excited for some reason.

To hear the truth.

Hear about everything that he imagined.

Because I think I'll like it too. Like I did when he'd told me the story behind this bed and what he wanted to do to me in it.

"Because I need to send a message, don't I?" he continues, lust swirling in his gaze. "I need to make it clear to them, to my teammates, that this firecracker of a girl belongs to me. That you belong to the captain. You're not public property. You're not *theirs* to look at, to salivate over, to fantasize about. They're not supposed to jack themselves off in the shower, thinking about your tits. They're not supposed to imagine how perky they are or how high they ride on your body. Or what color nipples you've got. And if they sucked on them, how hard will they get, how dark in color, how juicy.

They're not supposed to do any of that. Your tits aren't theirs to think about. And neither is your milky skin, your cotton candy lips and that gap between your creamy-as-fuck thighs. Where they can stick their pencil dicks and hump your tight little body until they jizz all over your panties.

"And that's because only *I'm* supposed to do that. Only the captain is supposed to think about thcsc things. Only the captain is allowed to pluck this perky little girl who doesn't go to our school but still shows up to practice like it's her job, and carry her to the locker room. Only he's supposed to make her kneel at his feet, tear her flimsy fucking dress down the middle and expose her tits that are responsible for every hard-on in a ten-mile radius. Only the captain, you understand? Me."

I nod. I think.

I also say something that sounds like, "And do what with her?"

"That's hard to choosc, isn't it?" he murmurs as he roves his eyes all over my kneeling body. Kneeling and rocking body, and I don't think I'm being subtle anymore. I think I'm really going at it now, humping the air, pressing my legs, looking for friction.

Asking for it, like he'd said.

"While I do wanna give you what you've been asking for, I also want to use your mouth. Stretch your lips around my big cock and make you smile up at me that way. And I also want to stick my cock between your thighs and ride them like I would your pussy and cream all over your panties. But only because I'm not going to show them what your panties are hiding. Because if I do, no amount of show and tell that I've got planned in the locker room is going to keep them away from you. If I show them your juicy cunt, they'll all be descending on you like a pack of wolves. And of course I can handle them all and protect you but I'm more interested in fucking than fighting. So we're going to have to make do with your panties on.

"And maybe that's why I'll do all three. I'll fuck your tits. I'll fuck your mouth and then I'll fuck that gap between your thighs."

"B-but… But what about…"

"What about *what*?"

"My brother," I whisper. "He's there too and…"

He narrows his eyes again, looking thoughtful. "Well as I said, I could either crush him and leave him to die on the field. Or I could just lock him outside the locker room. Only to spare you the embarrassment. I could give a fuck if he watches though. Or if he pounds on the door or tries to kick it down, call security or whatever. I'm not gonna stop. In fact, that will only get me going harder. Maybe I'll fuck your titties to the rhythm of his pounding. Maybe I'll fuck your mouth that way too. And maybe when I come, I'll groan louder than he's calling for help.

"And trust me when I say that it has nothing to do with revenge. It's not for his benefit. Not what I'm doing right now. It's for them. The guys.

Who'll be standing around and watching me molest you. Who'll be standing around, probably beating off their dicks like I'm beating up that gap between your thighs. Which of course will make me angry, but I guess I'll let them live. Because I'm trying to prove a point here. I'm trying to send a message that you belong to me, don't you? And only I can use you. Only I get to soothe myself with your body, come on your body, abuse your body to find peace. Only *I* get to make your heart race or make it slow down. Only I get to snatch it out of your chest or play with it. Only I get to keep it safe and treasure it for as long as I live. Only me." Then, scoffing, "Which I probably should've done today as well."

"Why didn't you?" I whisper.

Probably because I've lost my mind.

Or maybe because if he's right, that his teammates *were* staring at me today, then I do want him to send a message. I do want him to tell the world that I'm not theirs to look at. I'm only his.

Now and for as long as I live.

That it's completely irrational and of course untrue is not something that I want to think about.

What I want is to exist with him in this moment.

Exist and reminisce about our history.

Our story.

That's not a romance novel, but it's still a story of love and hate and heartbreak and revenge. We may not get our happily ever after but I will forever remember these days that we've spent together and our past fraught with tension and longing as something to be happy about.

And maybe I'll tell them too, one day.

My babies.

About how Mommy and Daddy met and what Daddy means to Mommy.

"Because things are different now," he says, pulling me out of my own head.

"Different how?"

"Different because you're my wi —"

He stops abruptly and I prod, "I'm your what?"

His eyes go down to my belly again that I'm still cradling, still rubbing in circles. "You've got my babies in your belly."

"Yes."

Lifting his eyes, he rasps, "So no one else gets to look at you. Or them." With that, he finally, finally takes a step toward me and I breathe out in relief. "No one gets to look at what I've done to your body. How I've made it softer and rounder. More ripe and swollen. No one gets to see the way your tummy is stretching and growing every day to keep my babies safe. How you and your body are making sacrifices, how you and your body bear every pain and ache that I've given you, just to nourish and treasure my babies.

It's because your body's a temple now, isn't it? And only I get to worship at your altar." Then, when he's only a couple of steps away, he says, "Well, it was a temple before too, but I guess I'm less of a sinner now than I was back then."

Finally he's close and I raise my hand to cup his cheek. "You're not a sinner."

He scoffs, his breath escaping him in a rush. "No I'm not. I'm more than that. I'm the sin itself."

"That's not —"

"Show me."

"What?"

He licks his lips. "Your body."

Now my breaths are escaping me in a rush. Not that they weren't before, but still.

Now my breaths are even more excited and rapid.

As I go to do his bidding.

I don't even wait to show him my new body. I can't. I want him to look. I've been wanting him to look. To *see* what he did to me. What I look like now.

All proudly and eagerly.

Because I know he'll like it. I know he'll like my expanded curves, the pooch in my belly. He'll like my bigger tits, my darker nipples. All the little veins and moles that keep showing up every day now.

And *that's* because he wants this as much as me.

Yes, he's been angry at my symptoms and all the pain I've had to endure, but I know that he wouldn't have it any other way. In fact, now that we know we're having twins, he wouldn't want anything less.

And the moment my dress is off and my bra is gone, I'm proven both right and wrong.

Wrong because he doesn't just like it, he loves it. And right because he does want it as much as me.

In fact he wants it so much that his knees go weak.

Something that I never thought could happen to a guy and such a masculine guy at that.

But I guess I should have known.

If anything can weaken his knees and make him come down on them, it's these babies that are growing inside of me. Because that's where he is: on his knees on the floor, his rough hands gripping my rounded hips and his mouth on my swollen belly.

As I said, I'm only fifteen weeks right now and my clothes hide the bump. But I'm also carrying twins, which means my bump is bigger than a normal fifteen-week bump.

And he's doing exactly what he said before.

He's worshiping it.

With his mouth. That he at first simply presses on my skin before opening it and breathing on my bump. But that's not where it stops, no. It's only the beginning. After simply breathing on my tummy, he then licks it. As if tasting my skin. As if he thinks it tastes different now because of the babies.

Because my body is growing something for him.

Maybe it is, I don't know. He certainly feels so, because after that first long lick with the flat of his tongue, he groans. And he does it again.

And again and again.

Like it's his new favorite thing, the taste of my pregnant belly.

After which he goes on to suck.

Which is when things get crazy and feral and all I can do is bury my fingers in his hair and let him do to me whatever he wants. Let him suck at it, lick it and nip it as he rubs his hands all over my bump and my hips. As he touches and caresses and mauls and memorizes everything about my new body, from veins to moles to little silvery lines at the bottom of my bump.

At first I try to keep track of everything he's doing to me.

So I can think about it later when he's at practice or even later, when I'm gone.

But soon I lose track of everything. There's just his mouth and his groans. My fingers in his hair and my moans to match his sounds. I especially don't care about anything when he moves away from my belly and goes up to my chest.

My tits.

That have also grown and changed.

While my boobs used to get sore in the beginning, now they're pain free and gosh, extra sensitive.

Because the moment his lips find the underside of my tit and vacuum the flesh, I shudder and arch my back, probably already orgasming from only his mouth on my breast. My 'probably' becomes 'definitely' when he moves on to my nipple. Because he opens his mouth wide, wider than he ever has, and pulls in as much of my plump flesh as he can and then goes to town on it.

He practically has my entire tit in his mouth as he sucks and suckles and works it in his mouth, his hands plumping it up meanwhile. His fingers rhythmically squeezing and squeezing as if he's milking it.

As if he's milking my tits and drinking out of them.

It has to be the most erotic experience of my life, hands down.

And that's saying something because I fucking squirt every time we fuck.

While I'm not squirting right now, I'm certainly orgasming and climaxing and moaning and writhing the longer he stays attached to my breasts.

Other than his mouth, his groans and his hands on me and the fact that my channel is pulsing and pulsing, drenching my panties, I have very little awareness of what's happening around me.

I can feel movements here and there, changing sensations.

Like my world tilting on its axis before I feel something soft on my spine. I guess he's laying me down on the bed. Then I feel his heat hovering over my body, meaning he's propped himself up on me. And then I feel his hands tugging and pulling at my panties, probably trying to get them off. So I try to help him, even though it's very hard to make sense of my own limbs that have turned to jelly and my spine that's turned liquid.

In any case, I think I'm naked and now it's his turn.

Because he's stopped playing with my breasts and moved himself away from me.

Blinking my eyes open, I notice that he's standing at the foot of the bed, pulling his t-shirt off, pushing his pants down. And he's doing it in a very mechanical way. In a way that's fast and efficient so he can get back to me soon. Something about that, his impatience and mechanical movements, make him even sexier to me.

A man stripped of all finesse and style.

A man after one thing and one thing only.

Me.

And my pussy.

Which he gets to only a microsecond later when he gets on the bed, his hard and dripping studded cock bobbing and slapping his abs, and knocks my thighs further apart to make space for his large body.

But then he pauses.

Right at my entrance.

His leaking cock poised to enter.

Licking his lips, he rasps, "I want to do something."

Licking mine back, I whisper, "What?"

He swallows, his eyes strangely both intense and concerned.

Before he bends to the side and produces something in his hand.

A phone.

His phone.

And without him having to say it, I understand.

I understand everything.

But he goes ahead and says it anyway. "I want to capture it. The first time."

My pussy clenches in response.

"The first time I fuck your pregnant pussy."

"Do it," I tell him as another pulse that goes through my channel.

He flares his nostrils as if he can smell it.

He can smell my arousal leaking out of me.

Then, "You sure?"

"Uh-huh."

His chest heaves. "It's only for me."

"I know."

"It's only for when…"

"When what?"

He clenches his jaw for a second. "When I'm all frustrated and angry at practice and…"

I fist the sheets. "And you can't get to me."

Another clench. "Yeah."

"So you can take all your frustrations out on me and calm down."

He throws me a short nod in agreement. "So I can watch you and your rounded belly and jerk off thinking I did one thing right. Thinking that on the other side of all this bullshit that I have to go through every day, there's someone waiting for me. That *you* are waiting for me. My beautiful and pregnant Firefly. My peace."

Again I don't know how it's possible to feel this aroused and lustful while your heart is breaking inside of your chest.

I don't know how it's possible that my eyes are tearing up while my pussy is all juicy and wet.

But maybe it's possible with him.

With my Beautiful Thorn.

Who's made of a world of emotions and who makes me feel every one of them every second of every day.

So again, I say yes and tell him to hurry.

And he does.

He fiddles with the phone, turning the camera on, and I widen my thighs even more. Eager and ready and dying to do this. To be his beautiful and pregnant Firefly.

His peace. His everything in fact.

But the moment he thrusts inside, making me moan and arch my back, I think he becomes *my* peace. He becomes my *everything* and there is no need for words.

No need to say anything or commemorate this moment with words.

It's all there on our faces: flushed and euphoric.

His eyes half-closed, his mouth parted, his cheekbones ruddy. And my blushing cheeks, my teeth nipping my lips at the sudden flare of pain, my eyes pinned on his kneeled form.

And of course, it's all there on our bodies.

His tanned and sweaty muscles, flexing and so completely masculine as he starts to move inside of me. And mine, pink and creamy, dotted with his bites, jiggling and shaking at his every thrust.

He starts out slow at first.

Probably because he's holding his cell phone in one hand, pointed directly at where he's moving in and out. And he wants to capture the moment and he wants to do it perfectly.

356

But when I start to lose my mind, when I start to buck and push back, trying to snap my thighs closed because it's too much — not only his long and lazy strokes but also the fact that after the initial shot of his cock inside my pussy, he's now moved on to my whole body, recording my pregnant belly, my swollen tits, as if he doesn't want to miss anything — he goes crazy as well.

His thrusts pick up, his hips slamming into me, his heavy balls slapping against my ass. He even has to prop himself on his free hand as he comes down over me. Because I think it's getting harder and harder for him to hold himself up.

It's getting harder and harder for me too. To hold on, to keep my eyes open and watch him watch us on the screen. Watch him go crazy, the more he watches. Watch sweat drip from his body, his jaw clenching and unclenching, his abs going tight, his chest vibrating with grunts.

So I understand.

I also understand when he can't hold the phone anymore, and has to drop it on the bed.

So he can watch me in real time.

It's probably my fault because I'm arching and arching my back, and I'm pushing back against him at every chance I get. I'm also rubbing my body with my hands, my belly, my hips. My tits and my nipples.

All because I want to give him a good show.

I want to give him something that really soothes him when I'm not there.

But I guess my efforts were a little too good and they defeated the whole purpose, and now he's propped up on both hands, watching me do all this in real time. And now I can't decide which is hotter: him watching me through a screen as I writhe and grind my body for him or him watching me like this.

I guess my body decides for me in the next second.

When an orgasm steals over me out of nowhere.

One second, I'm tugging at my nipples and rubbing my pregnant belly, and the next I'm holding onto his biceps, scratching at his skin as thunder rolls over me.

A thunder that shakes me from the inside out.

That makes me moan and scream, which he then captures in his mouth.

While going over the edge himself.

As he comes with me and inside of me.

And even through my own revelation of an orgasm, I clutch him to me. I wrap my thighs around his bucking hips and my arms around his flexing shoulders, and let him burrow into my neck. I let him groan and grunt into my skin as he comes and comes, sounding stoned and pained.

But it's okay.

I'm here to absorb it all.

His climax, his cum.
His pain, his torture.
His violence.
And turn it into something beautiful.
I just wish I could do it for the rest of my life though.
I just wish that I could be there for him at the end of all his shitty days.
And not just for the next six weeks.

Chapter Thirty-Four

Her Beautiful Thorn

"SO HOW'D YOU DO IT?"

At his question, I look at my friend Reign. "Do what?"

"Knock her up," he explains.

I regard him silently as I take a sip of my beer. We're at a bar in the city, celebrating a teammate's birthday. For the record, I'm not real familiar with the guy and I usually don't do group activities. But Dr. Mayberry thinks it's good for me to mingle, and since her regular progress reports are what's keeping me on the team, I'm her puppet until she cuts my strings. Gio is extremely happy about it.

Anyway, Reign just got drafted to a team in Florida, but he's visiting for a couple of days. And since he knows most of these guys, he was invited.

"If you don't know how to knock up a girl, I don't know if we should be having this conversation."

He gives me the finger. Then, with a frown, "I mean, how the fuck did you do it so fast? And with twins no less."

My lips twitch. "Why, you looking to get your girl knocked up?"

His frown thickens. "I shouldn't."

"Yeah? Why not?"

"She's only eighteen, dumbass."

"So?"

"And she's in college."

I tip my bottle toward him. "You barely got out of college."

"But she just started. She has goals. And I'm supposed to be a good boyfriend and support those goals. I shouldn't be thinking about…" he trails off in a grimace.

My lips twitch harder. "Thinking about what?"

"Planting my baby in her. Seeing her all," his eyes glaze as if he's actually imagining it right now, "soft and round. All mine."

"Well," I tell him, trying not to laugh. "She already is yours."

He comes back to the moment with a sigh. "Yeah, but not like that."

I know what he's saying. I know what he means.

I felt that too.

In fact I still feel it. And I *have* knocked her up. With twins no less.

But then again, I have done other things too, haven't I?

Other despicable things.

Which means that she's not mine. Even if I wanted her to be. Even if *she* wanted to be.

"And it's gotten worse now," he says.

"Ever since you moved away."

"Yeah." He shakes his head. "We're trying to get her to move down to Florida, but it won't be until next semester, so yeah."

Sighing, I put him out of his misery. "It's not all it's cracked up to be. Pregnancy is hard." He's listening raptly so I go on, "It was fucking torture, man. Those first few months. She was throwing up left and right, couldn't keep anything down. She'd cry just like that. Weird smells knocked her off her ass. Her boobs hurt. Jesus," I shake my head, "and the worst part was that I couldn't do anything. They say ginger helps but it did jackshit for her. She couldn't even keep water down, lost so much weight. And all I could do was stand there and pull her hair back while she emptied her stomach."

"Holy fuck," Reign goes.

"So you better think really long and hard before you do something drastic," I tell him. "In fact, the moment you get the urge to go bareback and knock her up, you go for a run. You work out. You run drills. You drink yourself to sleep. You do whatever you can to fight the urge. And you support her, you hear me? In all her goals. Do what she says. Give her what she wants. Treat her like she's your queen and don't be a selfish dick."

Before Reign can respond, someone else joins our little two-some.

Riot Rivera.

One of my only friends on the team and a striker like me.

"What are we talking about?" he asks, settling himself on the couch with a beer of his own.

Reign turns to him. "Ledge over here is giving out love advice."

Riot's eyes go wide. "For real?"

"Yup."

"Let me guess, it all has to do with having a big dick and knowing how to use it."

Reign chuckles. "Apparently not. *Apparently*, our legendary lover boy does have some pointers about how to be in a relationship."

Riot pauses sipping on his beer and look at me like he's so fucking surprised. "You're shitting me."

Reign's lips twitch. "Nope."

"But he did slip his dick in the conversation at least once, right?"

"Not once."

"Holy fuck," he breathes much like Reign had done only a few moments before.

"You talk to your daughter with that mouth, asshole?" I address Riot.

Who has the audacity to chuckle. "No, I do wash my mouth out before talking to my daughter whenever I curse. Don't worry, I'll teach you when you have yours."

I flip him the bird, which only makes him chuckle more.

Like me, Riot is also new to the team. But of course, he wasn't the last pick like I was. In fact, he was one of the first ones. With his soccer player Puerto Rican father and uncles, soccer practically flows in his veins. Although for a while there it looked like he might not be able to make any team or go pro. Because a one-night stand he'd had in college ended up pregnant — without his knowledge — and dumped the baby on him. There's a lot of drama involved, including her trying to get money from him in exchange for the baby, threatening him to go to the press and whatnot.

But in any case, I'm glad he ended up here or I'd hate literally everyone on the team.

Which is not a problem for me, but having a friendly face is nice.

It's also the only reason that I stay for another beer when I want to get out of here and go back home. Since it's my turn, I go to the counter to get us another round. But while I'm waiting for my order, I run into the last person that I thought I'd see here. Not to mention, the last person I *wanted* to see.

But from the looks of it, I was the only person *he* wanted to see.

I steel myself for whatever it is he wants to say as he settles himself beside me at the bar. He signals to the bartender and asks for whiskey — the choice of liquor for my oldest brother — before turning to me. "It's good to see you mingling with the team."

"Doctor's orders," I tell him.

His lips quirk up slightly. "Well then, it's good to see you following her orders."

I shrug. "Kinda don't have a choice, but sure."

The bartender places both our orders in front of us and I'm about to take my leave. If he wants to discuss my therapy sessions, he can do it in depth with the doctor herself. I'm not going to stand here and analyze my shit with him.

When he says the one thing that has the power to keep me here.

"Tempest's nice," he murmurs, taking a sip of his whiskey.

Leaning away from the counter, I instantly go on alert. "What do you want?"

He looks at me, a frown on his forehead. "What do I want?"

"Yeah." I stand with my feet apart. "What is it that you want from me? You came here to see me, didn't you? Because there's no way you're here to celebrate someone's birthday. That's not your style. You send your lackeys to do that."

"My lackeys."

"Stellan." I tip my chin toward the corner he's standing in with a couple of players and another assistant coach. "Right over there."

Shep isn't here tonight, which I'm glad about. Because if he were, it would be tough for Stellan to mingle on Conrad's orders. He would've done it for sure. But it would've been a chore, or rather, *more* of a chore for my other big brother.

Looking away from Stellan, I focus on Conrad. "So what is it?"

He regards me silently, my straight spine and my battle stance. Then, shaking his head, "Nothing. Just wondering how I missed it."

"How you missed what?"

He shrugs, taking another casual sip of his drink. "That you're in love with her."

I suck in my gut.

The impact of his words is so strong, it's like a sucker punch.

An implosion even.

Jarring me to my marrow, jangling my bones.

Stealing words, stealing thoughts from me.

When I don't say anything — I can't, he goes on, "You are, aren't you?"

I still don't speak.

I still haven't gathered enough sense to form words, let alone put them in the right order to spill out sentences.

Turning to me, he keeps going, "Because I've never seen you this way. Well, I've seen you angry and agitated. But I've never seen you be that way for anyone outside of the family."

At 'family,' I bite out, "That tends to happen when everything I've heard from your mouth regarding her has been bullshit of the biggest variety."

I'm not lying.

I still don't know what he said to her the day she visited me at practice about a week ago. I've asked but she won't tell me. She keeps insisting that she's fine and that Conrad didn't say anything objectionable to her. Which is kinda hard for me to believe, given how much of an asshole he's been about her pregnancy.

I knew that would be the case though.

My brother gets really triggered any time he hears the word 'pregnant.' He flipped his shit when Callie got pregnant last year. I'm ashamed to say that I was with him at the time. Only because of whose baby it was.

But Conrad has deeper reasons.

Our mother had him when she was only eighteen, a high schooler, and Conrad thinks that that was a mistake. That if she hadn't had him that young, maybe things would be different now. Although I don't know how that's possible. Our father would still be an asshole and our mother would still be dead.

But anyway, when I broke the news about Tempest's pregnancy — even though it was none of his business, I wasn't going to hide it either — needless to say he didn't take it well.

He did what he always does, judge and lecture.

While looking extremely disappointed in me and my 'rash and thoughtless decision-making process.' That would not only 'ruin my life but now someone else's too,' including those two babies that she's carrying in her body. And did I really need that when my focus should be on getting my almost-destroyed career back.

Granted, all of his disappointment was directed at me, but still it's not a stretch to think that he may have said the same things to her as well. And if he has, I'm not going to be held responsible for what I do to him.

"But all that bullshit's been about you though," he says, looking at me pointedly.

"Which is the only reason I haven't made the news again."

At this, he surprises me with a small smile. "Thank fucking God for that, huh."

"I'm —"

"Do you know what our father's problem was?" he asks me abruptly.

"What?"

He takes another sip of his whiskey and then stares down at the glass. "Apart from alcohol."

I'm not sure why we're talking about this but I reply nonetheless, "Women."

Which is true.

Our dad liked to sleep around. In addition to drinking his days away and blaming all his misfortunes on his wife and his children, that for the record, he never had a problem making.

"Christ," he mutters. "Yeah, I forgot about that."

"Well, he had a laundry list of problems. Not your fault."

He chuckles lightly. "Yeah, he did."

"Why are we talking about him?"

His jaw clenches for a second as he regards the dark liquid pensively. Then, "Because I fucked up."

My brows bunch together. "Fucked up how?"

Finally he turns to me, his face etched in determination and believe it or not, remorse. It instantly puts me on edge. Because I guess now we're coming down to the real reason why he showed up to see me at the bar tonight.

"I hated our father," he says in a low but fierce voice. "I hated him so fucking much that I was glad when he left. I was glad that it was going to be just us, Mom and me and all of you guys. Sure, it was a big responsibility but I would've gladly taken it. I did gladly take it." Then, "Even though I started resenting a lot of it as years passed. But that's not the point. The reason I hated our father so much wasn't because he slept around or woke up in his own vomit more often than not. I hated him because of what he did to Mom. Physically."

"What?"

His jaw clenches again, this time I know in anger, as he says, "He had a temper. And it was mean and it was cruel, and he liked to take it out on Mom, sometimes me. I don't like to think about it. I don't like to... revisit it, even in my head. But he did. And when you guys came along, I did everything that I could to shield you guys from that and I'm happy to say that you guys never saw it. Maybe Stellan here and there, even Shep, but mostly I did everything I could to run interference. And you know what, there are days when I'd feel proud about that. That I protected you guys, my family, against a monster. But apparently, I didn't. There's one person I didn't protect from him, all the bullshit, and that's you."

There's a buzz in my body.

The same one that I've felt for as long as I can remember.

The army of red ants crawling under my skin, making it tight and itchy. Making me want to scratch it, break something, wreak havoc. And if I don't get a handle on it, it's going to paint the world red and make me wreak havoc.

Make me vomit and split me down the middle.

Is that why?

Is that why I feel this incessant agitation? Is that why I'm always ready to burn down the world and blow it apart?

Is that why I tricked her into signing those papers and is that why I feel so unhinged and jealous any time I think about her leaving me and running into someone else's arms?

Because of genetics, because of our piece of shit father.

Regret is swimming in my brother's eyes as he continues, "He may not have touched you but I made sure that you felt the impact of it. I made *sure* that you suffered the consequences, you felt the sting, the pain. And the only pathetic excuse I have is that I put you in the same category as him. I lumped you together with him. I..." He swallows thickly. "Every time I'd get a phone call from your school or someone knocked at the door to complain about their crying kid because you punched them on the playground or their ruined rose bushes because you ran them over with your bike, I'd be reminded of how our father was. I'd be reminded of what he'd do and how there were days when we'd be terrified of him and I... I was hard on you, Ledger. I was critical of you. I judged you before you even knew what that word meant. And I thought I was doing it for your own good. I thought I was doing it so you didn't end up like him, so you didn't become the monster that our father was. And I guess I was so blinded by that, so fucking tunnel-visioned that I never saw all the differences between you and him.

"I never saw, I never appreciated the things you did for the family. All the ways you stood by our side, all the ways you always had our back. The ways you helped out even when you were a kid. The ways you'd assume responsibilities without having to be told. How you'd make grocery runs without having to be asked, pick up Shep's slack when he'd be busy with soccer practice. In fact, it should've been obvious to me back when you'd run away and —"

"You knew?"

His eyes bore into mine. "Of course I did. You're my little brother. Of course I knew you'd run away." Then, scoffing, "And of course like a shitty big brother, I assumed it was because you were angry and throwing a tantrum."

"I *was* angry."

"Yeah, but you had a right to be," he says. "I rode you hard that week. At practice. Chewed you out just because you missed a goal and never appreciated the fact that you'd made the net every single time before that. All because deep down I was afraid that if I let you slip up once, it was going to happen again and again and what if you end up like him. And what if I could've prevented that but I didn't. What a sorry excuse for a brother, huh."

"No," I say immediately, my chest feeling tighter and tighter. "You were a good big brother. You *are* a good big brother. You did the best that you could."

"Not with you."

I chuckle harshly, my breaths getting strangled, my muscles locked tight. "But what if you were right? What if I am —"

"You're not," he says firmly, his eyes flickering with conviction. "Because if you were, you wouldn't want to kill me just because I said her name."

I grind my jaw. "But that still —"

His hand shoots out and he grips the back of my neck like he used to when I was a kid and he wanted me to not only hear something but under-stand it as well. "Listen to me, you're *not* like him. I spent my life thinking that. I spent my life punishing you for it and I know what a huge mistake that was. I *know* how big my regret is, and trust me when I say it's not a good feeling. In fact, it's the worst feeling in the world, misunderstanding my own brother, and I refuse to let you do that, got it? I *absolutely refuse* to let you misunderstand yourself. You're not like him. You were never like him. You're more of a man than he ever was. You *were* more of a man at twelve, when you'd run away but came right back because you couldn't abandon your family, than he ever was, yeah? That's why you came back, didn't you?"

I clench my jaw, unable to respond in this moment.

But turns out he doesn't need me to say anything. He simply tightens his hold on my neck, almost shaking me, and says, "And if you still have doubts about it, I want you to think about her. I want you to think about the girl you love who made me see it."

"What?"

His nostrils flare with a sharp breath. "I wish I could say that I had this epiphany all by myself. But I didn't. It was her. She told me to stop fucking around and really think about things. That day. She told me to really look at you and I did. And I'm fucking embarrassed to say that it was easy. More than easy to see the differences."

While I'm watching him, stunned, he delivers his last blow. "So if it becomes difficult for you to see the differences too, I want you to think about her. The girl you love and who loves you back just as much if not more."

She doesn't.

She does not.

She did once, yeah. But she can't be foolish enough to love me now.

And I don't love her either.

Do I?

Because if I do, then what does that make me? If I love her, how could I do to her what I did?

How could I lie to her?

How could I *keep* lying to her, knowingly, consciously? Just because I know that if I told her the truth, that I tricked her into marrying me, she'd run.

And how is it that that's not the worst thing that I've done to her?

Despite my good intentions, despite the massive guilt that keeps getting bigger and bigger as the days pass without me telling her truth, I took advantage of her trust and fucked her. Not only that, I recorded it too.

Actually, I fuck her every night and record it.

I fuck her every night like a depraved animal and then record the shit out of her so I can watch it at practice and jerk off. So I can look at her face, stare at her body. Because I don't know what I'd do if I didn't get to do that. I don't know how I'd breathe, how my heart will beat and my blood will pump.

I don't know how I'd live from one second to the next.

And if I love her, how could I be so selfish?

This is not the first time that I've wondered. How could I do these things

– among other things from the past – to the only girl who's ever given me peace? The girl who's going to give me the two most precious gifts anyone has ever given me.

My Firefly.

My wife.

Chapter Thirty-Five

EVERY NIGHT we have the same discussion and I love it.

"You know, it's not going to happen just because you want it to," I tell him, amused, playing with his crazy hair.

He presses his hand on my belly. "It'll happen."

"Maybe they're as stubborn as their daddy," I point out.

He palms my belly harder. "Maybe their mommy should shut up so Daddy can concentrate."

I roll my eyes and tug at a strand lightly.

Then, "You know, maybe they don't like the fact that their daddy's guessing their gender wrong."

He grunts, still focused on my belly.

I bite my lip then, taking in his frown of concentration. We're lying in bed: he's freshly showered and wearing only his gray sweatpants, and I'm wearing a tiny and silky black-colored slip; just for the record, they do have some really sexy maternity wear that accentuates your bump and your bigger boobs.

Anyway, his head's propped up on his elbow, his eyes on my rounded tummy as he rubs it gently, going from one side to the other, his fingers still almost spanning me from the bottom of my tits all the way down to my belly button. As if he's coaxing them, trying to wake them up and do what he wants them to do.

"It wouldn't be such a problem if you just asked the doctor," I sing-song, pulling at his hair some more.

Because he still hasn't, for some reason.

Which I never thought would be so fun, the not knowing.

But I love to tease him about it.

And even though he's totally focused elsewhere, I keep going, "I bet they're boys. Both of them. Oh, imagine if they were. I could be their queen. Their only queen and —"

He finally looks up, his fingers bunching the fabric on my tummy. "You'll be one of three."

God, he's so handsome, isn't he?

So beautiful.

All relaxed and flushed after his shower, his crazy hair even messier and damp, trying to bond with our babies.

"One of three of what?"

"Princesses."

"Yours?"

"Fuck yeah."

I smile, tracing his high, kingly cheekbones. "Why, because you're Ledger Thorne and the whole world bows down to you?"

"No, because they're mine and they know what I want."

"That's —"

"And the whole world *does* bow down to me, but I only bow down to them."

To his two baby girls.

And me.

I swallow, trying to tamp down the butterflies in my pregnant belly. Or maybe it's them, rolling around in happiness inside of me, fluttering around like my little butterflies at their daddy's conviction and love.

"Remember what the doctor said though," I whisper, "and all those other websites? They aren't going to move until at least week nineteen or twenty. And I'm only like, seventeen weeks."

His frown comes back. "Fuck doctors."

"Are you still mad at her for not coming to my rescue during the first trimester?"

"Yeah," he says in a *duh* tone.

My lips twitch. "You're crazy, you know that?"

His eyes bore into mine. "Better than being a useless asshole who lets his pregnant Firefly suffer and does absolutely nothing." Then, resuming his gentle motions on my belly, "Although I am that too."

I turn to him, my skin trembling.

Because this time around, his touch isn't for our babies but for me. It's there simply because he wants to touch me and because he knows how crazy I get for him these days.

"You're not," I tell him.

"No?"

"No," I whisper, rubbing my thighs together. "You *do* do things to alleviate my suffering."

His thumb hooks into my belly button and his eyes grow half-mast. "You suffering, baby?"

I press my thighs together. "Uh-huh."

"Where?"

"You know where."

A smirk flickers on his beautiful mouth. "Let's pretend that I don't."

I move my legs restlessly, whining, "Ledger, don't be mean."

His smirk gets bigger. "Yeah? But you like it so much."

"I don't."

"I think you do."

"I do not."

"The fact that you went so crazy last night that we had to change the sheets says otherwise."

Oh God, I cannot believe that he's bringing it up.

I was so embarrassed.

Because last night was something else.

He kept me on edge for what seemed like hours and when he let me come, I came so hard I *really* drenched the sheets. And I'm not even kidding. It's like ever since I got pregnant I feel everything differently. First trimester was all about scents and tastes and getting sick at the slightest things. But this one, my second trimester, is all about hunger.

Hunger for food. Hunger for him.

I even get horny while reading him my romance novels.

Which I have to say is not really a surprise, because I used to get that way before too. But while I could hide it before, now I can't. I absolutely cannot hide my blush, my breathiness, the way I keep licking my lips and squirming.

But honestly if this is the only symptom of the second trimester, I'll take it.

Although I'm not sure how I feel about his teasing and stupid edging.

"That wasn't me," I tell him, my hand going to his obliques and latching on.

"I think it was you," he replies, his own now stroking my side, going from my waist down to my ass, my upper thighs even. And every time he goes back up, he inches my slip higher and higher, scraping the silk against my skin, making it break out in goosebumps.

"It was the hormones," I insist, stroking his skin back.

He's so close to me on the pillow that his cinnamon-y breaths waft over my lips. "No, I'm pretty sure it was you."

I scratch him with my nails. "I —"

He inches closer. "I'm pretty sure you've always been this way."

"What way?"

"Slutty."

I moan and he pushes me on my back again, this time rolling over with me, his hand still tugging on my slip, moving it up and up, exposing my panties. And like the slut he just called me, I rock my hips and spread my legs, begging him to fill the space between them.

"You have, haven't you?" he rasps, dragging my slip up and baring my pregnant belly. "You've always been a whore."

My head goes back and forth on the pillow. "No."

"For me," he adds a qualifier.

I blush. "N-not true."

I think he smirks at my denial, but I've got my eyes closed and so I can't say for sure.

"All I ever have to do is look at you and you start leaking. Your pussy starts juicing up, running down your thighs. You get weak behind the knees, barely able to stand up. Because you know where your place is at."

"Where?"

"On your back and at my feet. With your mouth open, your legs spread and your ass arched. So I can take turns on all your holes."

All of this is already happening, I think.

My legs are already spread. I'm already arching my ass up and my mouth is parted as I drag in breaths upon breaths, but still not able to breathe.

"No," I deny, blinking my eyes open and closed. "You d-did this to me. It's because I'm p-pregnant."

He runs his nose along the column of my throat, humming. "Well, you can't blame me, can you? I mean if you walk around looking like such a good whore for me, reeking of pussy like a ripe fruit, of course I'll take you up on your offer. Of course I'll stick my dick in that sloppy cunt of yours and put a baby in you. Not one but two. Because you've got the sweetest and sluttiest pussy that I've ever fucked. And if it were possible, Firefly, I'd fuck another baby into you right fucking now."

I'm mauling the sheets at this point, whining and writhing so much that I'm actually rocking the bed. Or maybe all that's happening inside of me.

"Ledger, I —"

My words turn into a gasp because he chooses that very moment to stick his cock into me. And he does it hard. Because I know that he's been edging himself as well and now his patience is gone. And all he wants to do is fuck and rut inside of me. Which he does until I squirt all over him.

And then because he's really turned on right now, he fucks me again. But this time he rolls me to the side and gets behind me. He lifts my leg up over his arm, and cradling my belly with one hand while grasping my neck with the other, he thrusts inside me that way, hitting totally different angles with his bejeweled cock.

When I come for the second time, he changes position again. He gets me up on my knees and fucks me doggy style. I know it's his favorite position because like this my ass is exposed and so is my asshole. Where he sticks his thumb, because he likes me full of him in every way possible. His cock in my pussy, his thumb in my asshole and his babies in my belly.

I love it too.

Although I would love it more if he found a way to fill my mouth too.

Like always, I come at just the thought of it and this time he can't resist my core pulsing around his dick and comes with me. After that he cleans me up, runs me a bath and we sleep in each other's arms.

With him clutching my stomach and our babies.

And always I secretly send a wish up to the sky that they move.

For him.

That he finally feels them rolling around under my skin. Something that he so desperately wants.

Something that I so desperately want him to feel.

Before I go.

Because I have to, don't I?

Shut up in this cabin, with his arms around me at night, whispering about our babies, watching his love for them, it's very easy to pretend. To dream. To think that yes, I'll be one of three.

Three princesses.

That he will pamper for the rest of our lives.

That he will cherish and treasure.

But of course that's not true.

There is 'no rest of our lives,' only four weeks.

Until my wedding.

And every day that passes, I get more and more convinced that I don't want to get married. That I don't want to leave here, leave *him* and marry someone I don't love.

I don't want to marry *anyone* period.

However, it's not possible.

Especially when I have to go for my wedding dress fitting.

Something that hadn't occurred to me that I'd have to participate in. Especially when I told Ezra's assistant, Alice, that she could contact my mother for any and all wedding details.

As expected, my mother has been very happy about it. So much so that she never even bothers to check anything with me and makes all the decisions by herself. Which kinda bothers Alice because she thinks that I should have a say in my own wedding. And therefore she sends me regular updates about what's happening. Even after I told her that I don't really care and that my mother knows best.

And the fact that I have to be involved in even *this* makes me want to vomit.

Because I don't think I'll be able to handle seeing myself in the mirror, wearing a white dress when I don't even want to show up at the venue my mother had chosen.

Not to mention, I'm carrying twins.

Meaning my belly is growing at an alarming rate and it's going to very hard to hide that from my mother.

At a *fitting*.

Although I shouldn't have worried.

Because my mother defines self-absorbed and vain. While the whole bridal shop knows I'm pregnant — I told the salesgirl that it's a secret and my mother is very old-fashioned, which she very enthusiastically accepted — my mother thinks that I've merely grown fat. And I should really watch what I eat until I get married.

"You don't want to look all puffy in your wedding photos, do you?" she says after she insists that I have lunch with her.

I stab at the lettuce because again, she insisted that I have salad. "No, Mother."

She looks at me critically. "And I do think you're developing a double chin."

"Well, sorry," I say, clearly not sounding sorry at all.

Because I really don't care.

I don't.

The only person that I want liking my body does.

In fact he's crazy about it, about my swollen tits and my rounded belly, and he proves it *every single day*.

So I don't really care what my mother thinks.

Besides, my life's falling apart right now. I just tried on dresses for my wedding.

The wedding that I don't want to participate in.

I don't give a fuck if I'm growing fat.

She sighs sadly. "Exercise and diet, my lovely. You need to go on a strict regimen. If you want I can hook you up with my yoga instructor."

"The one I saw at the house?" I ask, recalling a sweaty muscular guy who was giving my mother looks.

"He's very good."

I smile that I'm sure comes out as a grimace. "I'll think about it."

Probably in another life, I add silently.

In this one, I want this stupid lunch to be over so I can resume my normal routine.

Which is to go see him.

Like nights, my mornings have a regular routine as well.

He leaves for practice early morning while I'm still in bed, where I lounge around for another hour or two. These days sleeping in always sounds like heaven. Then I wake up, eat breakfast because I'm always hungry and start prepping for lunch and then leave to go see him in the city.

Something that he didn't like very much initially. And not only because he still thinks his teammates can't stop looking at me but also because he thinks I'm super delicate and need to be treasured because I'm pregnant.

I simply rolled my eyes at him and kept on showing up.

I mean, I don't go to his games ever since they started him back on the team because he doesn't want me to — too crowded and dangerous — and there's no way he's budging on that so for this, he was the one to compromise. I do watch them on TV and call him though, after every game. And let me just say that I love watching him. Not only because he's been doing so well since his comeback — they won against Arrow Carlisle's team a few days back; oh and it was so fun to go to dinner with him and Salem — but because he's just so alive on that field, see.

So in his element.

Such a god.

That dominates not only the field but the entire stadium as everyone's eyes are on him.

But anyway, when the impromptu lunch with my mother is over, I grab a cab and race across town to go see him.

To hug him and smell him, and just be with him.

Because all this, trying on wedding dresses not only made me sad about my future but also felt like… cheating.

Like I was cheating on him by wearing dresses with the thought of another man.

Which is ridiculous.

Because we're not in a relationship.

We don't even *want* to be in a relationship.

But every time I saw myself in the mirror, a stabbing pain went through my chest. A crippling pain and I swear my belly grew tight. As if my babies knew and they disapproved. They were agitated in my womb because of what I was doing to their daddy.

So as soon as I see him, I launch myself at him.

I bury my nose in his chest and breathe in his musky, cinnamon-y scent. And since he's used to me being all mopey and emotional these days, he doesn't question me. He simply hugs me extra tight, rocks me back and forth like *I'm* a baby.

I look up after a bit. "I want you."

And again, he's used to that, me wanting him all the time. Because he was right the other night; I *am* a slut for him.

A complete whore.

Every time we touch, I get horny and restless.

But I'm not alone in my lust, am I?

Because every time I come over for lunch, he first drags me to a lonely place — sometimes the treatment room, the overnight rooms with bunk beds, one time it was in a corner of the locker room after everyone had gone off to the field and once it was in the gym — and makes me get on my knees and suck him off.

In fact, somedays his lust is so big that I barely get him in my mouth and lick the tip. I barely jiggle those bars against the roof of my mouth, and he's coming. He's throbbing and jerking on my tongue like he's been waiting for me ever since he left me sleeping in our bed, and watching me on his phone wasn't enough.

And other days, like today, we're in an empty office and I'm on my knees.

While he stares down at me.

At my tits that he scoops out of the neck of my dress and my pregnant belly that he makes me expose by lifting my dress and making me clutch in between my teeth as he fucks his fist in long and lazy strokes. That quickly become short and fast.

Until he blows on my stomach.

And then I'm rubbing it all over my skin.

Just the way he likes it.

"Fuck," he groans as he watches me do that. "You're a goddess, aren't you? A beautiful, cock-sucking, pregnant goddess."

I shake my head, rubbing my nipples that are hard and slippery with his cum. "No, I'm your beautiful, cock-sucking, pregnant Firefly."

His licks his lips as he watches and watches me greedily. "Yeah, and now you smell like me."

"Is that why you like it, when I rub you on my skin? Because it makes me smell like you."

He lifts his eyes, pitch black and swimming with emotions. "And because it'll warn the other guys off you."

Always my jealous and possessive Thorn.

Something about that thought soothes my own ruffled feathers.

It makes me feel calm after the morning I've had.

His agitation over someone else coming in and snatching me away.

It makes no sense but I always feel safe when he gets like this. But instead of focusing on all these angsty emotions, I focus on the fact that he helps me stand on my feet and turns me around, his hand going under my dress, groping my ass, looking for my panties that I know he'll shove to the side before he enters me.

"Although it hasn't worked so far, has it?" He manages to expose my pussy and positions his dick at my wet hole. "They still look at you. At your pregnant body. They don't care whose babies are in your belly. They just want you for themselves."

I go to say something but he pushes inside and all my words die.

All my thoughts become his and his only.

Like he's purging all the ugliness from inside me and making things beautiful again.

And since I don't have a lot of time, I try to do the same for him.

I try to make sure that before I go, I give him something beautiful back. Like his family. His brothers.

So a week later with Callie's help, I organize a picnic kind of thing.

At the cabin.

I know it's a big step, revealing to his brothers that Ledger has not only been keeping up the cabin but is now living here. At least for the time being. But it needs to be done. He can't hide this fact forever. Plus I will be there for him if anything goes south.

Ledger, of course, is not happy.

He's been grumbling about it ever since I told him my plan.

But it's testament to the fact — yet again — how much he pampers me that he doesn't refuse. He lets me take the lead. Which means I invite everyone: all his brothers, Reign, his friend, even Riot from his team with his little girl and all my St. Mary's friends: Callie, Wyn, Poe, Jupiter and Echo. I also invite *my* brother, or rather have Callie invite him,- but he doesn't show up. Callie says it's because he's busy at the garage but I know the real reason. He still hasn't forgiven me for everything.

It makes my heart ache but I'm not going to think about that right now when I have other things to focus on.

Such as how Ledger is faring with his brothers.

They already had some clue about the cabin; Callie told me it was best to ease them into the information so she had a family meeting at her house — without Ledger, which bugged me because he's just as much part of the Thorne family as the rest of them, but I understood — and told them about the cabin. And from what I hear, Shep was very mad and very vocal about it. Stellan was quiet and pensive. But Conrad was as vocal as Shep but in Ledger's favor. And then they all had a long discussion about how unfair they'd all been to Ledger, with Conrad leading the charge in the blame.

And God, I'm ashamed to say but I broke down crying even before Callie had reached the end of it. I can't even imagine what they all went through at the hands of their pathetic loser dad. And how my Ledger suffered for it even after their dad was gone, and he did it all alone.

Which makes me want to break down crying once again.

But I've got company and as I said, I need to focus.

Although my focus does waver with the arrival of this one unexpected guest.

Isadora Holmes.

Shepard's infamous girlfriend, and well, Stellan's not-so-secret secret crush.

"So this is her, huh," Callie murmurs from beside me.

We're standing at the picnic table that Ledger put together. It's laden with all the food Callie and I made. Since we're both fiends for cooking and baking, we didn't let anyone else bring anything. Plus I know how much

Ledger loves the things I make for him and so I wasn't going to give him something cooked by someone else. Not today of all days.

"And she's stunning," Poe says. "I love her dress."

She's wearing a bohemian style chic maxi dress with a loose crochet cardigan. Her dark, wavy hair's bound in a loose bun with a few tendrils framing her very exotic-looking face. Even if Shep hadn't mentioned that she's half South Asian — her mother was born and brought up in India — her almond-shaped eyes and her tanned complexion would've given her away.

And Poe is right; she is stunning, even more so than her dress.

"Well, she seems nice," murmurs Echo, who's standing on the other side of Callie.

When Callie glares at her though, Echo mouths *sorry*.

"Okay, fine," Callie gives in. "So she does look nice. Which is really sad because I want to hate her."

So far, she's been really polite, if a little reserved. Probably because she doesn't know anyone here except Shepard. Who, to his credit, is sticking close to her side.

"You could never hate her," Poe says from beside me.

"Why not?"

"Because I don't think you've hated anyone in your life," she says with a shrug.

"Oh, like you have?"

"Yeah. Alaric."

Alaric Marshall is Poe's ex-guardian and her current and forever boyfriend. The term, Poe says, he doesn't like very much. Makes him feel like a teenager instead of a distinguished history professor in his mid-thirties. Which is exactly why Poe likes to use the term.

And yes, once upon a time, she did hate Alaric.

With a passion no less.

Until fate forced his way into her life as St. Mary's interim principal, which is where their hate story changed into a love story. He's not here today — he's out of town for a guest lecture at a university in Chicago — but we can all safely say that he worships the ground Poe walks on and pampers his diva endlessly.

"Please," Callie rolls her eyes, "that was just sexual tension, waiting to explode."

"No it wasn't," Poe denies it. "Not in the beginning. In the beginning I really wanted to kill him."

"And aren't you glad that you didn't?" Wyn chirps in from where she's standing on the other side of Echo.

Poe smiles. "Yeah. Very, very glad."

"You know what, guys," Echo says. "I think we're staring at her and it's extremely rude."

She is right though.

We're all standing over here, single file, and staring at her like she's some kind of a zoo animal. And while it was okay before — we were all shocked at her sudden appearance; no one had seen her before this and Shep never said that he was bringing a date — it's not anymore.

Because we aren't the only ones staring at her.

Stellan is too.

But in his own subtle way. A glance here, a look there. And every time he does it, his entire frame tightens up. He gets agitated and angry and I'm sure she can tell because believe it or not, she's staring back at him. Although her looks aren't as subtle and every time she does it, we all hold our breaths, thinking that this is the moment Shep is going to catch on that his girlfriend is staring at his twin brother.

"I don't care," Callie says stubbornly. "She's driving a wedge between my brothers."

"Maybe there's a perfectly good explanation for it," Wyn placates.

"Yeah? What do you think makes a good explanation for coming here as Shep's date and then staring at his twin brother?"

We all shrug and shake our heads.

Even so, it's Wyn who puts her foot down and separates herself from our group. "You know what, I think that's enough. We should really make her feel welcome." Then, turning to Callie, "And that's your department, isn't it?"

Callie purses her lips.

At this, I finally say something. "You always made *me* feel welcome."

"Yeah, me too," Echo agrees.

"Yup, come on," Poe says, reaching out for Callie's arm and dragging her away.

Thereby dispersing this meeting.

While they all head toward Isadora, I head in a different direction, and approach our other friend, Jupiter. She's been standing on the other side of the table, carefully keeping away from our group. And I know why. Even if I hadn't seen her exchange strange looks with Echo — who she's closest to in the group — I still would've known.

I prop my hip against the table when I reach her. "Hey, you okay?"

"Uh-huh. These crab cakes are really good," she says, developing a sudden interest in the said food item while up until now, she's been watching Isadora like the rest of us.

And well, also Shepard.

"You don't have to lie to me," I tell her.

"No, they really are."

I give her a look. "I mean, I know."

"Know what?" she asks, still keeping her eye on the plate of crab cakes as she keeps piling them on hers.

"What it's like to fall for a Thorne brother."

That gives her pause and her eyes jerk up at me.

Emerald green and shiny, they're some of the most stunning eyes I've ever seen. And they look so sad even though she's trying to hide it.

She lowers her plate full of crab cakes. "I'm not —"

"I've seen how you look at him," I say in my kindest and friendliest tone. "Every time he's around you get this sad look in your eyes. Well, there's happiness first but then slowly it gets eclipsed by sadness."

For a few seconds it looks like she's going to argue, but then her shoulders sag and I whisper, "I'm sorry he has a girlfriend."

With her eyes downcast, she mutters, "It wouldn't matter even if he didn't."

"Why not?"

She looks up again but this time I know she isn't going to answer me or clarify what she meant. Instead, she swivels her gaze over to where all the girls are chatting up Isadora. Who's starting to look more at ease.

"I like her skin," she says abruptly. "Tanned and pretty."

I glance over at Shep for a second before saying, "I like your skin too."

She gives me a look. "No, you don't. No one likes the kind of skin that burns too easily."

"No," I admit, "but people are known to like strawberries and cream."

Which is exactly how Jupiter looks with her red hair and porcelain complexion.

Jupiter looks at me weirdly before shaking her head and going back to the crab cakes. So she doesn't see it. But I do: Shep eating cream-dipped strawberries while his girlfriend is busy with the girls, while *watching* Jupiter. And the way he's watching her, he's definitely thinking the same thing as me: there's something alluring about strawberries and cream.

Which makes me super happy.

I don't know what's happening between all these people, Shepard and Stellan and Isadora and now, Jupiter as well. But for the first time ever, I have hope for my friend and I couldn't be more thrilled.

I also have hope for my guy over there.

Who's standing beside Conrad at the edge of the lake and seeming to be having a pleasant conversation. Or rather, they're not arguing or looking angry at each other, which is a win in my book. And after a while, when all the boys decide to play a game of soccer, my happiness doubles because Shep and Ledger are on the same team and even though Stellan and Conrad end up on the opposite side, it still looks like all four Thorne brothers are playing together instead of against each other.

I'm smiling the rest of the day and crazily thinking that nothing could ever dim the joy that this has brought when I get a text.

From Ezra.

And he says that he's free to meet with me day after tomorrow.

Two DAYS LATER, I'm getting ready to meet Ezra for lunch and tell him everything. So that we can come up with a plan to handle it all with his father and mine and even in the public eye, if need be.

I can't believe that I'm saying this, but I'm glad Ledger isn't home.

He isn't even in town.

He's gone for an away game, and as much as I hate this first separation between us, I don't want him anywhere near me when I do tell Ezra and inevitably come back home, upset and crying. I know it's going to happen even if he receives the news of my pregnancy without me having to ease him into it.

It'll just be a final nail in the coffin, and then there's nothing stopping me from telling Ledger that our time's up.

That it's time for me to leave our little dreamland and for us to rejoin real life.

And go our separate ways.

Only connected by these little two beings I'm carrying.

I just hope that he trusts me enough to know that I'm *not* taking his babies away from him. That he'll still be a part of their life even though I'll be married to another man. Not to mention, I've decided – once I'm married and my brother and Callie are safe – that I'll tell Ledger everything. About my father's scheme; why I married Ezra; why I had to keep it a secret from him even though he had his suspicions about something being wrong in my life.

Everything.

And again I just hope that he understands that my hands were tied. And that I did it for family, for his and mine.

I'm almost out the door to meet with Ezra when my phone rings. It's Callie and distractedly, I pick up, "Hey, I'm just heading out the door. Can I —"

"Tempest."

Her voice, sounding so feeble and small, brings me to a halt. I pause in the process of shrugging on my spring coat that will hide my belly until I manage to tell Ezra and ask, "What's wrong? Is it Halo?"

"No," she says, sniffling. "I… It's Reed. His shop."

At this, dread settles in my chest and my own voice almost matches hers. "What?"

"There…" she begins, but trails off for a second. Then, "There were some people who came over this morning for an inspection. I-I mean, I didn't even know there was going to be one. Reed didn't know either and… And they're saying that he doesn't have the required paperwork."

"What required paperwork?"

"I don't know. I don't... All I know is that it's apparently a big deal and..."

"And what?"

She waits for a few seconds and even though I understand that she may be trying to gather her thoughts — my own seem pretty scattered right now — I still want her to hurry.

"Tempest," she begins, her voice still as shaky, "they're saying that they could close down the shop and there may be an inquiry on Reed. And that they might suspend his license," she gulps, "forever. I don't... I don't know how it happened. He loves that shop. That shop is his life and he's so particular about it. He's always stayed on top of things and his business was starting to pick up now and... I didn't know who to call and I'm... I'm freaking out."

I wish I could say something to her.

God, I don't know what to say to her.

She's right.

My brother loves that shop. It's been a big part of his life ever since he was a teenager and Callie is right. He's so particular about everything, even more so now that he owns it rather than simply working there. He's always on top of keeping up to date with his licenses, equipment, keeping the other guys who work there in line and...

Oh fuck.

Fuck, fuck, *fuck.*

Is it... him?

Is it our father?

But why would he do that? I've done everything he's asked of me and...

"Listen, Callie," I say, my voice sounding foreign to me. "I'm going to figure this out, okay? I'm going to ask around and see what's... happening. Just wait for my call, okay? Don't... Don't freak out."

I'm not sure if I did anything to soothe her fears, especially when I sound so scared myself. But I unfortunately don't have the time to worry about that right now.

As soon as I hang up, I call Dad and he picks up before the first ring is even complete, making me think that maybe he was expecting my call.

Which sends dread right up to my throat, strangling me.

"Someone's up early," he says chirpily.

I'm at the front door of the cabin so I lean against it for support as I growl into the phone, "What did you do?"

"This morning?"

I close my eyes for a second. "What the fuck did you do, Dad?"

Again his voice is casual as he answers, "Well, I woke up, had breakfast —"

"Dad, do not fuck with me right now," I cut him off, pressing my spine against the door. "Just tell me what you did to Reed."

"Oh that." He sighs. "Well, nothing yet and that's the truth. But I'm thinking about it."

"I don't…" I swallow, my throat going dry and scratchy. "Why the hell would you do anything to him? Why now? Why —"

"Because my feelings are hurt."

"What?"

"First, it's your brother," he goes on, making absolutely no sense to me. "And now it's you."

"What are you —"

"What have I done to deserve this treatment? Why do you both insist on keeping me out of your lives? Out of my grandchildren's lives."

My purse falls to the floor with a thump. "What?"

There's silence on the other end.

Dreadful and scary.

Not able to bear it, I'm about to speak when my father decides to make it even worse by going first. "You didn't think I'd find out, did you?"

"I —"

"You didn't think that you could hide this from me, did you, baby girl? You didn't *fucking think* that you'd screw me over and I wouldn't retaliate," he says, his voice getting louder with each word. "Did you?"

I shake my head frantically. "I didn't. I didn't screw you over. I was —"

"You think Ezra's going to marry you like this, huh? A fucking slut pregnant with a loser's baby. Do you think his father would approve of it? Do you think he's going to hand over that money to me now, after months of dragging his feet?"

"Dad, I —"

"Ledger Thorne, isn't it? That's his name."

I didn't think I could be any more terrified than I was but I was wrong.

Now my terror is eating at my bones.

It's eating at my muscles and skin, making me shaky, making me want to throw up, attacking my breaths, my words, my thoughts.

"You sure know how to pick 'em," he goes on. "A soccer player with anger issues. You do know his career's in the shitter right now, don't you? They're talking about ditching his loser ass. Not that I care who you choose to spread your legs for. Like mother, like daughter. But I do care when it fucks me over."

"I wasn't…" I begin, pushing words out. "I'm not fucking you over. It doesn't matter that I'm pregnant or whose babies I'm pregnant with. I —"

"Babies," he interrupts, his voice dangerous and creepy. "Didn't know that."

I clench my eyes shut then.

At my stupid, stupid mistake.

I never wanted my father to find out. Not until I told Ezra and we decided on a plan as to how to deal with the situation. And even then, if there was a way to keep the news hidden from his evil self, I would've done it. I would've done anything and everything to keep my babies away from my father.

From my mother too.

From everyone in my other life.

People who don't understand the meaning of family or love or anything remotely pure.

Never did I think, not even in my wildest imagination, that he'd find out this way. Not only that, but that he would retaliate when I least expected it. When I have done everything in my power to bow down to his wishes.

"It doesn't matter that I'm pregnant," I repeat. "The wedding's only three weeks away and I'm still going to marry Ezra. I'm still going to hold up my end of the deal. You just have to let me do things my way and —"

"You are."

"What?"

"You are going to marry Ezra, but not in three weeks. Day after tomorrow."

"D-day after…"

"Yeah, because now I'm doing things my way," he declares.

"What does that… What does that mean?"

"It means, baby girl," he says in a soft, threatening voice, "that I'm done playing around. I'm fucking done letting you fool me, do you understand? Now if you want your brother to be able to keep his useless shop and his useless fucking license, you'll do exactly what I tell you to do. You'll stop shacking up with that loser and you'll show up at the party tonight, in honor of your wedding. And you'll show up in a way that no one will have a clue about what a little tramp you are. Do you understand what I'm saying to you? *No one* will know. Not until you're good and married to that faggot piece of shit and that money's in my bank account. Because trust me, if anyone finds out and this wedding is called off for any *fucking* reason, I'm going to put your brother in a world of hurt. And I'll throw in your lover boy too. Two for the price of one. It wouldn't be hard; his career is already hanging in the balance. One phone call to New York City FC's owner who I'm friends with and he's gone. And it will be all your fault. Yours and those bastard babies in your belly."

Chapter Thirty-Six

Her Beautiful Thorn

SHE'S GONE.

My wife's gone.

I should've known. I should've fucking known something was wrong when she not only didn't call me after the game like she usually does, but also when she didn't pick up my call. And simply sent me a text saying that she was too tired to talk.

She's never too tired to talk.

In fact, these past couple of days since I've been away, I had to be the one to tell her to hang up and get some rest. So yeah, I should've known.

At first I think that she knows.

She knows what I did, how I lied to her, tricked her, and that's why she broke her promise and left without telling me.

And as I said, I wouldn't blame her.

But the papers that prove that she's mine, the marriage certificate, is safely tucked inside the safe in the bedroom where I left it. So it's not that.

What is it though?

Why the fuck would she leave?

Why the fuck would she break her promise to me?

Is it her dad?

It's her dad, isn't it? And it's that guy. The guy she insisted is just a family friend.

Shaking with fury, with fear, my vision both blurry and red, I call the only person I know who can tell me what the fuck is going on.

Reed picks up on the third ring and I bark, "Where the fuck is she?"

"What?"

"Where the fuck is my wife?"

Chapter Thirty-Seven

Her Beautiful Thorn

MY WIFE IS GETTING MARRIED.

And the guy's name is Ezra Vandekamp.

Apparently she's been engaged to him since last summer. Which means she was engaged the night I ran into her at The Horny Bard and then again, at that swanky fucking restaurant. That's why she was smiling at him in that way, in her special way.

She was engaged the night I kissed her in her brother's kitchen.

She was engaged the night I took her out to her favorite bookstore and then later when she asked me to fuck her so she could get closure. She was engaged when I took her to the cabin, the whole time we were trying and the time after that.

She was fucking engaged.

She.

Was.

Fucking.

Engaged.

And I know it's her dad.

I know it.

I knew it back then and I know it now.

But what I don't understand is why? How? What does he have on her?

Why the fuck hasn't she told me about it?

I climb out of my truck just as my phone rings. I wanna let it go to voicemail but the asshole did help me look for my wife so I hit accept. "What?"

"You there yet?" Reed asks.

I look at the posh wedding venue on the outskirts of Bardstown, the address of which Reed gave me only a couple of hours ago. After my frantic phone call, he contacted his 'old people' as he likes to call them, and that's how he found out about her wedding today.

His sister's and my wife's.

"Yeah," I say.

"Listen, this whole fucking plan reeks of my father, do you hear me?" he growls. "Pest would never do this. She'd never marry someone picked by him. I know my sister and —"

"My wife," I growl back. "She's my *wife*. And where the fuck were you when she was sick and miserable and throwing the fuck up all the while hurting because her asshole brother couldn't get his head out of his ass?"

I hear him breathe in and out for a few seconds, as if he's calming himself down.

Maybe I should do the same.

Dr. Mayberry would approve. She's been teaching me breathing exercises. Along with rationalization techniques to take my anger apart and study it from all angles. She calls it the classic 'think before reacting.'

But I can't think.

Not right now.

Not when she's in there somewhere, close to getting snatched away from me.

"I'm not talking about that with you," Reed seethes.

"Good, because I don't have the fucking time."

"But we *will* have words about the other thing. About how it is that my sister who up until now was just having your babies — as fucking tragic as that is — is suddenly your fucking wife?"

It's a good thing that he had to stay back because of some hiccup at his shop or I would've strangled him with my bare hands.

"No, we're going to let our fists do the talking and when I win, I'll let you decide whether you want me to let you live or die."

"You fuckface, I'm going —"

"And you know why that is, Jackson?" I cut him off. "Why I'm going to win. Because this isn't some dick-measuring competition for me. I'm fighting for my fucking wife and I'll destroy anyone and everyone who comes between me and her."

With that, I hang up and go to find her.

First, I'm going to take her away from here. I'm going to get her to safety.

And then... *Then* we will talk about all her lies.

We'll talk about how she's been lying to me for *months*. How she deliberately misled me about Ezra. How she said that he was only a family friend.

With every step that I take, I remind myself that I've been lying to her too.

That I've been betraying her ever since I had her sign those papers.

Not to mention, is that what he felt when he was angry, when he wanted to lash out at the world? I know Con said that I'm not, but does this make me like my father?

But nothing seems to penetrate.

Nothing seems to make even a lick of a difference.

My world is cracked and painted red.

And nothing will make it right until I find my wife and take her home with me.

Chapter Thirty-Eight

I LOVE HIM.

I'm in love with him.

With Ledger Thorne.

The world calls him angry but I call him beautiful. To the world, he's hotheaded and reckless. But to me, he's the most thoughtful and caring man I've ever known.

The safest. The strongest.

The most misunderstood.

The man who gave me these two babies in my belly just because it was my dream. It ended up becoming his dream too but still.

The knowledge slammed into me when I left him a little over forty-eight hours ago.

The reason why I wanted a piece of him for the rest of my life. Why I wasn't able to move on after what had happened between us. Why I don't want to marry Ezra, or anyone for that matter. Well, other than the fact that I'm being forced into it.

It's because I love him.

I never stopped loving him. And I don't regret that.

I absolutely do not feel ashamed or stupid or any kind of remorse.

The only remorse I have is that I didn't realize it sooner.

When I was there, with him.

As it is, I didn't leave a note or a message as to where I was going or that I was going anywhere at all. I simply packed my clothes, took my things and left.

I know I'd promised him that I wouldn't leave like that.

That I'd tell him first.

But I didn't have a choice. I had to do it. To not only keep my brother and his family safe, but him too. And he's always made me feel safe, hasn't he? So this is me making sure that everything he's dreamed of, everything that he's worked for stays safe as well.

And just to double check that I'm doing everything that I can to obey my father's commands, I look at myself in the mirror for the thousandth time. Thanks to my mother's vanity, we'd decided on a dress that can perfectly hide my eighteen-week belly. It's got ruffles for days and an umbrella sort of waistline that starts right beneath the bust, making sure that no one knows about the secret I'm hiding.

Last night too, at the party, I wore something similar and pretended to sip on champagne while our fathers, Ezra's and mine, had us make rounds around the room as the happy couple. Everyone was pleasantly surprised at the hastiness of our wedding, especially after the invitations had already been sent out. But under our fathers' direction, we played the part of the happy couple that couldn't wait to get hitched, and especially after how Ezra had been delayed in Korea these past few months, it made sense to advance the date.

But of course the real story is that thanks to my father, Ezra's father got his hands on certain photographs of Ezra in a compromising position with another man. According to my father, he'd received the information that these photos could be in the paper any day, which of course Ezra's father didn't want. So in honor of their friendship, my father proposed that the wedding take place as soon as possible, granted Mr. Vandekamp also announce the merger of two companies at the reception that very night.

My father is a snake, isn't he?

It's not the first time that I've felt bad for Ezra. Not only is he getting cheated out of his money, it's going to be a hell of a surprise for him when he sees me with a swollen belly on our first night together.

But if I have to choose between him and keeping my family safe, I'll always choose my family.

I'll always choose him.

God.

He must be going crazy right now. He must be losing his mind, his peace. And gosh, he was just getting it back, wasn't he? The picnic was a success. I could see that he made some real progress with his brothers. Meaning, going to practice every day with them wouldn't be such a chore for him anymore. And maybe, just maybe, he'd start taking more interest in his mandatory therapy.

But now with my leaving, I feel like he'd be back to square one.

His flight back was super early this morning and by now he must know that I'm gone and is he mad that I broke my promise to him? Is he worried? Does he think this has something to do with my dad? What…

I hear the click of the door opening and I fiddle with my skirts to make sure that my bump is still hidden.

But I shouldn't have bothered.

Because the person I see in the mirror, who's just entered the room, is someone who knows.

He was the first person to know actually.

That I was pregnant with his babies.

And he looks...

So good. So amazing, such a balm to my aching soul with his dark t-shirt and washed-out jeans, his hair messy and falling on his brows, his cheeks clean-shaven. Making me think that he must've shaved before boarding his plane because he knows how much I love seeing the beautiful arches and curvature of his face.

I swirl around just as he closes the door behind him, his eyes the darkest I've ever seen and pinned on me. And the first thing I do, after turning to face him, is take a step forward, knowing in my heart that he'll solve everything. That he'll take me away from here.

My heart finally starting to beat for the first time since I left the cabin and my mouth stretching into a smile.

But then I stop.

And *think*.

He's here.

Here.

And I'm getting married in less than an hour.

And I *need* to make sure that I get married in an hour.

For his sake and my brother's.

So I can't go to him. I can't throw myself in his arms and ask him to take me away. I need to get him out of here. I need him to leave.

"What... What are you doing here?"

His jaw tics and in response, he starts to walk toward me.

"H-how did you know where to find me?" I ask, starting to walk backward.

His response remains the same as before, advancing toward me.

Except now he's taking me in, from top to bottom.

In my wedding dress.

And he's doing it slowly. Very, *very* slowly. Purposefully and deliberately.

And I realize two things in this moment.

One: his perusal, even though slower than usual, is what he usually does when he comes home after a long day of practice. To make sure, for his peace of mind, that I'm okay. And that just breaks my heart even more.

And two: he looks exactly the way he did that night. The night he came to me with revenge on his mind, and that completely shatters my heart.

It's in the air. It's swollen and heavy. Charged up and electric with his anger.

Something that I missed but it's very apparent to me now.

And it's even more apparent that he's angry because he's hurt. I've hurt him with my actions. I've hurt him by breaking my promise to him.

I've hurt him.

And I wish I had the time to fix it.

But I don't.

Because it's even more imperative that I get him out of here.

Angry Ledger is not a good thing. Angry Ledger destroys things like he did that night. I need to somehow placate him enough that he leaves without causing damage to himself and my brother.

"Look, I know…" I raise my hands up in a calming gesture. "I know you're hurt. You're pissed. I know that. I can see that, feel that. I *know* you must have questions. I left you. And I didn't leave a note and I didn't…" I lick my lips. "I worried you. And that was exactly the thing that I said I wouldn't do. *Exactly* the thing that I'd *promised* I wouldn't do. I broke my promise to you. I know that. But I swear… I swear to God, Ledger, I'll answer every question you have, okay? I'll do whatever you want me to do. I'll take any punishment that you want to deliver. And I… I was going to anyway. I know you have no reason to believe me, but please trust me when I say that I was going to explain everything to you. I was going to tell you everything, confess everything once I was…"

I swallow, hating that I have to use the word in front of him. "Once I was married. I hadn't figured out a way yet. But I was going to. And I know you h-hate even talking about him but he's a good guy. I was going to talk to him and Ezra would've —"

My words come to a halt when my spine hits the cool window.

Not to mention when his ticking jaw stops and he grinds his teeth at the name 'Ezra.'

Swallowing again, I whisper because now he's close enough to hear me. Now, he's close enough that all I see is him and his carved-in-granite face and smell his cinnamon scent. "Please, Ledger. I know you're angry. I know that. But please don't do anything. Not right now. Just please hold off, okay? Just leave. For now. And I promise, I'll find you after the wedding and explain —"

This time I stop because he grips my arm. Tightly.

Painfully.

And before I can draw a breath, he spins me around and makes me face the window. The drapes are partially open and I can see the courtyard from here. I can see the altar. The chairs, the flowers, the little votive candles that my mother simply insisted we had to have enough though the wedding was pushed up by three weeks. The guests have started to take their seats. The band is set up in one corner. The minister is in his place, chatting with my father.

This is why my mother hated this room.

Because you could see everything and there should be some mystery before the wedding.

I feel him behind me, his body so close but not touching yet. And despite everything, I step back so I can touch him. So I can feel his hard muscles against my body. See how we fit together.

Because this is quite possibly the last time.

I'm getting married now and even though I can explain to him why, I don't think he'd want to have to do anything with me. I can never imagine him as someone's side piece.

I can never imagine him not being the center of someone's universe, and I wouldn't want that for him anyway.

Not to mention, he never said he wanted forever with me.

Even though I lied about that too.

I do want forever with him.

But I'm not going to get it. And it looks like I'm not going to get to back into him either because he stops me, flexing his grip on my arm and rasping, "Show me who he is."

The very first words he's spoken, and they give me shivers. "Ledger, please. Don't do this. Don't —"

"Tell me who he is."

"My mom could come in any minute now. Please, you have to —"

His other hand strikes and wraps around my throat, making me arch up as he says in my ear, "As much as I like hearing your voice, I don't want to. Not right now. I only want you to use that cock-sucking mouth of yours to tell me what I'm asking you. Nod if you understand."

I swallow, dread coursing through me.

Dread and arousal.

At how possessively he's holding me. My throat.

I nod.

"Good," he praises, his thumb pressing against my freckle. "That's good. Now, tell me who the fuck he is."

With choppy breaths, I whisper, "T-there. By the… By the altar."

He's standing with my dad now. Plus the minister *and* his dad as well.

He hums. "Now show me your father."

"On his… On his left side."

At this, he exhales a sharp breath but otherwise doesn't explain why he's asking me all this. So again I try, "Ledger, I —"

"Shh," he coos in my ear, making me whimper. "I didn't ask you to talk, did I?"

"B-but —"

His grip on my body tightens. "Don't piss me off, okay? Not when I'm hanging by a thread. If you do as I say I'll let you go."

I close my eyes for a second. "P-promise?"

His grip tightens even more. "Yeah."

"I —"

"But then again, I don't think we have a good track record for promises." My heart clenches as he goes on, "But you don't have a choice right now, do you? Not with so many people out there, waiting for you to walk down the aisle to marry another man. So you're going to have to do as I say anyway and it'll go a lot easier on you if play along."

My breaths are even more broken than they were before.

Not because I'm afraid.

I'm not. Not of him.

Even though he's angry. As I said to his brother, I know what he's capable of. I'm not blind to his flaws and I know he won't physically hurt me or our babies.

It's the pain lurking in his voice that makes it harder for me to breathe.

The pain I caused.

So isn't it on me to fix it? Or if not that, then alleviate it a little.

Which makes me nod and I feel his chest move with a breath. As if in relief.

But that only lasts a second because he speaks in a tight voice. "Now tell me who's standing behind you."

I open my mouth to answer him but I get delayed.

Because the next thing I know his hand on my arm is moving and it's going down. Down and down until he reaches the poofy skirt of my wedding dress and starts to drag it up. And again, I want to ask him what he's doing but this time he beats me and speaks again.

"Tell me who's pulling your wedding dress up, Tempest."

I feel him groping my ass, my thighs as I say, "L-Ledger."

He manages to get it all up as he says, "Good."

"Now I want you to tell him."

"I-I'm sorry?"

I'm not sure what it is, why I didn't understand what he's asking me, but I think it has to do with the fact that he's now going for my panties. He's groping the edges of them and pulling them down and I momentarily forget everything but his rough fingers and the fact that I'm so wet for him.

When he's pushed them down to the point where they simply fall to the ground and it's only a matter of me stepping out of them, he replies, "Tell your daddy who's pushed your panties down and who's spreading your legs right now."

"I don't —"

"Say it." He pulls my head back. "'Ledger's pushing my panties down, Daddy. He's making me spread my legs.'"

God.

God.

This is so wrong.

Isn't it?

394

Him asking me to do that.

And yet it feels so tempting.

"Say it," he bites out, shaking my head. "And keep your fucking eyes open, yeah? Look at him when you talk to him."

"L-Ledger's pushing my panties down, D-Daddy," I whisper, keeping my eyes where he wants me to. "He's making me spread my legs for him."

He presses a soft kiss on my forehead, so contradictory to how he's behaving right now. "Good girl."

But even so, I bask in his praise.

I get even wetter.

"Now tell him," he goes on as I feel him shuffling behind me. "Tell him what I'm doing."

I lick my lips as I hear him pulling his zipper down. "He's… He's opening his pants and I think…"

"You think what?"

I shudder when I feel his hot trunk of flesh coming to rest on my bare ass with a smack. "I-I think he's going to put it in me."

"Put what in," he asks, this time really smacking my ass with his cock.

Smack, smack, smack.

And I feel those studs, the already wet tip of his dick stinging my flesh.

"H-his dick," I whisper.

"Yeah? Is it big, baby?"

I nod, still keeping my eyes on my father, who's just burst out laughing. "Yes, Daddy."

"Does it hurt you when he puts it in?"

"Uh-huh. So much."

"But you like it, don't you?"

I nod. "I love it, Daddy. I love it so —"

My words become whines and mewls as he thrusts his dick in with a jolt. And my arms shoot out, my palms pressing against the window. My heart almost leaps out of my chest too.

Because I think they know.

All the people out there. Ezra. My father. The minister.

Everyone.

They know that someone has stuck his dick inside the bride. That someone is violating her right now as he makes her stand at the window, overlooking the altar she's about to walk to in under an hour. As he makes her talk to her daddy.

How can they not?

It's seismic, these filthy things he does to me. It's life-changing, his first thrust. It's a phenomenon as always.

That starts out with pain, a soreness, a stretch and turns into something so beautiful that I can barely keep my eyes open. That I can barely figure out what's happening around me.

But of course he knows that.

Of course he knows how mindless I become when he fucks me.

How thoughtless like a doll.

His doll that only exists for his pleasure and amusement. To do his bidding.

Because he delivers a sharp thrust as he squeezes my throat and spanks my ass. "Eyes open, Firefly. Keep your fucking eyes on your daddy as I fuck you in the dress he paid for."

My eyes pop open. "Ledger —"

"He paid for this, didn't he? Your fucking wedding dress."

I nod. "Yes."

"And this room."

"H-he did."

"What about the wedding? Did he pay for that too?"

I claw my fingers on the glass. "Yes. I-I think so."

"Good." He squeezes my throat again. "So I want you to look at him as you spread your legs for me. I want you to tell him every single thing that I'm doing to you, that I've *done* to you, like you should have before."

"I —"

Another smack on my ass, this time really making it hurt as he keeps moving inside of me. "Like you *should have* when he was forcing you to marry that piece of shit." I jerk. "He is, isn't he? This is what he's doing to you. Forcing you to marry someone you don't want, yeah?"

And much to my dismay, I nod my head. "Yes."

"So you should've told him, shouldn't you?"

"Ledger, I —"

"*Shouldn't you?*" he growls, his hands on my body growing vicious, as vicious as his thrusts.

And despite his commands, I have to clench my eyes shut for a second.

With guilt. With pain.

I have to breathe even though he's making it harder and harder when he won't stop squeezing my neck, mashing my pulse with his thumb. When he won't stop fucking me. When he won't stop drowning me in his scent, whispering things in my ear.

When he just won't stop.

"Yes," I reply.

"So you'll tell him now," he says, delivering another sharp thrust, making me jerk and arch up against him. "You'll tell him everything I'm doing to you as I'm doing it and maybe then, *then*, I'll let you tell me why the fuck you would do this, why the fuck you would break your promise to me and steal my peace."

With that, he goes for my neck.

He sinks his teeth into my skin and sucks on the freckle, my pulse that he loves so much. And my eyes sting even as I moan. A lump forms in my throat even as I push back against his thrusts, my pussy so wet that the juices are running down my thighs, soaking into my lily-white garter.

And I can't help but whisper, "He's… He's leaving his mark on me, Daddy."

Ledger grunts in my skin, satisfied and approving.

"And I think… I think he's doing it on purpose."

Another grunt. But this time he lets my skin go with a pop and asks, "Why's that?"

"So when I… When I walk down the aisle and stand in front of the minister a-and the m-man I'm going to marry, everyone can see who I belong to. Everyone can see what he did to me."

He grunts for the third time and takes a few moments to simply fuck me. Simply move inside of me with abandon.

And I let him, not only because I don't have a choice right now, but also because the more he makes me say these things, the less shocked I become.

Less shy and more free.

Because why shouldn't I?

It's the man I love and if I can't let him claim me proudly in front of the world, then I'll do it here. Standing at the window, watching the whole world as he fucks me from behind.

"You're loving this, aren't you?" Ledger whispers like the devil in my ears.

The devil who's my god. "Yes, Daddy. B-but I…"

"You what?"

"But I love it more when…" My breath hiccups when he hits me right on my G-spot, his piercings doing a number on me. "When he comes inside of me."

He breathes out a puff of air that sounds suspiciously like a low chuckle. "Yeah, you do. It's obvious, isn't it?"

His hand leaves my ass and slides up to my belly. The belly that you can't really see in the dress but you can feel it when you touch me.

And he does.

He splays his palm wide, cupping my bump, cupping his babies that are resting inside, and my pussy clenches over his rod at the blatant display of his possession and dominance.

At the blatant display of his ownership, not only of me but of them too.

"It's obvious what you let him do to you," he says, digging his fingers into my bump. "And look what happened."

"Uh-huh, I got p-pregnant."

"Yeah, you did," he rasps, his hips slapping against my ass. "And now you've got a swollen belly that you run around hiding from the world."

"I-I don't want to though."

"No?"

I shake my head, my vision blurry. "No."

He moves his hand from my belly up to my chest. "And what about these fat tits, huh?"

I moan when he squeezes one. "They won't…"

"They won't what?"

"They won't fit in my dress, Daddy."

Another puff of air as he plumps up my flesh. "Of course they don't. Because that's what happens when you spread your legs for a guy and let him come inside you, isn't it? You get bred. You get your belly full of his babies and your tits full of milk."

I move my head back and forth, barely able to keep my eyes open now. Barely able to watch my father laughing with Mr. Vandekamp, completely oblivious to what's happening to his daughter. Completely oblivious to how I'm breaking his rules and letting the daddy of my babies fuck me before I march down the aisle.

While he pinches my nipple and I whine again, jerking and jerking against him. Even so, I say, "Not yet, Daddy. My tits…"

"It's going to happen soon though, yeah?" he whispers and then groans as if he can't wait for it to happen, for my tits to get even fatter with milk. "It's going to happen, and trust me when I say that guy, that fucking asshole, who put his babies in you, he's not going to leave you alone. He's not going to fucking let you go. He's going to be on you, do you understand? As soon as you're done feeding his babies, it's going to be his turn to feed. And he'll latch onto you. To your tits and drink and drink and fucking drain your titties."

And I imagine that.

I can't help but imagine that.

His mouth on my milky tits, suckling and drinking from me. While our babies sleep after being fed.

It pushes me so over the edge that I can't help but claw on the glass and warn him, "Oh God, Ledger, I think I'm going to —"

"But you don't have to worry about that now, do you?" he rasps, his breathing heavy and his strokes getting faster and faster. "You've still got time. For now, the only thing you have to worry about is how your cunt is going to be full of his cum as you walk down the aisle. How you'll reek of him as you stand before that piece of shit fiancé of yours and he'll have no clue that someone already got there first. Someone already beat him to your pussy. Someone already filled your womb and your cunt and made you his whore."

And I don't know how I get the strength to do this but I turn my head to look into his eyes.

They look drugged and stoned and lustful and agitated all at the same time.

Letting go of the glass, I bring one hand up to his ticking jaw and say, "But it's okay. Because I *am* his whore. Only his and no one else's. Marrying someone w-won't change that. And do you know why, Daddy? Because you're not my daddy anymore. He is. And I'm his princess. One of three."

And then I just let myself go.

As I watch his face, his eyes losing their agitation, becoming completely eclipsed by lust, I let myself rest my head on his shoulder and succumb to the orgasm that's been threatening me for a while now.

I let myself come and come, drenching my wedding dress and my garter.

Probably drenching his clothes too.

I let myself shiver and writhe against him, moan and cry out at all these sensations inside of me. Sensations and emotions. Emotions that I better understand now than I ever did before.

They're love, aren't they?

All of these things that he makes me feel.

The good, the bad, the ugly.

Everything that I feel for him starts with an L and ends with an E.

Like always.

Since the beginning of time.

My wayward thoughts break when I feel him grow thicker inside of me, harder and bigger, alerting me that he's going to come. And he does, I feel hot lashes of his cum and tight throbs of his dick, but only for a little bit. Because in the middle of his orgasm, he whips his cock out and aims it at the tightest hole in my body that he's only breached with his finger yet. He gets the head inside, mixing my pleasure with pain until he's coming inside my asshole.

Until he's filling it with his cum.

And I understand why he's doing it.

It's the same reason why he leaves my throat and thrusts his fingers inside my mouth, going deep, deeper than ever before. It's because he wants to fill me everywhere. He wants to lay claim to every hole in my body.

Before I marry someone else.

And the thought is so sad that it's all I can do to not break down crying.

It's all I can do not to become a puddle on the floor, or worse, tell him to take me away.

But I can't do that.

I need to step out of this dreamland and walk into the real world. I only have a little bit of time before they come for me so when he's done, I spin around on shaky legs. I look up at him, ready to tell him to leave and that I'll explain everything later, when I notice his focus is on something else altogether.

Something over my shoulders and out the window.

Something that's caused his features to harden once again. But there's also a sense of something else lurking on his face. Something that looks very much like satisfaction and victory and triumph.

I've seen that look on his before.

Especially at his games or when he'd fight with my brother.

But I don't understand why he'd look like that now.

I'm about to ask him when I hear the worst sound in the world.

The sound of my door opening and footsteps, lots of them, thumping and pounding inside the room. I've still not looked away from Ledger though for some reason. Maybe because I'm frozen.

I'm terrified.

I'm fucking petrified right now.

He isn't though.

He's calm.

Still victorious. Like he wanted this to happen. Like he wanted people to barge into the room.

"You knew," I whisper. "You knew they'd see us. You wanted them to."

I see it on his face. That yes, he knew and yes, he wanted.

But before he can answer me, a hand appears on his shoulder, gripping his t-shirt and spinning him around. And I know who that hand belongs to. I know who that voice belongs to too.

"Who the fuck are you? What the fuck are you doing to my daughter?"

Instead of answering him though — my father — Ledger takes his time zipping up and buttoning his pants. "I think it's obvious what I'm doing to your daughter."

"You —"

"And I'm the guy whose babies she's carrying."

"What?"

"The real question though, *Daddy*, is who the fuck do you think you are? And why do you think it's okay to marry her off to some rich prick when she's already married to me?"

That's when I look at the room.

Until now I've been staring at his broad back, his straight but arrogant posture.

But now I notice that my room is filled with people: Ezra, his dad, my mother, the minister, a few other people I don't know and have never seen before.

They're all here.

They're all watching this. And they're all shell-shocked. They all look horrified.

And as disastrous as that is, them watching me get fucked, the fact that my wedding could be ruined now and thereby all my dad's threats may come true, I can't focus on that.

I can't even focus on the fact that in the next second I hear a thump.

A crunch.

Of fist connecting with bone.

And it's Ledger's fist connecting to my father's jaw and it doesn't stop there. These sounds, these thumps, no. They keep going and going with my father taking the brunt of it all. With people stepping forward, trying to stop Ledger, trying to separate him from my father, trying to dislodge him.

But to no avail.

He keeps beating and beating on my father.

At some point, he even beats on Ezra and I feel a compulsion to go stop him.

I feel a mild urge to put a stop to all of this.

But I don't.

I *can't*.

The only thing I can think about as I stand on the sidelines, watching Ledger beat the shit out of my dad and turning the room upside down, is that he said married.

He said we're already married.

As in, I'm married to him.

Married.

That's not true though, is it?

That's not…

It can't be true.

It can't.

I can't be his… wife.

I can't be…

Oh God.

I'm his *wife*.

Part V

Chapter Thirty-Nine

TEMPEST THORNE.

My name is Tempest Thorne.

Well not technically. Not yet. Not until I formally change my name, but still.

And I have a husband.

Something I didn't know about up until a few hours ago.

Until he — my husband — snuck into my room before my wedding and fucked me.

In broad daylight. In plain sight of the wedding guests and my future husband. And my father. Trying to get caught. Trying to stake his claim on me, and when we did get caught, he beat up my father.

And my future husband.

I hear they're going to be okay though. That's what they keep telling me. Something that I probably should've known since I was in the room at the time of the beating.

But I guess I was preoccupied.

And not by the fact that probably the whole world watched me get fucked and that was his intention. But by the fact that I was getting fucked by my husband.

My *husband*.

He later got arrested — someone had enough presence of mind to call 911 — and is now being kept in a holding cell. Because they both pressed charges, my father and my fiancé. Plus there were numerous witnesses who saw the whole thing.

In any case, I'm here at the police station.

Because I want to see him.

First, I want to ask him things. And then, I need to tell him some things too.

Believe it or not though, it's not an easy thing to do, to meet up with an alleged criminal. But thanks to all the connections my brother has and the reputation *his* brothers have, they're making an exception. So here I am, walking through the police station, escorted by a uniformed cop. He takes me to the back of the station, way past all the desks, and buzzes a door open that apparently leads to all the holding cells.

Well, there are only four.

And all of them are empty except the one at the end.

He directs me to it and leaves me with the instructions that I only have ten minutes and how to get out when I'm done.

But I only half hear it because I'm staring at him.

The guy who slowly comes up to his feet, his bloodshot eyes on me, his face bruised — probably not as much as my father's or Ezra's, but still — his hair and clothes a mess.

My husband.

Under the dim lighting, he appears almost haunted. Destroyed. Regretful even.

Of what, I don't know.

There are so many crimes he's committed recently that it's hard to pick which one he's remorseful for. For doing what he did today. Or for what he'd already done: making me his wife without me even having a clue.

As it is, I'm not interested in his remorse.

Or his concern.

Which is apparent when he runs his eyes up and down my body.

I'm wearing a black dress, and unlike my wedding dress and all the other clothes that I've been wearing for the past couple of weeks, it doesn't hide my bump. It accentuates it, displays it to the world. For which I'm thankful, if I'm being honest. All this sneaking around, hiding my babies from the world, was leaving a sour taste in my mouth.

It felt like I was ashamed of them when I'm not.

So at least one good thing came out of this — I don't have to hide my belly anymore.

"You shouldn't have come —"

"We're married," I say, cutting him off, sounding stern and emotionless for once.

And I'm proud of that.

It's always him who holds his cards close to his chest. But for once, I'd like to have the upper hand.

I think I deserve it after everything.

He flinches slightly.

But otherwise remains blank as he repeats, "You shouldn't be here right now. This isn't the place for you. This isn't —"

"Aren't we?"

His nostrils flare and his hands fist at his sides. "We are."

We are.

We're married.

He's my husband. And I'm his wife.

And not for the first time today, ever since I found out, I think…

I think we're a family.

A *family*.

Something that I always wanted. Something that *he* always wanted.

But not like this, right?

Not by lying and deceiving and tricking.

Breathing in deep, I ask, "Since when?"

His jaw tics for a second before he replies, "Since the day I asked you to sign the insurance papers."

I frown, thinking back to the day he came to me with the papers.

I do remember it was after dinner and he came to me looking all grumpy and impatient. I didn't mind though; I was happy and nothing could dim my happiness. I was on cloud nine, thinking that all my dreams had come true. Not only that, but the guy I chose to make my dreams with was so responsible, thinking about the future, taking care of things.

And well, he was.

Just not the way I thought.

I shake my head. "But they *were* insurance papers. I… I saw them and —"

"They were," he tells me, his eyes flicking back and forth between mine, probably trying to read me. "But there was something else in there too. In the stack that I gave you."

"But I can't believe that I didn't —"

"You were busy with your list."

Ah, okay.

My grocery list. Something that I forgot about.

"And you knew how I love making those lists," I say.

"Yes."

"So you picked that moment deliberately."

He doesn't respond but he doesn't have to. I get it.

"Like you picked that window today. *Deliberately*," I keep going.

Again, no response other than the tightening of his jaw. But again, I get it.

"Why?" I ask then.

He exhales a breath like he doesn't want to say. But he does. "I saw something on your phone."

"What?"

Again, it looks like he doesn't want to answer me but he speaks. "The day you told me you were pregnant, I… Your phone was on the nightstand. And while you were in the shower, I saw your text messages. With him."

By now we all know who *he* is. And how he — my husband; God, my *husband* — reacts whenever he comes up in any conversation, so I don't waste my time appeasing him or questioning him.

I simply ask, "And?"

At this, he exhales so sharply that his nostrils flare; his fists twitch at his sides. Actually his entire frame twitches. Then, "And what do you think? I got jealous."

"You got jealous."

"Yes."

"Even after I told you that you shouldn't. Even after I made you promise —"

His hands come up and grip the bars tightly. "Well, you can't blame me, can you? Apparently I *had* something to be jealous about. Because he wasn't just a family friend. He was your fucking fiancé."

Now *my* exhales are sharp and loud.

My heart is racing and *racing* in my chest.

And I can't believe it but despite my immense anger at him, I still feel bad that I twisted the truth. That I deliberately used the words in a way that would deceive him.

That I did anything at all to hurt him.

I wave those thoughts away though.

I'm not here to feel sorry for him.

"So you married me because you got jealous."

God, it sounds so childish. So immature.

So fucked up and twisted.

That you could marry someone just because you got jealous and angry and…

I take a deep breath before I explode.

Before I go up to him and start attacking him, beating on his chest, smacking his face. Scratching his skin, drawing blood.

All because even though I'm mad at him about how he lied to me and deceived me for all these weeks, I'm waiting.

I'm *still* waiting for him to deny it.

For him to tell me that no, he married me because he loved me.

Because he couldn't live without me and he didn't know what else to do.

He didn't know how else to make it happen other than breaking laws and forgoing morals.

Because I love him, don't I?

I'm his Lovelorn Firefly and I crave him with every breath that I take.

I crave him in all his toxic, fucked-up glory.

My Beautiful Thorn.

When I know that no answer is forthcoming — no answer is needed

You Beautiful Thing, You

anyway though because yes, he did trick me into marrying him because he was jealous, I ask, "Why, so I didn't run off to him and leave you?"

"No," he bursts out, vehemently, with all the conviction in the world. "Not because of that. That was never my intention."

"So what was your intention, Ledger?" I ask, sarcastically.

I watch his fists flex around the bars, his knuckles going white, the veins of his forearms standing up. I watch as he grinds his jaw and his eyes narrow as he replies, "To not fucking kill him."

"What?"

If I thought he was flexing his grip on the bars before, then I was wrong. He's flexing his grip now and he's doing it ten times harder. He's doing it with the purpose of forcing them apart. He's doing it with the purpose of busting through them and getting to me.

And I should end this discussion and leave.

I should end it forever and fucking leave.

But I'm a glutton for punishment.

I'm a glutton for him.

Because I stand rooted to my spot, my heart almost — *almost* — wishing that he could manage to do it. That he manages to break free and come to me.

"Every time I thought about him," he explains roughly, "it made me want to commit murder. It made me want to hunt him down and fuck him up. And I knew it had something to do with your father. I knew it. I knew him and your fucking father were somehow connected and… That was the only thing I could think of. That was the only thing that would calm me down, that would make me not lose my mind. The only thing that would keep you safe from them. Because if I married you, they'd have to go through me to get to you. To get to them."

No.

I'm not going to think about that. I'm not going to focus on that.

That he was trying to keep me and our babies safe even though he didn't know what he was keeping me safe from.

That it's so ingrained in him — his sense of protection — that he did the only thing he could think of. He gave it to me. Literally. He gave me his protection in the most traditional way possible.

"But I wasn't going to keep you," he continues, his gaze boring into mine, screaming the truth. "I wasn't going to force you into staying when I know I can't give you the things you want."

"What things?"

He cringes.

He actually cringes when he growls, "Love."

"Love."

"Yes."

"Why not?"

I don't know why I said that.

Why there's a need to rehash things when I already know the answer. When it's only going to hurt me — all over again — what he has to say.

"Because I don't fucking know how," he snaps, looking frustrated, looking like a beast with bruises all over his face, trapped in a cage that he doesn't know how to escape from. "I don't fucking know how to love, all right? I've never loved anyone before. I've never *wanted* to love anyone before. Love is not the first thing on my mind when I wake up in the morning or the last when I go to sleep. That place has always been reserved for soccer. For my ambitions, my career, my championship trophies, drills and plays and fucking practice. And even though my priorities have changed now, I still don't know how to change the fact that I know nothing about love. I don't know how to change myself. I don't…"

He trails off and I notice his eyes flickering down to my belly.

To where his babies are sleeping inside of me.

His mouth parts then. As if he's trying to drag breaths. And he renews his efforts to break free. He renews his efforts to pull those metal bars apart.

Lifting his eyes, he rasps, "I don't know how."

Which is when I move back.

I have to.

His eyes hit me like a punch.

Right in the center of my belly.

In my womb.

There's so much longing in them. So much longing and hunger. So much desperation and craving.

To learn. To change.

To know what love is.

And I want to tell him that he already knows. He already knows how to love. He loves his babies down to his bones, his soul, his very marrow. He loves his brothers, his sister, his family. His mom who died, who was abandoned by their father long before he actually left.

And I understand that it's different from romantic love.

The kind of love that I want from him, but I bet, if he let himself, he can do that too.

But I'm not going to.

Because it won't matter even if I do tell him.

This is something he needs to figure out on his own. This is a problem he needs to solve for himself. Just like his anger issues and his therapy and his relationship with his brothers.

I've done all I can.

Now it's time for me to go.

Which is what I came here to tell him.

That I'm leaving.

I promised him that I'd do that, and even though things got a little side-tracked, I'm here to say goodbye.

"You're right," I say then and he flinches. "You can't give me what I want. Because I don't think you can give *yourself* what you want. I don't think you've even figured out what you want yet. You haven't figured out why you react the way that you do. Why you do the things that you do, that people call you Angry Thorn for. And I was one of them. I mean, I didn't like the name but I still bought into that. I still thought that you were this angry and revengeful guy who could think of nothing else but winning. Nothing else but coming out on top, getting your trophy, your glory, success. And after what you did that night, the night you showed up at my dorm room, I don't think anyone can blame me. But like many, many people, like your own brothers, I was wrong.

"You're not angry. I mean you are. Of course you are, but you're so much more than that. You're alone. You're isolated. You're hurt. You're misunderstood. People judge you so quickly. Your own brothers judge you so quickly. They make rules for you, try to bind you in a cage. They try to control you. What they don't do is give you a chance. What they don't do is give you the benefit of the doubt. They don't listen to you; they don't see what you need, what you want. And maybe that's why you don't see it either.

"Maybe that's why you haven't figured out that you're not angry at your brothers, you're hurt by them, their actions. That the night you came to my dorm room, to exact revenge on my brother, it was an act of loyalty. Yes, you made a mistake by trying to take your anger out on me, but you were doing it for your sister. And today," I bark out a laugh, broken and harsh. "What you did today, staking your claim on me, deliberately sabotaging my wedding, my dignity, is because you were hurt. By me. Something that I never wanted to do, not to you. But I did anyway. I kept things from you. I deliberately used words to twist the truth. I ran away, broke my promise. So today was you reacting to that."

I shrug, my eyes welling up with tears, blurring him out. "But none of that matters now. I didn't come here to psychoanalyze you. I know how much you hate that. I came here to tell you that I'm leaving. And just for the record, I had every intention of always telling you before I left. But then things happened and…" I shake my head, a tear falling down my cheek. "I couldn't. But I'm here now. And I'm telling you that I'm leaving. And no, I'm not going to him. He isn't my fiancé anymore. They called off the wedding after what happened, which is understandable. And well, I told him what my father was planning, how he wanted to get his hands on their money, so yeah. That ship has sailed."

It has.

After Ledger was taken away by the cops and the crowd had dispersed, I went to Ezra. While they were tending to his injuries, I told him everything.

The whole truth — my dad's plan and how he was forcing me to help him; my pregnancy, who Ledger is — and of course, he was angry. He had every right to be. And as much as I hate what happened today, I'm glad that I came clean to him.

I'm pretty sure that my father knows by now.

That I blew his cover.

Even though he was rushed to the hospital immediately and I'm sure his retaliation is coming. And I don't know what I can do to stop him now. I don't know if my brother's shop can be saved. I don't know if *his* career can be saved either.

"And the reason I was going along with it all was because he was threatening my brother, his shop. And you. Your career. I was trying to give you your dream like you gave me mine. Oh, and just for the record, he's gay. Ezra. So what I told you, that nothing could happen between us, was a lie but also wasn't. As for the babies, I promised that I wouldn't take them away from you and I won't. But I don't want you at my doctor's appointments anymore. They're too… personal. Unless there's a problem with the babies, I don't want you anywhere near me. Once I give birth though, we can work out a schedule or something. But until then, there's no reason that we should see each other."

I shrug again and wipe my tears off.

Which is when I finally see him.

I finally see his face, his skin that's usually tanned and flushed with color is stark white and his bruises look even more dramatic. More painful and bloody. Or maybe it's just how strung tight his features are. How taut and carved from granite, pulled over his bones that makes him look as if he's in pain.

In actual, physical pain.

I sigh and brace my own body for my next words. "I trust you'll take care of the paperwork. Since you're so good at it. So I'll just expect my divorce papers in the mail soon and —"

My breath catches in my throat.

And I jerk, my hands coming up to cradle my belly.

Was that…

"What is it?" he asks, his voice urgent.

I would answer him but I feel it again. And this time I know what it is for sure.

A foot.

Kicking me. In the same place as before.

And then there's another kick, in a different part of my belly and I think it's from the other baby. Who like her sister, kicks me again at the same spot.

"Tempest," he goes again. "What the fuck is it? What the —"

I look up, a smile blooming on my face before I can even think. "I think it's… I think it's them. They're kicking. They're… Whoops." I chuckle, clutching my belly. "There's another one. And oh my God, it actually feels like a kick. I mean, they're only eighteen weeks and…"

His eyes are wide and pinned to my belly.

And he's breathing slowly, as if he doesn't want to spook them. As if he doesn't want them to stop kicking and go away. And before I know what I'm doing, I'm halfway to him so he can put his hand there too and feel them.

He's been waiting and waiting for it, right?

And look, he was right.

He knew they'd kick before the usual time and they did and he should definitely feel that.

But just as I'm about to reach within touching distance of him, the same cop who brought me here appears at my side.

"Time to wrap it up," he says and I remember where we are.

I remember that he's behind bars and I came here to say goodbye.

And didn't I just say that I don't want him anywhere near me?

So I should leave him. Right now.

But still I hesitate.

They're his babies. He loves them. Shouldn't he feel what I'm feeling? Just for a second and…

"You should leave," he says, his tone neutral, a muscle beating on his cheek.

But I can see a thousand emotions in his eyes. I can see him swallow, his chest shuddering with his choppy breaths.

And I know that he doesn't want me to.

But I do.

I leave because he's right.

I *should* leave.

Even though it's painful to feel this kind of joy without him. To feel them roll around and kick and not share that with the one person who can understand the depth of my joy.

It's for the best though.

As I turn around and leave, I want to call myself an idiot.

For loving him.

For never stopping loving him.

But I won't. Because even though I haven't yet learned how to not love him, I've at least learned enough not to abuse myself for it. I've at least learned enough to know that I'm brave.

Which means I'll survive this.

I'll survive without him.

I will.

Chapter Forty

Her Beautiful Thorn

"I DON'T WANT you in there," I tell Reed as soon as he stops his car in front of his big-ass mansion.

I've only been here once.

The night I caught her stalking me behind the bushes. And I'm not going to lie, I didn't like the look of it. I didn't like the differences between us. How she lived in a palace while the paint was peeling off the walls of my bedroom.

"Too bad," Reed says from beside me.

"You —"

"She's my sister," he snaps, his fingers tight on the steering wheel.

"She's my *wife*," I snap back, in the process of unbuckling my seat belt.

But then I stop.

Because she's not.

Or at least, not for long.

Two days ago, she asked me for a divorce. She told me that she was leaving and none of that was unexpected. I knew when she found out what I did, she'd leave. And she'd take my babies away.

By some miracle, she hasn't.

She won't.

And I don't know how to feel about that. I don't know if I deserve that mercy.

After everything.

"Are we doing this or not?" Reed snaps impatiently, breaking into my thoughts.

"Yeah, we are," I say just as impatient.

Because as I said, it's been two days and that shitstain – their father – is still breathing. From what I hear, the fucker only got a few broken ribs, a neck brace and a bent nose. So now it's time to finish the job.

It's time to put him into the ground.

I would've been here sooner. But he pressed charges, and since he has every judge and cop in his pocket in this town, it was difficult to make bail. No judge was willing to hear the case until Con found an old lawyer friend of his who brought the case in front of quite possibly the only judge who has a beef with Jackson. He heard the case, set the bail and here I am.

I have to say though that even after things have started to smooth out between us, I wasn't expecting Conrad to come to my rescue. Not with the bail and definitely not with the team. But he did. He talked to the board, took my back and explained to them why I did what I did.

While they aren't happy, they're still letting me stay on.

Given Conrad vouched for me.

I'm not sure how I'd ever repay him for this but I know that I won't let him down.

Anyway, the charges are still alive and kicking but that's going to change tonight.

A lot of things are going to change tonight.

We both climb out of Reed's white Mustang and stride over to the front door.

"I'm going to kill him," Reed says.

"Not if I kill him first."

He's fisting and un-fisting his fingers as if warming them up. "I should've killed him a long time ago."

"And since you didn't, I should've killed him two days ago when I found out what he was doing."

"Well, we're going to finish the job tonight."

With that, he pushes the front door open and enters his own house for the first time in probably over a year. Or even more. I'm not real familiar with their history except to know that Reed's always hated his father and the feeling is mutual. Anyway, he makes a beeline for what I assume is his father's office and bursts through that door as well.

And there he is.

The asshole who's been hurting her.

He sits in a throne-like chair, his neck encased in a brace and his face pockmarked with bruises. Even though as I said my beating didn't do the job of putting him six feet under, I'm still proud of the fact that I did him some damage. And I think it made an impression because at the sight of me, his eyes widen and he draws back in his chair.

Afraid.

Good.

He recovers quickly though and says, "What the fuck are you doing here? How the fuck is he out?"

"Turns out, you don't own every judge in town," Reed replies, coming to a stop by his desk.

"How did I not know about this?"

"Maybe you're not paying your lackeys enough anymore." He smirks. "I hear you're having money problems."

His father goes for his cell phone, his eyes narrowed. "I'm calling the fucking cops. And then we can talk about money problems. Because I see that in your future."

Reed reaches forward and takes the phone from his grip. Throwing it across the room, he says, "Let's talk about your future first. Because it's looking bleaker than mine."

His father grinds his jaw. "You think you can intimidate me, boy. I could crush you with my bare hands."

"Christ, you've been saying that since forever," Reed mutters.

"One phone call and everything's gone. Everything that you worked so hard to build. Everything that you did to get out from under my fucking boots and —"

"All right," I interrupt, already bored with his yapping. "You don't need to talk for this part. So why don't you shut up and listen?"

He turns toward me then.

His eyes are bloody and shooting fire, and I don't like the fact that his fear is gone.

No matter, I'm going to put it back in there, in his very soul, where it belongs.

"Who do you think you are, huh?" he spits out. "Who do you think you're talking to, you —"

"Told you, all you need to do is listen," I cut him off. "It's for your own good."

"My own good, huh."

"Yeah, and by that I mean, if you wanna live through tomorrow."

"You —"

"The bottom line is: I want you to leave her alone."

"Leave who alone?"

"My wife."

"Your *wife*."

"Because I don't like it when someone messes with her."

"Yeah, he gets real angry about that," Reed supplies.

"And I don't care if that someone is her scum of the earth father," I finish.

He watches me for a few beats. Then smirking, "And what makes you think I'll listen to you and leave her alone after she fucking destroyed everything?"

Ignoring his cocky statement, I go on, "And then I want you to make the bullshit inquiry into your son's shop go away." At this, he chuckles but I keep going. "And when you're done with all that, I want you to drop the charges against me too."

He loses his shit and laughs at that.

I give him time to get over his mirth.

It may be a while before he laughs again.

"Well that was hilarious," he says, still chuckling.

I cock my head to the side. "As I said, it's for your own good."

"Is that so?"

"Yeah, because I hear these Russians are ruthless." Then, addressing Reed, "Aren't they?"

Finally I see fear sneaking back into his eyes.

Just the way I wanted.

Reed shrugs. "That's what I hear too." Then, turning to his father, "And don't you owe them a bunch of money, Father? The money you don't have."

"The money you *never* had," I say.

"And you were never planning on giving them anyway," Reed adds.

"What?" the asshole barks.

"That's what they're going to think when I tell them that the daughter you were planning to marry off in exchange for selling your pathetic company is already married. She's been married for months now. Not only that, she's pregnant. With my babies."

"Which can only mean one thing, Dad, can't it?" Reed asks with something akin to glee in his voice.

"That you were lying to them all along," I fill in. "That you had no intention of ever giving them what you owe."

"And lying is a bad thing," Reed says. "It's a really bad thing when you do it to those Russians."

Reed's dad looks at us for a few moments, his eyes going back and forth between us, fear jacking up in his eyes, on his face. His mind whirling.

"You fuckers," he breathes out. "What, you think they're gonna believe you? I've dealt with them for years. They know me. They —"

"Which is exactly the point," Reed says, leaning forward. "They know you. They know what a piece of shit you are. They know that you'd do anything for the money, including being stupid enough to dupe them."

"Do you think marrying her off was the only trick I had up my sleeve?" he spits out. "That whore may have —"

Putting my hands on the desk, I lean forward and he flinches. "You don't listen, do you?"

"You —"

"And apparently, you don't have a very good memory either. So let me explain some things to you, yeah?" He opens his mouth again but I don't let him talk. "You're not the boss here. Not anymore. Not when you mess with her and definitely not when you keep messing with her. Because I've got half a mind to cut the middleman and finish what I started two days ago myself." I glance down to his neck brace. "You at least remember that, don't you? I could very easily break the rest of your ribs and leave you gasping for breath in your million-dollar mansion. So I'd be very careful what you say next. Because if I hear one thing against my wife coming out of your filthy fucking mouth, I'll also yank out your tongue and make you eat it."

He's vibrating with rage now.

And fear.

True and pure panic.

"And trust me, Dad," Reed tacks on, "it would be my pleasure to help him. In fact, I'd enjoy this more than making that phone call to the Russians. There's just something about doing the job yourself instead of having someone else take care of it."

His father is mashing his teeth now, hatred dripping from his eyes.

"You have a day to decide," I say to him. "And should you choose to make a decision we're unhappy with, you better start planning your funeral. Because I don't think anyone would care enough to do it for you."

With that I turn around and leave.

Reed follows, because I think he's as done with his father as I am.

We step into the night and I can finally breathe now. I can breathe because I did it. I at last did the job and protected her.

Something that I should've done two days ago.

Something that I went there to do in the first place. But as always, my anger, my selfishness took over and I ended up destroying everything.

"That was epic," Reed breathes out, probably feeling the same thing.

"Your father should eat glass."

"You won't hear any objection from me."

I glance at him. "You have good contacts."

He glances back at me. "I worked with my father for years. I know where he hides his dirt and who to get it from."

Which is how we came to know about the Russians and his gambling debts, and why he was using her in the first place.

"But it wouldn't have worked without you," he finishes on a shrug.

Maybe not.

Maybe at least one good thing came out of my fucking crime.

"Well, I'm still glad," I say.

He shrugs. "You're welcome."

"I didn't say thank you," I reply more out of habit than anything else.

"You wanted to," he shoots out, probably more out of habit than anything else too.

I turn to face him. "I don't think so."

He faces me as well. "Well, you're right. You'd need to learn manners for that. And I think you skipped school when they were teaching that."

"Yeah, I did. Right alongside you."

We stare at each other for a bit.

Then, I say, "She says we're similar."

"Who?"

"My wife."

I probably shouldn't be saying it but I guess I want to say it as much as I can before it stops being true.

Reed's eyes narrow as if he doesn't like it. "My wife says the same thing."

I know he doesn't.

Because I don't like it either. That my sister is his wife.

"We're not friends," I tell him.

"Fuck no."

"But if he ever comes back."

"We'll deal with it."

"Together."

He gives me a short nod. "Absolutely."

"For Firefly."

"For Fae." Then, "Although I don't know if I like the name you've got for my sister."

"I know I fucking hate the name you've got for mine."

"Let's agree to disagree then."

"Let's."

We stare at each other some more. Then, Reed speaks. "I can't believe you married my sister."

"Yeah, I can't believe I did that either," I say, my voice sounding wooden, my chest feeling tight.

"She's beyond pissed," he adds.

"I don't blame her."

"You really going to…" He grimaces. "Divorce her?"

The tightness intensifies but I manage to reply, "Yeah."

"That's fucked up though." He shakes his head. "You guys… You're having babies together."

"And from what I recall, you weren't too happy about that."

"Can you blame me? It's you."

I chuckle humorlessly. "No, I don't think I can."

"Listen, maybe… Fuck." He sighs. "Can't believe I'm saying this, but maybe I can talk to her, make her —"

"Just take care of her," I tell him.

I want to say so much more here.

I want to say *help her heal if you can. Help make it all go away for her.*

Wipe her tears. Make her smile. Make her forget me.

Make her forget that she ever met me.

Just fucking make her forget…

419

Because I can't do it.

I can't be the one to heal her when I'm the trauma in her life. I can't stitch her heart back together when I'm the thorn that has stabbed it and pierced it over and over again.

Because I'm no good for her, am I?

I mean I always knew that. But there's one thing that I hadn't realized before. Not until she told me two days go.

That I'm no good for myself either.

I don't think I've ever been.

I always thought I could handle my anger. That my anger was mine and hence under my control. I could rein it in if I wanted to. I could curb it, tame it.

But I don't think that's true.

And while my anger has fucked things up before – my career, my relationship with my brothers – this is the first time that it has fucked up with something that I was born to do. This is the first time it has fucked up something that I think is my God-given job.

This is the first time I've hurt my family.

My one true family.

It's something that I've been feeling more and more over the past few months but I've been afraid to even give it voice. The fact that she's my family.

She's the one who always stood by me. No matter what. Since day one. In fact, she stood by me even after I broke her heart and her trust. She stood up for me in front of my brothers. She stood up for me in front of *her* brother. She stood up for me because I'm her family too.

And instead of taking her away from her sham of a wedding when I had the chance, I saw her in that wedding dress and lost my shit. I gave in to my selfish urges and staked my claim the only way I knew how.

I got angry and jealous and selfish.

I hurt her. And those innocent babies in her belly.

I hurt them all.

Stepping back from Reed, I start to walk away.

"Where the fuck are you going?" he calls out.

"Feel like taking a walk."

People say taking walks can be cathartic. Taking walks can make you think.

And time has come that I really, truly think about who I am.

What kind of a man I am.

And if this is the kind of a man I want to be. Who hurts his family – like my father did. Who hurts the babies that aren't even born yet. Who hurts the girl he loves.

I love her, don't I?

I do.

Probably from the first moment that I saw her. Which is exactly how long I've been abusing her and hurting her. All because of who I am.

It's been the easiest and toughest realization of my life.

So yeah, I'm going to take a walk and figure some shit out.

I'm going to figure out how not to hurt people that I love. Because apparently, abandonment is not the only way you hurt the people around you. Sometimes staying is worse than leaving.

So I'm doing just that.

Chapter Forty-One

"OH MY GOD," I breathed out on our FaceTime call the night before everything blew up. "These are so *cute*."

His face appeared unsure as he looked down at the cutest onesies ever. "Yeah?"

"Duh."

He looked up. "I still think they're a little too big."

Is he insane, that's what I thought.

What was he talking about?

Because I couldn't stop smiling at those little things. I couldn't stop my heart, my belly, from clenching and clenching with love.

Of course, back then I hadn't known that it was love for him.

I just thought I loved the fact that he bought those things for our babies. That while he was at an away game, that was what had been on his mind. Our babies. And so he bought them their very first gift.

Propped up on pillows, I was lounging on the bed. "Ledger, for the third time, this is the right size, okay? Babies grow up really quickly. So shut up about it already and take off your t-shirt."

The light frown between his eyebrows cleared up and he shot me a look from across the screen. "Take off my t-shirt."

"Yes." I nodded. "And put those on your chest. I want to see."

"See what?"

"How they look." I bit my lip, pressing my thighs together, imagining what our babies would look like resting on his corded chest.

He stared at me for a beat, his lips twitching before he went for his t-shirt and took it off in one go, causing his hair to fall on his forehead in a messy tangle and thereby making me squirm on the bed.

But that was nothing compared to what I felt when he put those two little onesies — pink and blue, with 'Dada's bestie' written in glitter — on his bare chest. I think I almost exploded with hormones at the sight of those colorful little baby clothes.

"Oh God, I think…" I whispered reverently.

"You think what?"

"I think I came a little," I told him.

His lips twitched even more. "A little."

I shook my head. "A lot. More than a lot, I don't know. I just know that you look like such a daddy right now."

"A daddy, huh."

"Uh-huh."

"Theirs or yours?"

I looked up at him. "Theirs."

He lips pull up in a smirk, his gaze arrogant and cocky. "But that's not what you wanted to say though, was it?"

Biting my lip, I shook my head. "No."

"So then what was it that you wanted to say?"

Blushing furiously, I bit my lip harder. "Mine."

His eyes flared and I thought that probably this was the first time I'd said the word 'mine' in his context. And it was kind of a turn on for him. For someone as possessive as him, I never thought that that would be the case.

But I liked it.

I liked it so very much.

"So does that mean you're going to be a good girl and do what Daddy says?"

I began with a nod but then changed my mind and shook my head. "Maybe."

"Maybe."

"Depending on what happens if I don't do something Daddy says."

"If you're looking for a punishment, Firefly, I don't have to be your daddy to give it to you."

"Then what do you have to be?" I asked breathlessly.

"Your Thorn."

I clenched my thighs together again. "My Beautiful Thorn."

And then the same thing that always happens to me, happened to him. His eyes turned liquid with so many emotions while his breathing turned noisy with arousal. Making me realize that maybe I do the same things to him that he does to me: make him experience a spectrum of emotions all at the same time.

"So why don't you be my good little Firefly and take that useless nightie off," he said with a lick of his lips, "and show me those tits that I know are dying to get fucked by me."

And of course I did.

We also indulged in a little phone sex — well, a lot of it, given that I came twice — and then I went to sleep, thinking that I'd be doing it all over again tomorrow night and the night after. And when he came back, I was going to put those baby clothes on his chest again just to memorize how he looked before doing all the things to him that we'd just done, in person.

But that never ended up happening.

What happened was something else altogether.

Something unexpected and surreal.

I mean, not the part where I had to leave him — I always knew that was going to happen — but everything else. Him showing up so unexpectedly and breaking up my wedding. Him beating up my father and Ezra. Him ending up in jail and somehow still saving me *and* my brother from our father.

Yes, I know about that.

I know how he came to my rescue the minute he was bailed out.

Some days I'm extremely thankful for it. Other days I think there's nothing to be thankful for. He was the one who ruined everything in the first place. If he hadn't gotten the urge to show me off as his freaking property, I would've saved the day myself.

But then I'd also be trapped in a sham of a marriage and would now be living under my father's thumb.

So really I don't know.

I don't know if I want to strangle him or wrap myself around him so we're never apart.

But of course I can't do any of those things because it's been nine weeks since that godforsaken day and our lives are different now.

My life is different now.

Yes, I live in the same apartment in Bardstown and I have the same circle of friends who visit me as much as they can, and I do the same. Thankfully, things are okay with my brother now. He came around and apologized profusely and of course I forgave him. He's my brother; he was only looking out for me. Which means I get to see Callie and Halo like I used to before.

Anyway, I still read romance novels and bake as much as I can. I go shopping when I can, pamper myself with spa days and whatnot.

But I also do different things now, like I go for a lot of walks these days. At first it was because it was recommended to me by the doctor: light exercising, getting fresh air to keep my blood flowing, et cetera. But now I think I like it. It gets me out of my apartment and forces me to empty my mind and simply be.

And even though I read romance novels like I used to, these days I read them to my babies. Or more like I talk to them while reading, teach them about things such as knowing your worth, being brave and courageous enough to be vulnerable and have feelings. Most importantly I teach them to fall in love with the right person, or if they don't, then have the strength to leave and put themselves first.

But the biggest change in my life has been when I started working at my bookstore: Burning the Midnight Candle. I'm one of the sales reps, an expert in the romance genre. I never really thought about getting a job before. I guess for all my efforts to be different than the rest of the crowd surrounding me, they did rub off on me some. No girl around me has ever worked; they've never needed to. We all have trust funds and rich fathers or husbands. And even though I always hated my father and never wanted anything from him, I didn't have the same problem with touching my grandfather's money.

But now that I'm going to have my babies soon, it finally occurred to me that I need to lead by example. If I want them to be responsible and independent and a force to be reckoned with in this day and age, then I need to show them how it's done. Granted, getting a sales job at a local bookstore isn't exactly the top of the career ladder, but we all start somewhere, don't we?

And I like it.

I like talking to people about books, sharing my favorite books, giving someone the gift of a favorite writer or a story. I'm also finding that apart from romance, I also love children's books. Probably because I love interacting with children and manning the children's section gives me an opportunity to do that.

But yeah, life's different and I think I like it.

Well, *mostly* like it.

Or again, somedays I do and somedays I don't.

Today's been kind of a bad day and I knew it would be. Because it's game day, and another one of the things that I've started doing differently — or rather, haven't stopped doing after picking up the habit of it while living with him; similar to resuming reading my romance novels — is watching his games. I think it's important and I should get used to it for our babies' sake.

They should know who their daddy is.

What he does. What he loves and how good he is at that.

And he is good.

He is.

His comeback has been good for the team. They're on a winning streak and it looks like they'll take the championship trophy this year. Something that hasn't happened in a long, long time. And it's all thanks to Ledger. In fact, the press is saying that Ledger has proven to be the shiniest star from the Thorne clan this season and it could arguably be said that it's not the Thorne brothers' magic but his and his alone that's making a difference.

And I'm so proud of him.

So fucking proud of him that I'm literally bursting with it.

Our babies are proud too because every game night, they move like crazy. They roll and kick and punch, sometimes hiccup too, making a ruckus. And I always have to soothe them by rubbing my swollen belly while telling them how amazing their daddy is. How he loves them both and I know that he's away right now — mommy told him to be — but once they're out of me, he'll come visit.

Which inevitably makes me cry and sob.

Tonight though, something else is happening in addition to my waterworks.

Something that can only be described as pain.

Stabbing and bordering on excruciating.

Actually it's been happening all day now, attacking my pelvic region and spanning back to my spine; attacking my pubic region too and radiating out to my thighs. Plus my belly, on and off, has felt like a heavy bag of cement. My doctor did warn me about Braxton Hicks contractions and since I'm carrying twins, they may be more painful and have an early onset. But Jesus Christ, she never said that they would be *this* painful.

I'm about to call her and check in when a pain so bright and flashing grips my middle that I have to lie on my side and curl into a ball.

When it looks like it won't pass at all like the other stabbing pains I've had all day, I somehow reach for my phone and call my brother. I don't know what I say to him but I think he understood me because he barks, "I'm coming, all right? Just hang on."

And then I black out.

———

I WAKE UP GROGGY.

Way groggier than I usually am.

And at first, I have no clue where I am and why every part of my body is sore. But then I hear a mechanical beeping sound, the sounds of rubber soles squeaking on the floor, the quiet whooshing of doors opening and clos- ing, and I realize I'm in the hospital, lying on a bed.

But more than that, I think I'm not alone.

In my room, I mean.

I think there's someone here.

And that someone is holding my hand.

I already know who it is before even looking at him.

I already know him by his touch. The way he's gripping my hand so hard, his large, dusky fingers wrapped around my small, pale ones. Even in his sleep.

I take a second to look at him, at his messy hair, both his arms thrown on the bed, his head resting on them, his face mostly hidden. The only things that I can see are his brows and his closed eyes and a little bit of his stubborn nose.

Something about that makes me smile.

But then I realize I shouldn't be smiling or rejoicing in his presence.

Which I have to admit that I am.

I told him to stay away and this is not away.

I try to extricate my hand from his grip and separate myself from him. But even in his sleep, he doesn't let me go. His grip tightens and I see the smooth brows bunching. And then a second later, his eyes snap open and clash with mine.

He jerks upright then and despite myself, I can't help but adore the sleep lines on the side of his face.

Like before me jerking him awake, he'd been sleeping so hard.

He'd been sleeping so comfortably, which is ridiculous because he was half sprawled on the side of the bed while sitting in the most uncomfortable seat I've ever seen.

"You're awake," he says in his sleep-roughened voice.

The voice that I'd come to treasure when we lived in our dreamland.

It sends a shard of pain through my chest. It's different from the pain in my middle but I think it's no less excruciating. I glance down at our joined hands and again try to get free.

He looks at our hands too, notices my struggle to break free from him and a second or two later, lets me go. Then, "How are you feeling?"

Staring at his stubbled jaw that's clenched right now, I ask a question of my own "You... What are you doing here?"

He straightens up even more, his eyes strangely alert for a guy who's just been jerked awake, and takes me in. In his usual way. "Yeah. I... They called me."

I try to ignore how good it feels to be looked at like that.

How familiar and comforting.

And safe.

I definitely try to ignore it when his eyes linger on my very visible mound and his fingers become fists. As if he wants to touch my belly and he wants to touch it really, really badly. Reminding me of that day in jail when our babies moved for the first time and he couldn't feel it.

"Who?" I ask, trying to distract him from the sight of my swollen stomach.

He jerks his eyes up to mine. "Your brother."

Right.

Apparently my brother and him are BFFs now. Another one of the unexpected consequences of that horrid day. They talk on the phone. Reed gives him full reports on my health and tells him about my doctor's appointments. Moreover, my brother also sends him ultrasound pictures and keeps him informed on our babies' weights and things.

I had a discussion with him about this and he told me in no uncertain terms that as a father, Ledger had every right to know about the well-being of his children. That whatever happened, happened between the two of us and our babies shouldn't suffer. Not that I was going to make them suffer, but I see his point.

Besides, as long as Ledger isn't there in person, I'm okay with him knowing about my appointments.

"I thought…" I say, frowning. "You had a game tonight and —"

"Home game. I came right after."

I swallow, my throat feeling dry. "What… What happened?" My hand goes to my stomach, pressing on my mound. "Are they —"

"They're fine," he tells me. "You're fine too."

"But I —"

"It was Braxton Hicks." He swallows. "Apparently one of the more severe cases. But everything looks normal. You just need to take it easy for a few days."

"Oh," I breathe out in relief, my hand still pressing on my bump.

"How do you feel?" He's still looking me up and down, concern evident in his gaze. "Do you need anything?"

I swallow again. "I think… I think I need to pee."

At that, he stands up so abruptly that it startles me a bit. But then I understand why.

When he bends down and helps me sit up. He even goes so far as to bring my legs down to the floor like I'm some kind of an invalid.

I don't mind it as much as I probably should. I'm pretty sure my brother told him about my reduced mobility as well and I'm secretly thankful for it. Because getting up from the bed, especially after lying down for so long, has become a chore.

I'm about twenty-seven weeks now and hugely pregnant.

And when I say hugely, I mean it.

I'm like a whale.

My back aches more often than not. I've got swollen feet. Rolling over in bed feels like I'm climbing a mountain and I have to pee practically all day long. Carrying twins is no joke and in my moments of irrationality, I've blamed him for that as well. If only his stupid dick wasn't so powerful, I probably would be cruising through my second trimester like the rest of the women out there.

But no, he had to have super fertile sperm that gave me twins in the first shot.

Anyway, he walks me to the bathroom, where I do my business and throw some water on my face. When I'm done and open the door, he's right there waiting for me.

But instead of going with him, I simply stand there.

And look up at him.

428

It's been almost nine weeks since I last saw him in person. I've of course seen him on TV though, focused and dominating the soccer field. I've seen his interviews where he keeps things short and to the point, always looking like he's in a hurry to leave and extremely focused on his game and nothing else.

Of course I've been happy for him.

Soccer has always been his dream and I'm glad that he's getting all the glory that he deserves.

But I'm not going to deny that I've also felt a little sad and hurt and — well okay, downright miserable — that he moved on so quickly. That I told him to stay away and he did and now he's thriving.

It shows on his face too.

Apart from the stubble on his jaw and his crazy, sleepy hair, he looks good. He looks healthy and well-rested even after the game tonight. And I look like someone close to me has either died or taken really sick and I spend my days crying over them because my dark circles are more like dark depths of despair; my hair hasn't been styled in weeks and my skin has more pores and oil than ever before.

And I just...

I'm so mad at him all of a sudden.

So fucking mad.

For looking so fucking beautiful; for moving on; for being here when I told him that I didn't want to see him. For actually listening to me — for once — and staying away for weeks on end. When all he's ever done is bull-doze his way into my life over and over again.

Like, what the fuck?

So I clench my teeth and look away from him because I can't stand his put-together beauty when all I've done in the last nine weeks is cry and agonize over him, and start to waddle away myself. And he picks this moment to disobey my wishes and lends me a hand anyway. He puts a hand on the small of my back and grabs my elbow and walks me back.

I hate him for this.

I do.

But I keep my silence because well, I did need a hand, plus if I'm going to argue with him, I'd much rather be sitting than standing.

Once I'm situated on the bed and he's propped the pillows up enough, I tell him, "Thanks for coming. But you don't need to stay."

He gives me an inscrutable look. "Are you hungry?"

"Where's my brother and Callie?"

He stares at me for a beat. "They went home. Couldn't find a babysitter this late so they had to leave."

I nod in understanding. "Well, you should leave too. There's no need for you to stick around now that I'm awake. I'm sure a nurse will be coming around soon and —"

As if I summoned her with my words, a nurse does come in to check my vitals. She says the same thing that Ledger told me. That I had a severe case of Braxton Hicks but everything looks normal now. I should take it easy from now on though. No stress, no anxiety. Try to rest as much as I can, and my doctor will come by to check on me in the morning.

I'm nodding my head at everything but Ledger, as always, has questions.

Like he used to when we'd go to my appointments together.

And his question has to do with what I can or can't eat right now. When the nurse gives me the all clear to eat whatever I want to but focus on protein and fiber, she leaves.

"You don't —"

"I'm going to bring you food," he cuts me off with a determined expression, "and I'll be in the visitor's lounge."

He looks like he's about to leave and I say, "No, you won't."

"I don't want to argue with you —"

"Then don't. Just do as I say." Then, because I just can't help myself, I add, "It's not as if it would be the first time."

"What?"

"Nothing." I draw the sheets up my body, trying to look all relaxed and casual. "As I said, there's no reason for you to stay. Everything is fine now and…"

"And what?"

I tell myself that I shouldn't say it.

I absolutely should not say anything at all.

But since I don't know how to keep it inside, my anger and my words, I do say it. "And the visitor's lounge is for family only. In fact, overnight stays are for family only."

His jaw tics.

Standing at the foot of the bed, his hands fisted, his posture ramrod straight, he looks so large and intimidating. Like he could browbeat anyone to get his way. And I know he can.

Well, except when it really counts, right?

"And you're not my family," I tell him, raising my chin.

His jaw clenches harder and I think I see him flinch.

And if it's true, then great.

I want my words to hurt him. I want him hurt and in pain.

Just as much as I've been in.

"Noted," he says, his lips pursed.

"Good. So then you should —"

"But you're mine."

I fist the sheets so tightly that I know I'm cutting off my own blood circulation. "I'm not yours. Never was and never will be and —"

"My family."

And that just makes me fly off the handle.

Because what a fucking asshole, huh. I remember the last time he said it. In the woods, and since then there hasn't been a peep about this. And this is the moment he chooses to say that. *This.* When I'm so mad at him. When I want to smack his face.

When before this, despite myself, I waited and waited and *waited.*

For him to say that to me again.

"I'm not," I tell him sternly.

"You —"

"I signed the divorce papers."

At this, I know he definitely flinches. I know his body definitely staggers back a bit.

Although I have to say that it doesn't feel as good as I thought it would. When I finally told him about the papers. When I finally threw those words in his face.

Yes, I was the one who asked for it and yes, he gave me what I wanted.

But again, *when* has he ever done that?

When.

Exhibit A: he won't leave like I'm asking him to.

But he couldn't wait to send me the divorce papers. Just like he *couldn't wait* to leave me and go back to his precious soccer.

"Just because I haven't gotten around to sending the paperwork back to you doesn't mean that it isn't done," I tell him. "So there. I'm not your family anymore. *If* I ever was to begin with, so —"

"You think a piece of paper makes a difference whether you're my family or not?"

"It certainly did, didn't it? Before. When you had me sign those marriage papers," I taunt.

His jaw tics and tics, causing the lines of his face to stand out in stark relief, causing his skin to get all flushed and ruddy. As if his blood is pounding inside his veins, rushing and hurtling and causing mayhem.

Then, "You should rest."

With that, he looks ready to leave again and I've had it with him.

With his conveniently choosing to do what he wants and what I tell him to do.

"Good, great," I say, clutching the sheet in my fists. "Leave! That's what you love to do, don't you?"

"What?"

"What, *what?*"

His nostrils flare. "If you have something to say to me, why don't you just fucking say it?"

"Oh, you want me to say it, okay then." I throw him a mock smile. "Let's see: The very first thing you did after you made bail was to save me from my dad like some kind of hero. When you were the one, *you*, who ruined everything in the first place. So if you think I'm going to say thank you —"

"Didn't do it for the thank you," he rumbles.

I take a deep breath. "And then the second thing you did was file for divorce and had them mail me the papers —"

"You asked for a divorce," he interrupts me again. "And asked me to have them mailed."

"Right, and you do everything I ever ask you to do, don't you?"

"I —"

This time I interrupt him and say, "And did I also ask you to leave town?"

His jaw is going back and forth but he otherwise remains silent.

"Did I?" I ask again. "Because you certainly couldn't get away fast enough, could you? As if you couldn't wait to get out of here. As if nothing was tying you to this town. As if you were leaving *nothing* behind. Nothing at all and —"

"I left," he says, his voice lashing, "because leaving everything behind was my only option."

I watch him then, study his face.

Or rather, his put-together face that doesn't look so put-together anymore.

His skin doesn't glow with health and his eyes don't look so alert anymore. In fact it looks as if he's shed his façade. Suddenly his polished persona is gone and he appears haunted and broken. Gaunt even, with sharp cheekbones and an even sharper jaw.

"What does that," I whisper then, "mean?"

He takes me in with those once-alert eyes that look tired now.

Tired and shiny.

He takes me in from the top of my head to the bottom of my sheet-covered feet.

Lingering on my bump again.

This time I don't distract him though. I let him look.

I let him gather strength from it because that's what it looks like he's doing.

Then, in a raspy, vulnerable voice, he says, "All my life I thought the worst thing a person can do is leave someone behind. Like my father did. Like my mother did after him. I know it wasn't in her hands or in her control but it still felt like abandonment. It still felt like being left behind, left alone, discarded. And somewhere along the way, I developed something called abandonment issues." Then, shrugging, "At least that's what my therapist calls it. Issues with being left behind, left alone. It's all very complicated and scientific but... She says that's where my anger comes from too. This need to always be on the edge, on the defense. My need to keep people away and... That's what I did with you. In the beginning."

He pauses and looks me in the eye. "The day you came to my game almost four years ago now, that wasn't the first time I'd seen you. I'd seen you before. A *year* before. Sitting on the hood of your brother's Mustang. You had a pink dress on. You were eating cotton candy, smiling at people, and of course, everyone there noticed you. Everyone on the street. They couldn't *help* but notice you, and I was one of them. There was a group of guys there too. Just some annoying teenagers who were..." He clenches his jaw. "Who were checking you out, making crude jokes and all the other crap that guys do, that I've done. But for some reason, I wanted to pop their eyes out. For looking at you. I wanted to smash their teeth in for joking and laughing about you. And I... I felt something that I'd only ever felt for my family until then. This grave need to protect. This urgent *need* to keep you safe and away from all the dangers of the world, all the assholes. It was just instinct, see. I didn't even know you and yet I wanted to protect you with every fiber of my being, like... Like it was in my blood. Like I was born with it. With this job to protect you, this constant need to look after you. I'm not really sure but I think that's why I got so... spooked. Of you."

"Me?"

"Yeah, that you could make me feel this way. That you could have so much power over me. That you could make me want things that I didn't want to *want*." He ducks his head then, shaking it. "But of course, we both know how I dealt with that, don't we? I refused to let you get close to me. I could see that I was hurting you but I refused to do anything about it. I denied that I wanted you. I kept saying to myself that it was revenge, or I was protecting you from myself or that I didn't have time for anything but soccer or whatever the fuck came to my mind but... I think it was all me. It was my issues. Something that I hadn't realized up until now. And... Jesus." He rakes a hand through his hair. "It gets worse. It gets *so much* worse because when I got tired, fucking exhausted of wanting you and denying myself, I did something drastic. I did something so selfish. I... came to your dorm room. At the first opportunity that I could."

"But I forgave you," I cut him off, unable to keep my words in, unable to watch him torture himself for something that I've long since moved past. "For that night. I forgave you, Ledger, and I meant it. And I want you —"

"But you don't know what you're forgiving me for," he says.

"What?"

He thrusts his hands inside his pockets, shifting on his feet.

Making me think that he's preparing for the worst.

That he's preparing to drop a bomb, not on me, but on himself.

As though he's a suicide bomber who knows when he presses that button, not only his whole world will burn but he'll burn with it.

"That night when I came to you," he says, "revenge wasn't the only thing on my mind. In fact, after thinking about it for so long and talking it out with my therapist, I don't think revenge took up even half the real estate on my mind. I thought it did but... Yes, I was angry at what your brother did, but I guess by that point, I cared so little about him and so much about you that revenge might've gotten me there. It might've been my excuse, but I had a different purpose. A completely different agenda when I came to you, and it was..." A deep breath again followed by a muttered curse. "It was to breed you. For myself. Not your brother."

"What?"

I notice him making fists inside his pockets.

The vein on the side of his neck pulsing.

Then, "I wanted to put a baby in you so I could tie you to me. So I could keep you. So no one — *not even me* — could've torn us apart. After two years of keeping you away and denying myself what I really wanted — you — I got so crazy, I got so blinded by that primal need that I didn't think about you even for a single second. I didn't think about what you wanted or how my reckless need would affect your life, I just... I just wanted you. Wanted to show the world that you were mine. That you belonged to me. I wanted to make it so that you could never leave me. Like the rest of them.

"And then a year later, you asked me to do the same thing and *Jesus Christ*, I thought I'd hit the jackpot. I thought all my dreams had come true and I kept telling myself that it was only for you. That it wasn't for me. I didn't deserve to feel any happiness over this and I couldn't be selfish. But I was, wasn't I? I tricked you into marrying me. I told myself that it was because I needed to calm my anger, my jealousy. I told myself that it was my need to protect you. And while that may have been true, the real reason again was me. It was because that was what I wanted. I'd already put a baby in you, two babies, and I just... I couldn't go another day without making sure that you were mine. Completely and irrevocably and permanently.

"And again, it gets worse, doesn't it? Because of what I did on the day of your wedding. I knew, I fucking knew, that it wasn't your choice, marrying him. That you were being forced by your father and that there must've been a motherfucking good reason as to why you were ready to sacrifice your own life. And I'd come to rescue you, I swear to God. I swear to fucking God that was my intention but I... I saw you in that wedding dress, looking like a dream, looking so beautiful that it fucking broke my heart just to look at you, that I couldn't stop myself. I couldn't stop this rush of possessiveness, this hot rush of anger, and again, I fucked you over.

"So the reason I left, Tempest, something that I promised myself that I'd never do, was because you were right. Because for the longest time I didn't know what I wanted. I didn't know why I did the things that I did. But I do now. I figured it out. I finally fucking figured it out. It's because I love you."

So this is the bomb.

And it drops.

And I explode. I die.

I'm killed in this moment.

Murdered. Annihilated and destroyed.

"I've loved you since the first moment I saw you and wanted to protect you," he rasps. "And I will love you until the moment my heart stops beating. But unfortunately, that doesn't bode well for you. Because imagine being loved by someone like me. Imagine being loved by a man who's so broken on the inside that ever since I saw you, I've been hurting you. That I've been making you cry and bleeding you dry. Imagine being loved by someone whose insides are snarled and twisted up like a coarse rope or a barbed wire. Whose heart is a ticking time bomb. Whose soul is made of thorns and thunder. Imagine being loved by someone who's so controlled by his fears, his issues that," he swallows, "he can never make you happy. I can never make the girl I love happy. The girl who's my one true family. Because you're that, Tempest. I've been afraid to say it. I've been afraid to even think it, given how broken my family has always been but… You've been the truest family that I've known. You stood by me and had my back when you didn't have to. When you shouldn't have at all, and I… I hurt you and abused you and traumatized you exactly like my father did to my mother, to us. And so leaving you was the only good thing I could do for you. Because my love isn't the stuff of romance novels. It isn't the stuff of dreams. It's what tragedies are made of. It's what they talk about when they talk about cautionary tales. To survive my love is to survive a war. To love me is to destroy your peace. And the only way I could make sure that you didn't have to was to leave. Staying away from you is the only way I can love you and keep you safe at the same time."

Chapter Forty-Two

I KNOCK at the door and wait for it to open.

When it doesn't even after a couple of minutes, I knock again. Well, I bang my fist on the door until it's snatched open, and there he is.

Frowning.

And naked.

"Why are you naked?" I ask, looking at his sweaty and heaving chest.

"What —"

"And panting?"

That frown of his thickens. "What are you doing here? Why aren't —"

I put a hand on his chest — mostly just to cop a feel because he's always been hard to resist when he's all sweaty — and push him back so I can enter.

His childhood home.

I've been here before, of course.

Lots of times when Callie and I were in high school, and I never missed a chance to come over and watch her big brother like the perv I was. And I always thought that their home was beautiful. Not because they had fancy things but because all the things that they had were accumulated through the years. They were well-used and loved. They meant something to the people who lived here.

A perfect house for a perfect family.

But now I know how wrong I was.

They weren't a perfect family. They were — *are* — just that: a family. With their own flaws and cracks and issues. While I still like this house, I don't like the fact that he's stuck here alone. With all the memories and history.

I hear the door snapping shut. "Why aren't you at the hospital? You —"

I turn around to face him. "You never answered my question."

"What question?"

"Why are you naked? Well," I look him up and down and find that he's wearing his infamous gray sweatpants, "half-naked. And panting."

He's still doing that by the way, his chest going up and down with his harsh breaths. As he watches me like I've lost my mind. I raise my eyebrows at him when he still hasn't answered my question.

Then with a sharp breath, he does. "I was out back, running drills."

"Why aren't you back in New York, running them with your team? You've got an away game in a few days," I ask, even though I know the answer; my brother told me.

He said that Ledger will stay here for the next couple of days and will sit out the next game. Apparently, Conrad and the others were completely onboard with it.

"I'm taking a break for the next couple of days."

"Why, did you punch someone again?" I quip, trying to yank his chain.

His jaw clenches. "Unfortunately, no."

"So then —"

"Why do you think?"

For me.

I knew that too. No, my brother didn't have to tell me; I figured it out on my own.

Turns out, there are a lot of things that he's been doing for me.

This latest one is because of the scare I'd had day before yesterday. They kept me under observation for twenty-four hours and let me go with clear instructions to relax and take it easy for the next few days. My brother and Callie picked me up and had every intention of taking me home with them.

But I had them drop me off here instead.

Something they both were very happy about, if Callie's breath of relief and my brother's muttered, 'about fucking time' were anything to go by.

"Show me your room," I tell him next.

"What?"

"It's upstairs, isn't it? Second floor."

"What the —"

I spin around and start to waddle toward the stairs. It's kinda intimidating, climbing all those stairs by myself, but I don't think I'll have to worry about that. Because someone is going to come to my rescue.

And in the next second, he does.

He grabs my biceps to stop me, and he does it so gently that I have to consciously keep myself from sighing. From leaning into him, his strong, heated body. Into his care.

He turns me to face him, again gently, which is in total contrast to the expression on his face.

Tight and thundering.

A frown on his forehead. A tic in his jaw and the hollows on his cheeks standing out.

"What the fuck are you doing?" he growls.

"Going up to your room," I tell him, trying to smell his cinnamon-y scent mixed in with his musk.

"Why do —"

"Because I want to see it."

I do.

I have wanted to see it for as long as I can remember. Back then, because I was so obsessed with him and everything that he did. Now, because during one of our bath time conversations, he told me that whenever he comes to visit, he always stays in his room. Even though there's no need for it. It's just something he does out of habit and he hates it.

Almost as much as he hates the house.

"Okay." He pinches the bridge of his nose, his fingers tightening and loosening around my arm. "Why the fuck aren't you at the hospital?"

"Because they let me go."

He exhales a sharp breath. "Why in fuck's name would they do that? I told them —"

"I know what you told them," I say with raised eyebrows. "But when they came to check on me, they thought there wasn't any need for me to stay there longer. So they let me go."

They were a little hesitant about it, given that the Angry Thorn had instructed them to keep me there for another couple of days. With him footing the bill, of course, because as I said, there wasn't any need for me to stay there any longer. Anyway, I insisted that I wanted to be released and go home. And despite what they'd been instructed to do, they did.

His eyes narrow. "The fuck they did."

"You —"

"I'm giving them a call."

"No, you're not," I tell him calmly.

"I am."

He's ready to let me go when I blurt out a warning, "If you call them, then I'm going to climb these stairs all by myself."

He stares down at me for a few seconds, his face a mask of displeasure. "You are."

"Yes, and look," I glance at them for a second, "there are so many of them. I'm pretty sure it's a stressful thing to do in my condition. Exactly what the doctor said I shouldn't do."

He takes a second to respond. Then, "Are you threatening me?"

"Yup."

The displeasure on his face goes up, causing his eyes to narrow.

"So you better decide what you want to do," I continue when he keeps studying me silently. "I don't think you —"

Instead of words, I squeal.

Because he bends down to pick me up and carry me in his arms.

Bridal style.

Again, all gently and cautiously like I'm the most precious treasure he's ever held in his arms.

It reminds me of that one time when he carried me over the threshold into our cabin. The day I went to see him practice. It felt like such a significant thing, and of course it was.

Significant and traditional.

What a groom does with his new bride on the night of their wedding.

God, I can't believe I was married to him back then.

This powerful guy who's climbing the stairs with me twenty-eight weeks pregnant without breaking a sweat. For a second when he started, I wanted to tell him to put me down because I'm so heavy now. But then I figured it's his job to carry me around, isn't it?

It's his *job* to take care of me.

That's what he said to me yesterday. Among other things of course.

So I'm not going to stop him.

But he can't stop me either then. From taking care of him.

We'll get to all that in a second though.

First, I want to see his room.

When we enter, he slowly puts me down and I look around. This is the first time I've been inside it. In all my visits to their house, I never once set foot inside his room. Not because I didn't want to or I wouldn't have taken the opportunity to sneak into his room if it had been presented to me.

But because it was always locked.

Either with him inside it or without.

Anyway, I don't think much has changed over the years. From what I can see, it still looks like the bedroom of a teenage boy. There's a desk in one corner and even though there aren't any books on it, I can still picture it laden with them. There's a chest of drawers, again empty on top but I can imagine Ledger piling up his clothes on it. Or on the floor, like he used to do back at the cabin. There's a twin-sized bed that I don't think can accommodate him now, if it even could when he lived here full-time.

It's a room stuck in history.

And the more I see of it, the more I'm convinced that I can't let him do this alone.

Sighing, I look at him. "Hmm. We're going to have to do something about the bed."

He's standing at the door still, rigid and tight.

At my words, the tension in his frame only grows. "What?"

"There's no way all four of us can fit here."

"I…" He swallows whatever he was going to say and stays on topic. "Four."

"Well yeah," I tell him. "You and me and our two little butterflies. Oh, and my body pillow. I have like, a huge one that supports the bump and my back at the same time. So I guess five."

"Wh…" He swallows his words again. Then, "Where's your useless brother? What was he doing when they were discharging you? Why the fuck didn't he call me and tell me when he knew I was —"

I narrow my eyes at him. "When he knew you were what?"

His first response is to draw in a breath.

Probably because he slipped up just now.

Then, shaking his head and scrubbing a hand down his face, he says, "It doesn't matter. He —"

"When he knew you were going to drive over to the hospital and wait in the visitor's lounge until they kicked you out, without ever letting me know that you were there?" Then I add, "Like you did yesterday."

Like a silent sentinel or something.

A guardian. A protector. A warden.

Who watches over things without letting anyone know that he's there.

Which is what he did yesterday; again, something my brother told me when he came to pick me up today.

After Ledger told me all the things, things that I never could've imagined in my wildest dreams, he left.

He simply left me there.

And if I hadn't been so shocked and stunned and fucking floored by what he'd revealed, I probably would've stopped him. I don't know what I would've said to him though because it was a lot to process, all the information that he dumped on me. But yeah, I would've stopped him.

I would've somehow kept him there, in the room with me.

Probably to make sure that it was real and I hadn't dreamed him up.

"If you still think that my brother controls any aspect of my life whatsoever, then I don't know what to tell you," I say, looking him in the eyes. "And while they were discharging me, my brother was in the parking lot, bringing the car around so he could pick me up at the front entrance. And since the doctor told me that I needed to go home and rest, I told my brother to bring me here."

"Here," he says, staring back at me.

"Yup." I nod again. Then, "But fair warning: I need constant care right now. Foot rubs, back massages, belly rubs. Carrying twins is hard. I'm only twenty-eight weeks, but I look so huge. Plus I'm clumsy and —"

"You're not huge," he interrupts.

"That's very sweet of you to say but —"

"Or clumsy."

I give him a look. "You always thought I was when I wore my heels."

"I was an asshole."

"Was?"

"Am."

My lips twitch. "People move away from me on the street because they think I'm ready to pop any second now."

"People are assholes too."

I stare up at him and he stares down.

I'm the first to break my silence. "And I need guac and chips twenty-four seven. So you have to stock up on that. And this amazing mango passion-fruit juice I found at the store a few weeks back. I need you to stock up on that too. But first, as I said, this is the wrong bed and —"

"No."

"What?"

Grinding his teeth, he watches me for a few seconds. "Absolutely fucking not."

"Absolutely fucking not what?"

"You're not staying here."

"I —"

"That's what this is, isn't it? You barging in here like this is your house and —"

"This *is* my house."

"Yeah, how do you figure?"

"Because you live here."

One sharp breath later, he growls, "This is because of yesterday, isn't it? This is because of what I said."

"And if it is?"

"Then, you're —"

"I'm what?" I cut him off, stepping toward him.

Clenching his teeth, he automatically steps back.

I advance on him nonetheless. "I'm what, Ledger? Say it. I dare you to say it to me, insult me when I'm pregnant." His back clashes with the wall and I am here, trapping him with my pregnant body. "Not with one but two freaking babies. Because you can't do things half-measure, can you? Because you just *had* to go and put two babies in me in one shot. Because your stupid freaking sperm is super fertile and a menace."

He raises his hands up in a 'calm down' gesture. "Look, I wasn't kidding yesterday. I wasn't…" He sighs, scrubbing a hand down his face again. "I'm all fucked up, you understand? I'm all twisted up and ugly on the inside and I don't know if I'll ever be…"

My heart is clenching and clenching for him. "Ever be what?"

He swallows, his eyes even more vulnerable than they were yesterday.

Vulnerable and molten and shiny with everything inside of him.

"Normal," he rasps.

My heart aches so much in this moment that I don't know how I'm not screaming from the pain. How I'm not hunching over with it. How does he not know that he's killing me in this moment.

"I don't know if I'll ever be," he swallows again, "*not* fucked up. *Not* self-ish. I don't know if I'll ever be like those heroes you read about. In fact, I know I won't be. I can't be. It's not something that —"

"You are right." His breath breaks at my declaration, but I keep going. "I don't know if you'll ever be like the guys I read about. And yes, you hurt me. You make me cry. You break my heart. You make me want to smack you and punch you and be angry at you. But you don't do that by being who you are. You do that, Ledger, by being who you *aren't*. You do that by denying who you are. By denying the things that you want. By being afraid.

"You are, aren't you? That's what you told me. That you're afraid of people leaving you, people abandoning you. You're afraid to go through the same pain that you went through when you were a kid and that's why you did all those things. Hurting me, keeping me away, clinging to lies and excuses. So I'm here to tell you something."

His breaths are still broken but they're noisy now.

Noisy and chaotic and harsh.

So much so that I wish I could take my words back.

I wish I could shut up and leave him in peace.

But the thing is, he's never going to be at peace without me.

Because he wants me. He's wanted me for a long time. Apparently even before I wanted him. His obsession with me is longer than mine with him. And I know, I *know*, just how torturous it is. To want something and never have it. Actually it's even more torturous than wanting something but denying that you want it in the first place.

And it's not just me, is it?

It's everything else in his life too.

His relationship with his brothers. His family. Maybe even friends.

So I'm here to give him all that. I'm here to give him me.

"Don't you want to know what it is, Ledger?" I ask, prodding him, tempting him.

And for a second, it looks like he's going to nod.

He's going to ask me what.

It's in every line of his face, the way he swallows again like he's thirsty. The way he takes me in with such hunger in his eyes. The hunger so powerful that it eats at me. It eats at my heart. My organs. My very soul and marrow.

"You need to leave," he says abruptly, getting ready to dislodge himself from the wall.

But I advance on him, getting so close that if he wants to avoid touching me, he needs to stop breathing or take smaller breaths. Good thing I have no such objections and my next breath is a long sigh that drags my engorged breasts and puffy nipples along his chest.

Which shudders.

"It's the fact that I lied," I whisper, dragging my breasts along his chest again.

Another shudder goes through him.

This one more violent than the first one.

"Tempest, I —"

I grab hold of his hot obliques, my fingers latching onto his muscular flesh. "Didn't you ever wonder why I asked *you* to give me a baby?" He opens his mouth but I keep going. "I'll give you a hint: it's not because I wanted closure."

His body tightens; I can feel it in his muscles that thrum like a string.

"It's because I lied to you. I lied when I said that I hated you. That I stopped loving you when you broke my heart, my dreams. I lied when I said all I wanted from you was a baby and nothing more. The truth is that I never stopped loving you. I loved you even when I hated you. And I do want something from you. It's what I've always wanted from you. *Always*. Can you at least guess what that something is?"

He looks afraid.

God, he looks terrified and I once again think that I should stop but I can't.

I won't.

For both our sakes.

"It's for you to love me back. To *let* yourself love me back, Ledger. Without excuses and lies. Without ulterior motives. Without fear. Because I do. I love you like that. I've loved you like that since the first moment I saw you and I'll love you like that until my heart stops beating. And let me tell you something else too. If your love is a war, then my love is peace. If you're what tragedies are made of, then I'm made of fairy tales. If you're toxic, then I'm the cure. Because I'm the girl made of candies and cream, remember? And I'm the only one who can handle the boy made of thunder and thorns. I'm the only one who can take care of him like he deserves. The only one who can wrap him around in my arms and keep him safe. I'm the only one who can protect him. Because he's my family. Like I'm his. Which means that if you want to stay here, in this house that you don't like, I'm going to stay here with you. If you want to do therapy and work on things, then I'm going to be here to listen to you after every session. Or if you don't want to talk to me, then I'll sit with you in silence and just hold your hand."

At this, I slide my hands up his body and press my fingers on his chest, splaying them over his heart.

That's pounding.

So much so that I can see the vein on the side of his neck pulsating.

I can see it throbbing and I have to admit that I like this role reversal.

I like the fact that it's me pinning him in place. It's me who's watching that pulse like a predator.

It's me, his Lovelorn Firefly.

Although not so lovelorn anymore.

"I love you, Ledger," I whisper just to make it clear.

A wince goes through his system.

In fact, every breath he takes makes him shudder and jerk, as if he's this close to falling apart. So I give him strength. I give him my weight, touch our bodies, my steadily breathing chest aligning with his shaking torso. My hands reaching up to grab his shoulders, my fingers spreading and my thumb pressing on his fluttering vein, trying to calm it down.

But most of all, I give him the strength of these two little beings in my belly.

The beings that we made.

Out of love.

Whatever we may have called it in that moment, it was always love.

For each other.

"Say it," I command with my rounded belly resting against his pelvis.

"Tempest —"

"Say that you love me too, Ledger."

He swallows quite possibly for the millionth time. That's jerky as well.

His Adam's apple bobs thickly, awkwardly.

"I'm…" he breathes out, his eyes boring into mine.

I give him a small, serene smile. "You don't have to be afraid. I've got you."

"I'm not good at this."

"It's okay. I'll hold your hand and keep you safe, until you do."

His forehead comes to rest against mine. "I-I'm going to hurt you. I know that."

"I'll tell you when you do so you can make it better."

His hands spring into action and grab my thickened waist. "I can't… I can't promise you that I won't make you cry."

"We'll make sure to stock up on tissues and cotton candy ice cream."

"I don't know if I can be what you need me to be."

"You already are."

"I —"

"Say it," I command again, this time *pressing* my belly into his pelvis.

And his fingers spread open on my waist as he whispers, like he was dying to and all he needed was a little push over the edge, "I-I love you too."

Before I can respond to that, he does something else like he was dying to do that as well.

Kiss me.

And because I've been dying for it as well, I let him do it.

I let him devour my mouth so I can devour his back. I let him taste me so I can taste him back. So I can feel him invade my mouth like he's invaded my heart and my soul since the first moment I saw him.

444

So I can be in his arms for the first time ever without anything separating us.

Not his lies, not mine.

Not his fear, not mine.

Just us.

Although just us isn't true, is it?

Because we do have some things between us.

Two things, in fact.

And those cute little things decide that this is the time to make their presence known, making their mommy smile and their daddy break apart from Mommy's mouth.

Startled, he goes, "What was…"

I chuckle when I feel them kick just beneath my belly button, startling Ledger again. "Them."

His kiss-swollen lips part. "The b-babies?"

"Uh-huh."

I feel another kick and this time he moves apart a little and looks down at my swollen stomach. And he looks at it in a way that makes me think he's actually waiting for them to pop out of there any second now. He's actually waiting to see a real foot poking through my clothes.

When it happens again, he breathes, "Fuck me. They're…"

"Very active, yeah." I grin. "All the techs always tell me that they're the most active babies they've seen in a while."

His eyes jerk up to mine then, his fists opening and closing around my waist. "He never… Reed never told me that. I –"

I put my hands on his, making him let go of my dress and bring them up front.

Where his babies are making a ruckus.

Then, "Reed doesn't know everything."

His fingers shake and grip my belly like he'll never let go.

Good.

I don't want him to.

Then in the next second, I'm the one getting startled because he's down on his knees. Just like the time back in the cabin when he was touching my bump for the first time. Like he couldn't hold himself up any longer. And before I can absorb that, he leans forward and rests his forehead against my bump as if in worship.

I sink my fingers in his hair and he looks up. "Thank you."

"For what?"

"For letting me touch them. Even when I'm not –"

I press a finger on his lips. "You are. For me. For them."

At this, something happens that I've never seen before. That I never even imagined I'd ever see. His usually dark brown eyes – pitch black right now though – fill with something akin to tears. They go red-rimmed and his jaw clenches with emotion.

And then he presses a kiss on my belly.

I don't know if this is divine intervention or if the universe is just so beautiful sometimes that you get all your dreams coming true. Because at his kiss, I feel another kick in my belly right at that spot and this time, he chuckles.

And does it again and again and again.

Until he's covered my entire belly in his sweet kisses and I'm laughing and crying and flying in joy. Like he is. Picking me up then, he puts me on his old bed and keeps kissing me over and over until I'm all liquid under his hard body.

"I could get used to this bed," I say, chuckling when he lets me come up for air.

He stares down at me with languid eyes. "This bed fucking sucks."

I play with his hair. "Did you think about me, while you were lying in it?"

He runs his thumb along the side of my face. "Fuck yeah."

My fingers in his hair stop. "You did?"

He shoots me a look. "Why do you think I always had the door locked when you came over?"

With wide eyes, I reply, "Because you were… thinking about me?"

"And doing other things."

"What other things?"

"What do you think a guy does when he's obsessed with a girl? Who's right next door, laughing with his little sister while gabbing about the most useless things anyone's ever talked about."

I smack his shoulder. "Hey, not the –"

"I jerked myself off," he says, cutting me off.

My momentary ire goes away. "Oh."

"To your voice. To your laugh. To the cotton candy scent that you always left behind in the hallway."

This time my *oh* is silent and gasp-y.

He smirks. "I might be the only person who's ever jerked off to Chanel's fall line of handbags."

I bite my lip. "I can't believe you did that."

"Me neither."

"I can't believe you saw me a year before I saw you."

"Probably just like I couldn't believe that the girl I saw was the same girl who started stalking me a year later."

"I can't believe you came to my dorm room because you wanted to get me pregnant for yourself and not for revenge," I continue.

"Again, probably same as you wanted me to breed you a year later. For yourself and not for revenge."

I shake my head, taking his beautiful face in. "We're soulmates, aren't we?"

His playful expression goes away and an intense look takes over his face. His eyes.

My heart starts to pound something fierce, afraid that our fragile happiness is going to be broken any second now. But before I can ask him what's wrong, he lets go of me and comes down on his knees on the floor.

I prop myself up on my elbows – soon I won't be able to do that with how fast I'm growing – and ask, "What… What are you doing?"

He stares at me for a second or two before breathing deep. "I don't have fancy words. I don't even know if I could ever find them, even if I went looking, but…" He clears his throat. "But I want to do this right. For the first time ever, I want to do something because I *want* to do it. Bravely and without fear." Then, "Well, maybe with fear but still."

Another deep breath later, "You already know that I've loved you since the first moment I saw you and I've hurt you more than any man has ever hurt the woman he loves. You've seen my ugly parts and if I have any beauty in me, you've seen that too. I've broken a lot of promises while I've kept the others. I've made you cry. I've made you laugh. I've scared you and made you feel safe. I've broken your heart and tried in my twisted way to heal it. And knowing all that, knowing how fucked up I am and how far I still have to go, I'm asking you to marry me. I'm asking you to be my wife, and Tempest, I'm not going to make any promises to you because I don't want to break them. I'm not going to say that I won't make you cry because I probably will. I'm not going to say that I'll hide my ugly parts because again, I'll probably fail to do that as well. But I will say that I will always be there for you. I will burn down the world for you. I will kill for you. I will lie on broken glass and walk on grenades for you. I will live and breathe and die for you." He glances down at my belly. "And for our babies." Looking up, he asks, in the most vulnerable display of emotions, "Will you marry me?"

He's blurry right now because my eyes are filled with tears.

But still I see something sitting in the palm of his hand.

A blue velvet box.

I have no idea where he produced it from or when. All I know is that it's sitting there, and slowly, he opens it to reveal the most beautiful ring I've ever seen.

A princess-cut diamond on a white gold band with two little diamonds flanking it.

And I immediately know that those two diamonds are our babies. That he thought of them when he bought it.

"When did you…"

"The day I went to your father."

"Y-you mean, after you were released from jail?"

"Yeah."

"B-but I'd already asked for −"

He shakes his head once. "I just… wanted to do something right. For once." Then, "I tricked you into marrying me, without ever asking you or giving you a ring or doing all those traditional things I know you dreamed of. So I bought this ring, knowing that I probably would never be able to give it to you, and that it would burn a hole in my pocket for the rest of my life. Which is…"

"Which is what?"

"Me never getting to ask you that one question after selfishly not asking you before was," his eyes flick back and forth between mine, "exactly what I deserve."

There have been many moments like this with him. Where he breaks my heart while simultaneously healing it, and I still haven't gotten used to it.

I still have no clue as to how to handle all these emotions at once.

So it pains me to say, "I can't."

He blinks.

As though stricken.

But it only lasts momentarily because after that a resigned expression washes over his face. Like me breaking his heart is okay. It's what he deserves and gosh, that chokes me up so bad that a tear falls down my cheek.

And I vow − even though he's told me that he wouldn't make any promises himself − that one day, I'll make him believe that he's worth every inch of my love. That he's the most beautiful thing I've ever seen.

For now though, I wipe my tears off and cup his jaw. "Because we're already married."

He takes a few seconds to respond. Then, "What?"

"I never signed the divorce papers."

Again a few seconds of pause before he repeats, "You never signed the divorce papers."

Slowly a smile blooms on my lips. "I lied."

"You lied."

"Again."

"Again."

Nodding, I ask, "Still think I can't handle your ugly parts, Ledger Thorne?"

Slowly, his mouth stretches into his signature arrogant smirk. "You're a firecracker, aren't you?"

"No, I'm a Firefly."

"My Firefly."

"And you're my Thorn."

This time, I go in for a kiss and devour the delicious smirk on his lips. And of course, he devours me back.

And of course, our babies have to create a ruckus because they're like their mommy, I think. Always dying for Daddy's attention. Who goes to grip my belly and rub it, trying to soothe them. Trying to tell them that he's finally here.

That he will be here for the rest of our lives.

Which reminds me…

Breaking the kiss, I whisper against his lips, "By the way, I know what we're having."

Chapter Forty-Three

Her Beautiful Thorn

THERE ARE silvery lines on the bottom of her rounded belly.

I think they came back when she was fifteen weeks or so. And while back then they were hardly visible, I can see them clearly now. I can see clearly how her body has changed ever since I last saw it.

How it has grown and stretched to make a cozy home for our babies.

And so I kiss it.

I kiss every single one of her silvery stretch marks.

Lying in my shitty bed, all naked, she giggles, her belly shaking. Which makes them shake as well and so I watch, very carefully, as they roll in her body, just underneath her creamy skin, making it flutter and twitch.

Exactly like two little butterflies.

"Does that hurt?" I whisper, still staring at how they're moving and flitting.

In fact, I've set up camp by her belly, my head propped up on my hand as I examine her new moles, new freckles that she's gotten in the weeks that we've been apart.

Yes, her brother – who's somehow become a friend; still fucking surreal to say that – kept me updated about her health even though I told him not to. I told him it was invasion of her privacy but he wouldn't listen.

And I can't deny that I soaked up every single thing he told me.

But it's nothing compared to actually seeing it with my own eyes. Seeing her, our babies rolling around in her magical, goddess-like body.

She curls my hair in her usual way. "No. Not yet. It tickles sometimes."

At this, the left side of her belly moves and she chuckles again. And I go in for another kiss, making her moan.

Then she asks, "So? You never said what you thought of the names."

I look up. "Dove Thorne."

She nods. "For the girl, yes."

"And Warden Thorne."

"Well, War," she corrects me. "For the boy."

"Dove and War."

"Isn't that perfect? Dove stands for peace, and Warden means protector. So people may call him War but on the inside, he's going to be the biggest softy and he's always going to protect his sister with everything he will be. Like his daddy."

"Like his daddy," I whisper as something digs into my throat.

"Like his daddy, yes," she replies with shiny blue-gray eyes.

Swallowing, I rasp, "I love them."

"Yeah?"

"Yeah."

"And I love you."

The more I say it, the easier it becomes.

The easier it becomes to believe that this may not be a dream after all. That she's really here. She really is wearing my ring on her finger. That she still is my wife. I know I have a long, long way to go when it comes to dealing with my issues. And again, it's surreal to say that I'm liking talking to Dr. Mayberry but I'm willing to put in the work.

If soccer has taught me anything, it's that hard work and focus always pay off.

So I'm going to work hard. I'm going to focus. I'm going to fight my demons.

But most of all, I'm going to let her hold my hand as she guides me in our new life. I'm going to let her protect me like I'm going to protect her. I'm going to let her keep me and our babies safe like I'm going to keep them safe. I won't be irrational and fuck up like I did before, when she was trying to protect me from her father and put her in jeopardy.

I still can't believe that she was trying to do that though.

For me.

But she was.

And that's because she's my family, isn't she?

Her and these babies.

Dove and War.

"I love you too," my wife whispers, making my fucking heart race.

And I go back to studying her goddess-like body. Ripe and swollen and flushed. The dark line going from the top of her pregnant belly down to her pink-as-fuck pussy. Her engorged tits and darkened nipples. Her cute swollen toes and fingers that I kiss probably for the tenth time in the last half an hour.

I kiss and worship every part of it until I'm settled between her thighs and I'm devouring her sweet cotton candy mouth. Until I'm sliding into her pregnant pussy, making her moan.

Against her mouth, I say, "Mine."

Looking up with dazed eyes, she whispers, "Yours."

"My wife," I groan into her mouth.

Gasping, she replies, "My husband."

At which point, I kiss her again.

With love. With relief.

With fucking peace that I will get to kiss her for the rest of her pregnancy. For the rest of our lives. Because she's mine, isn't she?

My girl. My Firefly.

My wife.

And I'm hers.

Her man. Her Thorn.

Her husband.

And we have both war and peace between us.

THE END

About the Author

Writer of bad romances. Aspiring Lana Del Rey of the Book World.

Saffron A. Kent is a USA Today Bestselling Author of Contemporary and New Adult romance.

She has an MFA in Creative Writing and she lives in New York City with her nerdy and supportive husband, along with a million and one books.

She also blogs. Her musings related to life, writing, books and everything in between can be found in her JOURNAL on her website (www. thesaffronkent.com)

Milton Keynes UK
Ingram Content Group UK Ltd.
UKHW011047231123
433129UK00005B/352